·· Myths, Gods & Immortals ··
Loki
New & Ancient Norse Tales

This is a FLAME TREE Book

Publisher & Creative Director: Nick Wells
Editorial Director: Catherine Taylor
Editorial Board: Gillian Whitaker, Catherine Taylor, Jocelyn Pontes, Jemma North, Simran Aulakh and Beatrix Ambery
Special thanks to Karen Fitzpatrick

FLAME TREE PUBLISHING
6 Melbray Mews, Fulham,
London SW6 3NS, United Kingdom
www.flametreepublishing.com

First published 2025

Copyright in each story is held by the individual authors.
Introduction and Volume copyright © 2025 Flame Tree Publishing Ltd.
Note: stories within the Introduction ('Introducing Loki') are written by Matt Ralphs.

25 27 29 30 28 26
1 3 5 7 9 10 8 6 4 2

ISBN: 978-1-83562-269-8

All rights reserved. No part of this publication may be reproduced, stored in a retrieval system, or transmitted in any form or by any means, electronic, mechanical, photocopying, recording or otherwise, without the prior written permission of the publisher.

Publisher's Note: The stories within this book are works of fiction. Names, characters, places, and incidents are a product of the authors' imaginations. Locales and public names are sometimes used for atmospheric purposes. Any resemblance to actual people, living or dead, or to businesses, companies, events, institutions, or locales is completely coincidental.

Content Note: The stories in this book may contain descriptions of, or references to, difficult subjects such as violence, death and rape, but always contextualized within the setting of mythic narrative, archetype and metaphor. Similarly, language can sometimes be strong but is at the artistic discretion of the authors.

Cover art by Flame Tree Studio based on elements from
Shutterstock.com/Fotokvadrat.

A copy of the CIP data for this book is available from the British Library.

Printed and bound in China

Myths, Gods & Immortals

Loki

New & Ancient Norse Tales

FLAME TREE
PUBLISHING

Contents

FOREWORD
Prof. Tom Birkett 6

ANCIENT & MODERN: INTRODUCING LOKI
by Matt Ralphs 10
1. The Norse World 11
2. Loki's World 43
3. Loki 72
4. Impact and Influence 112

MODERN SHORT STORIES OF LOKI
Loki: The Movie
Chris A. Bolton 125
Loki's Confrontations
Drew Conners 140
The Norn's Offer
S. Cameron David 151
Means to an End
Stephanie Ellis 165
Eitrdropar
Corey D. Evans 178
The Ties That Bind
Ariana Ferrante 191

CONTENTS

Parent-Aesir Conference
Cara Giles 199

Fraternized: The Enemy Within
Sara Gonzalez-Rothi 202

The Apple of Her Eye
Kay Hanifen 211

Captain of the Ship
Justin R. Hopper 220

Degrees of Truth
Michelle Kaseler 236

Loki Meets His Match
Mark Patrick Lynch 248

A Knot for the Hawk
Nico Martinez Nocito 264

**Loki and Pickled Herring
at World's End**
Mark Oxbrow 276

Just Because
Diego Suárez 294

The Shape of Mischief
Jeffery Allen Tobin 308

Laufey's Son
C. Adam Volle 328

The God of Lead and Blood
M.M. Williams 344

BIOGRAPHIES 360
MYTHS, GODS & IMMORTALS 367
FLAME TREE FICTION 368

Foreword
Prof. Tom Birkett

here is no character quite like Loki. Often described as the 'trickster god', this label really doesn't do justice to his myriad roles, or to the complexity of his characterization in the body of stories that comprise Norse mythology. This complexity begins with his lineage. Loki is uniquely referred to by reference to his mother, as son of Laufey, due to the fact that his father Fárbauti is a giant. Using the matronymic Laufeyson draws attention to the taboo of giant patrilineage and his unorthodox position, and makes it difficult to place him within the family of the gods. If considered a giant like his father, then why does he appear so often as a companion of the gods, and if a god, why is he so openly hostile to the Aesir? While the fact of his birth might explain his divided loyalties on a structural level, it doesn't explain why the people who worshipped the Norse gods felt the need to insert such a troubling character into their pantheon, or why he plays such a prominent role in the surviving mythology.

The number of stories involving Loki is truly remarkable, particularly when compared with Freyr – often considered one of the 'big three' alongside Odin and Thor – who only has a single story dedicated to him in the Eddas. Loki walks with Odin

FOREWORD

when the world is young, killing Ótr and instigating the story of the gold of the Niflungs. He is the catalyst for the crafting of the most precious objects of the gods, for saving Asgard from ruin by a giant builder, for (inadvertently) bringing Skaði into the pantheon. He's responsible for stealing the apples of immortality and cutting off Sif's hair, and most infamously, for killing the most perfect god Baldr (as well as ensuring he can't be returned from Hel). He also plays a key role in Ragnarök, the great cataclysm that brings an end to the world, escaping from his captivity and torture to lead the armies of the dead to execute his revenge, and personally dispatching Heimdall, with whom he has particular beef. His children are even more closely associated with the destruction of the world. Combining the nature of Loki with a giant mother is – apparently – enough to create monsters that threaten life itself. Hel, who rules over the realm of the dead, Jörmungandr, the World-Serpent, whose unravelling from the depths of the sea presages Ragnarök, and the wolf Fenrir, who ends Odin's life. Loki is also chained up with the entrails of one of his legitimate sons with his loyal wife Sigyn, after being captured with a net that he designed himself. If the gods are implicated in their own destruction, none so literally conceive the means of their own demise as Loki.

It might be worth noting that in literature from pre-Conquest England the most represented character is the devil, playing roles that include challenging the established order. It might be that Loki's ubiquity is related to his broadly similar role, as a character who constantly tests the (im)morality of his peers and asks difficult truths, as well as simply acting out of unrestrained malice at times (Loki's killing of Baldr, and manipulation of the blind Höd to carry it out, is a chillingly sadistic act). Like Satan, Loki also hides his true identity by regularly disguising himself, and he's as slippery as the salmon he turns into to evade capture. But the comparison with Lucifer has its limitations too. Most of the time, the impression we get of Loki is not of a Manichaean 'evil', but of a more sympathetic character whose actions we can understand and even empathize with. Who wouldn't make a deal with an eagle if faced with being dashed to pieces on the ground? It's also true that the gods often treat Loki with callous and elitist disregard, blaming him instead of recognizing their own culpability, and throwing him to the wolves on more than one occasion. Perhaps the reason why Loki holds such an appeal for modern readers is that in a system as deeply flawed as that of Asgard, he doesn't engage in the hypocrisy of the other gods. When he instigates an exchange of insults at a feast, none of the insults thrown at him land. Yes, he's a murderer, an adulterer, a shapeshifter and (in the eyes of medieval Scandinavians) a pervert. Yes, he gave birth to a horse and tied his testicles to a goat to make Skaði laugh. But he meets all those accusations with a shrug.

Although it is always tempting to read Loki as a disruptor or a catalyst – a kind of chaotically productive force – there are many instances of Loki simply tagging along in the adventures of other gods, whether dressed as a bridesmaid as a sidekick of Thor's, or losing an eating contest in the halls of Útgarða-Loki. His quick thinking sometimes saves the gods, often at a personal cost, not least when he allows himself to be impregnated by a stallion to

FOREWORD

prevent the gods losing a bet. He often seems to be included in stories centred on the other gods because – as something of a wild card – he adds interest and colour to any narrative. This might be one reason why he continues to prove irresistible to artists and writers using the Norse myths as inspiration. Reimaginings of his character range from Wagner's manipulative Loge, to video games casting him in a much more positive light, including as a teenage hero helping to bring an end to the tyranny of the gods. The fluidity of Loki's gender, and the ease with which he changes his appearance, is often emphasized in modern interpretations, including in my own recent profile of the gods for young readers. But it is perhaps his rebellious streak, his potential for renewal through action – however extreme – that is most attractive for contemporary writers, including those responsible for Marvel's Loki, the dominant reference point in popular culture. With this new collection of stories we need to put aside Tom Hiddleston's character and return to a far more multifaceted and disturbing figure. As a (demi-)god who shifts and changes every time we try to pin him down, perhaps Loki is best represented by a collection of short stories that each capture him in a slightly different light.

Prof. Tom Birkett
Professor of Old English and Old Norse, University College Cork

MYTHS, GODS & IMMORTALS: LOKI

Ancient & Modern: Introducing Loki

by Matt Ralphs

1.

The Norse World

Behold, the church of St. Cuthbert
spattered with the blood of the priests of God,
despoiled of all its ornaments;
given as a prey to pagan peoples.
– Alcuin of York, Letter to Ethelred, King
of Northumbria

et's try an experiment. What's the first thing that comes
to mind when you see the name Loki?

I'll bet one hundred silver coins and a horn of mead
that words like 'cunning', 'deceitful' and especially 'trickster'
flitted through your mind. And you'd be perfectly correct. Loki
is all of these things. I'd also throw in liar, capricious and cruel,
as well. But, like anything or anyone worth our time, there's a
lot more to it than that.

Norse myths are full of huge, multifaceted and distinct
characters: Odin, the wise and ruthless All-Father; Freya,
beautiful mistress of magic; Thor the troll-thrashing
Thunder God, to name only a few. And yet Loki stands
apart from this stellar cast as being even more multifaceted
(multi-multifaceted?), and more attention-grabbing, than
his peers.

Think Hans Gruber in *Die Hard* (1988).

Loki appears early in the Aesir God's timeline (*see* page 48 in 'The Walls of Asgard') and reappears regularly right up to and including the bloody, action-packed climax of Ragnarök – the apocalyptic Twilight of the Gods. He's an important character who clearly fascinated the Norse, who retold these stories countless times over the centuries. His restless, capricious nature and his active propensity to *set things in motion* make him a storytellers' dream.

As a storyteller myself, I believe the best (and most fun) way to get a handle on Loki's character, motivations and quirks is to examine the stories in which he plays a part. My source for these is the priceless *Prose Edda*. Compiled and edited by the medieval Icelandic scholar Snorri Sturluson (1179–1241), it's the most complete collection of Old Norse tales we have.

For the purposes of this essay, I'm going to take the liberty of rewriting some of these tales. However, I'm adding nothing to the plots except my own dialogue and description: characters, events, twists and turns are all as they originally appear in the *Edda*. From them we can build a profile of Loki, the Trickster God of Norse mythology.

But first, some context.

THE VIKING AGE

We can't really get to know Loki and the Norse gods without first gaining an understanding of the people who believed in them: their homeland, culture and the effect they had on the wider world. (And the Norse had one *hell* of an effect.)

Given the constraints of this essay format, I can only provide a surface look at a complex subject spanning several centuries, so you'll have to forgive my generalizations. However, this broad-strokes approach will at least provide some interesting and useful context before we dive into the myths themselves.

Some Interesting and Useful Context

The Norse (also called Norsemen) lived during the medieval age. In Europe, this period (also called the Dark Ages and the Middle Ages) sits between the ancient world (that of the Greeks and Romans) and early modern times. So, from the fifth century (the fall of Rome) to the fourteenth (the beginning of the European Renaissance).

One of the medieval period's subheadings is the Viking Age, and this is what we'll be looking at. This lasted from 793 to 1066. These dates are far from arbitrary (I'll explain them in a moment), but they do give the erroneous impression that important things start and finish in particular years (and that all historians agree on those years). This is obviously not the case: Vikings existed before 793 and after 1066; history's demarcation lines are rarely clearly defined, especially by those living through them.

For example, 793 was decided as the 'beginning' of the Viking Age because it's the year of the infamous Norse raid on the monastery at Lindisfarne. This is an important date, a watershed event and, to quote *The Lord of the Rings* character Saruman, it serves as a beginning. (That Saruman quote isn't arbitrary either

– we'll be visiting the works of Professor J.R.R. Tolkien [1892–1973] later.) Except it's not *really* the beginning, because the Norse had been raiding and pillaging for decades before this.

And it 'ended' in 1066 when Harold Godwinson (*c.*1022–66), the Anglo-Saxon King of England, defeated an invading Norse army led by King Harald Hardråde (1015–66; 'Hardråde' means 'hard ruler') at the Battle of Stamford Bridge. This was the last Norse attempt to invade the British Isles.

An ironic footnote: three weeks later, Harold was defeated at the Battle of Hastings by another invading force, this time the Normans led by William the Conqueror (1028–87). The Normans were descended from Vikings, who in 911 were given a portion of northern France (which became Normandy) as a payoff to cease their continuous raiding into the European interior. So, in the end, poor Harold defeated one Viking army, only to be defeated himself by (of sorts) another.

Norse or Vikings?

The Norse lived in Scandinavia, which is now comprised of Norway, Sweden and Denmark. Back then, this rugged land of forests, fjords and crystal lakes was home to a fragmented group of localized chieftain-led tribes (collectively: the Norse). Fiercely independent, each tribe had their own identity, and they allied, traded and fought each other depending on their own self-interests.

The term 'Viking' is often used as a synonym for 'Norse', but this is incorrect. 'Viking' comes from the Old Norse '*víkingr*', which means 'pirate', and refers only to those Norse who set out on ships to cause their particular brand of homicidal mayhem. So, all Vikings were Norse, but very few Norse were Vikings. (Side note: no one at the time – including the Norse – called them Vikings.)

The Wider World

From their north European strongholds, the Norse looked west to Britain where, after the Roman withdrawal in the fifth century, the Germanic Anglo-Saxons had settled and formed several kingdoms. While fortunes fluctuated between these kingdoms, the spread of the Christian Church continued unabated until the 600s, by which time the old pagan religions had been largely replaced. This meant lots of wealthy monasteries and churches to plunder...

To the south, across the Baltic Sea, was the European continent. The collapse of the Roman Empire left much of Europe in the hands of various Germanic tribes. In 800, after years of campaigning, the Frankish King Charlemagne (Charles the Great; 748–814) had conquered most of Western Europe and was declared Holy Roman Emperor by the Pope. In 843 his Carolingian Empire (800–877) divided into West Francia (later France) and East Francia (later Germany).

To the east, the vast landscapes of what is now Russia and Ukraine proved tempting targets for trade and eventually conquest.

THE NORSE

Fragmented as it was across Scandinavia, Norse society was still pretty organized: within each local kingdom was contained a government (the effectiveness of which depended on the ruler and nobility), law courts called 'things', and a rigid social hierarchy where everyone knew their place.

Top dogs were the *konungar* (kings), who had complete power over the lands they owned; everyone beneath owed their loyalty to them. Next down were the jarls (earls): nobles who owned land and ruled the people who lived on it. Then came the *karls*: freeborn farmers, traders and craftspeople. At the bottom were thralls: enslaved people often captured during Viking raids, who had no rights and lived pretty miserable lives.

Home Life

Most Norse were *karls*, and many *karls* were farmers. They toiled the land growing wheat, barley, rye and oats, and kept cattle and goats for meat and milk, sheep for meat and wool, pigs and chickens. Deer, bear and seal were hunted for meat and pelts, and the sea, rivers and lakes scoured for fish and crustaceans.

Whole families, from grandparents to grandchildren (and in winter sometimes even the livestock) lived together in large, single-room thatch-and-timber longhouses. After the day's work was done, everyone gathered around the fire to eat, gossip and tell stories. There were no windows, but with a roaring fire and furs and wool hangings adorning the walls, a longhouse could be a cosy homestead.

Dogs were kept for hunting and tracking, and cats to catch vermin. Some Norse kept bees for their honey, which was highly prized as a sweetener and an essential ingredient for mead – perhaps the most ancient alcoholic drink.

Arts, Crafts and Entertainment

Like the mythical dwarves of Nidavellir, the Norse were exceptional craftspeople who poured skill, pride and a bold aesthetic style into their weapons, jewellery, tools, pottery, glasswork and textiles. Gold, silver, bronze and pewter were worked into beautiful bracelets, brooches, torques and rings, and tableware such as dishes, plates and chalices; wood was carved to make carts, sleighs and their exceptional ships; wool woven for clothes, blankets, wall hangings and sails.

Clothes were hardwearing and sometimes waterproofed with fish oil, but they weren't always drab. Dyes made from plant extracts were used to colour the wool yellow, blue, purple and red. Outfits could be finished with fur cloaks, leather accoutrements, and belts and brooches to keep everything together.

All work and no play makes Ragnar a dull Viking, and the Norse knew how to entertain themselves. Gathering to feast and drink was a common social pastime. They loved music too, and played pipes, flutes, lyres and drums. Skalds (poets) created and recited poetry for their audiences. There were two kinds: Eddic poetry told tales of gods and monsters; skaldic poetry dealt with contemporary figures (usually kings, jarls and warriors) and recounted real historical events.

THE LANGUAGE OF THE NORSE

Imagine being shown the first manuscript of *Beowulf,* the epic poem about heroes, monsters and monsters' mothers. Now housed in the British Library, this precious artefact was written in Old English by two unknown transcribers around 1000. The parchment is thin, burnt at the edges, stained throughout. The text is peat-brown and boldly written – each letter clearly defined; perfectly legible even after ten centuries (and one fire).

Here are the opening lines, one through to eleven:

> *Hwæt! We Gardena*   *in geardagum,*
> *þeod-cyninga*   *þrym gefrunon,*
> *hu ða æþelingas*   *len fremedon.*
> *Oft Scyld Scefing*   *sceaþena þreatum,*
> *monegum mægþum,*   *meodo-setla ofteah,*
> *egsode eorlas.*   *Syððan ærest wearð*
> *feasceaft funden,*   *he þæs frofre gebad,*
> *weox under wolcnum,* *weorðmyndum þah,*
> *oðþæt him æghwylc*   *ymbsittendra*
> *ofer hron-rade*   *hyran scolde,*
> *gomban gyldan.*   *Þæt wæs god cyning!*

Unless you speak Old English (which, no offence, I doubt you do) the meaning of the above will be a mystery, and your link with the original writers sadly tenuous: *Wow. Amazing to see the actual words written down by these long dead transcribers! I wonder what they mean…?*

However, in our amazing technological age, a quick Google search brings up this translation by American literary scholar John Lesslie Hall (1856–1928):

Lo! the Spear-Danes' glory through splendid achievements,
The folk-kings' former fame we have heard of, How
princes displayed then their prowess-in-battle.
Oft Scyld the Scefing from scathers in numbers,
From many a people their mead-benches tore,
Since first he found him friendless and wretched
The earl had had terror: comfort he got for it,
Waxed 'neath the welkin, world-honour gained,
Till all his neighbours o'er sea were compelled to
Bow to his bidding and bring him their tribute,
An excellent atheling!

Fantastic. The meaning is clearly expressed for us in English (except perhaps for searches to find out what 'scathers', 'welkin' and 'atheling' mean), and thus our link to the original writers is strengthened.

And Yet...

And yet I'm looking at this translation rendered in a font on a computer screen – a far less evocative experience than seeing the original words as scratched out in Old English. More importantly, I'm reading the opening of *Beowulf* as translated by Hall, a modern scholar. And, like all translations, no matter how skilfully done, there will be discrepancies, slippages of meaning, between the original and translated texts.

This is highlighted by the fact that Hall's translation is different to others. For example, R.M. Liuzza's opening (*Beowulf*, 1999) goes like this: '*What! We of the Spear-Danes in days-of-yore of the people-kings glory heard, how the noblemen valour did.'*

And here's John McNamara's (*Beowulf*, 2005): *'Hail! We have heard tales sung of the Spear-Danes, the glory of their war-kings in days gone by, how princely nobles performed heroes' deeds!'*

'Lo! What! Hail!' Even the first word differs! I'm taking nothing away from these estimable scholars and their great works, but these abstractions can't help but keep the reader at a distance from the original transcribers' exact intent of meaning.

Now, imagine looking at the original Old English *Beowulf* and being able to understand it pretty much word for word, without needing an ancient language degree or relying on someone else's translation. How wonderful that would be!

Well, prepare to be envious, because that's exactly what a modern Icelander can do when presented with something written in Old Icelandic. But how?

Old Norse

During the Viking Age, Scandinavians spoke what we now call Old Norse, which stems from even older Germanic languages. There were different dialects (two being East Old Norse and West Old Norse), but people understood each other just fine no matter where they hailed from. East Old Norse was spoken in what is now Denmark, Sweden and the Baltic; West Old Norse in Norway. As the Norse settled beyond their borders, they took their language with them and, at its broadest extent, Old Norse was spoken (not always exclusively) in Scandinavia, Greenland, Iceland, the Faroe Islands, the British Isles, continental Europe, Russia and Byzantium.

ANCIENT & MODERN: INTRODUCING LOKI

Languages are in a constant state of change as imposed or imported social and cultural influences take their toll. Thus, the modern languages spoken in Norway, Sweden and Denmark are very different to Old Norse. Not so in Iceland.

Settled in 874 by West Old Norse-speaking Norsemen from Norway, their language developed into what we now call Old Icelandic. In the roughly 1,200 years since, Iceland's relative isolation in the northern Atlantic and fierce protection of its Norse roots has ensured that the language spoken there now is very similar to Old Icelandic, which in turn is very similar to Old Norse.

So, give an Icelander a thousand-year-old book written in Old Icelandic – the *Prose Edda*, for example – and they're all set for a cosy evening's read.

Old Norse is Still Alive and Kicking

Iceland aside, Old Norse faded from the world...but it did not disappear. Modern English and the map of England are positively awash with Old Norse words and names. Weekdays, for example. Tuesday is Tyr's day; Wednesday is Odin's day; Thursday is Thor's day; and Friday is Frigg's day.

Place name endings: -thorpe = settlement (e.g. Cleethorpes); -thwaite = woodland clearing (Brackenthwaite); -toft = site of a building (Lowestoft); -keld = spring (Threlkeld); -ness = headland (Skegness); -by = farmstead, village or settlement (Whitby); -kirk: = church (Falkirk); -dale = valley (Rochdale).

And here are a few ordinary words: *angr* = anger; *happ* = happy; *odda* = odd; *klubba* = club; *slatra* = slaughter;

rannsaka = ransack; *bylög* (village law) = bylaw; *beck* = stream; *húsbónd* (house occupier) = husband; *myrr* = mire; *rotinn* = rotten and so on and on.

Runes: The Norse Written Language

The Norse wrote using runic alphabets. From around 150–800 they had a 24-rune alphabet called the Elder Futhark. ('Futhark' comes from the first six letters: f, u, th, a, r, k.) By 800, the beginning of the Viking Age, they had streamlined to the 16-rune Younger Futhark.

'Rune' means (evocatively, I think you'll agree) 'secret' or 'mystery', and they were designed to be easily carved into hard surfaces such as stone, wood and metal (Norse didn't write with ink on parchment). We don't really know how widespread literacy was, but probably fairly low. However, we can be sure that those who understood and utilized runes were respected as recorders of law, history and stories.

Runes carried far more weight than the utilitarian Latin alphabet we use today. Sure, they functioned as letters that formed words when put together, but individually they carried symbolic meanings that connected them to consequential forces and concepts, both natural and divine. For example,   is 'sea'; is 'ride'; is 'wealth'; is 'sun'; is T̲ý̲r̲ (the God of War) and is 'iron' or 'rain'. This meant people could use runes to interact, understand and even influence the forces they symbolized. Runes were etched into weapons, tools and jewellery to add potency, and were central to Norse magic (more on this later).

In short, runes held *power,* and nowhere is this more ably

demonstrated than the story of how Odin, leader of the Norse pantheon, learned the runes and what he put himself through to do so.

'Odin Learns the Runes'

Odin brooded.

"The fate of the gods is written," he muttered. "*My* fate is written."

A vision of the future, of dread Ragnarök, swept like a storm through his mind. Famine. Fire. Death. Asgard torn asunder. Kith and kin annihilated. Fenrir's foaming jaws snapping shut over his head...

"But if I can learn the runes with which this fate is foretold, perhaps I can rewrite the story to my advantage."

So, the All-Father travelled to the roots of Yggdrasil, where the fate-weaving Norns abided. He watched hungrily from afar as one carved marks onto the World Tree's bark, one drew glowing symbols in the air, and the other sat on the ground throwing dice.

Runes they were, but his untrained mind couldn't grasp their shape or meaning.

Odin stepped into the open, and as he did so the bark healed, the symbols scattered, and the dice were swept into a bag.

"Hail, Odin," the Norns said as one. "We knew you would come this day."

One plucked a thread attached to a spindle, and Odin's soul vibrated. "I wish to learn the runes," he said.

"To stave off your fate," one replied.

"It will not work," the others added.

Odin gritted his teeth. "Nevertheless."

"Such power is not free," one said.

"A sacrifice is required," two said.

"What will you give?" all said.

"The only sacrifice worthy of the prize," he declared. "Myself."

Odin produced a rope. He tied one end around his ankles and passed the other to the Norns. "Throw this over a branch and hang me over the Well of Urd," he said. Expressing no surprise, the Norns did as he asked.

Once dangling upside down, Odin produced his spear and impaled himself right through. Blood flowed, painting his face red and clotting in his hair – but he made no sound. Spinning on the rope and wracked with pain, he looked down into the swirling well.

For days he hung – pale as a corpse, eating not, drinking not, sleeping not – as the well turned red with his blood. Throughout, Odin glared unblinking into its depths. Meanwhile, the Norns scratched, drew and cast the runes of fate.

On the ninth day the pain-price was paid and what had been hidden was at last revealed: the runes appeared on the water's crimson surface. Upon seeing them, Odin gave a cry of exultation, withdrew the spear from his side and used it to cut the rope.

"I understand," he gasped. "I understand it all."

"You may use the runes to heal wounds, make enemies' weapons useless, free yourself from bonds, defeat weavers of dark magic, win any lover you desire, and speak to the dead," the Norns chanted. "But in the end, Odin All-Father, it will avail you not. Ragnarök is coming, as is the ravening wolf."

Odin turned his back on the Norns. "We shall see."

NORSE INFLUENCE ON THE MEDIEVAL WORLD

Let's play our game again. What do you think of when you see the word 'Norse'? I expect 'raiding', 'plunder' and 'pillage' may well have popped in there, along with visions of bloodthirsty warriors leaping from boats and laying waste to screaming Saxons. The Norse are indeed famous for their lightning-fast raids – after all, they did it a *lot* and they were *very* good at it.

The Raid of Lindisfarne Abbey

The year 793 started badly for the monks of Lindisfarne Abbey, as evidenced in the late ninth-century *Anglo-Saxon Chronicle*: 'This year came dreadful forewarnings over the land of the Northumbrians, terrifying the people most woefully: there were immense sheets of light rushing through the air, and whirlwinds, and fiery dragons flying across the firmament. These tremendous tokens were soon followed by a great famine.' (Translation by Reverend James Ingram, 1823.)

Not good. But worse – *much* worse – was yet to come.

Founded in 634 on a small island off the east coast of England, Lindisfarne Abbey was an important religious site. Home to monks, as well as the interred remains of the venerated Saint Cuthbert, this was a sacred place of healing and pilgrimage. The church was constructed from lead-lined timber and surrounded by smaller wooden buildings that the monks lived and worked in.

The monks led a cloistered, quiet, contemplative life in service to their Christian God; it's likely they felt deeply fortunate to live in such a holy sanctuary, safe and sound under His protective gaze. Treasures they had, including gold crosses and jewel-encrusted chalices – but the monks believed that no Christian would risk the wrath of God by stealing them, let alone laying hands on their devoted custodians.

Pagans, however, had no such compunction.

Signs and Portents Fulfilled

The fateful day occurred in June.

Three dragonships landed on the shores of the island, and a few dozen heavily armed Vikings disembarked and descended on the defenceless abbey. It's hard to imagine the sheer horror felt by the monks as their idyll was shattered: unarmed men of peace being set upon by axe-wielding men of violence. Room to room the Vikings went, smashing down doors, looting, slaughtering, slicing.

Contemporary accounts are short and to the point (*Anglo-Saxon Chronicle*, 1823): 'The harrowing inroads of heathen men made lamentable havoc in the church of God in Holy-island, by rapine and slaughter.' The 12th-century chronicle *Historia Regum (History of Kings)* by Simeon of Durham states: '[The heathens] laid everything to waste with grievous plundering, trampled the holy places with polluted steps, dug up the alters and seized all the treasures of the holy church.' The contemporary Northumbrian scholar, Alcuin of York (*c.* 735–804) wrote: 'The church of St Cuthbert is splattered with the blood of the priests of God, stripped of all its furnishings, exposed to the plundering of pagans.'

All accounts are from the Christian side (there exist no known Scandinavian records of the event), so it's biased against the Norse. However, we have no good reason to believe that what these appalled chroniclers wrote is inaccurate or even exaggerated. This was an at-the-time unprecedented raid of great brutality on a holy site, and it scared the pants off every Christian who heard about it.

Those monks not killed in the initial wave of terrifying violence were either drowned in the sea (presumably because it amused the Vikings) or taken as slaves to Scandinavia. Imagine waking up on an ordinary morning, praying, having breakfast with your brothers in faith...and a few hours later, perhaps with the blood of those brothers soaking into your robes, being taken on a ship to spend the rest of your life in servitude in an unknown land filled with murderous heathens.

Of the few monks who managed to escape, the only scrap of comfort left for them was that the Vikings had at least left the remains of St Cuthbert behind – probably because they saw no material value in them.

A Raid Heard Around the World

As previously mentioned, this was not the first Viking raid on English shores, but it was the first to target a holy site, and that was enough to send shockwaves through the Christian world. Much handwringing followed. Why did their merciful God let these pagan barbarians attack such a sacred place? Why did men who had dedicated their lives to God's service meet such horrendous fates? What can be done to stop it happening again?

The contemporaneous answer to that final question would probably have amused no end any Viking who heard it. Alcuin of York, who I mentioned earlier, was at the time of the raid working in the court of Charlemagne. He wrote, 'Never before has such terror appeared in Britain as we have now suffered... Is this the outcome of the sins of those who live there? It has not happened by chance, but is the sign of great guilt.'

So, according to Alcuin, it was the monks' own fault (classic victim blaming) – the Vikings were a punishment meted out by God for (unspecified) sins. Alcuin suggested the best thing to prevent this from happening again was to lead a more pious life.

Spoiler alert – Alcuin's suggestion didn't work.

Soft Targets and Rich Rewards

Far from being a one-off scolding by God, the attack on Lindisfarne proved to be the first of an ongoing campaign of painful thrusts into Britain's coastline. In 794 Jarrow Abbey (also in Northumbria) was assaulted, and a particularly unlucky monastery on the Hebridean island of Iona in 795, 802 and 806; it's testament to the fortitude and resilience of the residents there that they stayed put despite these lethal visitations.

Vikings singled out abbeys and churches because they were easy targets and guaranteed a haul of slaves and portable wealth to cart off home. Such places were often situated on islands, headlands and coastlines – so easily reached by ship. They were often isolated, allowing the Vikings to land, plunder and disappear before aid could arrive. And they were usually entirely undefended.

Standing armies were rare at this time – they were too expensive to maintain when not serving a purpose, and the workforce was required to farm and do the usual things society needed to function. Armed forces were mustered as and when required, and this took time and organization. Besides, even if there were armies knocking about, it was unlikely they would be at the right place at the right time to turn back a raid.

In short, abbeys and churches were easy pickings for determined raiders.

We can only imagine what it was like for anyone living in or near such tempting targets. Aware of their vulnerability, always watching the seas for telltale dots on the horizon, praying that the day never came when the dreaded dragonships scraped up the shingle to offload their barbarous crews.

By the mid-800s much larger fleets carrying Norse armies of conquest were hacking bigger, more permanent chunks out of Britain, but we'll get to that in a bit. For now, let's examine why the Vikings were so damned effective at their job.

Dragonships

We've all seen it in films, TV and video games: a sleek-hulled dragonship skimming across the water. Oars rising and falling in perfect rhythm. A red sail billowing, fat with wind. Standing at the prow, arm wrapped around a carved figurehead, a Viking warrior peers into the distance. It's iconic stuff: dramatic, kinetic and exciting...and historically accurate.

The Norse had long been a waterborne people. Their land was a rugged one: hilly, mountainous and heavily forested. It was also surrounded by a long coastline of fjords and naturally sheltered harbours, so the quickest and most reliable method of getting around was often by sea and river. Because of this, they took maritime technology seriously and designed seriously good ships. Put simply, Norse dragonships (also called longships) were state-of-the-art – no other nation had anything to rival them, and this remained the case for most of the Viking Age.

If you want real evidence of what the Norse could do with some wood, rope, iron nails, wool, simple tools and a whole lot of skill, check out the Oseberg ship. This vessel (a fairly short type of longship called a 'karve') was excavated from a burial site in Norway and is perfectly preserved in the Museum of the Viking Age in Oslo. With its elegant prow and curvaceous hull, it is that rare feat of engineering that manages to combine striking beauty with perfect functionality.

Dragonship Construction

Dragonships were built by highly skilled shipwrights. Trees to make them were carefully chosen, cut, treated and shaped. The keel – the structural element at the bottom that runs the boat's full length – was made from carved oak strong enough to support a single mast. From this foundation rose the hull. This was built from long planks of overlapping wood fixed with iron nails (a method called 'clinker-built' or 'lapstrake'), which created a strong yet flexible structure; gaps between planks were stuffed with moss, animal hair and wool, and a layer of tar added for waterproofing.

Over Sea, River and Land

One of the most remarkable aspects of a dragonship was its shallow draught. It meant that rather than having to bully its way *through* the waves, it could more easily skim *over* them to reach speeds up to around 25 kph (13 knots) – much faster than other vessels at the time.

And that's not all. A shallow draught meant a dragonship didn't need harbours or jetties to moor up against; all it needed was a beach to slide up on, and when their business was done, the Vikings could push it back into the sea and off they'd go. This allowed Vikings to land almost anywhere they wanted, usually as close to their intended target as possible.

It also meant they could travel up rivers, meaning potential victims were not limited to those living on the coast. Raiding parties could sail deep into the interior, hopping off at trading posts and villages to kill and despoil at will. Some even set up camps so they could take their time sacking an area. After all, it was always best to return home with as much booty as possible.

And if that wasn't sufficient to make these vessels as sneakily penetrative as possible, they were also lightweight enough for the crew to lift them from the water and heave them across land. With brute force and logs to roll it on, a dragonship could be manhandled from one river to another. Truly no one was safe from these determined raiders and their spectacular ships.

A shallow draught didn't mean the boat was unstable – far from it. These were ocean-going ships capable of riding heavy seas for hundreds and even thousands of miles. Their hulls were relatively wide across the beam to reduce the chance of capsizing; low sides, and with a single mast, and gear and cargo stashed under the decks kept the centre of gravity low.

Tools of the Raid

Away from his arms in the open field
A man should fare not a foot;
For never he knows when the need for a spear
Shall arise on the distant road.

So reads advice from Odin, as translated by editor Henry Adams Bellows (1835–1939) in the Old Norse poem 'Hávamál' (meaning 'Words of the High One') that appears in his version of the *Poetic Edda* (1923). This is a dangerous world, he's saying, so be prepared. In fact, all Norse were expected to keep weapons and fighting gear in readiness for any military action deemed necessary by their war-chief, and everyone, including women and children, would have had at least a rough understanding of how to wield them properly.

The spear was the average *karl's* favoured weapon because they were cheap to make and effective at stabbing and keeping enemies at bay; lighter versions could be hurled. Axes were popular too. In battle they could hack flesh and break bones; skilled warriors could use the blade to hook around an enemy's shield and tear it from his grasp. Most axes were single-handed, but the Dane axe (or long axe) was a fearsome metre-long affair capable of unhorsing cavalry and lopping off limbs. (Check out the Bayeux Tapestry to see some contemporary depictions.)

Requiring a lot of high-quality metal and great skill to make, swords were the reserve of the wealthy. Norse swords were around 90 cm (35 in) long, double edged and with a fuller (groove) running their length to make them lighter. Often highly decorated, these objects held great significance to their owners, who sometimes gave them names; known examples include 'Leg-biter' and 'Viper'.

Metal armour was rare. It came in the form of long chainmail coats and, like swords, only the richest could afford them. The majority of fighting Norse made do with padded jerkins that might turn a blade but probably wouldn't stop an arrow. Helmets, as I'm sure you're aware, did not sport horns. Shields were round and made of painted wooden planks secured together with a metal rim; the holder's hand was protected by a protruding metal 'boss'.

Traders' Influence in the Wider World

I know I led with the Norse propensity for monk-murder and brigandry, but I want to stress that raiding was not the only thing the Norse did to influence the wider world. They were also excellent merchants who established long trade routes across water and land, and built bustling trade hubs all over Scandinavia and as far afield as Dublin, York, Bordeaux, Kiev and Novgorod. The Volga river took them all the way to the Caspian Sea; the Dnieper to the Black Sea, thus giving them access to the trading powerhouses of Constantinople, Baghdad and Jerusalem, where many a Norse fortune was made.

The Norse took full advantage of their lands' natural resources and the skill of their craftspeople, and set forth with holds and carts laden with furs, amber, leather, walrus ivory, honey, wood, wheat, timber, tin, iron, leather, weapons and jewellery. They also traded into servitude the poor souls captured during their raids (including British, Irish, Frankish and Slavic folk), prisoners of war and home-grown criminals.

Again, Norse maritime ingenuity came into its own. Clinker-built, cargo-carrying vessels called knarrs were shorter, wider and deeper than longships, and could carry around 30 tonnes of goods over rivers and oceans (and we're including the heavy, storm-wracked North Atlantic here).

Upon their return, traders might bring back olive oil, wine and pottery from the Mediterranean; glass, silk, silver coins, exotic fruits and spices from the Middle East; and via those eastern links, decorative items and jewellery from India, China and North Africa.

Norse Conquests

To quote the penultimate line in the film *The Terminator* (1984), 'There's a storm coming.' (I admit this quote *is* a bit arbitrary.)

And for ninth-century England, already bloodied after decades of Viking raids, black clouds were most certainly massing across the North Sea. Because the Norse had asked themselves the fateful question: *Why just pick at the edges of this resource- and cash-rich country? Why not grab the whole lot for ourselves?* It would certainly save a lot of sea crossings, and it was warmer too. Win win.

34

So, they did what all history's best prime movers do: they got busy and organized.

The Geography of the Battlefield

The conquest of England is quite the saga, so it's worth mapping out the lay of the Anglo-Saxon land before the Norse came along and rearranged it with axe and extorsion (mostly axe). For a start, it wasn't called England and it wasn't yet a unified country (although we'll get there before this section is done).

At this point, 'England' was split into seven petty kingdoms ruled by Anglo-Saxon kings, collectively called the Heptarchy. Northumbria is now Yorkshire and southern Scotland; Mercia was the Midlands; East Anglia, Essex, Kent and Sussex were pretty much where they are now, and Wessex was a big section of the West Country. They were a disunited bunch, constantly squabbling and snarling at each other – which the Norse took full advantage of.

In the Red Corner...

The Norse kingdoms were just as adept at fighting each other as the Anglo-Saxons, but in this grand mission of conquest they saw a mutual benefit and banded their forces together to create what became known as the Great Heathen Army. Estimates vary wildly on the size of this coalition, but it must have numbered at least in the several thousands. This bristling force was led by a chieftain called Ivar the Boneless. The Icelandic sagas say Ivar was the son of the semi-legendary Viking Ragnar Lodbrok (755–865) – the main character in the TV series *Vikings* (2013–20) – and we'll talk of him in a bit.

In 865 Ivar's fleet landed in East Anglia and the Norse set to the task of invasion with their now famous proficiency. Unable to fend off the Norse militarily, the locals instead gave them enough horses upon which to ride away, thus taking their unwelcome attentions elsewhere.

The Great Heathen Army cut a bloody swathe north up the country to Northumbria where they took York as a base of operations. Down but not out, the Northumbrians laid siege to York. However, their leaders were killed and the survivors forced to make peace with Ivar. Over the next few years, the Norse invaded the other kingdoms, sometimes allowing themselves to be bought off with gold before returning later to take the land and depose the kings anyway.

Alfred the Great

By 874, the only holdout was Wessex. Its ruler, Alfred the Great (848–99), knew it was only a matter of time before the Norse turned their full attention to him; the protection money ('Danegeld') he'd paid would only stay the invaders' wrath for so long. And so it proved when things came to a violent head at the Battle of Edington in 878.

A surprise Norse attack in January that year forced Alfred to take refuge in the marshes at Athelney. There he remained, building his forces until May, when he felt ready to counterattack. The forces met in Wiltshire, with both sides knowing that the fate of the Anglo-Saxons was hanging in the balance.

According to an account written by Alfred's biographer and friend John Asser (*Asser's Life of King Alfred*): 'The next morning at dawn he moved his standards to Edington, and there fought bravely and perseveringly by means of a close shield-wall against the whole army of the heathen, whom at length, with the divine help, he defeated with great slaughter, and pursued them flying to their stronghold.'

Alfred's crushing victory forced the Norse to negotiate terms, including to never threaten Wessex again – and this time the decisive nature of their defeat ensured they would keep their word. However, this setback aside, the Great Heathen Army had achieved its goal of subduing much of England in only a decade. Their portion became known as the Danelaw.

Snake Pits and Blood-eagles

Let's quickly digress from this (extremely compacted) history of Norse England into the realms of Norse myth, because they tell a different and more bloodily poetic story about why the Great Heathen Army was raised. According to their sagas, the great Viking leader Ragnar Lodbrok (Lodbrok meaning 'hairy-breeches') invaded England with conquest in mind. Unfortunately, he was captured by King Aella of Northumbria (c. 815–67) who, having quite the imagination, put Ragnar to death by throwing him into a pit of venomous snakes.

Hearing of their father's Spielbergian fate, Ragnar's sons (including Ivar the Boneless) decided to exact revenge, and that's why they forged their Heathen Army. After taking York, they subjected Ælla to a fate-worse-than-snake-pit called the blood-eagle. This execution method involved splitting the victim's ribs from the spine and pulling the lungs out through the resultant gaps, thus creating 'wings'. However, no contemporary sources attest to such a thing, and it might well be the result of a mistranslation or gross exaggeration by the Christian scholars who recorded the Sagas many years later.

Historically true or not, this excessively gory yet visually impressive method of revenge has ever since retained a place in the darker parts of our imaginations, and appears in video games such as *Assassin's Creed: Valhalla* (2020), *Hellblade: Senua's Sacrifice* (2017), TV shows *Vikings* (2013–20) and *Hannibal* (2013–15) and the Swedish-set folk-horror movie *Midsommar* (2019).

Creation of Engalond

King Alfred died in 899, but his progeny (son Edward, daughter Aethelflaed and grandson Athelstan) had clearly inherited his grit and skill in warfare, because over the next few decades they pushed the Norse out of England and took it back for the Anglo-Saxons. And so was created 'Engalond' – a unified kingdom of the English with Athelstan as its first ruler. But the Norse were not to be discouraged, and England would remain a battlefield for them and the Anglo-Saxons for many decades to come.

Invasion 2: The Revenge

The tenth century saw the return of Viking raids, with the Anglo-Saxons forced to pay in both blood and Danegeld. And then, in 1013, Danish King Svein Forkbeard (963–1014) landed an army. He retook all of England with astonishing speed, but annoyingly for him after all that hard work, died only a year later. The crown fell on the head of Anglo-Saxon Edmund Ironside (*c.* 990–1016), and there followed three more years of warfare that waxed one way, then the other. In 1016, Edmund was defeated by King Cnut (994–1035), Svein's son (who also ruled Denmark, Norway and southern Sweden), and England was once again in Norse hands.

And now a rush to the finish: Cnut and his sons ruled until 1042. In that time, Norse and Anglo-Saxon art and culture comingled. Viking raids fell off a cliff, leaving most ordinary folk highly relieved. Anglo-Saxon King Edward the Confessor ruled until his death in 1066, which brings us to Harold G., Harald H., William the C. and the end of the Viking Age.

Settling New Lands

The Norse's vigorous expansion was not limited to places already occupied. Sometime in the early 800s, a Norse called Naddodd from the Faroe Islands came upon Iceland when his ship was blown off course. He stayed long enough to call it Snaeland (Slowland) before leaving. The first permanent settler was Ingólfr Arnarson (*c.* 849–910) who in 874 founded a permanent home in what is now Reykjavík. More arrivals swelled Iceland's population and a Commonwealth of Chieftains was created. This is where the Eddas and sagas were recorded, and modern Iceland still holds fast to its Norse heritage.

In the tenth century, a Norseman called Thorvald was exiled from Norway for manslaughter and moved to Iceland, taking his son, Erik the Red, with him. In a strange coincidence, Erik was exiled from Iceland, also for manslaughter, so he decided to sail west. He and his comrades landed on the vast landmass of Greenland and spent a few years exploring before building a home. He named the country Greenland in the hopes that such an inviting name would encourage others to join him. It worked to a degree, and at its height the population was around 4,000 people, mostly farmers living along the southwestern coast. After around 400 years the Norse abandoned Greenland, probably due to the climate getting colder.

If further proof of Norse bravery and confidence in their ships and seafaring skills were needed, look no further than the achievements of Lief Erikson, Erik the Red's son. Having heard tales from other explorers of a new land further west of Greenland, Lief set sail in around 1000 to find it. After a gruelling voyage across the Atlantic, he became the first European to set foot on continental America. He found a lush, temperate landscape (in what we now call Canada) full of self-sewn wheat and grapes. He called it Vinland.

Harald Hardråde: King and Mercenary

Finally, let's go back to King Harald Hardråde, who led an extremely eventful life that took him far away from his native Norway to fight as a mercenary in another country. His actual name was Harald Sigurdsson ('Hardråde' was an epithet given to him in the Norse sagas) and he was pretty much born with a sword in his hand. At age fifteen, he fought alongside his half-brother King Olaf of Norway (963–1000) against the Danes at the Battle of Stiklestad. His side was defeated and Olaf killed in the melee, so Harald (who was himself wounded) and a few loyal followers beat a hasty retreat and ended up in Kiev, where they were taken in by Grand Prince Yaroslav the Wise (*c.* 978–1054), a descendant of Norsemen who had settled there years earlier.

Harald must have impressed the Grand Prince because he was made a captain in his army, a role he held for a few years before, after several military actions, relocating to Constantinople, the capital of the Eastern Roman Empire (the portion of the Roman Empire that didn't fall to the barbarians in 476, and which we now call the Byzantine Empire) to join the famous Varangian Guard.

This elite group of soldiers served as bodyguards for the Byzantine emperors from the tenth to the fourteenth centuries, and was mostly composed of expat Norse warriors (and a few Anglo-Saxons for variety). The idea from the Byzantian point of view was that foreign soldiers would be less mired in the sort of internecine scheming and shifting loyalties that were part and parcel of court life, and could thus be relied upon to deal with disloyal subjects and rebels.

As well as providing security, these long-haired, axe-wielding warriors (who were respected and feared for their ferocity and skill in battle) were deployed in military campaigns all over the place. Harald himself fought in Bulgaria, Sicily, the Holy Land, Anatolia and Mesopotamia. Serving in the Guard was a lucrative way for a Viking to make a living doing what he did best, and many returned to Scandinavia rich men.

And in 1045 that's what Harald did: using his new-found wealth and extensive military experience to end up ruling Norway, fighting lots more battles, taking control of the Orkney

Isles, Shetland Isles and Hebrides, antagonizing the Pope, until finally overreaching himself and falling to Harold Godwinson at the Battle of Stamford Bridge.

2.
Loki's World

Of old was the age / when Ymir lived;
Sea nor cool waves / nor sand there were;
Earth had not been, / nor heaven above,
But a yawning gap, / and grass nowhere.
– Poetic Edda (trans. Henry Adams Bellows, 1936)

'THE CREATION OF THE COSMOS'

efore mountains and seas and rivers and grass was Ginnungagap. A silent void. A blank canvas. An empty vessel.

Waiting.

To the north lay Niflheim, where fog roiled, winds howled and snow swirled; southward it crept on layers of rime. To the south, Muspelheim, where smoke billowed, fire raged and lava flowed; northward it climbed, on a bed of embers.

When they met, water flowed and sparks filled the darkness. From the water was born a frost giant – huge, primeval, chaotic. Named Ymir, he was so full of life that when he slept more giants emerged from his armpits and legs.

The water gave more: a cow called Auðumbla from whose teats flowed rivers of milk. Upon these Ymir gorged, growing ever stronger. Auðumbla was thirsty, so she licked a block of ice, and with her rough tongue shaped it into a god called Buri. And Buri begat Bor, who married a giantess called Bestla, and between them created three brothers: Odin, Vili and Ve. They wandered the primordial waste and liked not what they saw.

"This is an unwelcoming place," Vili said.

"And there's no order to things." Ve shuddered.

Odin flexed his mind and muscles. "Then let's do something about it."

So they set upon Ymir with axe and stone and fist. The frost giant bellowed, lashing left and right, but the gods leapt nimbly over him, avoiding his blows while landing their own, until Ymir fell dead to the ground. Blood poured from his wounds, drowning all but two of his progeny.

Flush with victory, the gods set about creating a place of order, using the slain frost giant for materials. His blood they channelled into seas and lakes. His hair they planted for trees and grass. His bones they stacked into mountains. His teeth they crushed into stones. His flesh they minced into earth. And so the land was made.

Next, Odin and his kin looked at the void above and, finding it bleak, cracked open Ymir's skull and raised it high to form a blue and pleasant sky. Then they grasped clumps of the giant's brain and cast them up to form clouds.

Satisfied, the brothers went for a walk. "We've created something special," Vili said.

"Although it does feel empty," Ve sighed.

"Then let's fill it," Odin said. "We can use this driftwood."

So they carved the wood into humans, and they called the woman Embla after the elm, and the man Ask after the ash. A land called Midgard the gods made for them, and around it formed a wall using Ymir's eyebrows.

Finally, from the shrunken remains of Ymir's corpse a great tree called Yggdrasil grew, and this formed the centre of the new cosmos. Odin was proud of this ordered world and looked forward to wandering its lands and meeting its denizens. But he was also fearful that chaos would return and bring an end to his creation.

And it was to that particular end that the two surviving giants slunk away to their own land, to procreate, nurse their hate and plan their revenge.

Creating Order from Chaos

The Norse creation myth, see 'Creation of the Cosmos' above, is a wonderful prologue for the many stories that follow. It is a wild and imaginative tale, perfectly reflective of the epic, intricate, twisty, thematically rich, often violent and sometimes downright bizarre stories that make up the rest of the canon (those that we know of, anyway).

One of the most striking aspects of the tale is how the gods use the raw materials of chaos (as represented by Ymir the frost giant) to create their preferred world of order. Killing Ymir provided everything the gods needed to not only form the cosmos into a place where gods and humans can thrive, it also (almost) rids them of the giants (and the gods' lack of regret or reflection on this homicidal act strongly suggests they felt it was entirely justified).

The creation myth sets up a gripping story arc where the gods' instigative act of killing Ymir and his progeny sows the seeds of their eventual demise at Ragnarök. Many of the stories that occur between these two cataclysmic events involve Odin's ultimately fruitless attempts to change the dark fate he's set in motion: 'Odin Learns the Runes' (see page 23) is only one example.

But before we fast-forward too far ahead, let's pause and explore the rich cosmos wrought from the corpse of a giant. It's a fascinating setting full of larger-than-life characters, monsters and one gossipy squirrel...

NINE LANDS OF YGGDRASIL

Yggdrasil, the World Tree, a sacred ash, holds from sun-dappled crown to shadow-filled roots all the lands, people and creatures of the Norse cosmos. There are nine lands, and each is distinct in geography and population: from lofty Asgard, realm of the Aesir gods, to the stygian mines of Nidavellir, realm of the dwarves. Travel is possible between these places, and many tales tell of various gods (including Loki) and giants crossing borders to (usually) cause some sort of mischief and mayhem. Let's start right at the top of Yggdrasil and work our way down.

Asgard

Asgard is a paradise of golden halls, temples, shrines and workshops, where the weather is always fine and the gods can enjoy themselves while looking down on all the other lands.

Asgard means 'enclosure of the Aesir'. The Aesir are one of two groups of gods in Norse mythology, the other being the Vanir who live in Vanaheim (more on them later). The suffix '-gard' comes from the concepts of 'Innangard' and 'Utangard'. 'Innangard' translates to 'inside the enclosure', which means a civilized place of order and rules, as represented by the paradise of Asgard. 'Utangard' translates to 'outside the enclosure', and means a chaotic, anarchic place where no rules apply. Anathema to the gods, this is represented in the giant's abode of Jötunheim.

Early in the timeline, Asgard was without a protective enclosure, and vulnerable to the predations of the giants...

'The Walls of Asgard'

Odin surveyed Asgard's shining temples, sweeping bridges and packed drinking halls with satisfaction. "Our home is almost as beautiful as you, Frigg."

But Frigg's brow was creased. "The world is full of creatures who hate us, husband. What's to stop them barging in and smashing it up?" She turned towards the distant sound of Thor at his favourite pastime of thrashing trolls in the far mountains. "Especially when our son's not around to protect us."

At that moment, a stranger leading a stallion arrived. "In three seasons I can build you a wall no giant will ever breach," he said. "All I ask in return is Freya's hand in marriage, and the Sun and the Moon."

Odin and Frigg exchanged a glance. "Can you give us a minute?" Frigg replied.

47

* * *

"No," Freya said. "I'm not marrying a total stranger."

"And imagine how dark Asgard will be without the Sun and Moon," Odin added.

"But we do need a wall," Frigg said.

"How about we give him one season, and he has to work alone?" Loki suggested. "An impossible task! And if he doesn't finish, he doesn't get paid."

"A partially built wall is better than nothing, I suppose," Frigg said.

"Very well," Odin replied. "Make the offer."

"This had better work," Freya hissed to Loki.

And so, on the first day of winter, the stranger set to his task, and the gods marvelled at how quickly he and his horse worked. As the weeks passed and the walls grew higher and stretched further around Asgard, so the gods' (and especially Freya's) disquiet grew.

"I don't understand how that horse can carry so much stone," Frigg said. "They'll be finished by tomorrow, and Winter isn't yet over."

All eyes turned to Loki, who returned a sickly smile.

"This was your idea," Odin boomed.

"How was I to know he had a magic horse?" Loki said, backing away.

"If I end up carted away by that filthy stonemason I'm going to *kill* you," Freya said.

Loki held up his shaking hands. "I'll fix it, I promise, no matter the cost to myself."

That night, the Aesir watched from the near-finished walls as the stranger led his horse to find the final load of rocks needed to build the gate. He gave Freya a cheery wave.

"Damn Loki's silver tongue," Freya growled.

Then, glorious in the light of the Moon, a mare pranced out of the forest, tossing her mane and twitching her tail. The stranger's stallion, inflamed and frantic at the sight, pursued the mare back into the forest leaving the astonished stranger alone.

Realizing he'd been thwarted and thus destined to be Sun-, Moon- and Freya-less, the stranger flew into a rage.

"Oh look," Frigg mused, "he was a Mountain Giant all along."

Odin clapped his hands in glee. "Perfect. Let's get our boy to sort him out."

So they recalled Thor who, fancying a change from killing trolls, used Mjölnir to crush the unlucky giant's skull.

Later, Loki emerged from the woods accompanied by an eight-legged foal called Sleipnir. "The best of horses," he declared with all the pride of a doting parent.

Valhalla

Imagine a vast hall standing on a hill. The sun glints on a roof made from a 1,000 golden shields, wolves guard its 540 doors, and an eagle hovers overhead. Inside, its rafters are made from spears, and the feasting tables from breastplates. This is Valhalla, Hall of the Slain, where half the warriors who die bravely in battle are taken after being chosen and plucked from the battlefield by female, winged entities called Valkyries. (The other half are claimed by the goddess Freya.) Called the Einherjar ('Army of One'), they spend their days sparring and fighting with each other. At night, their wounds heal and they feast on meat from an immortal boar called Sæhrímnir and quaff mead from a goat called Heiðrún.

This might seem like every Viking's ideal afterlife (drinking! feasting! fighting!), but it's not destined to last forever because Odin has gathered these elite warriors for a specific and long-prepared-for purpose. When Ragnarök comes, Odin plans to lead the Einherjar against Fenrir and the army of the giants...and perhaps – *perhaps* – defeat the dreadful fate they herald.

Midgard

Midgard is the human world where, from the point of view of the immortal (but not unkillable) gods, we mere mortals live out our short and petty lives. The name means 'middle enclosure', which may relate to the fact that it's located between the heavenly realm of Asgard and the underworld of Helheim. It may also refer to its position somewhere in the middle on the Innangard/Utangard scale: nowhere near as chaotic as Jötunheim, but not as civilized as Asgard. This gives us a nice indication of how the Norse saw themselves: flawed but striving to be better by using their gods as a benchmark.

Jötunheim

The antithesis of civilized Asgard, Jötunheim is the wild land of the jötnar (or 'giants'), the gods' mortal enemies. Winter never loses its grip on this inhospitable place of snow-capped mountains, dense forests and shifting plains of pack ice. Excepting Thor whose favourite pastime is slaughtering giants, few dare venture here.

The Jötnar

The jötnar are in constant conflict with the gods and are portrayed as a wildly contrasting race of creatures: the relationship between the gods and jötnar begins with murder (Odin slaying Ymir) and ends in slaughter (Ragnarök). However, god/jötunn (or 'giant') interactions between these two bookending events are not exclusively violent – nothing is that simple or uninteresting in Norse mythology.

The races often intermingle (Odin is part-jötunn, so all his offspring are too; Heimdall marries the giantess Gerðr; Loki is all-jötunn and he hangs out with the gods all the time) and in some stories they interact in a friendly co-operative way. Perhaps the relationship between Loki and the gods is the god/jötunn dynamic in microcosm: it's complex, always shifting between co-operation and antagonism…and destined to end *very* badly.

The term 'giant' is often used as a synonym for jötunn (including by me in this essay), but this can be confusing. Norse 'giants' are not giants as in 'bigger than everyone else'. Well, *some* of them are, but most are 'ordinary' size. Throughout the myths, some are described as large, monstrous and troll-like, while others are fair and beautiful. Just like the Norse, jötnar are not one thing only. That would be boring.

Vanaheim

There are two groups of deities in the Norse pantheon. The Aesir live in Asgard, and the Vanir in Vanaheim. The Vanir are closely associated with magic (known as 'seiðr'), soothsaying, wisdom, fertility and the natural world. At some point these two groups of gods fought a war against each other, with the Aesir pitting their martial prowess against the Vanir's magical skills. Neither side could gain a significant advantage and a truce was agreed using an exchange of hostages. In the end, both sides realized co-operation against their common foe, the jötnar, was the wisest choice.

Alfheim

This is the realm of the elves, luminous demigod-like beings described in the *Prose Edda* as 'fairer than the sun'; from this description we can assume that their land is also beautiful and tranquil. It is perhaps ruled by the Vanir god Freyr (at the very least he calls it home), which suggests an association between these two races, and a shared gift for magic.

Nidavellir

Meaning 'dark fields', Nidavellir is the home of the dwarves. This is a vast, subterranean complex of delving mines, echoing caverns and grimy workshops filled with the *tap-tap-tap* of pickaxe on rock and the *clang-clang-clang* of hammer on metal. Dwarves are expert miners and master craftsfolk who make many magical objects for the gods, including Odin's spear, Gungnir, which always hits its target, and Draupnir ('The Dripper'), a gold coin that replicates itself every nine days. Dwarves also forged Thor's hammer, the legendary Mjölnir, and in this tale Loki plays an important part.

'The Forging of Thor's Hammer'

One day in Asgard, while the other gods were doing useful things, Loki idled under a tree enjoying the warm weather. Sif, Thor's wife, passed by, and as she did so the sun glimmered tantalizingly on her golden hair. A bolt of jealousy tore through Loki.

"Why should that lunkhead get to be with such a beauty?" he muttered – and before he'd even finished the thought a petty trick formed in his mind.

Next morning, a horrified shriek followed by a bellow of rage shattered the peace, and all the gods and goddesses emerged from their halls to see what the fuss was about. Loki was among them, stifling a grin. Everyone gasped when Sif emerged from her home, face stricken, hands clasped to her perfectly bald scalp.

"My hair!" she cried. "My gorgeous golden hair! Where has it gone?"

"Perhaps a magpie stole it?" Loki said, struggling to keep a straight face.

Baldr shook his head. "Wow. My brother is going to be *pis*—"

Thor burst from his hall, face as red as his beard. He pointed at Loki. "YOU!"

Loki blanched. "Me…?" And before he could take a single step back, Thor had him tight by the neck.

"Who else?" Thor bellowed, spraying the trickster god in spittle. "Go on – admit it."

"I…thought it…would be…funny," Loki gasped.

"Oh Loki," the gods and goddesses sighed.

Thor squeezed. "I'm going to break every bone in your puny body."

53

"Wait," Loki gargled. "I can...fix Sif's...hair so...it's even... more beautiful."

"How?" Thor thundered.

"Better let him go, son," Odin said. "He's turning blue."

Loki dropped to the ground like a ragdoll. "I'll go see the dwarves. Strike a deal for the best wig ever made."

"You'd better, shit-heel," Thor growled, "or it'll be *snap-snap-snap* for you."

So Loki skulked off to Nidavellir and sought out the Sons of Ivaldi, expert metallurgists, and requested Sif's replacement hair. While they were at it, the Sons also make Gungnir, a spear that always hit its target, and Skíðblaðnir, a ship that folds up to pocket-size.

"Thanks," Loki said, accepting the gifts. "These extra tokens might even get me back in the gods' good books." He tapped his teeth with Gungnir's tip. "But what's better than two extra tokens?" His gaze turned towards a forge glowing much deeper in the mines. "Why, *five* tokens, of course!"

He headed towards the glow and found himself in the company of two soot- and-grime-covered dwarves sweating over a forge.

"Well met, my friends," Loki cried. "Brokkr and Eitri, is it not? The third and fourth best smiths in all Nidavellir!"

The dwarves scowled. "Third and fourth best?" Brokkr said.

"What idiot told you that?" Eitri asked.

"No idiot," Loki said, eyes wide and innocent. "It's just the Sons of Ivaldi made some items for me and I doubt any other dwarf could make anything close to as good."

"Show us."

Loki presented the wig, spear and ship.

"Toys," Eitri sneered.

Brokkr simply spat on the floor.

"Well, I suppose the only way to prove you're as good as you say is to make three even better devices," Loki said with the face of a perfectly cast ingénue.

Brokkr poked his dirty finger into Loki's chest. "We know who you are, Loki son of Laufey, and we trust you about as far as we could throw an anvil."

"We'll only take your wager if the price you pay for losing is your head," Eitri added. "And the gods get to decide on the quality of our goods, *not* you."

"Sounds reasonable," Loki beamed. "Just going for a wander. I'll come back when you're done."

The dwarves set to their labour, with Brokkr working the bellows as Eitri placed a pigskin into the forge. As they worked, Loki turned himself into a fly, settled onto Brokkr's hand and bit the soft flesh between his fingers. The dwarf yelped in pain but kept working until Eitri pulled Gullinbursti, a golden boar that ran faster than a horse, from the flames.

Next, Eitri placed gold in the forge and back to work they went. This time Loki landed on Brokkr's neck and bit even harder – but solid Brokkr kept working and Eitri pulled from the fire Draupnir, a gold coin that replicated itself.

Next Eitri placed iron into the forge. Knowing this was his last chance to mess up the dwarves' handiwork, Loki landed on Brokkr's eyebrow and bit so hard it opened a wound. Brokkr cursed and, just for a moment, took his hand from the bellows to wipe away the blood. Eitri pulled Mjölnir, a hammer that always struck its target, from the embers.

"There," Eitri said when Loki returned to human form. "Take these. We'll meet you in Asgard for the judging."

"That boar is incredible, and who wouldn't want a replicating gold coin?" Loki said. "But wait… The handle for this hammer – bit short, isn't it? Not very balanced."

Eitri shot Brokkr an accusatory glare. "Would have been longer if this fool hadn't stopped working the bellows."

"Still the best hammer ever forged," Brokkr said sourly. "Go on. Get lost, Loki. We'll meet you later."

Loki hot-footed it back to Asgard and presented the gods (who knew about the wager with Brokkr and Eitri) with all the items except Mjölnir. Sif was overjoyed with her golden wig; Odin took Gungnir and Draupnir; Freyr Skíðblaðnir and Gullinbursti.

"I'd say Brokkr and Eitri's work edges the Sons' by a golden whisker," Odin said.

"Maybe," Loki said, producing Mjölnir from his bag. "Or maybe not."

Thor's eyes lit up. "Give me that!" He snatched the hammer from Loki's grasp and hurled it into the distance.

"As you can see, the handle is way too short," Loki said. "That weapon is totally unbalanced."

To Loki's horror, Mjölnir returned, whirling through the air and landing with a *thunk* in Thor's meaty fist. He gave it a twirl and jammed it into his belt. "Seems alright to me," he said.

"Then Brokkr and Eitri win," Odin said. "Sorry, Loki."

The dwarves advanced on Loki, brandishing daggers. "His head will look perfect on a spike outside the workshop," Brokkr said.

"Now wait a minute," Loki burbled, "can't we talk about this first?"

"You talk waaay too much," Eitri said, grabbing Loki. "Time now for a long silence."

"Hold on," Loki said. "I wagered my head, right?"

"Right," Brokkr replied, pressing his dagger against Loki's throat.

"But not my neck. You can't damage my neck. Do that, and you break the wager."

The dwarves stared at him. "But we can't sever your head without damaging your neck."

"Exactly," Loki said. "So back off."

The dwarves stepped away. "You tricked us!"

Loki bowed. "My speciality."

"We should give the dwarves something," Thor mused, caressing Mjölnir. "We've done well by them."

"And Loki still deserves punishment for what he did," Freya added.

"I've an idea," Sif said, holding up some thread. "How about we shut Loki up with a bit of needlework to the mouth?"

"Now hang on—!"

"Excellent idea," Thor beamed. "I'll hold him down."

Niflheim and Muspelheim

The primordial realms were once separated by the great void, Ginnungagap. Niflheim, the abode of mists, is freezing cold, and

Muspelheim, a sweltering desolation of choking smoke and lava fields, is its opposite. Muspelheim is home to a fire giant called Surtr, a character who plays a fateful role at Ragnarök – we'll meet him when we get to that part of the Norse gods' story. In the meantime, this fearsome figure guards the border of his world with a flaming sword.

Helheim

Located under the roots of Yggdrasil and thus the lowest of all the nine lands, Helheim (from 'hel' meaning 'concealed' or 'hidden place') is the third Norse realm of the dead (the others being Valhalla and Fólkvangr). Helheim is not reserved for those who die bravely in battle, but instead of old age or illness. And unlike its Christian namesake, Hell, Helheim is not a place of torment and punishment for those who have sinned. Instead, it's more of a continuation of existence after death, a kind of limbo, functioning as neither reward nor punishment for the lives led by its inhabitants. It's presided over by Hel, one of Loki's offspring, and we'll visit her in her dreary domain later.

OTHER DENIZENS OF THE WORLD TREE

While most of the beings in Norse mythology live in the nine lands of the great ash Yggdrasil, some live outside these contained places, calling the tree's branches and roots their home. At the top resides an eagle bestowed with great wisdom, and between its eyes perches a hawk named Vedurfolnir (meaning 'wind-bleached'). An evil dragon called Nidhogg ('malice-striker') gnaws at Yggdrasil's roots, causing slow but serious harm. Between these contrasting creatures scurries a gossipy squirrel named Ratatoskr ('drill-tooth'), who antagonizes both by spreading slanderous rumours about them. Finally, four stags dine on the leaves, adding to the constant erosion from which Yggdrasil suffers. Entropy – the tendency of all things, no matter how powerful, to head towards eventual destruction – occurs throughout Norse mythology, with Ragnarök being the most audacious example.

All-powerful Norns

At the base of Yggdrasil, by a magical well called Urðarbrunnr, live the most powerful beings in Norse mythology. They are the Norns, three supernatural women who hold the fates of every living being – including, much to Odin's chagrin, the gods' – in their hands. By casting lots, carving runes and spinning thread, they determine the lifespan and destiny of everyone – and once these things are decided they cannot be undone.

Like us, the Norse knew that life wasn't fair, with some people having plenty and others nothing, some enjoying rude health and others sickness, some living to ripe old age and others perishing in the crib. So they also knew that the Norns were entirely unsentimental and could dish out either malevolent or benevolent fates, and all that could be done was deal with it in the best way possible.

The Norns also look after Yggdrasil by sprinkling water from Urðarbrunnr on the bark and pasting clay over cracks in the wood. Without the Norns' constant care, the World Tree would succumb to the forces of entropy, and the nine lands and everything in them would die.

Mímir the Wise

Although Mimir is an Aesir god, he is rather separated from his tribe. During the first stage of his life, he resided not in Asgard but among the roots of Yggdrasil as guardian of a well called Mímisbrunnr. Mimisbrunnr gives wisdom to anyone who drinks from it, and Mimir (being no fool) quaffed its water every day to ensure he was always the smartest god in the room.

With his eye on the main chance and seeking any edge that would help him thwart the giants at Ragnarök, Odin came to Mimir to request a brain-boosting swallow. Mimir told him he must pay a price, and that price was an eye. Without hesitation, Odin scooped one out and dropped it into the well. Price paid, Mimir granted him a drink, and by doing so Odin became much wiser and rose still higher in his own, and everyone else's, estimation. This notion of sacrifice to gain something of value (also demonstrated in 'Odin Learns the Runes', see page 23) is a regular theme in Norse mythology.

Things took quite the turn for Mimir during the war between the Aesir and Vanir. As mentioned earlier, the conflict ended with a truce guaranteed by an exchange of hostages, and Mimir was one of two Aesir hostages delivered to Vanaheim. The other was a god called Hoenir, and at first the Vanir were perfectly satisfied that the exchange was a fair one. However, after a time they realized that poor Hoenir was not the smartest sword on the rack and that the Aesir had duped them. So, in lieu of a strongly worded letter, they cut off Mimir's head and sent it back to Asgard.

Unsurprisingly (considering that it's Norse mythology we're dealing with here) this setback was not the end for Mimir – or at least not for his head. Recognizing the value of the wisest of all gods ('Mimir' means 'Rememberer'), Odin embalmed Mimir's head with herbs and revived it with magical incantations, thus allowing him to consult Mimir and ask his advice. We don't know how Mimir feels about his truncated state.

THE (INCOMPLETE) PANTHEON

The Norse worshipped many gods and goddesses. Some, like Odin, Thor and Freyr, we know so well that they feel almost real. We recognize their strengths and flaws as we recognize our own. We follow their stories from the cosmos's birth to its cataclysmic end – their intertwining friendships, feuds, fights and adventures. (The Norse really knew how to create compelling story arcs.)

However, others are less well known; records of them are fragmented, contradictory, and it's harder to translate the original meaning with certainty. Anyway, what we *do* have is an incomplete but precious cast of characters. Here are some of the better-known ones and a few stories they star in (usually getting annoyed by Loki for one reason or another).

Odin

Wise as an owl. Cunning as a fox. Farsighted as a hawk. Odin is the chieftain of the gods. He appears as an old man, bearded, hooded and cloaked, and spends much of his time wandering the nine realms, conversing, inveigling and beguiling others to gain an advantage of some kind. We've already seen in 'Odin Learns the Runes' (see page 23) and his sacrifice to Mimir that Odin thirsts for knowledge as Thor thirsts for troll blood. So obsessed is he with learning *everything* – including ways to see into and influence the future – that he is willing to mutilate his body as payment. And it's not only intellectual vanity that spurs him on in this painful, self-sacrificial journey. Oh no. His goal is no less than stopping the end of the world.

Although he is jötunn on his mother's side, Odin hates and fears the giants because it is they who will bring his and his kind's eventual demise. (Never mind the fact that Odin started it when, with his first conscious act, he murdered the primeval giant Ymir.) This fear is given an extra-fine edge because it's the cosmos he created and the gods of whom he is chieftain that will be destroyed. So, if anyone's got skin in the game at Ragnarök, it's Odin the All-Father.

Odin's Animals

Like all expert gatherers of information, Odin uses spies – in his case, two ravens called Hugin and Mumin. Every morning he sets them loose to fly around the cosmos and take note of all the comings and goings (especially what the jötnar are up to). They return before breakfast to report their findings. That is why Odin is sometimes referred to as the Raven God. He also keeps two wolf companions called Freki and Geri, and we've already met Sleipnir the eight-legged horse who was sired by Loki when he took the form of a sexy mare in 'The Walls of Asgard' (see page 47).

Frigg

Leader of the goddesses. Queen of the sky. Goddess of marriage. Like her husband Odin, Frigg is wise. Together they sit on the high seat Hliðskjálf to observe the cosmos. Like Freya, with whom she shares several traits, Frigg is a seeress, a practitioner of magic, which gives her knowledge of the future. She wears a blue cape that symbolizes the sky, and has three maiden attendants whom she confides in and sends off with messages. She is also the mother of Baldr the Bright and so is destined for unimaginable heartbreak – especially after all she does to safeguard him.

Thor

Son of Odin. God of Thunder. Loves a ruck. One of the most important of the Aesir gods, Thor appears in many stories and was widely worshipped. He is martial prowess personified: strong, brave, skilful in battle and happy to travel far and wide in search of adventure. His personal accoutrements reflect his warrior status and role as Asgard's protector: when thrown, his hammer Mjölnir ('The Grinder') always hit its target and returns to Thor's hand; gauntlets called Járngreipr ('iron-grippers') give him the ability to control Mjölnir; his belt Megingjörð ('power-belt') is straight out of a role-playing game (RPG) in that it doubles Thor's strength stats, and his chariot is drawn by two fearsome goats called Tanngrisnir ('teeth-barer') and Tanngnjostr ('teeth-grinder'). No one enjoys slaying jötnar more than Thor, so it's worth reflecting on the irony that he himself is part giant.

Sif

The Aesir goddess Sif is something of a mystery. Wife of Thor (her name means 'marriage'), she is famous for her beauty – and especially her golden hair that shines like sunlit fields of wheat… until Loki cuts it off as an off-colour joke. Interestingly, during a bout of flyting (an ancient form of rap battle, where people verbally sparred for bragging rights), Sif says to Loki that she alone among the gods has nothing remiss to hide, to which Loki replies: 'I alone know your lover beside Thor, and that was the wicked Loki.' We don't know if Loki's aspersion is a lie, but it would certainly be in character for him.

Baldr

Baldr the Bright. Baldr the Beautiful. Baldr the Just. He was the son of Odin and Frigg and beloved by the whole Norse pantheon for his joyful attitude and generous nature. Note the 'was' in the previous sentence. Perhaps it was his perfection and the deep affection in which he was held by all the other gods that so rubbed Loki up the wrong way…We'll see what happened to him soon.

Iðunn

Goddess of springtime, youth and rejuvenation. Iðunn means 'ever-young' – a fitting name because her vital task is to guard the trees that grow the fruit that bestows everlasting youth onto the gods when they eat them. However, nothing is too good or too useful for Loki to muck up with his selfishness, and such is the case for Iðunn's precious fruit.

'Iðunn and the Golden Fruit'

Odin and Loki were out exploring the wilder parts of the cosmos when they came across a herd of cows. Deciding it was time for supper they killed one, set it over a fire and waited for it to cook. Time passed. The moon rose. Patience thinned.

"I don't understand," Odin grumbled. "The meat's still raw. What's wrong with this fire?"

A harsh cry came from a nearby tree, and in the branches they saw a large eagle. It peered back at them with bright eyes; Loki thought he saw amusement in them.

"I'll tell you what's wrong with that fire," the eagle squawked. "I've enchanted it. You could sit there for a thousand years and that meat would stay stone cold."

"And why would you do a thing like that?" Loki asked.

"I don't like tourists. This is my home. If anyone deserves that cow, it's me."

"Well how about this?" Odin replied. "You lift the enchantment – nice work, by the way – and we'll share our meal with you."

"Yes, all right," the eagle said, and with a smug ruffle of its feathers, it lifted the enchantment and they all waited for the cow to cook.

Loki leaned forward, mouth watering. "I think it's done…"

"Great!" the eagle cried, and before Loki or Odin could move, it tore into the meat and gobbled down all the best parts. "Delicious!"

Enraged, Loki picked up a branch and swung it at the eagle, but before the blow landed the eagle grabbed the branch and, with a beat of its mighty wings, took to the air with a startled Loki dangling below.

Up-up-up it soared, to where the air was cold and the stars were close enough to touch. In the distance Loki saw the moon, pursued as always by the giant wolf Hati ('hatred'), and below the nine realms held aloft in Yggdrasil's arms.

"T-take me d-down," he chattered. "I'm f-f-freezing!"

"You disappoint me, Loki," the eagle said. "I thought you'd recognize a fellow shape-shifter."

"What are you t-talking about?"

"I'm not an eagle, I'm Thiazi of the jötnar. Heard of me?"

"Yes, you're a giant and you live in Thrymheim. So what? Take me *down*!"

"Thrymheim, that's right. A mighty but lonely place in the mountains." Thiazi sighed. "I wander its halls alone, you know, talking to myself. My daughter, Skadi, lives there too, but she's always off skiing in the mountains. What I'd like more than anything is company."

"Forget it!" Loki said. "I'm not interested."

"Not *you*!" Thiazi scoffed. "I want someone much fairer to gaze upon and more charming to converse with."

"Such as?"

"Iðunn would do very nicely."

"I'm sure she would," Loki said drily. "I see what you're driving at."

"Thought you would. So – will you do it? It's either that or I drop you."

"All right," Loki sighed, wondering how such things always happened to him. "I'll do it."

"I want her apples too. The ones that give the gods their everlasting youth."

"Fine. This is what we'll do…"

* * *

Keeping his dark bargain secret from Odin, Loki returned to Asgard and sought out fair Iðunn; he found her in her orchard.

"Hello, Iðunn," he said. "What are you up to?"

"Just harvesting," she replied, placing a plump golden apple into her ash wood box.

"I'm so glad I found you," Loki said. "I've discovered a tree that bears ruby coloured apples. Would you like to see it?"

"Assuredly!" Iðunn replied. "That sounds fascinating. Perhaps they're magic apples?"

"Very likely. Follow me!"

And so, like a spider luring a fly, Loki led poor, trusting Iðunn away from Asgard and into the forest where Thiazi in eagle form was waiting. With a triumphant squawk, he grabbed her in his talons and made off with her back to Jötunheim.

Not entirely without regret – Iðunn had never done him any harm – Loki slouched back to Asgard, hoping he'd get away with his latest act of treachery.

* * *

A few days later he ran into Thor, Sif, Freya and Heimdall. Thor was looking craggier than usual, and there were grey streaks in his beard. Sif's face was lined and there were bags under her eyes (her hair was as shiny and lustrous as usual though, because it was a wig), and Heimdall was leaning on a stick.

"Have you seen Iðunn?" Thor grunted. "I need some of her fruit right now. I feel weak."

"Nope, not seen her," Loki said.

"Why aren't you looking any older, Loki?" Freya asked. "Have you had a golden apple today?"

"He's a giant," Heimdall sniffed. "He doesn't need them."

"Oh yes. I sometimes forget that…"

"Anyway, I'd best be off," Loki said.

Heimdall grabbed his arm. "You've definitely not seen Iðunn?"

A bead of sweat rolled down Loki's back. "I've just told you, no."

"It's just I saw you the other day, walking towards the forest with her."

"Must have been someone else—"

Thor grabbed Loki's cloak and lifted him clean off the floor.

"Thought you said you were feeling weak," Loki said as he dangled.

"I'm strong enough yet to deal with you."

"What have you done with her, Loki?" Sif said. "If you've cut off her hair, I'll kill you myself."

So Loki told them what he'd done, and the gods were even less sympathetic to his reasons for doing so than he'd feared ("You don't understand – if I'd refused he would have *dropped* me!"). Anyway, after Thor had threatened him in his simple yet effective manner, Loki agreed to sort out the mess he'd created and, to that end, Freya gave him her falcon feather cloak that allowed the wearer to fly.

Wasting no time, the Trickster God flew to Thiazi's chilly mountain stronghold where he spied Iðunn, pacing like a caged cat around the topmost chamber in the highest tower. Ensuring the giant was nowhere to be seen, Loki swooped into the chamber, turned Iðunn into a nut, put her in his pocket, leapt out of the window and flew back towar\ds Asgard as fast as he could.

A harsh cry of rage from high above made his heart lurch. A shadow fell over him and he only just swerved out of the way as Thiazi in eagle form dove past, claws extended, beak open and ready to rend.

"Traitor twice over!" Thiazi cried. "Come back here or I'll tear you limb from feeble limb!"

Meanwhile, back in Asgard, the gods were keeping watch for Loki. Being the most farsighted, Heimdall saw him first. "There he is, the little sneak," he said. "And it looks like he's got unfriendly company. We'd better prepare a proper welcome…"

By diving, swooping, swerving and climbing, Loki just about managed to evade Thiazi's attacks; relief swept through him as the walls of Asgard emerged out of a thick bank of fog. Loki folded his wings and fell into a steep dive; a quick over-the-shoulder glance told him that Thiazi was right behind.

Wait! Not fog – *smoke*! Pouring up from inside the walls. And at its base, a roaring fire! Lightweight Loki jinked left and landed next to the bonfire; Thiazi, being far less manoeuvrable, gave a startled cry and cannoned right into the middle of the inferno.

🎆 69 🎆

There was an explosion of fire, a fountain of sparks and the air filled with the smell of burning feathers.

Before the sizzling giant even had a chance to put himself out, Thor fell on him with Mjölnir and put a very definite end to him. After turning Iðunn back into her usual pleasing form, Loki sloped away, hoping his absence would make the gods' hearts grow fonder of him again.

Heimdall

Watchman, guardian, herald of Ragnarök. Gold-toothed Heimdall lives on the borders of Asgard in a hall called Himinbjörg ('sky castle'). There he waits, gazing across Bifrost, the rainbow bridge connecting Asgard to Midgard, looking out for invaders. This son of Odin and nine mothers (not sure how that works) needs less sleep than a bird, can see a hundred leagues at night, and can hear the grass grow in fields and wool grow on sheep. Always close to hand is Gjallarhorn ('resounding horn'), which he will blow to warn the gods when the jötnar march across Bifrost…bringing Ragnarök with them. He's got beef with Loki, perhaps because of the Trickster God's giant blood, and they are destined to meet at the end of times.

Freyr

Brother of Freya, much-loved Freyr is a god of fertility, peace, sunshine and rain. So, a bit of a hippy. Like Thor, he's got some pretty cool bits of kit, including the golden boar Gullinbursti and the fold-up-able ship Skíðblaðnir (see 'The Forging of Thor's Hammer' on page 53). Freyr also provides us with a great example of how a rash decision can come back and bite you later.

The first part of this sad tale tells of how he falls in love with a giantess called Gerðr. However, the price for her hand is his magical sword, and Freyr gladly pays it. We'll see what happens next when we reach Ragnarök.

Freya

A principal member of the Vanir tribe, Freya is a goddess of beauty, love, fertility and sorcery. Magic is her speciality, and she ends up teaching Odin some of her witchy ways. She also owns various magical items, including the necklace Brisingamen and a cloak made of falcon feathers that allows her to fly. When she fancies a land trip she rides a chariot pulled by a pair of cats or a giant boar called Hildisvini ('battle-swine'). She also plays host to exactly half of the worthy warriors who fall in battle (the rest go to Valhalla); those chosen by Freya reside in Fólkvangr ('field of the host').

Seiðr

Following in the footsteps of their beloved goddess of magic ('seiðr'), magic-wielders in Norse society were always women. They were called 'völva', which means 'wand-carrier'. These wands were impressive wooden staffs decorated with bronze and semi-precious stones, and were used both to channel magic and set the wielder apart as a person of special social standing. Völvas travelled from place to place offering their shamanistic services, which included fortune-telling, curing illness, blessing warriors before battle and bestowing good luck. They were respected for their powers; sensible folk didn't cross a völva for fear of being cursed.

3.
Loki

Hard is it on earth, / with mighty whoredom;
Axe-time, sword-time, / shields are sundered,
Wind-time, wolf-time, / ere the world falls;
Nor ever shall men / each other spare
– Poetic Edda (trans. Henry Adams Bellows, 1936)

LOKI'S FAMILY AND OTHER ANIMALS

ow it is time to cut deep into the heart of the matter: Loki himself – his multifaceted and often contradictory nature, the jagged edges of his character, the light and darkness of his soul. All this will eventually lead us to the deeply profound and destructive effect he eventually has on the nine realms and all who dwell there.

In the stories told so far, we've seen how his rash decisions, petty cruelty and instinct for self-preservation resulted in others bearing the cost. But we've also seen him (under duress, it must be said) make right on his wrongdoings, and see the status quo returned. This is classic storytelling: character does wrong; character undoes that wrong; character learns something and become a better person.

Except Loki doesn't do that last bit.

But before we dive into more tales of Loki to see what else we can glean about him, let's first get a sense of where he comes from, and who (and what) he calls family.

Family One

Loki spends a lot of time hanging out in Asgard and going on adventures with the gods, and for the most part they tolerate him despite the various degrees of chaos he causes; Thor's threats of bodily harm aside, they are pretty darn forgiving of the Trickster God. (Until he does something way beyond the pale, but we'll get to that later.) This indulgence on the part of the gods towards Loki's misdemeanours suggests kinship; after all, people are often faster to forgive the bad behaviour of one of their own compared to outsiders.

And yet Loki is not really one of the gods. His father, Farbauti ('cruel striker'), was a giant about whom we know little, and his mother, Laufey, may or may not be a goddess or a giant, or neither. This parental ambiguity fits perfectly with Loki's ambiguous nature, and his ambiguous relationship with the long-suffering gods. Loki also has two brothers, Helblindi and Býleistr, and all we really know about them is contained in this sentence.

Loki is married to a goddess called Sigyn ('friend of victory'). We don't know how she feels about all the scrapes Loki gets into, or how her fellow gods judge her for getting hitched to such a disreputable character. We do know that she is far more faithful and dutiful to him than he deserves, as we shall see later in 'The

Gods Punish Loki' (see page 103). Together they have two sons, Narfi and Váli, and those poor souls pay a high price for their father's actions.

So, that is *one* of Loki's families. The – by Norse myth standards – ordinary one: the sitcom family with three generations of bipedal relations. Now let's take a look at Loki's second family: the far less ordinary, gothic horror one.

Family Two

It's safe to say that Loki gets around a bit. He's got his sitcom family that we've just met, and, lest we forget, while in horse form, he gave birth to an eight-legged steed called Sleipnir after having (mercifully off-screen) congress with a mountain giant's stallion. So far, so weird. But the weirdest is yet to come because somehow in his busy schedule Loki found time to couple up with a giantess called Angrboða and produce three (to say the least) distinct offspring. Angrboða means 'the one who brings grief', and never has a name been more appropriate.

Odin was deeply concerned when he learned about this trio of monstrous and powerful entities. He knew well the questionable natures of both parents, so their children were *bound* to end up being bad-uns. What mischief and disaster would they cause if allowed to grow to maturity and roam free? Best nip them in the bud, he decided, and deal with them one by one.

Let's go through Loki and Angrboða's strange children in leg-number order, starting with no legs.

Jörmungandr

Jörmungandr ('vast snake') is the biggest creature in Norse mythology – so big it encircles Midgard, which is why it's also called the World Serpent and Midgard Serpent. Upon seeing Jörmungandr for the first time, Odin feared what it could do in the future, so he cast it into the ocean hoping it would drown. But it didn't. Sharing its father's gift for survival, Jörmungandr adapted to its new watery home where it grew and grew...and grew. There it resides, wallowing in the sea, scales shining in the sun, clasping its tail in its tooth-lined mouth. Unsurprisingly, the Midgard Serpent hates the gods, but it reserves particular enmity for Thor...

'Thor's Fishing Trip'

Being the most daring of the gods, Thor often travelled to Jötunheim to explore its wilds and indulge in whatever adventure the Norns had weaved for him. On this particular trip, he'd been walking for many miles over ice-capped mountains and down wind-swept valleys, when he found a wooden hall in the middle of a field of bulls. Smoke poured from the chimney and light glowed through the windows. Feeling peckish and in need of some company, Thor knocked on the door.

It was opened by a giant who, upon seeing it was the mighty giant-slayer Thor on his doorstep, reached for his battle-axe.

"No need for that," Thor said, holding up his hands. "I come in peace. What's your name?"

"Hymir," the giant said, stepping aside to let Thor in. "I own all those bulls out there."

"A fine herd," Thor remarked.

"They're my pride and joy."

"And mighty tasty, I imagine."

Taking the hint, and mindful of Mjölnir, Hymir slaughtered three of his best bulls, roasted them and set them down on the table. Before he could cut one in half so that he and Thor would have an equal share, the ravenous Thunder God chomped his way through two of the bulls.

Taken aback at this rudeness, but remembering his role as host (and, again, the nearness of the giant-bashing Mjölnir), Hymir bit his tongue. "Will you stay the night?" he asked, hoping that the answer would be no.

Thor leaned back and put his boots up on the table. "I will, thanks."

"Oh. Wonderful."

"What's for breakfast tomorrow?"

"Perhaps a change from steak?" Hymir said, eager to keep the rest of his bulls uneaten. "How about we go fishing and cook what we catch?"

"Excellent idea," Thor said.

The next morning Hymir asked Thor to find some bait for their fishing trip, so Thor ripped the head off the giant's prize bull and stowed it in the boat. Cursing Thor under his breath, Hymir pushed the boat into the sea and rowed to his favourite fishing spot, where he quickly landed two whales.

"Look! One each!" he exclaimed, glowing with pride.

"They won't fill me up," Thor grumbled. "Let's find something bigger." And he grabbed the oars and took the little fishing boat so far out to sea they lost all sight of land.

Hymir looked nervously at the choppy waves. "We should go back. These are Jörmungandr's waters."

"So what?" Thor scoffed. "I can handle a snake, if it comes to it." And he fixed the bull's head to a hook-and-rope and threw the hook end into the sea. "Now we wait."

So they did: Thor with excitement, Hymir with fear. Clouds gathered. Rain fell in fat drops into the churning sea.

"Well," Hymir ventured, "looks like nothing's doing here, so why don't we—?"

The rope jerked so violently it nearly capsized the boat. Hymir gave a cry and fell backwards onto his rump. Thor grabbed the rope and began to heave it up, his bulging muscles testifying to the fact that something very large was attached to the other end.

Hymir trembled. "It's him – the World Snake! For Hel's sake cut it loose!"

"Never!" Thor roared. "There's no living creature in the nine realms I can't defeat! And I want to see the look on Loki's face when I present to him his disgusting offspring's head."

And then – with admirable timing, it has to be said – the mighty serpent broke the surface...and even Thor was struck by its immensity: its writhing body was covered with shield-sized scales of green, copper and gold; its mouth, stuck through with the hook, was wide enough to swallow a dragonship; its eyes were filled with bestial fury; geysers of poison foamed from its throat.

Thor, a mere speck before this leviathan, brandished his hammer. "Come over here, worm, if you think you can take me!"

Aghast at this unfolding nightmare, Hymir cut the rope and the World Snake slipped back beneath the waves.

Puce with fury, Thor turned on Hymir. "What did you do that for? I nearly had him!"

"He would have eaten us both!" Hymir protested.

"Nonsense! I'd have dined on him with salt and cabbage!"

"I just want to get back to my bulls," Hymir wailed. "Everything was fine before you showed up!"

Disgusted with his host's showing, Thor kicked him into the sea and rowed back to Jötunheim, taking the whales with him.

Hel

Although Odin feared Loki's two-legged daughter Hel as much as her siblings, he also saw a use for her. So, ever the opportunist, he cast her down into Helheim, the underworld located in the darkest place beneath the roots of Yggdrasil, to rule as queen. Among the dreary halls and sorrowful corridors, she governs all the dishonourable dead from all the nine realms. Her appearance is gloomy and downcast; one side of her face alive and flesh-coloured, the other dead with the pallor of a corpse.

But Odin's opportunism will come back to haunt him, because when Ragnarök begins, Hel will sail forth in a ship called *Naglfar* ('nail-farer') with an army of the dead, destined to clash with the gods in the final cataclysm.

Fenrir

Loki's four-legged offspring is Fenrir ('marsh-dweller'), an enormous wolf, and the best way to get to know him is to tell the first part of his extraordinary story.

'The Binding of Fenrir'

With Jörmangandr tossed into the sea and Hel cast down to Helheim, that left only Loki's wolf pup, Fenrir.

"He's a playful creature," Thor chuckled, ruffling the fur behind Fenrir's ears.

"Huh. So were you when you were his age," Odin grumbled. "And look how you turned out."

"He'll get bigger and more dangerous, for sure," Tyr, the god of justice, said. "I think we should keep an eye on him."

"Good idea," Odin replied.

Thor's face lit up. "You mean we can keep him?"

"For now. Let's see what happens."

What happened was Fenrir got bigger. *Much* bigger. His fur grew thick and spiky, his claws scimitar-long, and when he loped through the streets of Asgard the gods shuddered and turned away. All knew this was a creature of ill-omen, and disaster followed in his wake.

"Something must be done," Odin said. "This is not some wild beast we can kill or cage. Fenrir is clever and cunning, just like his father."

"We need to use our wiles," Frigg said. "Trick the beast into captivity. Perhaps he can be lured into a test of strength, one which he cannot win?"

"Excellent idea," Odin said, and the gods forged the strongest chain ever made and sought out Fenrir. They found him eating, surrounded by sheep bones; the great wolf watched them shrewdly as they approached.

"Greetings, Fenrir," Frigg said.

"I'm at supper," the wolf growled. "What do you want?"

"We wondered if you'd like to take part in a test," Frigg said. "My husband doesn't think you're strong enough to break this chain."

The wolf turned his yellow eyes onto the All-Father. "Doesn't he now?"

"No, I don't. Care to prove me wrong?"

"I've finished eating, so I might as well."

Odin and Thor wrapped the chain around Fenrir's legs as tightly as they could and stepped back.

"All right," Frigg said. "Try to escape."

Fenrir merely flexed his muscles and the chain flew off in multiple high-speed pieces.

"Oh, bravo," the gods cried, and they retreated more worried than ever.

"Well, that was a disaster," Tyr sighed.

"We can't give up now..." Frigg thought for a moment. "We need a stronger chain."

So they created another that was twice as strong as the first; so heavy was it, it took Odin, Thor, Frigg and Tyr to carry it to Fenrir's lair.

"Is it me or has he got bigger?" Frigg whispered.

"Time for another game, is it?" Fenrir rumbled. "You gods like your games, don't you?"

"We just enjoy seeing you showcase your prodigious strength," Odin said with a perfect imitation of sincerity.

Fenrir lowered his giant head so he was muzzle-to-nose with the chieftain of the gods. "Very well. Do your worst."

And, just as before, the gods tied Fenrir up, this time confident that their new chain would hold their nascent enemy for eternity.

"Done," Odin said. "Now do *your* worst."

Fenrir flexed and writhed, the veins on his neck stood out, and for a moment the gods thought they had him…but with a final epic exertion he flung off the chain and got to his paws, panting but triumphant. "That was fun," he said. "Imagine how strong I'll be when I'm fully grown!" And with that he loped away, leaving the disconsolate gods behind.

Frigg surveyed the shattered chain. "I think we need to outsource this problem, don't you?"

So Frigg travelled to Nidavellir to commission the dwarves to make an unbreakable chain, and, enjoying a metallurgical challenge more than anything, the dwarves set about their task. In the end they used no metal, for all metal can be broken. Instead, they chose things that don't exist, because how can you break something that doesn't exist? They called their creation Gleipnir – 'open one'. Well pleased, Frigg thanked the dwarves and returned to Asgard.

Odin, Thor and Tyr looked at the silken ribbon in Frigg's hands with deep scepticism.

"It's stronger than it looks," she reassured them.

"What's it made from?" Odin asked.

"The sound of a running cat, a woman's beard, a mountain's root, a fish's breath and bird spit."

"Clever," Odin muttered. "Very clever. Well then, let's try it out, shall we?"

"Fingers crossed it works this time," Tyr said. "I gave Fenrir a whole herd of sheep this morning and he thanked me for the snack."

When they offered Fenrir (who now towered mightily over the tallest hall in Asgard) another strength test he sniffed the ribbon suspiciously.

"I sense trickery," he growled, hackles rising. "I smell *magic*."

"No, no, no," Odin soothed. "It's just a new material that we're trying out, that's all."

"What's the matter?" Thor said. "Scared you'll lose?"

In reply the great wolf bared his teeth – and even Thor took an involuntary step back.

"I don't trust you, or your 'new material'," Fenrir said. "I want a guarantee. One of you must place their hand in my mouth. If I can't escape, and you don't set me loose, I take the hand in payment for your bad faith."

"It saddens me that you don't trust us," Odin said. "We who raised you and fed you *so* many sheep…"

"I saw what you did to my siblings," Fenrir rumbled. "So, sheep notwithstanding, no, I don't trust you. A hand, or nothing doing."

The gods gathered in a huddle, knowing that their impending treachery was going to cost one of them a limb.

"I've already sacrificed an eye…"

"I can't fight giants with one hand…"

"I need both to spin yarn…"

Tyr sighed. "Very well. For the sake of us all, I'll do it."

"Good man," Odin said, patting him on the shoulder.

And so, because Tyr was the only god he trusted, Fenrir allowed himself to be bound with Gleipnir, and because Tyr was a brave and worthy god, he placed his hand in Fenrir's maw. There he kept it, head bowed, braced for the pain he knew was coming, as Fenrir strained and struggled against the this-time-actually-unbreakable fetters. For hours the great wolf strove, thrashing this way and that, and all the while Tyr remained steadfast.

Realizing he couldn't escape, and knowing in his pounding heart that the gods had no intention of setting him loose, Fenrir snapped his jaws over Tyr's hand and tore it off at the wrist. Blood pumped from the stump, but even the god's cry of agony was drowned out by Fenrir's howl of fury.

"The prophesies said you were to be the end of me, Fenrir," Odin cried out in triumph. "But I have bested you, bound you, and by doing so altered my fate to mine own advantage."

"I know not of this fate you describe," Fenrir growled, "but with this treacherous act you've only made it certain. For I vow to thee now, faithless Odin, that I *will* break free and I *will* tear you limb from limb and feast upon your parts."

Odin paled and shuddered, just for a moment, then recovered himself. "I would have thee silent, puppy." He drew his sword and propped Fenrir's mouth open with it, then had him chained to a rock in the most desolate part of Asgard, and there left him to howl and shake and lament.

NOT JUST A TRICKSTER GOD

We've now met Loki's families and extremely varied offspring. I don't think I'm giving much away when I say that despite Odin's best and most ruthless efforts to kill or contain them, we'll be bumping into Loki's three 'monstrous' children again – they each have important parts to play during the gods' demise at Ragnarök. Whether we should blame Loki for the actions of his children is open for discussion. He didn't get much of a chance to influence them one way or another before Odin muscled in and chivvied them off to their respective far-flung parts of the nine realms. Who knows what would have happened if Loki had had a more active part in their lives?

In the end though, such debates are academic. As we know, the future is decided by the all-powerful Norns, and their intricate weavings cannot be unpicked no matter how much meddling, interfering and scheming Odin indulges in; Ragnarök is coming and (nearly) everyone dies.

Coming, but not here yet. There are other stories to tell, other pieces to move on the board, other fateful events to describe before we reach the final bloodbath, and each one tells us something different about the more-than-just-a-trickster-god Loki.

The following story, 'The Marriage of Njord and Skadi', begins not long after the gods killed Thiazi the giant, for kidnapping Iðunn…

'The Marriage of Njord and Skadi'

For no reason other than they fancied it, the gods had gathered in one of Asgard's greatest halls for a feast. The air was filled with laughter, song and the smell of roast boar. Odin sat with Thor and Loki, for once unpreoccupied by his wiles and schemes. Today, food, mead and good drunken company was enough for the All-Father.

So it's a shame that the Norns had long ago decided that today was to be a day not for mindless hedonism, but a reckoning.

Thor was in the middle of slurring a toast when the door was smashed in with such ferocity that shards of timber flew like javelins. The gods stared at the towering figure now looming, backlit by the sun, in the doorway.

Loki peered at the interloper and, upon recognizing her, muttered, "Oh, now this is going to be *awkward*."

The figure stalked into the hall. She was an impressive sight: tall, clad in armour and with a drawn bow pointing right at Odin's remaining eye.

"Skadi," Odin said.

"Yes, Skadi!" And her voice rang strong around the hall. "Daughter of Thiazi, who you killed! I am here for vengeance."

Loki, well aware of his role in the tragedy, retreated into the shadows.

"Your father kidnapped our beloved Iðunn," Odin said. "He brought his death upon himself."

"He just wanted some company!" Skadi cried.

"Then perhaps, as his daughter, you should have spent more time with him."

Skadi gasped in anguish, and her bow dropped a little.

"But I understand your anger," Odin continued, "and the need to balance the scales. Let's settle this peacefully. What can we do that will soothe your troubled heart?"

Skadi considered, then said, "Cast my father's eyes into the sky, so I can feel him watching over me."

So Odin did as she asked, and two new stars were born.

"Anything else?" Odin asked.

Like a punctured wineskin, Skadi sagged onto a chair. "Grief fills me. I want to laugh again."

Everyone knew Loki had the best sense of humour, so all eyes turned – with some trepidation – to him; as always, Loki weighed his options.

"I *could* do what everyone wants of me," he thought. "Or I *could* cause a little chaos by describing to Skadi how amusing it was when her father's feathers burned and how his beak melted in the heat… Imagine her reaction if I did that!"

But he cast that gleeful, intriguing option aside and instead did the right thing…although his 'right thing' was not what anyone expected.

Loki stepped from the shadows, bowed to Skadi, and let his breeches fall to the floor. He then produced a length of string, tied one end around his testicles and the other to the horns of a goat. Skadi and the gods watched agog as Loki slapped the goat's rump and sent it galloping bad-temperedly around the hall. The tension as the rope was played out was palpable.

When it eventually jerked tight, Loki let out a howl and careened around the room after the bleating goat, nether regions foremost, screeching in pain. He endured this until everyone, including Skadi, was weeping with laughter.

"That was very funny," Skadi said, wiping her eyes. "Now I just want one more thing: I want to marry a god."

Seeing her covetous looks towards his son, Baldr the Bright, Odin insisted she choose her mate by their feet only. So all the unmarried gods stood behind a strung-up tapestry so that only their feet were on show, and Skadi walked the line trying to decide which were Baldr's.

She picked the most beautiful feet of them all, but was disappointed to discover they belonged not to Baldr, but Njord, god of the sea. Still, a deal was a deal, and he was a proper god, so they went and got married and by all accounts it was a lovely ceremony.

Now, both Skadi and Njord loved their homes, so they sensibly decided to split their time between them. Unfortunately, Skadi hated the sea and Njord hated the mountains, so in the end they went their separate ways – so proving that selecting a spouse by their feet alone is rarely a path to marital bliss.

Loki the Playful

'The Marriage of Njord and Skadi' is one of the more frivolous Norse myths – frivolous in the sense that no one gets killed. Odin negotiates a peace and offers payment to a giantess because he clearly feels that Skadi deserves compensation. Here, giants and gods co-operate and sort things out in a non-homicidal way.

As for Loki, this is an example of him at his best. He behaves himself and helps solve a problem for the gods (although with the caveat that this is a problem that he himself caused by helping Thiazi kidnap Iðunn). And the method he chooses to make Skadi laugh (of all the non-painful and less humiliating things he *could* have done) shows that he's willing to play a price to avert disaster. In this tale he plays the jester, the buffoon performing for the court's amusement, and it goes a long way to explain why the gods like having him around. When he's in the right mood, Loki's a pretty fun and funny guy.

Now let's explore the tale when, following Loki's advice, Thor gets hitched to a giant...

'Thor's Wedding'

The doors to Odin's hall burst open and Thor thundered inside looking uncharacteristically distraught. Mjölnir – it's gone!" he cried. "Vanished!"

"Vanished?" Odin replied. "Are you sure?"

"Of course I'm sure! I laid it on the pillow next to mine as I always do, and when I woke up this morning all that was left was a hammer-shaped dent."

"Well, it must be *somewhere,*" Frigg said, patting Thor's arm.

"I don't want it to be *somewhere,*" he countered. "I want it to be *here!*"

Loki stroked his chin. "This feels like jötunn trickery to me."

"Well, you would know," Heimdall muttered.

Loki ignored him. "Freya, would you lend me your falcon cloak again so I can go to Jötunheim and see what's up?"

Freya agreed and Loki flew swift and sure to the wild and mountainous land of the giants. There he found Thrym, king of the giants, perched on a burial mound plaiting golden collars for his dogs.

To Loki it looked as if he was waiting for someone to come from Asgard... "I think I've found the culprit," he thought.

"Greetings, Thrym," he said, landing gently. "What are you doing so close to Asgard's borders? What if Thor comes along with a mind for splitting jötunn skulls?"

Thrym looked smug. "Who fears a wolf without fangs? Or an eagle without talons? Not me, that's for sure!"

Loki sighed. "Where is it, Thrym? Give it to me now and I'll try to talk Thor out of killing you."

"I've buried it in a secret place eight leagues under the earth, so if that bonehead kills me, he'll never get it back."

Marginally impressed by Thrym's reckless stupidity, Loki asked, "So what do you want in return?"

"I want fair Freya's hand in marriage. Get me that, and I'll return the hammer."

* * *

"Not this again!" Freya fumed. "Why do all these entitled idiots want to force me into marriage?"

"So, that's a no, is it?" Thor asked, clearly disappointed.

Freya rounded on him. "Of course it's a no! I'm not giving myself to some dullard giant because you can't look after your hammer!"

"But he is *king* of the giants..."

"It's out of the question," Odin said before Freya combusted with fury. "But we need to get Mjölnir back somehow. Any thoughts?"

Heimdal raised a hand. "I've an idea, but it is a bit... unorthodox."

"Anything, please – just tell us," Thor pleaded.

"All right, bear with me here," Heimdall said. "If Thrym wants a wedding, let's give him one. But instead of sending Freya, we send Thor instead."

Everyone, even wise Odin, looked at him blankly.

"Disguised, of course,'" Heimdall continued, "so he looks like Freya."

"How dare you!" Freya said. "No amount of magic could make *him* look like *me*!"

Frigg shook her head. "This sounds like a stretch, Heimdall…"

"I'm not so sure," Loki mused. "Loath as I am to admit it, I think old gold-teeth might be on to something. I know Thrym and he's not very bright. I reckon a decent disguise would do the trick, and when he produces Mjölnir at the ceremony Thor can take it back and…do what comes naturally."

Thor brightened at the thought.

"Worth a try, I suppose," Odin said.

"I'll see about an outfit," Freya added. "I'll need to let it out a bit…"

And so, a few hours later, Thor found himself clad in a gorgeous drop-waist wedding dress set off by some choice pieces from Freya and Frigg's jewellery collections. The Thunder God brooded as Freya plaited his hair and trimmed his beard so it wouldn't poke out from below the veil.

"How do I look?" he asked. "It feels a bit tight under the arms."

Freya nodded approvingly. "You look surprisingly good. But do try and walk as gracefully as you can when going down the aisle, would you?"

I don't really do 'graceful'," Thor grumbled.

"Follow my lead and you'll be fine," Loki said as he strode into the room in a fetching off-the-shoulder bridesmaid's outfit. "What? You didn't think I'd let you go alone, did you? This venture needs cunning, so I'm coming too. Come on, we'd best be off before your make-up runs."

* * *

The wonderful news that Freya had consented to Thrym's wishes was relayed to Jötunheim in advance, and by the time Thor and Loki arrived at the venue it was packed with giants already well into their cups.

"Rude to start without us," Thor sniffed, adjusting his dress.

"Typical of my kind, I'm afraid," Loki replied. "Come on – let's make an entrance!"

Upon seeing his bride-to-be, Thrym threw out his arms and beamed. "Freya! How happy I am to see you! My, you're so much taller close-up." A slight frown troubled his face. "Broader too... and such big hands..."

"Don't speak," Loki hissed. "Play the demure bride and let me do the talking."

Thor glowered behind his veil. "I don't do 'demure'."

"Greetings, Thrym," Loki said in a strong falsetto. "Freya is so lost for words I'll be speaking on her behalf."

"Very well," Thrym said, beckoning them through the merry throng. "Come sit by me. Let's eat, drink and be merry before we tie the knot, eh?"

Trying to control his temper, Thor plonked himself down next to the glowing giant.

Loki laid a hand on Thor's arm. "Peace, my friend. Your time will come."

The feast began and Thor tucked in; by the time Thrym had finished a single caper, the Thunder God had wolfed down an ox, a sheep and ten salmon.

Thrym looked askance as his bride-to-be drained an entire barrel of mead then set about another ox. "Does Freya always eat so much?" he asked Loki over the noise of Thor's chewing.

"Oh no," Loki said, fervently wishing Thor wasn't such a dullard. "It's just she's been so lovesick for you she's not been able to eat for ages."

"Ah, that explains it!" Thrym beamed.

Grateful that Thrym was even dimmer than Thor, Loki got back to his roast goose.

Thrym sighed and turned to Thor. "My darling," he cooed. "I ache to see your face and kiss your sweet lips."

Loki froze, mid-bite. "Perhaps after the ceremony?" he ventured.

"I cannot wait!" And before Loki could react, Thrym lifted the veil to reveal Thor's furious visage. "Goodness," the giant murmured. "What bloodshot eyes you have."

"She's not been sleeping," Loki said. "So nervous has she been about tonight!"

"I understand," Thrym simpered. "Perhaps a kiss will settle your nerves?" And he leaned forward, lips puckered.

Loki cringed when Thor replied in a voice only slightly higher than his normal growl: "After the ceremony."

"Then let us wait no longer!" Thrym cried. "We shall bless this union on Mjölnir and begin our blissful life journey together!"

And so the great hammer was set on the table, and Thor picked it up and held it aloft; and all the anger and tension drained away, to be replaced with a kind of lethal serenity; and Thor set upon Thrym first, splitting his head and spilling his limited brains; and Thor's gown turned red as he strode and swung and slaughtered until the floor was carpeted, the tables strewn and the rafters draped with dead giants.

And Loki thought, "Given the right circumstances, Thor *is* graceful."

Loki the Cunning

In 'Thor's Wedding' we see Loki exhibit the cunning for which he is most famed. Although the initial idea of Thor infiltrating the wedding is Heimdall's, it's Loki who ensures its success. Without the Trickster God's quick-witted explanations for Thor's distinctly unfeminine behaviour at the dinner table, things would have quickly gone south. Indeed, without his magical hammer, Thor may even have been killed by the giants.

Loki has guile by the bucket-load, and his ability to lie quickly and convincingly is a gift he uses time and time again. And in this instance, he uses his gifts for the benefit of the other gods. It's worth remembering that he's entering the lion's den here, and if their disguises were discovered Loki would be in serious trouble. He's not a warrior like

Thor, so we can assume the giants would batter him in a physical altercation.

However, caprice and disloyalty are other facets of Loki's character, and he sometimes uses his cunning against the gods too...

'The Death of Baldr'

Odin and Frigg were playing chess one day when Baldr came to see them.

"Hail, Baldr!" Odin said. "A fine morning, is it not?"

But Frigg knew straightaway that all was not well. "What's the matter, my boy? You look terrible."

"I had a dream last night," he said, "in which the sky was leaden and full of crows. And on the sea, caught in the waves, a ship. As it drew closer, I saw a body lying within. Stiff as a board. Pale as snow. Dead as stone." He looked at his parents with haunted eyes. "It was me."

Odin and Frigg exchanged worried glances and, after sending Baldr away with comforting words ("It's just a dream. Nothing to worry about!"), conferred in anxious tones.

"A troubling vision," Odin muttered.

"Could it be a portent?" Frigg said. "Is our son going to die?"

"I hope not, with all my heart. For we both know it's his death that heralds the coming of Ragnarök."

"We must find out. Disguise yourself and go to Helheim. Seek out the seeress – she'll be able to tell us if Baldr's vision was just a dream...or the beginning of the end for us all."

So Odin rode Sleipnir to the land of the dishonourable dead and entered a vast and chilly hall, where crimson drapes hung from the walls and tables were laid for a great feast. Odin approached the seeress, who sat on a golden throne looking pleased with herself.

"What's all this?" he asked. "I can't imagine anything down here worth celebrating with fine decorations and a feast."

"Shows what *you* know," the seeress said. "We're preparing for a new and illustrious addition to the ranks of the dead. Someone with *impeccable* breeding who'll do much to brighten this place up."

Odin gathered his nerve and asked, "Of whom do you speak, seeress?"

"Why, Baldr the Bright, of course! We're looking forward to making him welcome down here."

* * *

Standing tall, rigid and pale as a sword blade, Frigg listened to Odin's dread tidings. "Our boy," she whispered. "Our beautiful boy is going to *die*?"

Odin sank into his chair, haggard with despair. "And not just him. When he dies, Ragnarök follows, and that will be the end of us all and everything we've built." A vision of Fenrir rushing towards him over a scorched and blood-drenched battlefield filled his mind. "I don't know what to do…"

"I do," Frigg said. "I must travel all the nine realms and speak to everything I find: every living and dead thing, and even those things that have never had life. And from each I'll extract a promise to never harm or kill Baldr. In this way, I will make him safe...and thus save us all."

So Frigg asked the animals, the birds, the trees, the flowers, the air, the earth, the rivers, the rocks, the sand, the sky, the clouds, the mountains and everything else in all the cosmos to never harm her son. And because all things loved Baldr for his generosity and joyful spirit, all things agreed, and Frigg returned home with the good news: Baldr, the gods and the nine realms were safe.

Naturally, this demanded a celebration, and all the gods gathered to express their joy that beloved Baldr had been spared. They sang and danced for him, and gave him the choicest cuts of meat.

During the revelry a new game was invented: Throwing Things at Baldr. Frigg's epic quest had essentially made him invulnerable, so it amused the gods no end to hurl lethal objects – axes, rocks, spears, even Mjölnir! – and watch them bounce harmlessly off his person. Baldr, being a patient sort, put up with it good humouredly.

But Loki did not join in. Quite frankly, he was sick of all the fawning and flattery being heaped on Baldr. He sat on the periphery, brooding and bad-tempered, letting envy and resentment build over his heart like caustic rust. He glowered as the gods laughed at another arrow ricocheting off Baldr's chest and leaving not a scratch.

"Pretty boy Baldr," he muttered. "What's he ever done worth noting? Nothing, that's what. And yet they all think he's so *bloody wonderful*. Well, we'll see how they feel when I turn the tides of fate back in their rightful direction."

Loki transformed himself into an old woman and sidled up to Frigg. "I hear you asked everything in the cosmos to make the promise," he said.

"I would do anything for my son," Frigg replied without taking her eyes off Baldr.

"But surely you didn't speak to *everything*, did you?"

Frigg pondered. "Actually, I didn't bother with the mistletoe, because how could that harm anyone?"

Only just managing to hide his glee, Loki disappeared into the forest.

* * *

The sun was setting and still the gods had not tired of Throwing Things at Baldr. Loki, now back in Loki form, approached another of Odin's sons: Höðr, who was blind and stood disconsolately apart from the merrymakers.

"How now, Höðr," Loki said in friendly tones. "Why so glum?"

"Alas, I cannot join in the fun," he replied. "I can't see Baldr to throw things at him. And besides, I have no weapon to use."

"Well, we can't have that now, can we? Here – take this javelin in your right hand. Got a firm grip? Good! Now, let me guide your aim. That's it...He's straight ahead, about twenty paces away. Now, remember to pivot as you throw – really get some power into it! Ready?"

"Ready!" Höðr said, beaming with anticipation.

"Then throw it as hard as you can!"

And Höðr hurled the javelin with all his strength. It streaked through the air and struck Baldr in the back – but instead of bouncing off, it pierced him right through. Baldr jerked, blood bubbled from his mouth and he fell stone dead to the ground.

The first and loudest shriek was Frigg's. She rushed to her son and cradled his head in her lap, weeping tears of grief. The other gods wailed and lamented – for Baldr and for themselves. Only two were silent: Höðr because he couldn't see what had happened, and Loki who was overjoyed that his plan had gone off so perfectly; realizing the finger of blame would soon be pointing at him, the Trickster God retreated elsewhere.

Odin plucked the javelin from Baldr's corpse and examined it. It was made from mistletoe.

Loki the Destroyer

'The Death of Baldr' is the point when the tales of Norse mythology turn sour. You can wave goodbye to the (comparatively) frothy stories of Loki shaving heads and getting Thor to put on a dress; from now on, it's revenge, punishment, death and destruction all the way.

It hardly needs saying, but in this watershed tale we see Loki at his worst. (So far, anyway – there's even more reprehensible behaviour to come.) Loki's depraved act is impossible to justify considering it leads to the death of an innocent victim, and the literally world-shattering event of Ragnarök, the end times, doom of the gods. It's akin to a world leader shooting their neighbour then launching nukes on their own country. What's more, Loki doesn't even carry out the murder himself, but instead tricks poor Höðr into doing it. That's malice with an extra topping of cruelty.

It's also self-destructive. Loki doesn't hide his identity when getting Höðr to use the mistletoe javelin, and even he can't believe there's any coming back from murdering the son of Odin and Frigg. It's an unforgivable act, and he must have known punishment would be swift and brutal.

But hey, perhaps Loki thought that Odin and Frigg, in all their wisdom, would find a way to undo the murder and thus pave a way for his redemption? Well, unsurprisingly, in the following tale, 'Hermóðr Visits Helheim', the gods *do* try to bring Baldr back from the dead. But Loki's actions in that tale are not those of someone seeking forgiveness or a way to undo the damage they've caused…

'Hermóðr Visits Helheim'

The gods mourned. Everything (except Loki the disloyal, Loki the malicious, Loki the murderer) mourned; even the mistletoe, who was not to blame for all this. Asgard was all the darker, all the less joyful without Baldr's presence, and the gods wept and walked with heads downcast.

"Death is so infrequent for us," one said, "I don't know how to cope with the loss."

Elves, dwarves, even jötnar attended his funeral, and when Baldr was laid to rest in a ship, Nanna, his wife, died of sorrow and was placed next to him. All watched bereft as the ship drifted into the sea and out even of Heimdall's long sight.

Frigg turned to the host of mourners and held her arms aloft. "Who among you is brave, loyal and true enough to negotiate with the Queen of the Dead in Helheim and ensure the return of Baldr?"

Odin pointed to the horizon, where lightning flickered and black clouds loomed like piles of soot. "Securing the return of our beloved Baldr might also save us from Ragnarök, our bleak and impending fate. Never has there been a more important task."

The first to respond was Hermóðr the Bold, Baldr's brother. "Fitting it is that it's you, my son," Odin said, and he gave Hermóðr Sleipnir upon which to make his journey. No more words were spoken, for none were needed.

Taking all the gods' hopes with him, Hermóðr rode non-stop for nine days into ever deeper and darker valleys until he reached the desolate borders of Helheim. He stopped at the mighty river Gjöll, over which all dead souls must cross. Spanning Gjöll's turgid black waters stood a bridge thatched with glittering gold. Hermóðr urged Sleipnir onto the ancient boards. In the middle of the bridge he was stopped by a fearsome giantess called Móðguðr, which means 'furious battler'.

"Halt, stranger," she cried. "You must give me your name and purpose."

"I am Hermóðr of the Aesir," he replied.

Móðguðr bent close to Hermóðr and examined him suspiciously. "Well, Hermóðr of the Aesir, you seem far too *alive* to be seeking passage into Helheim. I ask again – what is your purpose?"

"My purpose is to negotiate with Hel for the return of Baldr the Bright."

"Ah, that makes sense. He crossed Gjöll nine days ago accompanied by his wife." The giantess's armour clanked as she straightened up. "Very well, you may pass. But be warned, Hel covets her souls – especially his – and will demand a high price."

Nodding his thanks, Hermóðr spurred Sleipnir on and they clattered over the bridge and into Helheim. Breath pluming, horse and rider sped through gloomy passages and draughty chambers until they reached Hel's lofty throne room.

At the far end she sat, skeletal body wrapped in bone-white garb. One side of her face was alive and mobile; the other corpse-like, with blue skin, rotten flesh and a socket where an eye should be. Next to her, silent, head bowed, was Baldr. Hermóðr approached, feeling the weight of his task like a millstone around his neck.

Hel beckoned him closer. When she spoke, the words tumbled from her mouth like dead crows. "Why come you to my miserable halls, Hermóðr?"

"I come with an entreaty from Odin, Chieftain of the Aesir."

"Ah, Odin." Hel leaned back in her throne and sighed. "He who cast me down into this chilly and unhappy place."

"Erm, yes," Hermóðr replied, wishing he'd not brought his father into the conversation. "But it's not just Odin who wishes this favour from you, but *everything in the cosmos.*"

"And what is it *everything* wants?"

"We ask for the return of Baldr, who sits so sadly beside you."

"Only the gods would be so arrogant to think they can undo death." Hel shook her head, prompting a strip of flesh to slough off the dead side of her face. "Very well, but here is my price. If all things in the cosmos truly mourn for Baldr, then they must each and every one weep for him." She held up a bony finger. "And if even a single thing refuses, Baldr remains at my side."

And so Hermóðr returned to Asgard with Hel's offer and, filled with hope, the gods sent messengers to all corners of all nine realms to ask everything they found to weep for the return of Baldr. All things did so, until there was only one place left to explore: a remote cave in Jötunheim. Inside, the messengers found a giantess sitting by a fire. When they asked her to weep, she spat into the flames and said, "That pretty boy Baldr never gave me any joy, so let Hel keep him."

Loki Doubles Down

And thus Loki – for that giantess was him in disguise – dooms Baldr and the gods for a second time. He's given an easy opportunity to undo his previous maliciousness, and he cold-bloodedly turns it down. We know he had at least nine days to reflect on his murder and its catastrophic implications, and rather than feel regret he says "hang them all" and doubles down.

Loki must hate the Aesir to condemn them *twice*. Perhaps it's because of his jötunn blood – he may have lived among the gods, shared adventures, feasted and laughed with them, but he was never really part of their tribe.

Or maybe he got sick of them punishing him for his behaviour; they just didn't *get* him or his funny little ways. What was wrong with shaving a woman's head for a laugh? And where's the harm in organizing an abduction? The trouble with the gods was they had no sense of humour.

In the end, the end of all is all Loki's fault. Twice. But does Loki pay a price for this? Well, in that regard, the title of the next tale is a bit of a spoiler.

'The Gods Punish Loki'

Loki knew there would be no forgiveness this time, so he fled Asgard and found a lonely mountaintop far from everything and everyone. From this lofty place he could see all around, and what's more, a river teeming with fish rushed and tumbled nearby.

"Food and a clear view. Good. Now all I need is shelter and I'm all set."

After a few days' toil he'd built a cabin with a doorway in each wall so he could see people approaching from any direction. The downside was that whichever way the wind blew, it always got inside and made the place permanently cold. So Loki made a fire in the middle of the room then set about fashioning a net with which to fish.

Some may have taken this time of solitude to reflect on their actions, but not Loki. Instead, he wallowed in self-pity, blamed others for his reduced circumstances and cast endless nervous glances through all four doors. And well he might, because they didn't call Odin the 'All-seeing' for nothing…

Loki had nearly finished his net when he spied a whole group of gods led by Odin, Frigg and Thor marching up the mountain pass directly towards his cabin. Panic nearly overcame him, but Loki's powers of self-preservation took over and, quick as lightning, he cast the net into the fire, turned himself into a salmon and leapt into the river.

"Surely they'll never find me here," he bubbled.

The gods arrived and quickly turned the cabin over. "No sign of him," Thor rumbled. "Where is that wretched creature?"

"He's close," Frigg said. "I can smell his treachery."

Odin bent over the fire and pulled out the charred remains of the fishing net. "We know the slippery bastard likes to shapeshift," he muttered. "Perhaps he's taken fish-form and is hiding in that river yonder?"

"I think you're right," Skadi the giantess said. "I'll make a new net to catch him with. But let's not spook him – stay quiet until I'm done."

Meanwhile, Loki flitted and flashed in the river's crystal-clear waters, content to wait until his pursuers gave up and continued their search elsewhere.

"Fools," he snickered. "They think they're so clever but *I'm* the one with the real brains—"

There was a splash as a tightly woven net landed in the water right behind him. Again panic almost overcame him, but Loki kept his wits and swam as fast as he could upstream; a glance behind told him the net was keeping pace.

"The river ends soon," he thought, "and they'll easily catch me when I'm flapping about on dry land. My only hope is to jump the net and make a run for the sea."

With the first flick of his tail Loki changed direction, with the second more powerful one he leapt high into the air; the sun flashed on his silver scales, water flew from his flukes. The net was beneath him…behind him…and the river rose up to meet him!

"I'm going to do it!" Loki thought triumphantly.

Strong fingers closed over his tail and he was suddenly dangling in mid-air, staring helplessly down into the rushing water. And now panic did envelop the Trickster God, and he thrashed and wriggled and writhed, but to no avail: the grip remained, squeezing his tail until it was thin as a ribbon.

Loki's chickens had come home to roost.

* * *

Loki crouched by his dead fire, surrounded by the gods. Blocking all four doors, they stared down at him, lips curled, fists clenched, bristling with fury. He knew there was nothing he could say to get out of this jam; all the wiles in the world wouldn't save him now. All he could do was wait for an opportunity to escape.

"I should kill you for what you've done," Frigg hissed.

"Perhaps if I jumped up to that rafter and swung over their heads…"

"Have you any idea what damage you've caused?" Odin shouted.

"Or I could turn into a bird and fly away…"

"Baldr was the best of us," Skadi cried, "and you killed him!"

"Could I take one of them hostage and get out that way…?"

Realizing they were getting no answers or contrition from the still-scheming Loki, the gods dragged him inside a nearby cave. Dark and desolate it was, with a chill wind moaning among the stalactites.

"Do you mean to kill me?" Loki said, but in his heart he knew the gods had far worse in store.

Odin beckoned, and through the parting throng staggered Loki's terrified sons. Before the Trickster God could say a word, Odin turned one son into a wolf, which immediately disembowelled the other with a slice of its claws. Thor and Heimdall held Loki's thrashing arms and legs as Frigg and Odin used his dead son's entrails to tie him face-up on a rock.

One by one, the gods filed out of the cave until only Skadi remained. "This is for Baldr," she said, and set loose a serpent, which wrapped around a stalactite above Loki's upturned face; he screamed in agony as venom poured from its fangs and into his eyes; indeed, his reaction was so violent it set off an earthquake in Midgard.

"Unjust gods!" he bellowed. "Hacks! Hypocrites! How many jötnar have you slain, Thor? Just to slake your thirst for blood!"

Another dose of venom, more unbearable pain, another earthquake… And then relief, as Loki's wife Sigyn emerged from the shadows and sat beside him. In her hand was a bowl, which she held under the snake to catch the venom, thus sparing Loki pain – except when the bowl was full and she had to turn away and pour it out. In those brief but frequent moments the venom dripped into Loki's eyes and the gods had their revenge.

Who and What Is Loki?

And this is where we leave Loki: tied to a rock inside a lonely cave, with his long-suffering wife catching poison before it drips into his eyes. Whatever your views may be on justice and punishment, it's an imaginative response to Loki's crimes, but one which is unlikely to end in rehabilitation: the rift between Loki and the gods is now insurmountable.

So, what epithets can we assign to Loki from these tales? His risky deal with the giant in 'The Walls of Asgard' (see page 47) shows *recklessness*. He's *selfish*, too, because it's Freya who'll pay the price if the giant fulfils his end of the bargain. And by shapeshifting and sex-changing into a mare, mating with a stallion and giving birth to an eight-legged foal, he's pretty *imaginative* and *unorthodox* in his problem solving.

Cutting off Sif's hair in 'The Forging of Thor's Hammer' (see page 53) shows Loki being *petty, spiteful* and *cruel.* It's a prank no one else finds funny, so let's add *unself-aware* to the list. He also demonstrates *cunning* when he tricks the dwarves into making magical items; in this instance the gods benefit from Loki's trickery as they end up with lots of useful trinkets to play with. He's also a *shapeshifter* (another form of deceit): things he turns into over the stories include a fly, an old woman, a horse, a salmon and a giantess.

He exhibits *selfishness* and *self-preservation* when, to save his own skin, he agrees to help abduct 'Iðunn in 'Iðunn and the Golden Fruit' (see page 65). However, he exhibits *courage* when he mounts his rescue – although, again, he's also looking after number one because he knows he'll be punished if he refuses. So, let's add *dichotomy* to the list, too.

In 'The Marriage of Njord and Skadi' (see page 84) he's *playful*, a *jester*, a *buffoon*. In 'Thor's Wedding' (see page 88) he's *helpful*, *quick-witted* and *a master of disguise.* In 'The Death of Baldr' and 'Hermóðr Visits Helheim' (see page 94 and page 99) he's a *destroyer*, a *killer* and entirely *unrepentant.*

So, like all interesting and well-rounded characters, Loki is many (often contradictory) things. He changes from one story to the next, never letting us settle on one fixed opinion of him. He also causes a lot of stuff to happen; he's an instigator; a prime mover; a problem-maker and a problem-solver; a plot-twist generator; an ally and an enemy (often to the same person or group within a single tale); a creator and destroyer; a dynamic, fascinating and frustrating protagonist/antagonist. He most certainly is a Trickster God, but also much more.

Which brings us, at long last, to The End.

'Ragnarök'

Ragnarök was coming but did not arrive straightaway, and for a time the gods continued their lives as normal: Odin flitting hither and thither trying to avert the tides of fate, Iðunn tending her fruit, Heimdall watching for invaders, Thor eating, drinking and killing giants.

Until one year winter came and...stayed. Cold gripped the nine realms; black ice coated everything like armour; streams, rivers and lakes froze solid; blizzards howled from all directions; the wind stripped the trees of their leaves and huts of their thatch; hearths were snuffed out, never to be lit again. They called it Fimbulvetr – Mighty Winter.

Iron-hard earth could not be seeded, fruit withered on the branch, animals perished. Starvation and disease scythed through the cosmos; people became rag-clad skeletons killing kin for scraps of food; existence was a brutal struggle to survive.

Up in the heavens, the wolves Sköll and Hati at last caught up with the Sun and Moon and swallowed them whole. Darkness descended – a night never-ending rent by howls of despair. Yggdrasill trembled and shook, causing forests to collapse, mountains to crumble and cliffs to slough into the sea.

Earth tremors shook Loki's cave-prison so hard they snapped his fetters. Bent on revenge, he stalked into a world riven by torment and spied the death-ship *Naglfar* sailing out of Helheim. Hel's creaking hulk was made from the fingernails of the dead and inside stood an army of corpses, staring silently ahead through empty eye sockets. Loki leapt aboard and ordered *Naglfar* be sailed to Asgard.

Further out to sea, Jormangandr broke the surface. Water gushed from his scales and formed waves that sank ships, smashed shorelines and swept whole villages away. Higher and higher the great snake rose, searching for Thor, his mortal enemy, and spewing a geyser of poison into the air.

Frenzied by the smell of bloody revenge, Fenrir broke free of Gleipnir and ran amok. Mouth agape, devouring everything in his path, his lower jaw tore up the ground and his upper ripped a hole in the sky: and through that hole burst the fires of Muspelheim, and through that fire came the demon Surtr, and behind Surtr marched rank upon rank of fire giants clad in blackened armour, clanging swords on their shields and singing songs of vengeance.

Heimdall saw them first, and he blew Gjallarhorn to warn the other gods that war was on its way. He watched with dread as the serried ranks trudged past, and sorrow as Bifrost collapsed behind them.

Although realizing that all his scheming and sacrifice had been in vain, Odin did not give up. Ragnarök was upon him, yes, but hope was not yet lost. He consulted Mímir one last time then led the Einherjar from Valhalla to the battle they had for so long prepared. The place where the fate of the gods, the nine realms and all things that lived there would be decided on was called Vigrid – The Plain Where Battle Surges.

The armies formed up under a thunderstruck sky. On one side were the shining gods led by Odin and Thor. Behind them the ranks of the Einherjar, warriors who had once died valiantly and now prepared to do so again. On the other side, led by Loki and Surtr, the frost and fire giants, Hel's army of the dead, and the monsters Fenrir and Jormangandr. Both sides charged, rushing towards each other, weapons raised, magic swirling; when they clashed the noise was so loud it put the stars to flight.

Flinging fire and brandishing his burning sword, Surtr fell upon Freyr who, having relinquished his magical blade to win the hand of the giantess he loved, was the first to die.

Brave, one-handed Tyr faced off with Garmr, the dire wolf guardian of Helheim; both die after a desperate battle: one by iron, the other by claw.

Odin stands firm as he faces the nightmare that has long haunted his dreams: Fenrir, mouth gaping, eyes wild, racing towards him across the blood-drenched battlefield. Long they fight, slicing and snarling, until Fenrir fulfils the fate woven by the Norns and swallows Odin whole. As Fenrir throws up his head and howls at the pitch-black sky, Víðarr, one of Odin's sons, leaps into the air and stabs his sword downward into the great wolf's throat. Vigrid shudders as Fenrir collapses in a lifeless heap.

Jormangandr rears over Thor, but Thor is unafraid. Mjölnir flies and returns, flies and returns, striking the great snake again and again. The World Serpent hisses, encircling Thor in his coils and pouring venom all over him. In his last mighty act of war, the Thunder God crushes Jormangandr's skull with his hammer, takes nine halting steps before falling lifelessly to the ground.

Amongst the death and slaughter two bitter enemies meet: gold-toothed Heimdall and shape-shifting Loki. Long have they hated each other, and now they can finally put a bloody end to it. Loki twists and turns, sometimes a striking snake, sometimes a clawing eagle, sometimes a furious giant; doughty Heimdall swings and parries, thrusts and feints. In the end, both suffering a thousand cuts, they fall and perish together.

Surtr climbs to the top of the tallest hill of slain, and with his burning sword rends the hole in the sky even wider, and the fires of Muspelheim pour through to burn the land and boil the sea. Odin's creation is no more, his pantheon destroyed, his fate fulfilled.

And yet this end also serves as a beginning, and the few surviving gods – Víðarr, Sif, Höðr, and Iðunn, and even Baldr who returns from the now destroyed Helheim – can begin again as a green and pleasant land rises up from the ashes of the old one.

4.
Impact and Influence

*Hearing I ask / from the holy races,
From Heimdall's sons, / both high and low;
Thou wilt, Valfather, / that well I relate
Old tales I remember / of men long ago.*
– Poetic Edda (trans. Henry Adams Bellows, 1936)

nd there we have it. As foretold, the Norse myths end with nearly everyone and everything dead, and the entire cosmos destroyed: a hard reset with the promise of an updated version to follow. (Although how could any sequel live up to this epic predecessor?)

The stories I've presented are only a small portion of those recorded by Snorri Sturluson (1179–1241). I didn't even have enough room to write all those featuring Loki! But I hope they have given you some idea of the breadth of characters, ideas, themes and plots created by the Norse, and I strongly recommend diving further into their incredible myths. There are many translations and retellings available to choose from, which itself proves just how enduringly popular these tales are.

Let's look at why so many writers, artists, and film and TV directors are drawn to these centuries-old stories.

IMPACT AND INFLUENCE

WHY DOES NORSE MYTHOLOGY STILL INSPIRE US?

Throughout history, humans have told stories. Long before the written word, groups of our forebears recounted tales of heroism, treachery, love, hate, gods and monsters. They did this at night within the comforting glow of a fire, or to pass the time when out hunting and foraging for food. Tales were told and retold, endlessly amended, changed, edited and passed down from generation to generation. The invention of writing allowed stories to be recorded, preserving them for posterity, even after the society, culture or civilization that created them ended.

Nowadays we can enjoy stories portrayed through many mediums old and new: performed in plays, ballets and operas; written in novels, short stories, poems, comics and graphic novels, and onscreen in films, video games and TV. We consume stories to help us understand ourselves and the societies we live in; to gather insight into other cultures and life experiences; to gain comfort, education, inspiration or distraction in a world that can be frightening, confusing and overwhelming.

We also love stories because they entertain us. We keep reading, watching or listening because we *have* to know what happens next. This is often because we become attached to certain characters. We might relate to them because they're like us. We might root for them because they have qualities we admire. We might find them fascinating because they're complex, multifaceted and unpredictable (remind you of anyone...?). We might even fall in love with them. Whatever the reason, we want to know how their story plays out. Will they survive or die? Save the universe or fail? Find love or lose it?

Compelling Characters

Part of our fascination with Norse mythology must surely be down to their vivid cast of characters. They really are an inspiring and unforgettable bunch. Larger than life, each with strong defining characteristics, and made more human (and thus relatable) due to their mix of strengths and flaws; perfect beings they are most certainly *not*. (And in storytelling terms, there's little more boring than a perfect character.)

Take Odin the All-Father: the most wise and powerful of the Aesir. He, along with his brothers, created not only the entire cosmos but humans too. And yet he knows that he and it are doomed, because beings more powerful than himself (the Norns) deem it so. This sword dangling over his head consumes the rest of his life. He commits himself utterly to the (futile) mission of thwarting destiny: he cuts out an eye, stabs himself with a spear, and travels all around and yonder scheming, meddling, planning and manipulating to gain some kind of advantage. But in the end it is death he faces, and the destruction of all he created. We can admire Odin's determination, pity his failure, and understand his fear, because the tragedy of our own mortality is something we wrestle with too.

Then there's Thor – perhaps the pantheon's most recognizable god. The very definition of the perfect warrior: courageous, skilled in battle, protector of family and realm, and always looking for a new adventure. None too bright, what he lacks in brains he makes up for with brawn. He's got great equipment too: a magic hammer, gloves and belt, and a goat-drawn chariot, so he looks every inch the (super)hero.

And, of course, the inspiration and subject of this essay and book: Loki. The liar, the prankster, the shapeshifter; the joker, the traveller, the trickster; the creator of monsters, the killer of gods, the harbinger of the end times. Certainly one of the most compelling and confounding characters ever created.

There are many more characters other than those who appear in the stories retold here, and I envy you the joy of discovery if you choose to read more widely and deeply into the subject. It's also important to remember that to the Norse these were not fictional creations but real entities: gods and goddesses who existed alongside humans, and who had a direct impact on their world and lives; this mythology was inextricably linked to their practised religion.

Bold, Big and Action-Packed Stories

Characters and their motivations create stories. Odin wants to preserve his life and legacy. Thor and Heimdall to protect the realm from invaders and keep the forces of chaos at bay. Frigg wants to protect her children no matter what the cost to herself. Many of the stories in the Norse myths stem from these relatable character motivations – motivations we know mattered to the Norse as well, otherwise they wouldn't have created these stories in the first place.

Although the tales retold here represent only a small selection from the many preserved for us, they are still a varied collection ranging from existential tales of creation and destruction to amusing stories about fishing trips with hapless giants. Looking at the tales not included here provides us with an even clearer idea of their breadth of plot, tone and theme.

If you like epic high fantasy check out 'Sigurd and the Dragon'. This tells the story of a brave warrior called Sigurd, who slays a dragon with an enchanted sword to get hold of the treasure he guards. Sounds familiar, right? We'll be getting to Professor Tolkien's works in a bit.

Some, such as 'The Theft of Freya's Necklace', seem a bit weird and random. In this tale, Loki shapeshifts into a fly, enters Freya's chambers while she sleeps and steals a precious magical necklace called Brisingamen. *Very* on-brand. A distraught Freya asks Heimdall to find it and, using his excellent sight, spies Loki – now in seal form for some reason – frolicking in the sea wearing the necklace. So Heimdal turns into a seal too and they both slap and strike each other bloody until Loki gives up the necklace and goes off in a huff. This tale goes some way to explain why Loki and Heimdall hate each other so much.

The point is, the Norse didn't mess around when it came to telling stories. Like the characters who star in them, they are big, brash and bold. Stories hinge on acts of courage, stupidity, selfishness, treachery, kindness and love. There are action scenes galore: bloody battles, fights with monsters, aerial jousting with giants, and seal-on-seal action. They take place in exciting locations such as the shining halls of Asgard, the stygian mines of the dwarves and the windswept mountains of

Jötunheim. There are no half-measures: Norse storytellers went big or went home.

The Norse loved stories for the same reasons we do, and we can imagine what it must have been like sitting agog with our friends and family inside a hearth-heated longhouse, listening to these wild and imaginative tales being performed by a gifted storyteller!

The Story Arc: From Creation to Destruction... and Rebirth

As incomplete as the Norse myths that survive for us are, they still have the three fundamental ingredients needed for a satisfying story: a beginning, middle and end.

We witness the nothing before the beginning (Ginnungagap), the chaos of the initial creation, and the order imposed by Odin. (This also sets up the stakes for Odin – if he fails to see off Ragnarök, it's his creation that gets mushed.) In the middle we travel on many adventures, some standalone tales, others that feed into the wider narrative of Odin and the fate of the gods. And we are there at the end, when all that was created at the beginning and fought for in the middle is lost. It's about as satisfying as a story can be.

We can also see how well the Norse set up certain plot points early in the narrative that pay off later (the famous 'Chekhov's Gun' principle of storytelling). For example, Heimdall and Loki's enmity is set up in 'The Theft of Freya's Necklace', Thor and Jormangandr's hatred in 'Thor's Fishing Trip' (see page 75), and Odin and Fenrir's fate are tied together in 'The Binding of Fenrir' (see page 79). Freyr's sacrifice of his sword in the name of true love leads to his death at the hands of Surtr. These final standoffs are made more compelling and emotional because we know the history of them from the stories that came before.

And, like even the bleakest of stories we create today, the Norse provide a ray of hope at the end of all things. A few gods survive along with a couple of humans, and they can populate a green new land that rises from the ashes of the old...although I can't help thinking it's going to be a lot less interesting and fun without Loki in it.

MODERN INTERPRETATIONS

When author and philologist Professor J.R.R. Tolkien (1892–1973) wrote *The Lord of the Rings* he wasn't setting out to inspire generations of writers and readers to fall in love with high fantasy – but that is exactly what happened. Popular from the moment it was published in 1954–55, it's gone on to sell around 150 million copies, and with director Peter Jackson's commercially and critically acclaimed film trilogy (2001–03), there can't be many people in the world who haven't heard of Frodo, Sam and Sauron.

What Tolkien *did* want to do with *The Lord of the Rings* and his other connected works *The Hobbit* (1937) and *The Silmarillion* (1977) was create a pre-Christian mythos for England (something he felt the country had lost). This was a deep undertaking involving the creation of detailed maps, a pantheon of Aesir-like entities (the Valar), various races (including elves and dwarves), creatures and monsters (including dragons, trolls and wolf-like wargs), a creation story and a rich history going back millennia before the events of *The Lord of the Rings* occur, as well as several fully functional languages.

He drew inspiration from various historical sources, and especially Germanic and Norse mythology in which he was an expert. His 'Middle Earth' comes from 'Midgard' ('Middle Enclosure'). The wandering wizard Gandalf who provides guidance, wisdom and magic bears more than a passing resemblance to Odin. The elemental Balrog with its flaming sword is analogous with the fire demon Surtr. Tolkien's terrifying barrow-wights are similar to the undead Norse entities called 'draugar', which guard buried grave treasure. Even Sauron's plan to subdue all Middle Earth could be viewed as a sort of Ragnarök for the people who live there.

Like their Norse inspiration, Tolkien's dwarves have an affinity with stone and are master craftspeople. Indeed, every dwarf character's name in *The Hobbit* (excluding Balin) is lifted from the *Prose Edda*. 'Gandalf' comes from there too: 'Gandálfr', which means 'staff-elf' or 'wand-elf'. The dwarves' runic language and its connection to magic is taken from the Norse's Futhark. Tolkien's elves are otherworldly and almost god-like: tall, wise, luminous, ethereal and immortal (but not unkillable).

The idea of naming powerful weapons (such as Frodo's sword Sting, Gandalf's Glamdring and Aragorn's Andúril) mirror the Norse's predilection for doing the same. And, of course, Tolkien's magic rings are similar to Odin's gold-producing Draupnir, and a cursed ring called Andvaranaut that appears in the story 'Sigurd and the Dragon'.

Video Games

It's no surprise that video games (which for many people are the most immersive of all artistic experiences) have mined deep into Norse mythology. What the Norse created with their mythos translates brilliantly to this particular media: visually striking heroes and heroines, legendary antagonists, breathtaking locations and epic stories. The unique aspect of video games is that players don't passively watch and listen as things unfold before them. Instead, they participate by embodying the character onscreen, making decisions and using their skills to advance through the game. This active participation in the story is what makes games so immersive.

Santa Monica's *God of War* series began in 2005. The first batch of games are set in the world of Greek mythology and feature characters such as Zeus, Athena and Ares. The 2018 release saw a marked change in tone – a thoughtful story about fatherhood, responsibility, atonement and grief (as well as providing incredibly cool gameplay involving combat, exploration and puzzle-solving). It also saw a change of location, with the action set in Norse mythology, (some of) the Nine Realms, and featuring characters such as Freya, Baldr, Mimir and yes, Loki too.

Quick side note: one of the many gorgeous details that the developers ladled into their game is the way in which during quieter periods Mimir (just a head at this point, who travels with the two main characters throughout) relays many of the Norse myths in an avuncular and amusing way.

Anyway, the characters who appear in the game are in many ways only loosely connected to their real Norse forebears. For

IMPACT AND INFLUENCE

example, Baldr is far from the beautiful, joyful soul he is in the myths; although he *is* immune to pain. But such changes are justified because they are also fascinating constructs in their own right, help compose a deeply affecting story, while remaining respectful of the source material. *God of War*, and its 2022 sequel *God of War: Ragnarök,* go to show just how inspiring the original tales are, and how modern audiences can fall for them all over again.

Ninja Theory's 2017 *Hellblade: Senua's Sacrifice* (followed up with 2024's *Senua's Saga: Hellblade 2*) is a different beast to *God of War*. Much darker in tone, story and aesthetic, these games tell the tale of Senua, a young eighth-century Pict woman from the Orkney Isles. I won't go into too many plot details, but Senua's task (using a mix of combat and puzzle-solving) is to save the soul of her dead lover (killed by Vikings using the blood-eagle technique) by defeating (among others) Surtr, and seeking Hel (called Hela in the game) much like Hermóðr does to negotiate the return of Baldr. She also carries her lover's head around, a bit like Odin and Mimir.

As with *God of War*, a recurring character relates many of the Norse myths to Senua (and thus the player) as the game progresses, but in a far more apocalyptic and downbeat tone – proving just how versatile the original stories are.

Ubisoft's 2020 *Assassin's Creed: Valhalla* focuses more on the Norse/Vikings themselves rather than the gods. Set in the ninth century, it allows the player to take the role of a Viking warrior trying to gain a foothold in England by raiding, negotiating and building a permanent settlement.

Television and Films

Many people's first experience of Norse mythology will be from watching the hugely popular and entertaining Marvel movie depictions in *Thor* (2011), *Thor: The Dark World* (2013), *Thor: Ragnarok* (2017) and *Thor: Love and Thunder* (2022). Actor Chris Hemsworth (b. 1983) plays Thor as a rambunctious and likable character – a perfect hero to take on the various evil forces put in his way. Sir Anthony Hopkins (b. 1937) plays Odin as a powerful but fading deity, and Tom Hiddleston (b. 1981) portrays Loki as a delightfully charming antihero who causes total carnage for the gods but is also very difficult to dislike. (So, pretty similar to the Norse original.) So popular was Loki he got his own TV series, which premiered in 2021. Other characters and places are portrayed too, including Frigg, Sif, Heimdall, Hel (named Hela in the films) and the frost giants. Although there are many recognizable elements, these films heavily adapt the source material and include lots of changes and liberties to appeal to a modern audience of superhero fans.

Running for six series on The History Channel and Amazon Prime, Michael Hirst's TV show *Vikings* (2013–20) takes a more historical approach to the Norse and Viking Age. Although the show gets a lot correct, in some aspects it plays pretty fast and loose with the facts to create a cool aesthetic, increase drama and make the narrative work. For example, the clothes worn in the show are not entirely accurate, events that actually occurred many years apart are condensed in the fictional timeline, and certain historical characters who never crossed paths (mainly because they were not alive at the same time) do so in the show.

IMPACT AND INFLUENCE

But these are justifiable artistic choices to suit the medium and make the show accessible and enjoyable, so I'm not griping about them.

Director Robert Eggers (b. 1983) is famous for the intense research and historical authenticity he brings to his work. His debut, a folk horror film called *The Witch* (2015), is set in 1630s New England. The sets and costumes were made to be as accurate as possible, and the dialogue is an approximation of the language and speech patterns used back then. Eggers brought a similar kind of painstaking authenticity to his brooding historical epic *The Northman* (2022), which tells the story of a Viking prince, played by a jacked Alexander Skarsgård (b. 1976), on a quest to avenge the murder of his father.

A brutal Viking raid on a village is an undoubted highlight. This one-shot scene depicts the prince and his band of berserkers working themselves up into a frenzy before launching their attack wearing nothing but bearskins, scaling the walls and killing indiscriminately. After the assault, the village is plundered and the survivors taken off as slaves, just as they were in the Viking Age.

I expect we'll be retelling, rewriting and re-presenting Norse myths for a long time. The stories are compelling and have as much to say to us today as they did all those centuries ago. The themes are deep: what better example of hubris is there than Odin battling against the unforgiving tides of fate? The lessons strong: when someone shows you who they are (we're looking at you, Loki), believe them. The characters inspiring: as you will see when you read the brand new tales of the Trickster God (who is *so* much more than that!) contained in this book.

Modern Short Stories of Loki

Loki: The Movie

Chris A. Bolton

Hugh Tiddleman opens his front door and is already reaching for the bag of food before he realizes there is no bag, nor food, nor the delivery driver he expected. There is, instead, a tall, lanky man with straight, raven-black hair to his shoulders, green-eyed and wearing a purple suit tailored to fit like a second skin.

Shit. Hugh catches the word before it reaches his teeth. "Loki," he says instead, pulling on his million-dollar smile, "what a surprise! Brilliant to see you, mate."

"Hugh." Loki scowls at him. "I watched the movie. I saw what you did."

Hugh's breath catches. What happens when a trickster god disapproves of the way you played him in a movie? Nothing good, Hugh imagines. But how *bad?*

Loki's eyes light up and a smile splits his face. "AND I LOVED IT!"

Arms as strong as steel girders wrap around Hugh's shoulders. Loki pulls him into a hug that crushes the frozen breath from his lungs. He feels a wet smack on his cheek and realizes Loki just fucking *kissed him.*

"You knocked it out of the park. Even got my hair color right. Not sure why you changed it back, though," he adds, eyeing

Hugh's lemon-blond hair. "Those box-office numbers tell me there's going to be a *lot more Loki*. So, let's talk about the future, babe."

Loki breezes through the doorway before Hugh can stop him, marching across the marble floor of the foyer. Hugh races past Loki and tries to block him from proceeding into the living room. Fortunately, Loki is distracted by the luxurious surroundings of the rented mansion. (The one Hugh's *this close* to buying, if he can just land that $2 million payday.)

"What a palace!" Loki says, whistling at the vaulted ceilings. "These columns, are they faux marble or the real thing? Valhalla isn't even this grand! I kid, of course. Valhalla's a stinking shithole. Always was, and why not? Anyone stupid enough to die in battle for Odin deserves to spend eternity in an outhouse."

Hugh glances over his shoulder at the door to his study. Closed, thank God. Or gods. He doesn't really know anymore.

"I'd love to catch up, Loki," Hugh says. "I've been meaning to make a lunch date. Thing of it is, I've got a costume fitting at the studio, should've been out the door ages ago, Devin *hates* to be kept waiting. I'll call you after, we'll go for sushi—"

"You're their newest star. Let 'em wait."

Panic bubbles in Hugh's chest. "Better yet, why don't you ride with me? It's in Burbank, the freeway's a disaster, we'll take my Maserati and catch up on the way."

Hugh starts toward the door, wondering how he's going to talk Loki out of following him into a costume fitting he doesn't actually have. A vague plan starts to form: pretend he got the date wrong, play dumb, drive back after his *other* uninvited guest has a chance to slip out.

Loki stands under the chandelier, hands in his coat pockets, smirk on his face, and doesn't make the slightest gesture to follow Hugh out. "Dear boy, you must slow down. Enjoy the spoils of fame and adulation. Believe me, they don't last. I had them for hundreds of years, and then what happens? You kill one little god of light – *one bloody time* – and get imprisoned with a snake drooling in your face." Loki draws his gaze across a framed movie poster lying askew at the foot of the stairs. "How about that earthquake this morning? For a moment there, I thought it was the serpent crawling out of the earth to bring me back!"

"Right. Terrifying. Though I hear L.A. gets those all the time." Hugh feels himself fidgeting, tries to steady his hands. "Lovely day, though. Why don't we stroll in the garden?"

"I can't believe I waited so long to see *The Retributors*. It's been in theaters for half a year, became the all-time top-grossing movie, and I waited till practically the last showing. To be honest, Hughie, I might have been a wee touch nervous."

"Loki, nervous?" His laugh feels desperate, but Hugh hopes it *sounds* genuine. "I'm beginning to think you didn't trust my acting ability." What he's actually thinking about is the damage to the mansion if the study door opens. If it's anything like in the movies, it will be catastrophic – to his bank account *and* his career. "Let's chat about it outside—"

"It wasn't you, old shoe. When you met with me, I could tell you were hanging on every word I said. Your eagle eyes scanned every detail and filed it all away. And I Googled you first, so I knew how you pride yourself on thorough research for every role. It was the script. And Atlas Studios. I felt sure, no matter how authentically you portrayed my complex yet charismatic nature, those hacks would turn me into a bog-standard bad guy. 'Ooh, evil Loki, making mischief for no reason at all!'"

Loki whirls around so suddenly, Hugh flinches away. "But they did right by us! Yes, I could have wiped the floor with those ridiculous Retributors and their stupid powers. But I'm not some thick-skinned Asgardian dullard who can't recognize the value of good, solid escapism. Besides, *we* were the best character! The crowd laughed at our every joke, hissed at our dark deeds, even clapped when the Smasher beat the hell out of us. So did I, by the way! A fitting takedown for a godly villain, says I. And you – *compadre*, soulmate, brother!"

Loki pulls him into another chest-thumping hug. "You did me proud," Loki whispers into Hugh's ear. "Captured my essence in a way the poets and academics could never get right. You did it so well, in fact, that it's time we talked about what comes next."

As Loki releases him, Hugh launches for the door. "Wonderful! Can't wait to hear your thoughts. But I really must crack on and get to the studio. Ring me later—"

"Just a moment, old boy, old bean, old chap." God, Hugh *hates* when Loki tries to get chummy with fake Britishisms. "I've got something here that'll stop the clocks."

Loki reaches into his coat and pulls out a bulging sheaf of pages barely held together by three brads. After so many PDFs on his phone, Hugh hasn't laid eyes on a printed screenplay in a decade.

LOKI: THE MOVIE

"Loki: The Movie!" the god bellows, his voice echoing like peals of thunder.

He tosses the script, its voluminous pages flapping across the foyer on paper wings. It crashes into Hugh's arms and falls open to page 145, which Hugh is dismayed to see has gigantic paragraphs of descriptive text with no dialogue. So much for the one saving grace of having to read a script written by a friend or family member: they're usually 80% dialogue – most of it lousy but a relatively fast pity-read.

"That's right," Loki cackles, mistaking Hugh's open-mouthed dismay for awe-inspired shock, "it's time we got our own feature! No Retributors hogging the frame, sucking up our spotlight. Oh no, old chap, old fellow, old such-and-such, this is the *epic prequel* the fans are crying out for. So much bigger than life, even an IMAX screen will barely hold it all!"

"It's…it's all about you?" Hugh asks.

"A timeless tale – only in this telling, we're setting the record straight. It's the heart-rending story of a cunning, achingly handsome god who's unfairly maligned by history. I'm a *shapeshifter*, for Aesir's sake! That's a *real* power. Not like Thor, who can toss a hammer, or Balder, who could…what'd he do, wave a sword? He certainly couldn't change himself into another being."

"Well, in the movies, he shoots beams of light that melt Frost Giants and—"

"But can he shift his shape, Hugh?"

"No, certainly not. Bang-on with that one, Loki."

Glancing at the door to the study, his brow beaded with sweat, Hugh tries to remember when he'd been offered the role of Loki and thought it was a *good* idea to take it. Not just good – a blessing. He was building a portfolio of memorable roles in unmemorable films, stealing every scene he could wrap his gym-buffed arms around and chomping down on every chunk of halfway-edible dialogue. But many of his fellow British actors rocketed past him on the path to stardom. As he felt the clock ticking on his chance to become a viable leading man, Hugh realized he needed a huge breakout role – *right now.*

That's when Devin Craig came calling. He was the president of an upstart studio that was solely dedicated to turning Atlas Comics properties into hit movies by boosting its B-list heroes to A-list blockbuster status.

Devin wanted Hugh for the part of Loki in the *Balder* movie. That would be the follow-up to *Metallo Man*, which set the groundwork for the interconnected universe. As Devin pitched it to Hugh in his closet-sized office at the rented Atlas Studios building in a rundown corner of L.A., the third movie would be *The Retributors*, uniting Balder and Metallo Man into one team along with a handful of heroes Hugh had never heard of.

The whole concept gave off a stink of doom. But Hugh was ready to take a gamble because he *needed* that payoff. And besides, Devin promised him, "You'll not only be the perfect bad guy, but also a *god*."

That was music to Hugh's ears. He signed on the spot.

Metallo Man was a surprise smash. Then *Balder* was also a hit – and his deliciously sly performance as Loki put Hugh on the must-read list for casting agents all over Hollywood.

His whole body was humming when Hugh stepped into Devin Craig's new airplane hangar-sized office in the sprawling complex Atlas Studios now owned, ready to hear some good news about the *Balder* sequel. He got even better news.

"We want you as the big bad in *The Retributors*," Devin announced.

Hugh felt a lightning-like jolt as his eyes flooded with tears and a joyous sob clambered up his throat.

"Just one thing," Devin added, the smile retreating from his face. "I need you to meet with someone for the part."

"A fight coordinator?" Hugh asked, already shaping colorful stories of intensive training for the press tour.

"No, you need to meet Loki."

Hugh frowned. "Do you mean an expert on Norse mythology?"

"No, I mean Loki. The actual god. Well, *demigod*, but don't call him that to his face. Trust me on this."

A wave of concern crested over Hugh, who'd seen other high-powered executives and stars melt down from the pressure of success. "You're telling me Loki is not only an actual person, but that the Norse gods are real?"

"Again, he's a demigod, not a god – but again, don't tell him. And yes, I'm saying that." Devin dropped a hand on Hugh's shoulder. "Loki has a lot of thoughts about this role that he's eager to share." His fingertips dug into Hugh's flesh. "*Very* eager. In fact, he won't take no for an answer.

And he won't go away until he's happy. Even bodyguards, studio security, and a SWAT team can't get rid of him. The only way to appease Loki is to give him what he wants, Hugh, and that's to let him meet with you about playing him." Hugh's shoulder went numb as Devin's fingers sank deeper. "So, you're going to listen to everything Loki says. And make him very, very happy. And I swear to God, Hugh, if you ever bring him anywhere near me, I will fire you, burn this studio to the ground, and hire a team of assassins to hunt and kill every person you've ever known and loved in your life. Do you understand me?"

"Yes, quite," Hugh said, shrinking under Devin's death-grip. "One million percent. I'd simply *love* to meet Loki."

Devin's fingers released Hugh as a gale of relief blew from his quivering lips. "Thank you, Hugh. Bless you. And don't forget what I said."

Devin's words are ringing in Hugh's ears as he grips the solid-gold door handle. "Loki, I'm afraid I must insist that you leave at once, or I'll be forced to—"

Hugh yanks the door open and sees the Door Dash driver standing with his fist in mid-air, holding so many bags of Chicken Shack he can barely get his arms around them. "Uh, delivery for Mr. Hugh?"

"Yes, thank you," Hugh says, snatching the bags and slamming the door.

Loki studies the food with an unreadable expression. "Heading out for a fitting, but thought you'd order lunch first, hmm? For you and a guest, I'd say, unless you're eating for two."

Hugh sucks in a heavy breath. "Yes, I have a guest. And I've asked them to hide because if anyone saw them here, things could get quite…messy."

Loki leans close, waggles his eyebrows. "You sly dog. I meant to reach out when Taylor dumped you, but I needn't have worried – back in the saddle you go! Does she have a sister? Friend? Into three-ways? Never mind." Loki snatches the script from Hugh's sweat- and grease-slicked hands, nearly toppling the food bags. "I shall leave you to sup with your lady-friend, whilst I deliver this golden pitch straight to Devin Craig."

"NO!" Hugh blurts, dropping the bags as he imagines the apocalyptic fury Devin will rain down on him. "By which I mean, my guest can wait a bit longer. We should workshop it together. Hone this gleaming concept to its richest, *purest* essence."

"I love your enthusiasm, chum," Loki says. "Okay, fade up on the kingdom of Asgard. Not the gleaming golden spires we saw in the *Balder* movie – that's pure balderdash, if you can forgive an almost-pun. The real Asgard is a run-down shithole of rickety wooden shacks that are rotting and stinking from centuries of death and sweat. Ancient Norseman did *not* have good hygiene, I assure you."

Hugh keeps a nervous eye on the door of his study, careful not to let Loki catch his attention straying as he recites his entire history, from birth ("I was born in fire. It was hot. I don't remember much about it.") to his fateful first meeting with Odin, the Allfather: "Even as a young god, he was hairy and oafish. Stank of lutefisk and spoiled mead. The only difference between him and the jötunn was that trolls knew how to bathe."

A roar of laugher bursts from Hugh's mouth before he can contain it, which he prays will muffle Loki's last sentence. Loki beams, satisfied that Hugh is vibing with his every word.

"And now comes Balder," Loki says, "who is far from the bold, cunning hero in his movies. The real Balder was a little…dense. Bit of an understatement. Stupid, that's a better word. Braindead is an even more accurate one."

"Uh-huh, sure, I can see that. Dumb Balder." *How much longer can this possibly take?*

"Honestly, I'd rather keep him out of the whole movie," Loki sighs. "But here's the thing: the real Balder was stupid and mean. A bully. Even as the Asgardian gods unfairly blamed me for every little thing that went wrong, Balder made my life miserable. He'd torment the Aesir – especially his asshole brother, Thor – then pin it all on me. Why? He said it's because I was a 'trickster,' whatever that's supposed to mean. I say it's because I was smarter than all of them. I knew what soap was, and how to use it properly, and they were jealous that I didn't smell like the bloated asshole of a dead goat. So, when Balder chops off all the hair on Sif, Thor's equally slow-witted wife, who does he pin it on?"

"You," Hugh says, wondering how long before the door flies off his study – or the entire wall crumbles – and the mayhem begins.

"And when I protest my innocence, doth Thor believe a word of it?"

"No," Hugh says. *There's zero chance I'm getting my deposit back on this place.*

"Nay, indeed! And when Thor finds out who really shaved Sif's head, then shoots the mistletoe arrow that kills Balder, who gets blamed for that? And sentenced to eternal punishment in the bowels of the Earth with serpent venom dripping into his innocent eyes?"

"You," Hugh says, inching backwards, hoping Loki is too absorbed in himself to notice him sneak away.

"See? You get me, Hughie! We're going to set the historic record straight once and for all, and rake in a trillion dollars worldwide. We'll even throw in some of those dance moves you bust out on the talk shows. Those clips always go viral, get a million YouTube hits—"

"Yes, love it!" Hugh squeals as he dances to the front door. He's torn between what will happen to his loved ones if he brings Loki to Devin Craig's office and what will happen to Hugh if he doesn't get the bloody hell out of this house right now. "Off we go, to make history! And great art!"

"To Devin Craig," Loki bellows, "and the future!"

"That's far enough, Loki."

Though he speaks calmly, Odin's voice has a resonant boom that rumbles in Hugh's bones and rattles his back teeth. Hugh freezes with one leg in mid-air, his heart skipping so many beats, he wonders if it's ever going to catch up again.

The study door hangs open and Odin stands in the living room in a crisp linen suit. His beard is red and scraggly. Even if Loki doesn't recognize his face or voice after however many centuries since they'd encountered one another, the eyepatch and raven on each shoulder should give the broad, burly man away.

"*Odin*," Loki says in a choked whisper.

Hugh holds his breath. *Here comes the bloodshed...*

"I saw the movie," Odin says. "It was okay. A little hokey. Relied too much on CGI to fill gaping potholes in the plot."

Everyone's a bloody critic, Hugh laments, his hands quaking. Should he throw open the door and flee for his life? How far can he get on foot before an angry god *(demigod)* smites him?

"There were little details I recognized. Things that had never been written down by human hands, that only the real Loki would know about. I promised this mortal pretender that if he helped me recapture you, I'd grant him a seat at my table in the glorious palace of Valhalla."

"It's a shack, you idiot," Loki growls. "Covered in pig shit."

Like I had a choice, Hugh wants to bellow. When the god of gods shows up and demands your compliance, what options does a mortal have? Even one who desperately hopes to *not* incur the wrath of Loki?

"I'd hoped to forge a grand deception and amass an army to entrap you," Odin says. "It would be easy to assemble, for after all this time, there are still countless Aesir who yearn to roast you alive like a pig. But I was afraid I'd die of old age, hiding in that study while you blathered endlessly about your favorite subject: yourself. And so, I must improvise. *I'll* be the army that beats you senseless and drags you back to the serpent that longs to spit on you."

"What the actual fuck, friendo?" Loki hisses, turning his astonished gaze on Hugh. "You tricked me! Lured me here under false pretenses."

"I didn't actually *lure*, you just showed up—"

"I feel both betrayed and strangely proud," Loki says. "I didn't know you had it in you, old chummy-chum-chum. The soul of a trickster. Well-played! You've earned my admiration, and that's no small thing. Also, my everlasting hatred, which is an even less-small thing."

"Er, thank you? I think?"

Filling his chest with a mighty pull of air, Loki pivots toward Odin. "And now, Allfather, we have ancient business to settle..."

"Wait, please!" Hugh cries, jumping between them with his arms outstretched. "Before you start fighting, I beg of you... This is a very expensive mansion that I'm only renting, and I'm quite sure the insurance policy does *not* cover 'gods smashing each other and everything else to bits.' So, for the love of all that's holy, *please* step outside before you brutalize one another."

"Oh, there'll be no brutalizing," Loki says, sounding curiously reasonable. "I've had a good run of freedom these few hundred years since I escaped, but you finally caught me, Odin. I may not know when it's better to tell a truth than a lie, but I certainly know when I'm beaten. I'll go quietly. All I ask, strange as it may seem, is that you silence me."

Odin cocks an eyebrow at each of his ravens.

"I've accepted my fate in this moment," Loki says, raising his empty palms in surrender. "But as you haul me back to the serpent, I'm quite sure my temper will rise and my tongue will flap, and I'll say dreadful things we may both regret. Probably, mostly me. For my own good, gag my mouth so I cannot—"

The ground shifts abruptly, pitching Hugh off-balance. He slides across the tilting marble floor, past trembling walls raining posters, paintings, and plaster. *An aftershock*, he realizes as he whirls his arms. He tries to grab something solid to stop himself from slamming head-first into a marble column.

"Brace yourself!" Loki shouts. "The serpent's dancing with joy!"

The quaking ends as suddenly as it began. Hugh skids to a stop and grabs the column to stay upright, even as Odin rolls head over heels a few feet away.

When the ground settles, Odin rises to his feet. "I hate this damn city," he grumbles, looking straight at Hugh with a deep scowl. "All right, Loki, come along and I'll take you back to your cell."

Confused, Hugh turns to Loki – and is stunned to see the blond hair and shining blue eyes of Hugh Tiddleman staring back at him. "Don't forget," the other Hugh reminds Odin, "he asked you to silence him."

Hugh looks down at his own body, which is suddenly, inexplicably covered in a tailored purple suit! He turns toward the antique mirror above the fireplace and sees Loki's black hair and green eyes reflected at him.

Shapeshifter. OH, FUCK.

"Wait, Odin, DON'T—"

Odin flings something across the room – a small snake made of gold. It smacks Hugh's face and encircles his head until the mouth and tail latch at the nape of his neck. The golden snake covers his mouth, muffling his every panicked word so all that comes out is a whirr of desperate sounds.

As Hugh lifts his hands to pry it off, another golden snake flies from Odin's grasp. This one coils around his wrists, squeezing them tightly, unbreakably together.

He gawks at Loki, wearing Hugh's face and beaming with undisguised delight. "Well, old chum, I guess you'll be off. Fear not, I'll get this script into Devin's hands at once. And when our cinematic masterpiece takes the world by storm, Odin might show a touch of mercy and let you watch it in your cave?"

Odin shrugs. "I'll install a flat-screen TV and play it on an endless loop."

Loki-as-Hugh shakes Odin's hand, then claps Hugh-as-Loki on the back. "Best of luck to you," he whispers. "Remember, the venom dripping into your face only hurts for the first few centuries. After that, your eyes burn out and go numb. Mostly."

Ignoring Hugh-as-Loki's muffled pleas, Odin seizes his arm and marches him out the door, where a goat-driven chariot waits in the circular driveway next to Hugh's Maserati. The last thing Hugh sees, as the chariot ascends into the sky and he glances back at the opulent life that's no longer his, is Loki climbing into the Maserati, waving his script with a gleaming grin. "See you at the movies, mate!"

Loki's Confrontations

Drew Conners

Drip…drip…drip…

The sound of a dripping liquid echoed throughout the cave, but there was no stone splash that followed. Instead, what followed was a slight sizzling sound mixed with a man letting out a small groan of pain. That man's name is Loki, the God of Mischief. Suspended over the god is an offspring of the Midgard Serpent, also known as Jormungandr, a snake with venom that can kill a mortal man with a single bite. Due to Loki's crime, the snake is eternally dripping venom into his eyes as he is chained to an indestructible boulder, held by chains made from the intestines of his monster children. Yet, due to Aesir magic, they had the consistency of stone.

A question that I feel many would have about Loki's current predicament is: "What did he do to end up in this situation?" The answer is quite simple, really.

Loki killed Baldur.

Baldur was an Aesir God beloved by all and untouched by many. His mother, the goddess Frigg, cast a spell on him when he was born so that nothing in the world could ever bring him harm, in essence making him live forever. However, through some means, the mistletoe plant was not accounted for in this spell, but nobody knew. Nobody except for Loki, that is. Loki, ever a being of eternal

LOKI'S CONFRONTATIONS

mischief and tomfoolery, crafted an arrow of pure mistletoe and slipped it into the god Freyr's quiver during one of the regular "Watch-The-Arrows-Not-Hit-Baldur" games that the Aesir held. Needless to say, the plan went without a hitch, and Baldur was dead by the end of the day. Loki would have gotten away with it too, if he didn't drunkenly confess to the crafting of the mistletoe arrow during one of the Aesir's infamous parties. The resulting hunt and capture of Loki was unlike anything the Nine Realms had ever seen, and neither was his punishment.

So here, we find the man of the hour, strapped to a boulder and trying to regenerate his eyes before the next drop of venom reset his progress. Unfortunately, closing his eyes wouldn't do Loki any good, the venom seemed to melt through any kind of organic matter. Still, Loki persisted, his hatred for the Aesir that betrayed him growing more and more intense each passing day, which Loki tallied so far at 107.

The sound of footsteps echoed from the cave's entrance, and a warm yellow light slowly illuminated the surrounding walls of rock. Loki smiled, his wife, Sigyn, was here. Sigyn carried a bowl, a few sticks, and a torch with her as she casually marched over to her husband's place of torment.

"Aren't you a sight for sore eyes," Loki remarked, trying to hide the pain in his voice, "I thought you would have left me here to rot by now."

Sigyn let out a sigh that turned into a small giggle as she positioned herself next to her husband.

"As much of a fool I think you are, you are still the man that I love," she replied, arranging the sticks into a makeshift stand. She carefully set the bowl on top of the stand, positioned right above Loki's head. The venom from the snake began to slowly collect into the bowl, giving Loki a much-needed break.

The bowl was made from glass crafted from the coldest ice in the realm of Helheim, the land of the dead. One of Loki's children, the Goddess of Death, Hela, ruled over the souls that ended up there. Luckily, due to her usefulness to the Aesir, she had been spared from the wrath brought on to them by her father.

"How is Hela?" Loki asked, his fully regenerated eyes adjusting to the warm light of Sigyn's torch.

Sigyn let out a sigh, "As pensive as ever. She is trying to remain on the Allfather's good side by keeping Baldur's spirit safeguarded."

A snarky chuckle escaped from Loki's lips, "I would have assumed the mighty Odin to have snatched his precious son's soul and brought it to Valhalla."

"You know as well as I that that boy was no fighter," Sigyn responded, "one of the gentlest and kindest of the Aesir. He would not have lasted long in that eternal battleground. Besides, the Aesir had forgotten during their rabid search for the culprit."

A twinge of guilt snuck its way into Loki's mind. "Is this an attempt at guilting me?"

Sigyn sat down next to Loki. "No, but it is a reminder that no matter how much I love you, you are still a fool and an idiot for what you did." She reached into a pouch tucked away in her dress and pulled out a handful of grapes.

As she fed her husband, Sigyn sighed, "Why did you do it? You knew this was going to be the outcome, why betray them?"

LOKI'S CONFRONTATIONS

Loki finished eating a grape and lightly scowled. "Do you know what it's like truly living with them?" He asked, "Do you know what it's like to be the only Jotun in a group of beings that go out and regularly slaughter your own kind? Do you know what it's like to be expected to help them carry out such horrific deeds? Do you *know* how much I sacrificed for their happiness with little in return?"

His questions burned into Sigyn's brain, causing her to stop feeding him grapes and to truly listen.

"They treat each other horridly, and mortals even less favorably," Loki continued, "why should I ever have to abide by rules that benefit them and them alone. I'm surprised Freyr and Freya can stand being the only Vanir in their group, though I guess since they pass better as Aesir themselves nobody else cares."

As Loki talked, his red hair slowly began to morph into a burning fire and his ears began to grow pointier. His Fire Jotun traits were slowly starting to emerge, as per usual when Loki ever became truly upset. This issue got to him, and Sigyn knew it all too well.

"Nevertheless, this is what you get for toying with the Aesir," Sigyn replied, planting a kiss on Loki's forehead, "I wish it was not this way, but it is."

Loki groaned but accepted the kiss. Sigyn never usually showed affection physically, so this was a strange change of pace.

Just then, a noise coming from the path to the cave entrance startled both Loki and Sigyn. It sounded like footsteps, but uneven and peppered with profanities as a man of some sort stumbled his way down the path to Loki's chamber of misery.

Sigyn hurriedly disassembled the stand, causing the snake venom to drip back down onto Loki's eyes. Sigyn let out a small,

"Apologies, darling," and rushed to hide behind a rock formation on the other side of the cave.

Immediately after she did, the man finally found his way into Loki's cave. He was a large man, both in height and size. His dark red hair tumbled down to his chest, his messy beard matching in length. A one-handed hammer was strapped to a pair of pants that bulged out due to his beer belly, causing his boots to barely fit. The man eyed Loki up and down, a slight shimmer of lightning echoing through his eyes.

It was Thor, the strongest of the Aesir.

"Loki, son of Farbauti." Thor's voice rumbled like distant thunder.

"Thor, son of Odin." Loki responded.

Thor pulled a wineskin out from the other side of his pants and began to drink it.

The bastard's drunk. Wonderful. Loki thought to himself.

Thor brought the wineskin down and hooked it back onto his belt, eyeing Loki the whole time.

"Is there something I can help you with?" Loki spat, "If not, get out."

"Why?" Thor asked, his gaze still locked on Loki.

"Why what?"

"Why did you do it?" The question hung in the air for a moment.

"You're going to have to be specific, dear nephew," Loki responded, his signature snark shining.

Thor grew enraged, *"Why did you kill Baldur?!"* he roared, his voice echoing through the cave like a thunderclap.

"Ohhh, that," Loki answered when the last echo died down, "with how long I had spent with you Aesir, my sense of humor is

LOKI'S CONFRONTATIONS

something I thought would naturally rub off on you all. Perhaps I gave you too much credit—"

Thor's rage roared, *"WHAT'S SO FUNNY ABOUT MURDERING MY BROTHER?!"*

Thor's hand hovered next to Mjolnir with red-hot anger. If it were not for the Allfather's decree that no external harm shall befall Loki while he is imprisoned, Thor would have repaid his brother's murder tenfold.

"Who's to say," Loki started, "maybe it was the fact that his constantly kind attitude rubbed me the wrong way, maybe it was his preferential treatment by all the other Aesir. 'Do not make Baldur go on this quest, he may get hurt!' Maybe it was the utter hubris of the special incantation performed by Frigg to make him immortal, maybe it was the fact that you all treat him like royalty, yet when it came down to it, you all always relied on me to clean up your messes. Whether it was the gifts from the Dwarves, retrieving Idunn from Thjazi, retrieving Mjolnir for you, our adventure with Utgard the Jotun, the building of the Asgardian Fortress, you always counted on me to do the work that nobody else would! I am always the first one blamed, and the first one asked to assist with *no reward*!"

Loki breathed a bit, calming himself down, "Or maybe, I was bored and wanted some true excitement around here for once."

Thor's fury reached a breaking point, causing him to instinctively retrieve Mjolnir from his belt and aim it at the chained Loki, lightning crackling and surging throughout the hammer as Thor breathed heavily.

Finally, Thor's voice thundered, "Many of the issues you described are ones that you brought upon yourself! You made yourself untrustworthy so my kin would believe you stole Mjolnir, you made the deal with Thjazi to help him abduct Idunn, you cut my beautiful Sif's hair, which caused the Allfather to commission the Dwarves!"

"Hair grows back, you *blithering* oaf!" Loki sneered back at Thor.

"You create your own problems, Loki," Thor continued. "You claim to be a victim, yet you are a victim to your own decisions! Why do you choose to act the way you do? I have never understood it!"

It was at this moment that Loki realized something. For the first time in his unimaginably simple life, Thor was trying to relate to him. Instead of needlessly beating the problem to death with that beloved slab of metal he called a hammer, he was...trying to talk it out.

Loki began to grow enraged himself. All this time, all of these needless and fruitless battles, all of them could have been dealt with without so much as an ounce of physical effort from Thor if he had just put in this level of effort then.

"Do you have any idea what it is like living with you people, day in and day out?" Loki started, venom lacing every word. "Do you have any idea what it feels like to be one of the only intelligent people in a group where the average level of intelligence equates to that of a group of children? The only Aesir that could ever keep up with me was Odin, and he is so consumed by his own thirst for knowledge that he would never give anyone other than himself the time of day. All of you are a bunch of arrogant, idiotic, drunk, war-hungry monsters that use the world around you like it is your plaything. I guess there was some rubbing off, but you all seemed to give me your mannerisms instead of the other way around. I *loathe* the person I have become having known you all, and it will be a hot day in Helheim before I ever forgive any of you for the transgressions you have levied against me!"

Mjolnir seemed to vibrate, the energy coursing through it beginning to grow more intense as Thor's patience grew thinner. Suddenly, the energy stopped, Thor let out a deep sigh, and reattached his hammer to his belt.

"I see," Thor said, his voice surprisingly meek, "thank you for informing me. I thought that maybe you would remember all that the two of us had done together, and we could talk. I apologize for wasting your time."

Thor turned to leave, but Loki called out to him, "Where do you think you are going?"

"I...I am not sure," Thor replied, "maybe I will head back to Asgard and get drunk with Tyr, maybe I will stop by Helheim and pay my dead brother a visit, just anywhere other than here. Goodbye, Loki."

Thor left the chamber, leaving Loki alone in the darkness.

Sigyn lit her torch again and made her way back to Loki. This time, however, she was completely silent as she began to set the stand and bowl back up over Loki's face.

"Are you alright?" Loki asked her, concerned about her lack of enthusiasm.

Sigyn paused for a moment before asking, "Is that how you feel about the Aesir?"

In Loki's passion-fueled rant, he had forgotten that his wife was part of the very group he swore to loathe. He needed to think of something and think of it immediately.

"Sigyn, my love, I did not mean—"

Just then, coming from the mouth of the cave, the caw of a raven could be heard. Both Loki and Sigyn knew what that meant, and their attentions were immediately drawn to the noise.

Standing at the entrance to the chamber was a man. A long black cloak covered his entire figure, and a black hood hid his face. On each shoulder sat a raven, both of them looking around and examining the cave, almost as if taking mental pictures. The man raised two scarred hands and lowered his hood, revealing long silver hair that cascaded down his back, an almost equally long white beard, and an eyepatch over one of his striking blue eyes.

It was Odin, the Allfather, King of the Aesir.

Loki tried to swallow the fear that lodged itself in his throat, sweat beginning to collect on his brow.

Odin gently lifted a hand and beckoned with a finger. "Come now, Sigyn," he said, his voice equal parts gentle and manipulative, "if you return to Asgard with me now, then I shall forget that this ever happened."

Sigyn looked down at her husband, fear in her eyes. Loki silently begged her to stay, she was the only thing keeping him sane during his time in this prison. Sigyn looked back at Odin, still hesitant to join him.

Odin held up his hand, a dark purple rune shining on the back of it. Instantly, his two ravens soared off of his shoulders and collided with the makeshift bowl stand. The bowl toppled over, spilling its contents onto Loki's body. Loki exclaimed in agony; this was the most intense pain he had ever felt in his life.

As Sigyn looked on, helpless, Odin walked over and held his hand up to her, his one eye beckoning her to take it. She did. Odin

LOKI'S CONFRONTATIONS

carefully guided her over to the cavern entrance, his ravens landing on her shoulders in waiting.

Odin stood over Loki, his head just out of the way so the snake venom could still drip into his eyes. Loki recovered from the venom spilled on his body, staring up at Odin in anger.

"What do you want?" Loki asked, trying as hard as he could to repress his feelings, seeing if there was a way to lower the mental defenses of the God of Knowledge. Usually, there was not.

"I want you to suffer, Loki," Odin replied, a calm malice covering his words, "just as it was foretold."

"Is this still about that damned prophecy?" Loki asked, trying to blink the venom out of his eyes. Odin did not respond, he simply stared at Loki with that one, unblinking eye. "That prophecy will be your undoing, you mad fool." Loki's words seemed to have no effect on the Allfather, the mad god still standing over him.

"You will carry out the rest of your days in this cavern," Odin said, "you will never see the light of Yggdrasil or the Bifrost again. You have betrayed the Aesir and yourself. You are your greatest problem, Loki, and you will never see that for as long as you live. If there is any intrusion to your sentencing here, I will know. If anyone else tries to break you free of your chains, I will know. If you try and hatch some scheme to escape for revenge, I will know. I have always known, and I will continue to know. I am Odin, son of Borr, the God of Knowledge, the Eternal Seer. You are Loki, son of Farbauti, the God of Mischief, the Backbiter. Your name shall be written into the Tome of the Banished and displayed throughout the Nine Realms. You will never again know the freedom that comes with the morning sun, nor the relaxation that comes with the evening moon. This is

❈ 149 ❈

spoken on my authority as the Allfather, ruler of the Aesir. Begone foul creature, and torment this world no longer."

As Odin finished his speech, he placed a hand on Loki's chest, a different rune lighting up in red on the back of said hand. Once Odin pulled away, another drop of snake venom hit Loki's eyes, but this time the pain was worse. Though the effects were the same as before, the scale of pain that coursed through Loki's veins caused him to cry out in agony, twisting and contorting his body, making one last desperate attempt to free himself.

Odin gently placed a hand on Sigyn's shoulder, his two ravens placing themselves on his shoulders. Sigyn took one last sad look at her writhing husband, her caring turning into pity, then allowed herself to be taken away by Odin.

Loki's squirms slowly began to shake the cave around them, then extended out into Midgard above. The whole realm shook as his agonizing cries bounced off the walls of the chamber. Loki spat, and cursed, and yelled towards Odin as he left him alone in darkness.

"DAMN YOU, ODIN! DAMN YOU, SIGYN! NO MATTER HOW LONG YOU SENTENCE ME TO THIS HELLISH TORTURE, I SHALL ENDURE! THIS IS NOT OVER! ALL OF THE AESIR WILL FEEL THE WRATH OF THE JOTUN! I WILL MAKE SURE OF IT! YOU ARE, ALL OF YOU, BENEATH ME! I AM TRICKERY AND DECEIT, AND YOU SHALL KNOW THE EXTENT OF MY HATRED ONE DAY! YOU WILL ALL KNOW THE WRATH OF LOKI!!"

The light from Odin's torch fully faded, leaving Loki alone once again.

The Norn's Offer

S. Cameron David

It was dark in the cave…so dark, in fact, that were he a mortal he'd not have been able to see anything at all. But that was his problem, wasn't it? Were he a mortal, this torment would have ended long ago.

His screams filled the otherwise cavernous silence, causing his head to ache and his ears to trickle blood, and yet that pain was as nothing next to the agony of the venom dripping into his eyes and sliding down his cheek, sizzling as it slid along feverish skin. He lay trembling and spread-eagled on his back, his limbs and torso bound in chains.

He did not know how long it had been since Odin had cast him here – hundreds of years, at least. Thousands, perhaps. And he did not know how much longer he'd have to wait, how much more of this torture he would need to endure before the day his bonds were broken. Still, the thought of that day was one of the few things left that could bring a smile to his ruined lips.

For it had been said one day he would raise up a host – that he would bring Asgard to ruin, while his sons would visit death upon Odin and Thor themselves – and even after all these centuries had passed, he could still remember that morning he'd plied

MYTHS, GODS & IMMORTALS: LOKI

drinks on the Odinson, listening as Thor murmured on and on about the manner of his death.

Slain by the World Serpent. By poison of all things.

Loki's screams rang out once more as another drop of venom fell, reducing his eyeball into soup. He trembled and shook and spat out blood, feeling his tongue regenerate inside his mouth while his eye reformed in an aching socket. Oh, but if only he were free…if only he could gather his sons and parley with Surtr and feel the neck of Heimdall twist between his hands…

Then there was light, bright and blinding, forcing shut his atrophied eyes. Still, Loki could hear the rustling of the serpent slithering away, putting his agony on pause. It made for a queer thing, he reckoned. He had forgotten what the absence of pain had felt like. Vaguely, he wondered if his sons had come for him at last.

He was certain it had to be another of Odin's tricks.

Finally, after a long time spent steeling his courage – because for all the curses and reprimands that had been thrown his way, no one had ever accused the Liesmith of being a coward – Loki forced himself to look. But he did not see Fenrir baring his fangs, scraping his head against the ceiling of the cave. Nor was there Odin, one-eyed ruler of the world. Only a young woman in a traveling cloak. She looked barely old enough to carry a spear or sword.

"Skuld," he said in a haggard whisper. She may have looked young, yet she and her sisters were older than himself. "Come to gaze on the sight of Loki in chains?"

A thin smile drew across her face. "I daresay those you once named friends who have called it an improvement."

Loki chuckled. "I wouldn't take that wager, nor any other you might offer."

He sighed, relaxing against his bonds. His gaze drew upward toward a nook high up on the cavern wall, and he could see the head of his tormentor gazing back downward in his direction. With a flicker of its tongue, the serpent vanished in the shadows.

"Tell me," he croaked. "Does Odin know about this visit?"

"Not at all," said Skuld. "But do you believe my sisters and I, the three queens of the Fatespinners – do you believe we would submit ourselves so meekly to the Allfather's authority?"

Loki thought back to Odin's prophecy, the tale Thor had recounted so long ago. "And I imagine the doom of Ragnarok... that must have been your doing as well."

"You shouldn't thank us for that. Your fate will be a cruel one, this we dictated on the day you were born, long before the first temptations for mischief ever flashed across your mind."

And wasn't that a disturbing notion? There was a reason the gods tried not to think much on the Norns. Odin notwithstanding.

"Then tell me, Weaver, if it is not to mock me in my distress, what business brings you to my prison?"

"I come on behalf of my sisters to offer you a gift."

Loki found himself giggling, then cackling unrestrained. His laughter ricocheted back and forth between the walls of his prison, echoing even louder than his screams. "A gift, she says! A gift now, after condemning me to torture till the end of time. Oh, but that is a good jest. The audacity of it."

"I'm glad my words meet with your approval."

"As you should be." Loki found himself wishing that Sigyn had stayed. She'd have had a cloth ready to wipe away his tears. "But enough with this nonsense. What is this gift you speak of?"

Skuld sat herself down upon the cavern floor, and from somewhere within the confines of her cloak, she produced a pair of knitting needles and a ball of thread. Her movements were swift and well-practiced, and he watched as a kind of tapestry took shape between her fingers, one which strangely resembled a spider's web.

The needles stopped. Skuld looked up from her work. "You know of Ragnarok, correct?"

"Odin's prophesy."

"Yes." Skuld pursed her lips, and there was something in her expression – something in that sour, put-upon look that graced her features – that reminded him of Thor, usually in the minutes after he had played some trick or another at the thunder god's expense. "That prophesy." She set her needles down and raised up the spiderweb fabric, brandishing it before her like a banner. "So tell me, Loki. What do you think?"

"I admit, I'm no expert in weaving."

"And here I had been assured that the Liesmith has an opinion on everything. I suppose Ragnarok must be close at hand."

"If only we could be so lucky."

Skuld leaned forward, her gaze scanning his supine body. "You really mean that, don't you?" The Norn shook her head, and a lock of wheat-blonde hair fell across her youthful face. "Well, your brother has certainly done a number on you."

"I'd think that would be obvious," said Loki. He looked up toward the ceiling, trying to catch a glimpse of the serpent hiding away.

"I wasn't talking about the snake, nor about your imprisonment for that matter." Loki's head turned back, just in time to see her fiddling with her tapestry. "But he's always been a crafty one, isn't that right? Patient, manipulative, always running one scheme or another. I daresay he's got more in common with the spiders than those ravens he so loves."

That thought was enough to revive some of Loki's good mood. "Yes, I think you're onto something there, though I doubt Odin would appreciate the comparison."

"Or maybe he would," said the Norn. "The One-Eyed can be quite unpredictable, I'm sure you'll agree. It's a trait the two of you hold in common."

"Is there a point to this digression?" She'd crossed a line just then, comparing him to his brother in such a manner, and he could feel much of his fragile good mood already curdling back into spite.

"You're right," she said. "I should be getting to the point. Very well, then. Ragnarok. You're quite enthusiastic about your role in the destruction of the world."

"I admit, there's not much else to look forward to down here."

This time it was Skuld who barked with laughter. He watched with no little envy as she wiped away a tear. "No," she said. "Being immobilized like this, subject to torment every moment of every day…I imagine you wouldn't." She looked away from him, back in the direction from which she had come. "I see even Sigyn abandoned you in time."

"And was that also in your prophecies?" Loki asked. He noticed as Skuld kept her silence, refusing to answer.

"I don't blame her," he added. He could still remember an endless litany of hateful, piercing words, all the abuse and accusations which would commingle with his screams. "I'd have left too, if I were given the choice."

"An interesting bit of phrasing," said the Norn. A smile curled across her lips, showing a trace of her yellow-brown teeth. Loki didn't like that smile. It reminded him too much of his own. "Were I given the choice."

And with those words, the long-rusted gears of his mind began to churn. "Is that what you've come here to offer?" he asked. "Freedom? An end to this incarceration?" He laughed when he saw her nod. "Tell me, did Odin put you up to this? Is this another of his games. He sends you here to dangle the promise of freedom above my head, only to rip it all away the moment I agree…"

"As I said before, we don't answer to Odin."

"Is that so?" Loki asked. His voice was as toxic as any branch of mistletoe. "Then answer me this – regarding this so-called gift you brandish before me, this chance to walk away. I imagine it comes with a price."

Skuld nodded her head.

"Then name it. Tell me, what would I be sacrificing should I walk out with you from this cave?"

"Ragnarok," she replied.

THE NORN'S OFFER

"And there it is," said Loki. "You claim not to serve my brother, yet when I think upon your offer, I cannot help but notice that it benefits Odin above myself."

"We offer you freedom," she said.

"I want vengeance!" Loki roared, feeling all his emotions – all his sorrow and anger and pain and anguish – burst out from him at once. "I want to stand on the edge of the Rainbow Bridge with Surtr on one side and Fenrir on the other, and I want to be right there to see as it shatters and falls. I want to watch as Jormungandr entangles Thor within his coils, lowers his head, and sinks his fangs in the storm god's shoulder, and I want to be there, right there, when Fenrir ambushes the all-knowing Odin and swallows him down in a single bite. That, Skuld, is what I want."

"And if you should die? If you and all your children should die together, would your vengeance be worth it then?"

"Yes," he replied.

Skuld shook her head. "You'd die a fool then. You'd be playing right into the Allfather's hands."

"So you claim, but the prophecy is quite clear, isn't it? The Rainbow Bridge breaks. Asgard falls. Odin is devoured by the wolf." Loki smiled at the last bit. Yet for all his apparent confidence, Loki could not deny that the gears of his mind were still churning away, parsing through his recollections of that long ago morning, holding his nephew upright as he fell deeper and deeper into a stupor, spilling what he knew of the end of the world. But what had Loki missed? What secret trump could the Allfather have prepared?

"Have you figured it out yet?" pressed the Norn. "Have you discerned the nature of your error?"

"Why don't you tell me then, if you think it might make a difference in my decision?"

"Very well then. Your error was in trusting the Allfather's word to begin with. Surely you must have realized this by now – he's just as cunning as yourself."

He had no cutting words. No cruel rejoinders. For just one moment, the gears in the brain ground to a halt.

"I wouldn't say as cunning," Loki said, though the words sounded unconvincing even to himself.

Skuld could not stifle a laugh. "Of course not. However, could your vanity admit to having any equals? Still, I'm sure you must now realize what it is you've overlooked."

Loki licked his dried and chapped licks, feeling as his tongue drew over the scars. "Are you saying the prophecy was a lie?"

"More of a half-truth, actually. Odin took some liberties, excised some of the subtler details when he recounted it to Thor." She leaned over him, squatting down to better look him in the eye. "And Thor being Thor, so prone to histrionics and susceptible to drink...well, it wouldn't have been difficult to predict how Thor would react, which brings us then to you."

"He wanted me to hear it..."

Skuld's smile swept back across her face. "And now you understand. So tell me, Liesmith, do you wish to know the truth of the prophecy, or would you prefer to cling fast to the version Odin wanted you to hear?"

"I'm certain you already know my answer without requiring me to speak it."

"Fair enough. For all your flaws, and they are considerable, you've never been one content to stew in ignorance." She sat herself back on the cavern floor, returned to her needles, and added a few additional threads to her spiderweb pattern. "In its core shape, its fundamentals, things are much akin to the version you already know. In the beginning will come the cold – a terrible winter unlike any the world has ever seen. As you can imagine, it will be horrible for the denizens of Midgard. Entire generations will perish amid famine and war, billions snuffed out, many too young to put words to their despair."

"It seems they have your sympathy."

Skuld shrugged. "We Norns…we tend to live closer to mortals than to gods. We see the worst of them and the best of them as we weave their futures into shape." Here she paused her needlework, setting the tapestry in her lap. "Since I'm sure you've been wondering about our motive, this would be your answer. In this game you and Odin are intent to play, they're the ones who would suffer most."

"And so you would cross Odin…put a stop to Ragnarok itself. For them."

"You act out of a desire for vengeance, and I will admit, we're not entirely different in that respect. We never wished for our gift to be twisted so that the world would be burnt to ash. And yet when the Allfather came before us, we found it difficult to resist."

"Yes, well…he has his ways about him."

"Indeed," said Skuld. For just a moment, her voice held a combination of exhaustion and bitterness he found entirely too familiar. "In any case, as that great winter reaches its apex, when the glaciers of the Poles would sweep across the once fertile plains, then at last will Fenrir snap free from his chains to abscond to his father's side." Her eyes were wide and unblinking, and she looked as if in a trance. "The great cold shall be followed by a still greater darkness, as sun and moon vanish together from the sky. And on that day, the Liesmith shall be freed, and the great dragon Nidhogg shall snap his jaws through the World Tree's roots, seizing his long-desired prize."

None of her words were unfamiliar, yet Loki listened with rapt attention. It was one thing to learn of Ragnarok from the drunken mumblings of Thor, but it was quite another to hear it directly from Skuld herself.

And so she spoke of Surtr as he marshaled his legion of giants, and she spoke of Loki traveling beside them. She spoke of a vast army marching forth across the Rainbow Bridge while the Aesir made ready on the other side. She spoke of Heimdall and his horn, and of Odin and his spear, and she spoke of Jormungandr's poisoned fangs. She spoke of carnage and brutality, of Thor felled by poison and the Allfather disappearing down Fenrir's maw, swallowed whole in a single bite. And she spoke of Surtr standing alone in a field of corpses, raising his flaming sword to a branch of the World Tree, unleashing an inferno upon the world.

"Then there shall come a time of stillness, and the ravens will circle the ruins of Asgard, crying out for their former master. For nine days and nine nights, they shall repeat their calls, and for nine days and nine nights, not a voice will be raised to answer. But as morning dawns on the tenth day, then at last shall the children of Thor emerge from hiding and stumble on Fenrir's bloated corpse. Working in tandem, they will take up Gungnir, the Allfather's spear, to carve into the stomach of the beast, and from within that wound will the Allfather emerge, hale and healthy, to find no more rivals alive to oppose him. So will stand Odin, reigning amid the rejuvenation of the world, unchallenged and unconquerable for all of time."

Loki was trembling in his bindings and grinding his teeth. He wanted to disbelieve her, to accuse the Norn of lying, yet even so...

"Do you speak truly?" he asked, and Skuld nodded her head. "Then swear it. Swear on the branches of the World Tree that what you tell me is no lie."

"So I swear," was Skuld's solemn reply. "I swear on the boughs of Yggdrasil that what I say is true."

"Then the matter is settled," said Loki as he looked back up toward the ceiling of his cave. And where did that leave him? After all these centuries, stewing in rage and helplessness, dreaming of revenge. It had been his one hope and solace in this tortured existence, yet to know it had all been just another of Odin's manipulations, and that it would be Loki himself who would serve as the instrument for the Allfather's ascendance... yes, it made for a venom more noxious than that of any snake's.

"So where does that leave us now?" he asked.

"Come now, Loki. I would have expected you to know the answer to that one for yourself." He turned his head toward the

Norn as she pulled herself up onto her feet, raising that tapestry once more above her head. "If the Allfather wishes to entrap you in his web, then there's but one thing for the Liesmith to do."

With a grin on her face, she tore the weave in half, crumbled up the pieces, and threw them to the floor.

"You would have me give up my vengeance," Loki said, but not even he found the words convincing. Judging from Skuld's disgusted face, neither did the Norn.

"And what a glorious vengeance it would be."

"Indeed. I imagine the bards will sing songs about it, as will all those warriors gathered in Valhalla's dining halls." That crooked grin slithered back across his scars. "I imagine the Allfather would be most disappointed should I take you on your offer."

Skuld laughed. "I imagine he would be."

"And I've always made a habit of stealing his victories from under his nose, and you know, I do think that gallivanting off like this, giving up on Ragnarok and never returning for his prophesied final battle... I think that might well make for the greatest trick of them all." He looked over toward Skuld, and for the first time in a long time believed he might have felt some small measure of peace. "Oh, but if only I could see him, if even just for a moment, waiting out the remainder of eternity, making plans for a battle that will never be."

"I'm afraid you won't be able to do that," said the Norn with a shake of her head. "No, should you accept our gift, you'll need to submit yourself to a life of obscurity, to disappear into the margins of the world, never to be seen by god or giant or mortal man again."

THE NORN'S OFFER

Loki shook his head, remembering a time he had tried to do just that. The Allfather had found him in the end – found him and caught him and dragged him off in chains. "And can you guarantee that this time I won't be found?"

Skuld's response came without a moment of hesitation.

"Yes," she said. And that was that.

As the Norns had proclaimed it, so it would be.

Skuld stood over his unmoving body, setting her hands on his chains. "Now tell me, Liesmith, do you accept our terms?" she asked. "Will you take hold of your freedom, surrendering Ragnarok in exchange?"

"Yes," said Loki, and with a grunt of effort, Skuld pulled on Odin's bindings, and the chains of the Allfather crumbled in her hands. Loki watched passively as she freed first his wrists, then his ankles, and lastly ripped away the bindings on his torso, allowing him to sit upwards and pull himself to his feet. He reached with one hand up toward the ceiling, reached into that crevice where the serpent was hiding, and grinned as he felt it struggle in his grip. He pulled it toward him, holding its head between two fingers.

"Hello old friend," he crooned, and he took great pleasure in squeezing his fingers together, reducing its skull to pulp. He looked back to find Skuld waiting by the exit of his prison. He did not know if he saw approval on her face.

He found he did not care one way or the other.

Together they climbed upwards out of the darkness into the bitter brightness of the world outside. Loki looked upwards, taking in that endless expanse of sky.

"This is where I leave you," said Skuld. He watched as she departed, watched as she walked off across a frozen wasteland, her form growing smaller and smaller until it was no more than a speck of color on the tundra. Still her voice trailed behind her, echoing across the icy cold. "And I hope our two paths never have cause to cross again."

"Likewise," said Loki as he looked away, observing the jagged mountains of Jotunheim where the giants dwell. Far in the distance, he could hear the murmuring of the sea.

"So this is it," he said to himself as he took his first step forwards, leaving a shallow footprint in the snow. After so many years of infamy, this was to be his future. A life of obscurity, vanishing into Jotunheim's hidden reaches, never to be seen by anyone again.

He cackled to himself.

It would be the finest trick he ever played.

Means to an End

Stephanie Ellis

Loki stared at the water rushing by, thinking how much easier it would be to become a salmon and swim without thought of what Odin would get up to. He raised his gaze to the gentle blue sky and spotted a hawk hovering, intent on its prey below. He let out a sigh. With his luck, lately, he would be caught if he so much as showed a fin.

"What will you do?" asked Sigyn, coming to stand behind him, her hand resting lightly on his shoulder. Their reflections shimmered before them, a handsome couple, devoted, though they had suffered their share of trial and misfortune. Much, he had to admit, as a result of his own actions. "Such a horrible fate for both of us."

Odin, normally so protective of his consultation with the seeress had let slip to Frigg a portion of what he had been told. A conversation Loki overheard as he scavenged for the gossip which was his currency. He would have heard more except for his own mistake in taking on the shape of a mouse when Frigg's cats were around. They were fast but he was faster.

"You must find a way to bind Odin to you," said Sigyn. "Then he could never do anything so contemptible."

"Hmm. A blood oath would give us *some* protection, although he has too often shown a dismissive attitude to such things."

He felt Sigyn squeeze his shoulder.

"That may be true, but it is *something*, something to build on."

To be condemned to the eternal attention of a poisonous snake was not what either wanted. Certainly not what his wife deserved. He remembered Frigg's words, that such a fate was more than appropriate, and felt the anger rise.

Loki reached up and clasped Sigyn's hand. "Don't worry. I will find a way."

* * *

The next day proved equally fine and Odin, Loki noticed, seemed to be at a loss for something to occupy him. Even gods got bored.

"Perhaps a visit to the Iron Woods," he suggested. "A bit of hunting, catch up with family. We've heard little from the Jotun of late. Who knows what they might be plotting against us?"

Odin frowned, swishing a stick through the knee-high grass, then raised his gaze. "You're right. It *has* been too quiet. Forewarned is forearmed."

Yes, thought Loki, thinking back to the prophecy and what was supposed to befall him. He couldn't agree more.

The going was initially an easy ride, but then Odin said they should leave their horses so as not to announce their arrival. That suited Loki perfectly. When they came to a river, they swooped across as falcons, an open plain and they became wolves, covering the miles with their long limbs.

And then they were at Jarnvid's edge. The dense Iron Woods provided a forbidding border of ash and elm, birch and pine, but the two crossed the threshold without hesitation, although they kept their voices low and trod softly.

Loki could feel eyes upon him, sensed the presence of wolves, wondered if any were kin.

They hadn't gone very far before they came to a small clearing. A giantess was seated in its midst burnishing an axe which looked like a toy in her hands. Loki took in her form, her face, then thought of his wife and sought to look elsewhere – elsewhere being at Odin who seemed surprisingly uncomfortable.

"Not to your taste, eh?" he murmured. "Although I think you have caught her eye."

Loki was rewarded with a kick to the back of his calf, almost sending him to his knees.

"To whom do I have the honour of welcoming to Jarnvid?" asked the giantess.

"Byleist," said Loki with a small bow, happy to use his brother's name.

Odin opened his mouth to follow suit, but stopped as he realised the fame of his own brothers was as great as his own.

The woman burst out laughing. "Still as deceitful as ever, eh, Loki Laufeyjarson? And you, Odin, should be ashamed to follow such an example. Do you not remember me? Little Angrboda?"

Ignoring Odin, Loki stepped forward and took Angrboda's hand, kissing it lightly. Then he stood beside her and waited for Odin to approach. Giving Loki a sour look, he followed his example.

"Such manners!" cried Angrboda with delight. "Sadly, it is something I see little of amongst my brothers."

On cue, four monstrous wolves crept out from the trees and positioned themselves beside their sister.

"However, your arrival is somewhat fortuitous. My father wishes me to wed Ganglati in the absence of any other suitors."

Loki raised an eyebrow. "No suitors for one as comely as you?"

There was another peal of laughter from Angrboda causing the trees around them to shift and murmur in discomfort. "I have told him of Odin's long-ago promise, dismissed all the alternatives he has brought before me."

"Leaving you with lazy Ganglati," said Loki.

"Exactly."

By now, Odin had recovered himself somewhat, regained his confident air. "Angrboda, it has been many years and I am truly sorry that you have held to a promise made in the first flush of youth…"

Angrboda's eyes narrowed as she regarded her old suitor.

"But I cannot fulfil such a promise. I already have a wife "

"A wife can easily be discarded," said the giantess.

By this time more wolves had appeared, while the branches above were filled with crows. It would not be easy to escape, even if they could shift quickly. It looked as if whatever form the pair took, they would be devoured easily.

Loki sensed the opportunity he and Sigyn sought. "Will you allow me to consult with my…companion?"

Angrboda inclined her head graciously. "Of course, provided

you convince him to give the right answer. My bed has been too cold of late."

Odin and Loki moved a little way from the circle, kept their voices hushed.

"I have a plan," said Loki. "I can get us both out of here but I must be able to trust you —"

"And I you," interrupted Odin.

"Then we must bind ourselves with an oath...a blood oath." Loki looked Odin directly in the eye as he spoke, wondering what else he knew about the past, present and future.

It felt like an eternity as he stared into Odin's unfathomable gaze, and then the god gave a barely perceptible nod. Loki swiftly cut his palm open, pressing it to Odin's likewise spliced hand, their blood intermingling in their clasp.

Loki turned to Angrboda with a smile. "Odin has promised he will exert every...muscle...to give you the satisfaction you desire."

"Then you are both welcome in my halls," said Angrboda. "Come, let us feast your arrival, our future union."

As the pair moved to either side of the giantess to give her an escort, Loki sensed Odin's rising anger. "Don't worry," he whispered. "All will be well. Trust me."

Once inside Agrboda's hall, they were escorted to their rooms where they could wash and make themselves presentable. An adjoining door allowed Loki to slip through and take advantage of the absence of their hostess or any of her servants.

"So tell me, Loki," said Odin, barely concealing his fury. "Exactly how am I to get out of this?"

I, noted Loki, not we. "Easily. I will take your form and you mine. Our blood is now mingled so the giants will sense no true difference." He hoped.

"And what of Sigyn?"

Loki thought of his dearly loved wife. "She will understand."

"An understanding wife, eh? That's more than I have."

"Then perhaps, after all —"

"No," said Odin. "I will not betray Frigg."

Not tonight, thought Loki, thinking of other adventures. "So we will do as I suggest?"

Odin reluctantly agreed, certain the plan would not work, but for the moment it was the only plan they had.

* * *

The hall was full. Angrboda had Odin-Loki seated to her right and sent Loki-Odin to the other end of the table to entertain Kári, her father. The pair's subterfuge seemed to be working.

"You approve?" asked Angrboda, indicating her table, piled high with haunches of meat, flagons of ale and mead.

"You honour us," said Odin-Loki, placing his hand over his tankard to prevent a servant from refilling it. His action drew a suspicious look from the giantess. "Too much drink can impair..." He allowed his comment to trail away, letting his look add weight to the implication.

She blushed slightly. It was working, he thought with delight! As the evening wore on, he didn't stint on the food presented but continued to refrain from the drink. And when at last all was done and the time came to retire, Angrboda whispered she would come to him within the hour.

"My father doubts that you will honour your promise. This will ensure his acceptance of the situation. A father must guard his daughter's good name."

After the event, thought Loki, when a husband must be ensured.

Once Odin and Loki were back in their rooms, they resumed their normal appearance, taking advantage of the short respite.

"You must sleep in my room," said Loki.

Odin, ever sensitive of his position, frowned. "You forget yourself, Loki "

"Unless you wish to…entertain Angrboda?"

Odin shook his head but obediently headed into Loki's room. Then he looked back. "You are sure about this? You are sure you can…um…?"

Loki laughed, delighting in Odin's discomfort. "Oh, I can keep up appearances as needed. Don't worry."

The sound of approaching footsteps sent Odin scuttling into the safety of Loki's room, firmly closing the door behind him.

Loki quickly became Odin-Loki and opened the door as soon as he heard her first soft knock.

"To be husband and wife has been my dream," said Angrboda as Loki led her to the bed.

"Then let us make tonight, my lovely Angrboda," said Loki, "a night of dreams."

Candlelight flickered around them, softening her features, the flames of the fire dancing in the hearth illuminated her body, making her curves visible through the sheer fabric of her gown. Loki did not think of Sigyn, that would come later. He had already decided he would confess. And like always, she would forgive him, especially as his actions were necessary. He had little time to think of anything else as Angrboda pulled him onto the bed, all maiden embarrassment apparently gone.

Tumbling into the sheets, feeling her arms embrace him, Loki fought to retain his shape as Odin. Somehow, he managed, and when Angrboda at last released him, battered and bruised from her ministrations, she looked satisfied.

"To have such a husband as you to myself is truly wondrous."

"To have such a wife is more than I can imagine," said Odin-Loki. "But first I must return to Asgard, my love, and explain the nature of things."

"And then we will be together," said Angrboda.

"And then we will be together," said Odin-Loki, slipping a ring on her finger as a sign of his intentions. Angrboda gave him a final kiss before rising from his bed and wrapping herself in her robe. When she had gone, Loki curled up in the nest of sheets. "I am sorry, Sigyn," he whispered. "Forgive me." And then he fell asleep.

The following morning, Kári, Angrboda and their wolf family gathered to see them off.

"I will return," promised Odin-Loki, offering gold armbands to Kári as a gesture of good faith. "Nothing will keep me away from you."

Loki and Odin headed back through the Iron Woods, transforming as they had done before to run across plain, fly across river, until they reached their horses, happily grazing where they had been left. They rode, however, still in each other's form, just in case the giants had sent spies to follow.

It was only when they were safely in the realm of Asgard that they settled to their own shape and talk of events.

"Well, you certainly got us out of that mess," said Odin. "I'm sure Frigg will find the whole thing an entertaining story."

Loki held up his hand. "No. You cannot tell her. The tale will make its way to Sigyn and I do not want her to hear. Not yet."

After a moment's pause, Odin nodded. "For what you have done for me, I will keep my counsel. For now."

Their conversation was interrupted by Thor. "I have heard the giants desire to expand Jotunheim, claim more of our northern land."

"That is not something I have heard," said Odin. "But we have a way of finding out, spying a little. And I know just the person."

He was looking at Loki as he spoke, and Loki was suddenly aware of how his plan had come back to bite him. Day after day, he avoided Odin and Thor, took Sigyn travelling and exploring – south rather than north. But eventually, when three months had past, he could avoid Odin's command no longer.

* * *

His entry into the Iron Wood was met with unexpected delight. Kári accepted the treasure he had brought with him, slapping him on the back.

"I will say I was doubtful you would honour your word and what with the little one "

Odin-Loki stopped. "Little one?"

From behind Kári, Angrboda appeared, cradling a tiny wolf cub. "Here is your son, Odin. Fenriswolf."

Odin-Loki swallowed, fixed a smile on his face as he took the snuffling creature in his arms.

"I don't have all good news, I'm afraid," he said. "Frigg is proving somewhat difficult. I have to return tomorrow to finalise her settlement."

Odin had demanded he stay a week at least, but Loki could not face that, not having seen his son. He did not want to be bound to the giantess. He had Sigyn to consider. This was getting too serious.

But he could not avoid Angrboda's attentions that night, finding her already ensconced in his bed when he retired – this time with the approval of her father.

The following morning, he left with further promises of his return and more gold.

Once back at Asgard, however, Odin showed clearly his disapproval.

"You have found out nothing," he snarled.

Loki did not tell him of Fenriswolf.

Again, they pushed him to go back, again Loki fought against them. This time he held out for only two months, returning as before to a delighted welcome and another child.

"Odin," said Angrboda, "here is your son. We have called him Jormundgand."

Again, he enthused, again reiterated issues with Frigg. "But," he said, "the settlement is almost done. One more return home and all will be well."

Odin-Loki spent another exhausting night with Angrboda before escaping Jotunheim's woods.

"It's not good enough," said Odin when Loki appeared once more too soon. "You're not trying hard enough."

Loki glared at him. "Not trying? *Not trying?* Perhaps you should go in my place, *brother*. After all, they are expecting you."

He turned on his heel and stalked off, kept away from everyone, even Sigyn, who as yet, had no idea of her husband's latest infidelities.

But he could only say no so often and set out for Jotunheim, although this time with the proviso it was the *last* time. If Odin wanted any more information after that, *he* could get it himself.

This time he was greeted by Angrboda with a squealing child in her arms. A little girl.

"Your daughter, Loki. We have named her Hel."

It took a moment to register she had called him by his true name.

"You...*knew?*"

The giantess burst out laughing, as did her father. The wolf kin brothers howled alongside them. Nobody seemed annoyed.

"Of course we did. The end has been foretold has it not? We know of who and what will play their part at Ragnarok and my father told me long ago of the role I was prophesied to play. The honour *that* would bring me. As mother to those who would destroy the gods. You can return now, Loki. There is no need for you to share my bed, although I must admit you acquitted yourself...admirably." She paused as if conflicted about not spending a last night with him. "No, go back. And tell the All-Father that by his deceit he has brought that which will be his doom. And Loki. I suggest you tell your wife yourself. Word has already got out and you know how quickly gossip spreads."

Loki cast a final look at his three children and turned away, transforming into an eagle to get him away as fast and as far as he could.

He had to admire Angrboda. She certainly had him fooled. And Odin! He let out a shriek of delight. By agreeing to his plan, he had contributed to his own downfall. The only downside to all this was having to tell Sigyn. At least he could offer her the jewels and gold Odin had given him to gift Angrboda and which he had kept. He only hoped she would understand.

Loki spied his home below him, the door open. He swooped down, transforming as he landed. Then he took a deep breath and crossed the threshold.

Sigyn stood before him, arms folded, anger and sadness written in equal measure across her features. It was too late, she already knew.

Loki wondered whether he should get down on his knees. Then he looked at her again, saw her mouth twitch, a smile emerge – although a hint of sadness remained.

"You're not upset?"

"A little," said Sigyn. "What wife wouldn't be? But in the grand scheme of things, this was all but a means to an end. And you were only trying to do what we both agreed on, to bind Odin to

MEANS TO AN END

you. He is your brother now, whether he likes it or not and so he must tread more carefully."

"And…" He could barely bring himself to mention his unexpected offspring.

"The children? Let Odin worry about them. Angrboda certainly doesn't expect you to play any part in raising them."

"How…?"

"She sent a message, an apology, that she had used you in such a manner. Asked my forgiveness. And it gave me time to think things over. About our future together."

He was about to speak when Sigyn put a finger to his lips. "Don't make a promise you can't keep."

She knew him so well. He cupped her face in his hands and gazed into her eyes. "Then let me make one promise you know I *will* keep. I will never part from you. You are my wife and *only* love. We will *always* be together."

As he pulled her close, Loki thought he heard the hiss of a snake above his head. He looked up into the rafters, there was nothing there. But he felt its presence.

The future had reached back to claim him.

Eitrdropar

Corey D. Evans

There is a cave that lies between two worlds. Its floor is the basement of one realm and the ceiling of another. The cave is hidden beneath a waterfall that fills a deep pool where an impossible-to-navigate river originates. Only intrepid swarms of salmon can swim up the river to find the pool, but they lack feet with which they could step out of the water to walk through the falls and into the cave.

If one could navigate the river's windy meanders and knees all the way to the headwaters, one would be struck by the deep pool's beauty. Velvety moss grows on smooth river stones, and centuries-old beech trees cast shade over the deep waters with knurled and twisted limbs. The pool is clear enough to see to the bottom, but one could never sink to its deepest depths in a single breath. The sound of the waterfall's ceaseless rush fills the air like feathers stuffed into a down pillow and softly mutes the surrounding world.

Behind the deafening falls is the entrance to the cave that no mortal has found. It is not a small hole in the earth. In fact, it is large enough for both gods and giants to enter through. But the cave is not inviting. It is dark and belches more foul-smelling air than drunkards after a night of revelry. Jagged rocks line the cave walls, and thick ooze drips from the ceiling above. The cave mouth is as terrifying as the pool is enchanting.

Things do not get better after stepping inside. The sun and moon are quickly replaced by utter darkness, and the sound of running water is consumed by silence. Unlike most holes beneath the earth, the cave air is not cool. It is stifling. The deeper one goes, the warmer the temperature becomes until it is almost unbearable. Where the heat is the strongest, Loki, the god of mischief, dwells.

But ignore the god. He is harmless in his present condition. His hands and legs are lashed with charmed cords tied in unbreakable knots. He has been bound this way for years and will continue to be tethered until the end of days. Mind the snake instead. It sits above the god's head with open jaws as though it were ready to strike. Venom drips out of its fangs onto the upturned face of the incarcerated. The vile drops sear the skin and are most painful if they splash in open eyes. Loki yanks on the cords that bind him. He is strong enough to shake the earth in his discomfort but unable to free himself.

A goddess comes into the cave to give Loki aid. She has been near the cave for as long as him, though she is free to leave if she wants. The goddess is Sigyn, Loki's once fair and ceaselessly loyal wife. She carries a shallow pail with her.

"I'm back," Sigyn calls to comfort her tormented husband. She takes her place between Loki and the vile snake. Two divots are worn into the stone where she has stood over the years.

Drip.

Another drop of venom falls out of the snake's mouth, but Sigyn catches it in her pail. Loki breathes a sigh of relief. His skin will heal, and with Sigyn beside him, his prison is more bearable.

"Thank you, dear," Loki says. He wants to hug his wife, but the cords do not allow him that pleasure. They haven't touched in decades. They haven't kissed in centuries. Coming near is too risky, especially when more than a few drops of venom are in the pail. Instead, Loki embraces Sigyn with his words.

"I love you," Loki says. It is something he says often. Another woman might think he addresses his words to the pail that protects him, but Sigyn is not such a woman.

"I love you, too," she replies.

Drip.

* * *

Sigyn holds the pail over Loki's head day and night. She catches every drop of venom except when she must go outside to empty the pail into the pool. If she is fast, Loki only suffers two stings from the snake. But there are some days when she takes her time. Some days, Sigyn looks long into the wind and dips a toe into the waters of the pool before polluting it. Loki suffers in her absence, and the whole earth trembles from his mighty jerks at his tethers. He cries for the pail; he screams for her return.

"SIGYN! Come back, oh please come back."

Loki's voice is not easy to ignore. Not even the waterfalls can drown his anguish, so Sigyn takes her toe out of the numbing waters and turns her back to the wind. She drains the contents of the pail. The venom kills the fish in the pool. It's a wonder there are any fish left in the world, Sigyn thinks. Surely, she's poured out enough venom to kill them all over the years.

But her trips to empty the basin are less frequent than she thinks. As shallow as the dish is, filling it takes a long time. Sigyn returns to Loki's side in time to catch the seventh drip.

Loki and Sigyn are not without visitors in the cave. Some of the other gods and goddesses come to see them. Only Odin, the All-Father, neglects to visit. He cannot bear to see his once beloved blood brother in such misery.

When the gods come, they check Loki's bonds and give Sigyn a morsel of food and a draft of mead. She's grateful for the vittles and the company. None of the gods tend to Loki's needs. They have yet to forgive him for his mischief and misdeeds against them.

"Have you not proven your loyalty enough?" asks Tyr, the god of glory. While he speaks, Tyr strokes the stump of his arm where a hand once was. A hand he lost to Loki's son, the great wolf Fenrir.

"Loyalty is not shown once, but continuously," Sigyn answers. Drip.

"Let me hold the pail for a while," Tyr offers, "You must be weary of this task."

Loki looks at his wife with fear in his eyes. The same fear a lamb displays before the butcher. Loki knows Tyr would sooner dump all of the snake's venom onto his head than protect him.

"Tending to me is far too lowly of a task for a god like you," Loki reasons. His once cunning voice is rough and ragged. His lies are out of practice. "Surely you must be leaving us soon to watch some battle among the mortals?"

"The world is quite peaceful for now," Tyr grumbles. He does not look at Loki when he speaks. He has offered to take Sigyn's place before, so he knows what she will say and gets up to leave.

* * *

Time passes. The snake above Loki does not move. It does not eat or sleep and never shuts its vicious jaws. It is perched too high for Sigyn to reach, though she is sure that if she tried, the snake would bite her with its terrible fangs. If a single drop can cause Loki, a god and the son of a giant, to writhe in pain, what more misery might come from a bite?

One day, a most unexpected guest enters the cave. She is not a goddess – one of the Aesir – but the giantess Angrboda, Loki's first wife. She is wet from the falls. Her straight, dark hair clings to the sides of her face. Her pale blue skin glistens like ice thawing in the sun. A headdress made of stag antlers rests on her head, adding even more height to her imposing stature. Deep-set eyes scour the scene for anything other than the two pitiful gods. When nothing of interest is found, she looks to Loki.

"I see that the Aesir have treated you well," Angrboda says.

"They're going through a phase," Loki sighs. He pulls on his cords. They are as taught as ever.

"Why are you here?" Sigyn asks. She knows Angrboda. She knows Loki loved the she-giant first before he came to Asgard and returned to her embrace often enough to sire three monstrous children.

"Why are you here?" Angrboda asks in reply. "Why do you suffer with this fool?"

"Loyalty is not something I would expect a giant to understand."

"Ah, but you would be wrong. It is loyalty that brings me here." Sigyn raised a doubtful brow as Angrboda continued. "I have news that concerns the both of you."

"You have lies," Sigyn hissed.

"The only liar in this cave is the one you so desperately protect."

"I have not lied for some time. I think by average I might now be considered an honest man," Loki said with the smallest of smiles on his venom-scarred face.

"Bite your tongue and keep it that way," Angrboda said.

"I see my absence has not made your heart grow fonder of me."

"You're wrong, I have grown quite fond of your absence."

"I've missed you too," Loki sneered.

"Speak and be gone," Sigyn said. Loki's exchange with his former lover was too playful, in her opinion. It twisted her heart.

Drip.

The pail was near capacity. Sigyn adjusted her grip so that the splashes would not land on her. The skin of her fingers was calloused and scarred even more than the hammer-wielding hands of mighty Thor. The venom's touch was indeed painful; she had caught it with her own hands several times. Despite the occasional mishaps, Loki never once heard his wife cry out in pain.

"Ragnarok has come," Angrboda said.

"Ragnarok?" Loki and Sigyn said together. Angrboda nodded.

"Fenrir is free. Jormungandr rises from the tides as we speak." Angrboda's voice carried unhidden pride. The monstrous wolf and the world-sized serpent were her children – her and Loki's – two beasts fated to destroy the gods at the appointed time.

"Impossible," Sigyn said, but then the blast from a battle horn echoed through the chamber. The unmistakable call of Heimdall, the god's watchman, summoning the Aesir to battle.

"It is inevitable," Angrboda said. "The giants march on the Bifrost as we speak."

Drip.

"Why are you here to tell us? What can we who are imprisoned possibly do?" Sigyn asked.

"Only one of you is in chains," Angrboda answered. Her words were as cool as her frosty skin, "Since Loki could not come to me, I had to come to you. Besides, is it so unreasonable for me to see my husband one more time before the world meets its end?"

Sigyn scoffed, but she otherwise held her thoughts behind her teeth.

"You've had him all to yourself for so long," Angrboda said, "I can take your place if you wish. Give me a turn with my love, and you can run and fight with your fellow gods. Loki is, after all, my husband, too."

"And a good wife you've been," Sigyn mocked. She wanted to refuse, but Angrboda's proposal was the first to cause her to waver. Her hand jerked as though eager to accept. Her body betrayed the mind. Milky white venom swirled in the heavy bowl and threatened to slosh over the lip. Heimdall's horn sounded again, and a roll of thunder answered. The call to battle was difficult for her to refuse.

"Stay here," Loki's objection interrupted Sigyn's thoughts and caused Angrboda to frown. "Both of you. Stay here."

"Why?" Angrboda asked.

"Let Ragnarok pass us by. Let Asgard fall. Let the world burn, and from its ashes, we can start new. The three of us, together, with a blank slate."

Angrboda and Sigyn exchanged glances. Neither woman looked friendly to Loki's suggestion.

Drip.

"I'd rather spill this dish on myself than make such a cowardly decision," Sigyn said.

"Go, then," Angrboda said to Sigyn. "You are not bound nor a coward. Fight alongside your brethren. Leave me to protect the craven."

"Can neither of you see the opportunity we have?" Loki protested. More thunder rolled in the distance as Thor entered the far-off battle.

"Go," Angrboda encouraged, "you've been in the dark for too long. The gods need you."

Sigyn squinted. She and Angrboda ignored their spouse and the fierce sounds of war while they examined each other. Angrboda clearly bore ulterior motives for her visit. The giantess came near. Despite her size and crown of antlers, she made an attempt to appear endearing. Meanwhile, Sigyn was torn by dueling loyalties: to stand by Loki or leave and fight with her kin.

Loki watched without hiding his misgivings. He only cared about pain and avoiding it.

Drip.

"What is your goal?" Sigyn asked.

"I have been clear with my intentions. My goal is to speak to you about loyalty. I want you to remember that you are a goddess first, one of the Aesir, and married to Loki, the son of a giant, second."

"He is *my* husband."

"He is mine, too, and he is my kind. A son of a giant."

If she could, Sigyn would have stepped back. She desired more space between her and Angrboda, but the task of catching venom kept her anchored in place.

"This is silly," Loki said, "You can both have me if you want. Just stay here."

"You have already had both of us," Sigyn snapped. The contents of the pail threatened to spill out, but venom spewed from Sigyn's mouth instead. "This is all because of you, Loki. Those monsters you call children would not even exist if you could only keep to one bed. But nothing is enough for you. You have to take more. You might have a dwarf and an elf wife by now if you weren't locked away for so long." Sigyn took in a breath, "How can you receive my unrelenting attention for the ages we've been together in this cave and think for a second I'd share you at the first offer? Especially with her?" Sigyn jerked her head in Angrboda's direction. The giant did not look offended, only amused.

"Does that mean you're going then?" Angrboda asked.

"Why would I leave?"

"Because I am staying."

"That's what I want you both to do," Loki said. He gestured in exasperation as much as his bonds would allow.

"You are not staying," Sigyn laughed, "I won't allow it."

"How will you stop me? You seem a little preoccupied at the moment."

Drip.

"Leave," Sigyn commanded.

"I think I'll sit here," Angrboda said. She walked over to a ledge near one wall of the cave. A perch situated well out of arm's reach and likely too far for Sigyn to fling at with venom from the pail.

The tumult outside grew louder. The battle was undoubtedly fierce to be heard within the cave. Every giant, god, and monster was surely fighting in incredible duels. Sigyn considered the sounds. "Was every god truly fated to die at Ragnarok?" she thought.

"Why now?" Sigyn asked. "Why come today and not yesterday or the day before? Why come at all?"

"I've told you—"

"You're just as deceitful as him," Sigyn cut off Angrboda's words. "You are here in search of something."

"What is here that I could possibly gain? The realms are hours away from being dismantled, and all that is here is a bound god, a snake that drools, and a pouty goddess."

Drip.

Sigyn clucked her tongue. "Very well," she said. She glanced at the pail and then at Loki. Her husband's face was as white as the venom. His lips said, "Don't go," but something in his eyes spoke differently. She never knew what thoughts existed behind those eyes and had no hopes of deciphering Loki's intentions now. "The vessel is not yet full, but I'll empty it before I leave."

"I can take it," Angrboda said, standing up from her chosen ledge. "Go without delay. Your presence might turn the battle."

"That's what you want," Sigyn's brows raised. "You came here for the venom."

Angrboda's convincing facade fell. Suddenly, she looked concerned for the pail's contents. "Give me the bowl," she said coldly.

"What would you do with it?" Sigyn asked.

"Just leave." The giantess was very close to Sigyn and reached for the venom-catching pail. Sigyn could not move for fear of spilling the venom, but Angrboda's hand went above, not below. The snake's fangs yielded a drop, and it landed on the backside of Angrboda's wrist. She was not prepared for the resulting pain and howled like a wolf in her anguish. Her arm jerked back and knocked the bowl away. Sigyn dove after it in the air and crashed into her moaning rival.

Loki shrieked in horror at the descending wave of cream-white affliction, but the venom did not land on him. Instead, it splashed upon one of his bonds. The bewitched cord dissolved as soon as the venom touched it. Loki wasted no time to escape once he became unbound. With one limb free, he could shapeshift again. He took the form of a fish. His scaly body wriggled out of the bonds and flopped twice on the floor before Loki turned back into a man-sized god.

Sigyn and Angrboda untangled themselves from one another on the stone floor. The pail, which Sigyn held for so long, lay shattered where Loki once was. The god of mischief stepped on the shards with his booted foot.

"Look out!" Sigyn and Angrboda shouted in unison; the snake overhead uncoiled and struck at Loki, but the shapeshifter was quick to morph into something else to avoid his tormentor: a snake-eating wolverine. The snake's bite missed, and Loki attacked instead. As a beast, he was ruthless. He tore the snake like a ribbon and swallowed the tail end whole. The head tried to writhe away with the remaining body, but Loki pounced on it and painted the cave floor with red entrails.

Afterward, Loki took on his usual form again and looked at both of his wives. A bit of blood dripped from his chin, and his eyes were black and rabid like an animal's. He wiped his chin off on his wrist. The skin where the ropes had been was red and scarred.

"What now?" Angrboda asked. The antlered crown sat crooked on her head, and her wet hair was brown and muddy from the cave floor.

Loki looked down at the shards of Sigyn's dish. He picked up one of the larger ones and rubbed it with his thumb like a lucky totem.

"Thank you," he whispered, then he looked up at Angrboda. "You should have come sooner," he said before turning into a hawk and flying out of the cave.

"Did you know that the venom would do that?" Sigyn asked after a moment passed between them in the cave.

"I had a hunch," Angrboda answered.

"And did you think he would leave?"

"I was sure of that."

The Ties That Bind

Ariana Ferrante

I never leave my father's side.

My cold, dark metal loops thrice around him to bind him to the stones – about his chest, over his legs, around his shoulders. Mine is an unrelenting embrace, the longest he will ever come to know.

Before I was iron, I was flesh. Before I was brutal bondage, I was a boy. Before I was Loki's chains, I was Narfi.

Long ago though it was, the memory comes easily at my prompting. My father, fleeing reproach after his slaying of Baldr and the defaming of his fellow gods, escaped to one of the mountains of Midgard in the company of my mother, Sigyn. There, he hid away, sometimes a man, sometimes a salmon in the river, on a constant watch for any signs of the vengeful Aesir. Despite all his wiles and his disguises, the gods caught up to him. They plucked him from the rushing waters with furious fists and tossed him into this very cave, prepared to punish the trickster for his latest and greatest misdeed.

They would not dare sully their beloved bright home of Asgard with my father's blood. Midgard, on the other hand, would be a suitable site for their retribution.

Though Sigyn did her best to shield us, her efforts were no match against the all-seeing eye of the All-father. The Aesir rounded us up, Váli and I, and brought us to the same cave. I remember Loki's expression as we arrived even now. I had never before seen my father so pale. No one ought to see their father helpless, but the sight stings far worse when your father is a god.

With a single wave of one-eyed Odin's hand, Váli dropped to the cave's stone floor. His pained moans warped into bestial snarls, his body bursting all over with dark, coarse fur. Within moments, a wolf had taken his place, shaking out its pelt as the final throes of the transformation ebbed.

My brother threw himself toward me, not a glimmer of recognition in his golden, feral gaze. He gave me no time, not even to scream. The wolf's jaws closed around the soft pink of my stomach. He tore free my entrails with a single jerk, spilling viscera to the cold cavern's floor. My mother's wails echoed in the cave's confines.

The Aesir came upon my corpse the moment I struck the ground. They grasped my intestines and gathered them in their arms. Then, they coiled them tight around Loki's form – about his chest, over his legs, around his shoulders – binding him to three stones. With another wave, Odin enchanted my innards, hardening them to iron while my beastly brother devoured the rest of me.

In that moment, I stopped being my father's son and became my father's snare.

Finding bondage alone insufficient a punishment for my father's transgressions, the goddess Skaði placed a venomous serpent around a stalactite above his restrained form, the jaws of the suspended snake dripping burning poison toward Loki's awaiting flesh. Then, as easily as they came, the Aesir departed and left us to our fate.

Here we have languished ever since, father and son, prisoner and prison. Despite my slaying, I do not depart this realm for Hel. I dare not entertain the notion. No father, god or man, must come to outlast his child, and I will prove no exception. I lie across him in this cave, curling about his body and adhering him to the stones, and I will for as long as I am able.

We are not alone, my father and I. Sigyn stands above him, her arms held aloft. In her hands she holds a bowl to catch the serpent's venom and shield Loki from its torment. Váli, too, remains in the cave. Still a wolf, he fled at first to Jotunheim, his muzzle dripping with my lifeblood. Before long, however, he returned, a child expecting a punishment but finding none. My father and mother could not stand the thought of losing another child, animal though he may have become. To turn him away would have been equal parts hypocritical and inhospitable. Had our father not sired Jörmungandr, the great serpent that circles Midgard, or Sleipnir, Odin's six-legged steed? What was one more animal among his offspring?

Occasionally, like today, my beast of a brother rises from his spot on the cave floor and dares to approach our bound patriarch. Once there, he paws uselessly at my hardened entrails while his mother chastises his intrusion, a low, apologetic whine rumbling in his lupine throat.

He has long been forgiven, though such a sentiment is impossible to vocalize in my transfigured state. No, I can no more loathe my brother for his vicious slaying than I can blame the snake looming above my father for its venom. Wild things must rip and tear, must harm and hunt, and I was merely in his way.

Attempts fruitless as always, Váli recedes from our father's side with his tail between his legs. Our mother huffs, loudly lamenting that clumsy lupine paws cannot hold a bowl. My father murmurs some sly response, his laughter shaking my metal bonds.

They do not mention me. They haven't in years. The endless march of time has eroded any emotional connection they once possessed for their sibling-slain son, our present relations existing solely in the physical. I do not mind it. I am a chain, not a child, and we are still together, whether or not my name leaves their lips.

Any conversation conjured from the brief interaction comes to a quiet close, and silence permeates the cavern once again. These speechless stretches have only grown more numerous with each passing year. When you are confined in a cave for decades on end, you rapidly run out of things to talk about. The drip-drip sound of falling venom fills the wordless void, accompanied by the infrequent noise of flitting bats and dark-dwelling insects.

Without warning, Sigyn's face shifts. Her lower lip presses out, her brows creasing and nostrils flaring. I recognize the expression immediately; the bowl has grown full, and she must leave him momentarily at the mercy of the serpent to empty the burning contents.

She departs with a thundering of footsteps, but she is not fast enough. She never is. Drops of venom loose themselves from the looming snake's jaws, impacting the unshielded craters of my father's blistered and poison-pockmarked face.

THE TIES THAT BIND

I am used to many aspects of our arrangement, but I am yet unused to his screams. I am doubtful I ever will be.

Loki's screams are a nightmare to the senses. It sounds as if he is trying to expel his innards from his mouth from the force of his voice alone. His tortured cries ricochet across the walls of the cave, the smooth, curved stone surfaces echoing back his agony as if to mock him. The earth shudders and trembles as he reels and contorts, rattling all of Midgard with the trickster god's torment.

His ears swiveled back, Váli presses himself low to the cavern floor and buries his head in his paws. I do not envy him. I can only imagine what our father's cries sound like to an animal with such great hearing. The sound is harrowing enough to me, and I have no ears to speak of.

Another drop lands. Loki lurches forward in pained, contorted spasms, but I cling tight as I always have. The top layer of his skin rubs red and raw against the underside of my cool, constricting coils. Stones tumble from the ceiling, dashing the cave floor in a clatter.

Finally, Sigyn returns. She hurries back into her position, bowl outstretched. The venom lands in the empty receptacle, impacting the wood with a soft tap. Loki falls back against the stones, panting and cursing. His chest heaves, flush with my chains as he sucks in breath after breath. The agony is over – at least for now.

He will escape my hardened grasp one day, I remind myself, the sound of his already faded screams reverberating in ears long since consumed. He will not endure this pain and imprisonment forever. Centuries ago, I might have celebrated such knowledge, but now the notion is lonely and humiliating to consider; a chain

195

is worth nothing when it is broken. Regardless, such a moment has been set in stone before Váli and I were even born. Eventually, my father must leave me behind as all parents do, tear free from my clutches, and engender Ragnarök. But until then, I will cling to him like a frightened child, relishing in the certainty of our union. Sigyn, Váli, and I, we are his constant companions, soothing in our own ways; Sigyn relief, Váli remorse, and I restraint.

The days dribble on like the venom from the serpent above, singular and unrelenting in addition. They drip into the bowl of time, overfilling into weeks, months, years, and still we remain in this cave, kin and connected, links in a chain stronger than my iron. What more could a family desire?

Another day arrives as slowly as each before it, the first rays of morning streaming in from the distant mouth of our cavernous confinement.

Loki sleeps upon the stones, my chains his only blanket. Gods do not require rest, but I hardly blame him for indulging if it means he can stop thinking about the serpent and my stranglehold. Indeed, despite his meager amenities, he only ever looks at peace when he slumbers. Perhaps his reality is cruel enough that his unconscious brain cannot conjure worse.

I wonder what he dreams about. Ragnarök, perhaps – his promised time of freedom. Or maybe he dreams of nothing, just an empty blackness that nevertheless distracts him from the bleak present. I cannot say for certain. Iron is unpracticed in the art of sleep.

Above him, Sigyn's face shifts – nostrils flared, brows creased, lower lip jutting. Full. Again. She whispers a meek apology, then dashes to dispose of the venom.

As always, she cannot run fast enough.

His eyes fly open. The dream burns away to herald the living nightmare beneath. He thrashes against me, back arching off the stones as the venom strikes his face. All of Midgard quakes with him, the earth gouging open in identical agony.

My chains strain and buckle, each link pulled taut and tauter still. If I still possessed lungs, I might have held my breath.

Then, I hear it – a new sound, sharp and plaintive.

One of my links snaps.

The broken piece of metal strikes the stone floor, rattling before it settles. Returned, Sigyn gasps, and Váli's ears prick to attention.

A rush of cold fear shivers down a phantom, long-gone spine. Every century we spent confined flashes behind devoured eyes in an instant. This is it, I realize. This is the moment he is to leave me. I have contained him all this time, but I cannot hold him any longer.

And so, though I love him, I let him go.

My chains burst with a resounding clang, the noise of liberation echoed back in eager affirmation. The remaining iron bonds fall slack upon him and clink against each other, limp and useless at long last.

He shrugs my bonds away like a mantle, sending me clattering to the floor. He takes a single step, then stumbles, his movement uncoordinated from centuries of inactivity. Sigyn yelps and lurches forward, tossing aside her depleted bowl of venom to offer him support.

Her arms snake around his shoulders as he tumbles out from under the serpent. Her limbs form a newer, gentler bond – one that lifts him up instead of pinning him to the ground. Loki leans against her, weeping with relief. Tears mingle amongst the sweat and venom, coating his face in a glimmering sheen. Sigyn smothers him with kisses, her lips conquering his effort –reddened features as if to match every drop of poison that struck him.

Her amorous offerings draw a rasping chuckle from his throat, and, slowly, he finds the courage to support his own weight. His legs tremble at first, but quickly cease their shaking. Another laugh rattles out of him, and he scrubs away the slowing tears with the heel of his palm. The upward-twitching corners of his lips give way, a proud smile threatening to split his face in half.

I thought I might have despaired beholding this inevitability, but now, seeing my father stand, grinning and unfettered, a serene sense of satisfaction floods every inch of my limp, broken form. There stands the mischief-maker, the wolf-father, the harbinger of Ragnarök. My father. My prisoner. My meaning.

I have fulfilled my purpose – now he may do the same.

Loki and Sigyn turn to walk away, and my dearest Váli bounds to his paws. His tail wags as he pads eagerly behind them, departing down the tunnel. The three become silhouettes against the streaming sunlight as they reach the distant mouth of the cave, then wink out of my view forever.

I smile with lips long withered, and the world begins to end.

Parent-Aesir Conference

Cara Giles

Right, I'm Váli and Narvi's dad. Sorry about breaking your chair. I always feel like a giant with these kid seats. The teachers who aren't as slim as you must snap them like twigs!

Usually my wife Sigyn comes to these conferences, but she's at a herpetologists' convention this weekend, so the boys and I are roughing it. How are they doing in class? A handful, you say? Yes, I'm sure twins would overwhelm a less skilled teacher. Váli's lashing out at Narvi during dramatic playtime? That doesn't sound like him. Another student must have put him up to it.

Now for the rest…? I thought that stack of permanent records looked a little high for a couple of second graders. Dear lady, there's been some kind of mistake. My ex Angrboda, she has primary custody of our three. We agreed that she's supposed to handle all their school details – no? Angrboda didn't bother coming to last year's conference, either? Well, let's hear it.

Fenrir – he's been biting again? That's disappointing. I had a sticker chart going before separating from his mom, one gold star each day he didn't tear someone's flesh, and he was actually doing rather well. The divorce has been hardest on him, I think. We all cope in our own way. Angrboda's pretty frosty, so his homelife leaves something to be desired. Not a lot of treats and trips to the park, if you get my drift. I only have him two weekends a month, but maybe I can get Fenrir to chew his pencils. I believe you professionals call it redirecting the behavior? If you think changing classrooms is the fresh start he needs, I'm all for it. Yes, I'll be happy to have a chat with his new teacher. I'm sure Fenrir will settle down once Mr. Tyr takes him in hand.

Jormungandr – my middle child. I swear he's so well-behaved, I almost forget he's there. Quiet and keeps to himself? Red flag? I don't think you're giving this fine establishment enough credit for turning out a model student. His last report card was pristine. But his essays just circle around their topics endlessly? Where you see dithering, I see a bright career in academia. He never has his whole body in the classroom at once – now, that sounds like an accessibility issue. Perhaps more problems with the matchstick chairs? You think sports would help him engage more fully? I'll take a pamphlet. When are water polo tryouts?

Ah, Hel. Daddy's little princess is on the student council! Leadership potential, that one. Stubborn and standoffish? Well, she's at that age. Angrboda says she can hardly get her out of that basement bedroom. I think we broke the screens out a little too early with her. It's my fault. I did mean well – the apps were supposed to be educational. But she's been rather dead behind the eyes since she got her first tablet in hand, unfortunately. What's this about a boy? Baldur? She's never talked about him. He's missing? Why on earth a boy would wander away from a school where you teach is beyond me. You think Hel knows where Baldur is, and won't say? Why would Baldur go to Hel if, as you said yourself, she's so stubborn and standoffish? I think

PARENT-AESIR CONFERENCE

she's being framed. Who are this little troublemaker's parents, anyway? Odin and Frigg? Forget I asked.

Well, we've covered a lot of ground here. I'll certainly rest easier with such an exemplary educator in my children's corner. I know they have a complex family dynamic, and I appreciate all you do. Same time next fall, right?

Wait, lower your voice! That's private information. I registered Sleipnir at the stables, not with the attendance office! But yes, he's mine too, and this is not a co-parenting situation. The others don't know, and that could be awkward all around. I don't suppose parent-teacher confidentiality...? I wouldn't mention him to Sigyn, for example. What's this about track and field? Sleipnir's winning every race? He can run on water? And interest from Asgard's talent scouts – I'd never considered. I knew he couldn't have eight legs for nothing. That smells like a potential scholarship to me! I'm the proudest mother in the world!

Fraternized: The Enemy Within

Sara Gonzalez-Rothi

From Midsommar through Mabon, the brothers spent nearly every waking hour on the banks of the river Ífingr. They'd make camp in early June, gathering and drying peat to be soaked in whale oil. The dank result served as kindling for the bonfire they affectionately labeled "*staminarok*." If properly tended, the fire would stay alight for three months.

Laufey assumed that the Valkyries had lured the boys to the river. After all, Loki, Helblindi, and Býleistr were part frost giant, and known to ogle heavenly bodies. But it was a far more majestic creature that captured their attention in the waning days of sommar: shape-shifting silver swimmers abandoning the realm of Aegir and Ran to bring life into the uplands each year.

One million salmon would make the trek to the river that separated the quick and the dead. In the process, they too would cross the veil. But not before sacrificing their flesh as a living smorgasbord for the predators, Jöttnar, Aesir, and Vanir alike – all to spawn the next generation. The brothers wanted their fair share. As half-breeds they reckoned they were due at least a double portion for each brother, each meal, each day, for a year.

To succeed in their ambitious quest, the brothers met stiff competition. Wild creatures weren't keen to share. Loki's modus operandi was join them to beat them. Be it wolf or bear, he'd deceive the interloper into believing they'd stumbled on a peer's territory. To fully play the part, Loki had taken to voiding in and around the camp, much to the disgust of Býl. While Hel noted the putrid smell, he was unable to see that it was his own brother's doing, and assumed that the fauna who had gathered for the spawn were especially regular. Because their mediator matriarch assumed that her boys were off sowing their wild oats, Laufey gave camp a wide berth.

It didn't take long for Býl to recognize how wildly advantageous this power dynamic was. He had leverage over Loki: if he told Hel the real source of the smell, his brother would in turn seek reprieve from Laufey – the only person who had the power to shame any of the boys. Of the brothers, Býl was the most capable fisher. So, if Loki wanted to remain in his mother's good graces and with the flesh of the gods in his belly each meal, he'd better keep Býl happy.

Hel too had a specialized role at camp – an important one. Aside from vision, Hel's other senses were intensely acute. By touch alone, he could distinguish between sapwood and heartwood, seasoned fuel and green. He could smell peat from miles away. And he was massive and strong. And so it was that he became the firewood and peat sourcer for the camp – a grueling daily task.

Loki was a demigod of many talents, that he used to great effect (when it suited him). To please Býl, Loki would secure the whale oil needed to sustain *staminarok*.

One morning, as Hel retrieved peat from their cache, he found it particularly brittle and devoid of oil. The brothers inquired of their regular trading partner, who was fresh out. In a flash, Loki was gone – having transformed into a salmon himself. The other fish were confused as he swam *against* their tide of wriggling bodies, he headed *towards* the sea rather than from it.

Once there, Loki scouted a pod of orca whales with a particularly hungry look about them. He feigned injury to pique the interest of a young member of the school. Writhing this way and that, he swam towards the fjord against the receding tide. The unwitting orca followed. Just as Loki reached a deep pool, his performance intensified.

Appearing grievously injured and in danger, Ran took notice. Out of pity for the long-suffering of this confused salmon who had swam the wrong way, Ran sent her daughters to pull the tide out with great force, stranding Loki and the young orca in the pool. The salmon would flop a bit, and then lie still, prompting the orca to wriggle closer. When the whale was within arm's reach, Loki emerged in demigod form to plunge his dagger into the creature's blowhole. Ran was enraged by the deception, and embarrassed that she'd fallen for it. To appease the goddess, Loki vowed to share the spoils: meat for her daughters and blubber for his brothers.

Because Ran didn't trust that the trickster assailant would butcher the carcass fairly, she tasked daughters Kolga, Hronn, and Dufa to do the honors. Accordingly, the women sent Loki back to camp empty-handed. When he arrived, Loki assured his brothers he had accomplished the task, but they grew restless. At the approach of three goddesses bearing copious blubber, they soon forgot their doubt.

Staminarok burned bright and hot, as did the chemistry between Kolga, Dufa, and Býleistr. Hronn chatted politely with Loki, but Helblindi felt ignored. While it was a common experience to be left out, it wasn't a pleasant one – especially because though he could not see what he was missing, he could sense Hronn's beauty in her effervescent laugh and salt spray scent. Entranced by the women, neither Loki or Býl were fishing. Day gave way to night, and while two brothers feasted on good company, Hel was ravenous. He couldn't tell whether those were hunger pangs or jealousy.

By morning once the women had gone, it was clear as the morning sun: envy had devoured Helblindi. Býl was making up for lost fishing time, wholly focused on the water's edge. He didn't hear Hel's grievance airing – but Loki did. Never one to miss an opportunity to exploit division to his own advantage, Loki sat to listen.

"He already has all the fish in Midgard, now all the goddesses too?"

"You know, Hel, maybe that's just it. The girls were over the moon about the orca meat. Perhaps they aren't interested in Býl, but in his catch. We eat well, but the seagals? I bet Ran keeps them on a strict diet. Not everyone has access to the freedom and the bounty of camp."

"You think?"

"I know." Loki sounded empathetic, but definitive. "If you caught half as many fish as Býl, Hronn wouldn't be able to resist you. I saw her staring."

"You did?" Loki nodded. "Thanks for saying that, Lokes. But I can't even catch a tenth of his haul."

"*You* can't...but maybe *we* can."

"Do tell."

Loki spun a tale of a starving Valkyrie queen, separated from her sistren and her horse in an ice storm. Without a mount or a pack, Sigrun had no way to hunt and after many days grew weak. She came upon a small stream, devoid of living beings. Calling out to Odin, he directed her to stack rocks in the streambed. This seemed mindless toil, but as his most dutiful handmaiden, Sigrun heeded the command. When she placed the final stone, she stepped back to consider the purpose of this assignment. As she did, a corpulent salmon swam to the foot of the earthen dam. The fish stilled in place and it occurred to Sigrun: this was Odin's reward for her blind obedience. And so she feasted on the divine bounty, gathering enough strength to rejoin her sisters.

As Loki spoke, Hel formed a plan. Sure, he would gather sticks and logs for *staminarok*, but also for his newest masterpiece.

Days passed and the brothers all acted as usual. Býl complaining about the stench, Loki rendering blubber into oil, and Hel stoking the bonfire. But each night after they gorged themselves on the day's catch, Hel retreated downstream, alone. Býl asked Loki where he'd gone, and in true Loki form, he spun a believable tale: Hronn had requested Hel's company! Býl was impressed. Hronn was the fairest of the sea-dottirs, and good on Hel for wooing her.

By dawn on Frjádagr, the river which this time of the year ran more silver than clear was nearly devoid of fish. Býl was heartsick. Loki feigned concern, to keep up the charade. Neither told Hel.

FRATERNIZED: THE ENEMY WITHIN

Hours passed and no fish. Days passed, and Býl did not eat. He was puzzled that Hel and Loki weren't growing hungry or thin, while he winnowed with each passing mealtime. Býl surmised that Hronn was feeding Hel during their nightly tryst. He paid a visit to Kolga and Dufa.

"Ladiiieeesss, helllloooo!" Býl donned his most energetic flirtation.

"We missed you, Býl. Too busy fishing to call?" teased Dufa.

Crestfallen, he had to admit, "Nary a one. My net is as empty as Ífingr. I was hoping you had a meal to share, as Hronn has done for Hel these Fómhar evenings?"

The sisters looked at each-other quizzically, then back to Býl.

"It's still Sommar, Býl – the fish are swimming in droves through the fjord. The river should be full of them," explained Kolga, "and Hronn has been here with us every night, rebuilding the sandy beach before Fimbulwinter."

"And Hel too?"

"Only us sea maidens. Though Hel has kindly gifted salmon each night to fuel our efforts. Can't he share with you?"

Býl's face reddened at the rising heat from his bowels. Hunger, anger, and embarrassment are an explosive mixture. He left without a goodbye.

In a rage, Býl bulldozed all in his exit path. Clearing a particularly large pine, he noticed an enormous obstruction downstream of camp. At closer inspection, this was not the work of a lowly beaver. No, only an especially large and capable jötnar could have built such a structure. Only a giant the size and strength of his own brother. Why, after a lifetime of care, would Hel have turned on Býl, the great provider? Býl wasn't sure, but he expected Loki was to blame. Rage turned to apoplexy. And Býl turned the only place he could to punish his trickster kin: their mother.

In the meantime, Dufa and Kolga sought to warn Loki and Hel of Býl's apparent outrage. Upon the news, Loki elected to hide by shifting into a salmon once more and schooling within the piscine hoard behind Hel's dam. There, he relished the feeling of safety in numbers, the cool clear water of Ífingr fueling his belief that he had gotten away with this series of deceptions. He was confident Býl would blame Hel, of course, who else could have constructed such a barrier? He'd bitten the hand that fed him.

When Býl arrived, Laufey was pleased to see him, believing he'd taken a brief respite from Valkyrien dalliance to visit. He wasn't pleased to see her, though. In a sour torrent, words of disdain for his brethren poured out. She listened and hearing of the grievous deception that had left one son's belly empty, transformed into a fierce bear goddess before Býl's eyes. No sooner had he finished his tattle than she bounded off in search of Loki.

Once at the river, Laufey came upon Hel, pacing between the dam and camp wondering what had come of Loki and how he could explain his actions to Býl. He smelled bear, and did not realize that it was his mother. Without his trickster brother to lure the bear away, Hel jumped into the river for cover. Trying to retrieve her blind son, Laufey dove in at the face of the dam, which tore apart into splinters of wood pouring down river.

Her dagger-like claws pierced deeply through salmon scales and into flesh. At the sight of blood filling the pool and the intoxicating smell wafting above the mist, Laufey-bear couldn't resist. She drew the fish to her mouth and indulged, before securing Hel on the safety of the shore.

The meal and the scare having tamed Laufey, she returned to her goddess form. In her arms, Hel realized this was his mother and not a predator, and he too calmed. The mother and child connected, him telling her of the sea maidens, his jealousy, and Loki's idea.

Laufey's wrath resurfaced, this time aimed at her trickster son. An odd pain arose in her abdomen.

"Could the salmon have turned?" she wondered aloud. "Hel, help me." Her voice trailed off and her eyes rolled up as her body crumpled to the ground.

Tables having turned, the son cradled the mother and carried her to camp, where *staminarok* had simmered down to embers. He laid her down and went in search of firewood. All he found was wet from the now-opened channel flooding its banks.

By this point, Býl had returned to camp, where Laufey had awoken and rested her head in his lap. The pain came in searing waves. At times she lay quiet and still. But the bursts of agony increased in duration and frequency.

The embers of the once-intense fire gave way to ash. The surrounding earth cooled. Laufey trembled with the chill. Hel returned, empty handed.

"For Valhalla's sake, where is Loki?" he roared.

As the next spell came, water gushed from beneath where Laufey lay. The boys thought she had voided from the pain, but then came crimson. Their mother wailed and writhed for what seemed hours. In time, a blond fuzzy head emerged between her legs. The three were spellbound, as below the fuzz was an instantly recognizable face: that of Loki.

The fetal trickster, born again, with cries of laughter. Laufey reached down to pull him to her chest, sobbing and cursing all at once.

"YOU…! You? You…how did…? Is it really you, Loki…? I must have. It can't be…I *ate* you?? I consumed the flesh of my flesh??"

"Waaaaahhahahah," the baby replied, shivering and guffawing against the frigid autumn breeze.

"Well Loki, it serves you right," she continued. "You made this camp, now you have to lie in it. You want to deceive? You deceived your mother into eating you. Act as a feckless child? You've now been delivered as one. Void where you sleep? Now you have no choice but to. Undermine your caregivers? The flame is extinguished, and you'll face the dark and cold of Ragnarok and Fimbulwinter alone. Doomed to repeat your mistakes until you learn from them. And Fate will be your cruelest teacher."

With that, Laufey set the boy down in the ash, grabbed Hel's right hand and Býl's left, and the trio set off for Aegir's feast. "Until Valhalla, son, sweet dreams."

The Apple of Her Eye
Kay Hanifen

Though most of the Aesir had long left this world, there remained one. Legend had it that Idunn had hidden herself away in a mountain cave with her *eski* box of immortality granting apples. These apples could heal the sick and prolong life indefinitely.

Astrid grew up on that mountain, was raised by those stories, but had never truly believed. They were as real to her as the Jotuns that fought the Aesir or the trolls that lurked in caves and devoured unwary travelers. But Nessa always believed.

It was said that her grandmother was a völva, a shaman who could see the future, and that Nessa inherited some of that gift. She knew things she could not possibly know, from the location of a missing sewing needle to how severe the winter would be. But there were things even Astrid's beloved Nessa could not predict.

The illness that came over her was sudden and agonizing. One moment, she was fine, and the next, she was seizing on the floor of their longhouse. She spent the next few days drifting in and out of consciousness, clutching Astrid for comfort as the fever filled her mind with terror.

"Idunn's golden apples," Nessa muttered after a day of delirium.

"I wish I had them," Astrid replied. "They'd make you better."

Her eyes shot open, more lucid than they had been in hours. "The Dragon's Cave. One waits within and I shall be saved."

Astrid opened her mouth to protest, but the words caught in her throat. She wanted to stay by Nessa's side, but if these apples could save her...

Astrid kissed the top of her head. "I'll send for a healer to look after you. If these apples will save you, I'll stop at nothing to bring them back." Getting to her feet, she dressed in her warmest cloaks and slung a sword over her shoulder.

Before she left, though, Nessa snatched her ankle with a surprising strength. "Be wary and do not trust your eyes. It is not as it seems."

Kneeling before her love, Astrid gently pried the hand from her ankle and brought it to her lips. "I will be as clever as you."

Smiling at that, Nessa closed her eyes, drifting into an uneasy sleep. The healer's house was not far, so as soon as Astrid summoned them, she began her trek up the mountain.

The Dragon's Cave was a place where few dared to venture. It sat at the top of the mountain, and a great rumbling sound and billowing smoke emanated from it whenever anyone got too close. Not wanting to anger a creature that had otherwise been peaceable, they left the cave alone. No one knew what was in there, and no one cared to find out.

At least, not until Astrid began her journey up the mountainside. Not knowing how long Nessa had, she tirelessly trudged through the snow to this lonely cave. She refused to let Nessa die, not

THE APPLE OF HER EYE

alone and not in Astrid's arms. Nessa was going to live even if it killed her.

She made it to the cave by nightfall, her heart pounding in her throat as she drew her sword and slowly approached. Beneath her, the ground rumbled. Acrid smoke belched out of the cave's mouth. Astrid was no true warrior and wondered – with some regret – if it would have been a better idea to bring someone with her to watch her back.

It was too late for that now, and Nessa's life was on the line, so Astrid had no choice but to enter the cave. She had wasted too much time already.

The moment she stepped through, she found herself in a garden. It smelled of apple blossoms and sweet summertime, making her relax a little in spite of herself. This must have been the orchard where Idunn harvested her apples. Perhaps this was what Nessa meant when she said not to believe everything she saw. But if so, why would she tell Astrid to be wary of this paradise?

Without any other ideas about what to do, she ventured deeper into the orchard. Though the air smelled of apple blossoms, all the trees were bare. Whatever leaves were left on them had spots of blight contrasting the green. The land was not yet dead, but it certainly was dying.

The sound of something like crying drifted towards her on the breeze. Weapon ready, she followed slowly to the source: a fountain at the center of the orchard. An ethereal woman sat on the edge and clutched a box to her chest as she wept. A twig snapped beneath Astrid's feet and the woman's head snapped up.

The goddess, Idunn, was not how Astrid expected her to be. Though she was still breathtaking, she was not young looking. Her hair held streaks of grey and laugh lines had formed around her mouth. Idunn was older than the stories described but still looked no older than Astrid's own mother.

"Whoever you are, you shouldn't be here," Idunn said without getting to her feet. The air crackled with electricity like lightning about to strike, and Astrid was seized with a sudden panic.

What was she doing? Did she really plan to fight Idunn? It was suicide, but she couldn't do anything else. After all, she waltzed into a goddess's domain, intending to steal the apple without any real plan. Quickly, she sheathed her weapon and bowed her head. "Forgive my intrusion. The woman I love is dying, and the apples are the only cure. I've come to ask that you share your fruit with her."

The goddess gave her an incredulous stare. "Or what? You'll take it by force?"

Astrid shrugged. "If I must. Though I would rather talk. Why do you stay here when all the other Aesir have moved on?"

Idunn's back stiffened like a wooden plank. "I have vowed to watch over this orchard until they come back."

"And if they never come back? If they've left you all alone to feast in Valhalla?"

Her fists clenched and unclenched at her sides, and Astrid realized that she had struck a nerve. Though she could keep pushing, she didn't want to anger the goddess, who already seemed so terribly unhappy.

THE APPLE OF HER EYE

"I've been saving the very last one for myself," Idunn said. "It's not made for mortals like you."

"As I said, the apple isn't for me. It's for someone I love more than breathing. But if I may, the apple will prolong your life, but can you truly call this living?" She gestured to the blighted trees and the empty gardens.

Idunn cocked her head. "You speak with a silver tongue. Rare for one who holds a sword. They tend to be far less clever, and far more brutish. I've found your type to be more brawn than brains."

The hairs on the back of Astrid's neck prickled. Something about this was off. She felt like a deer stalked by a wolf, the threat out of sight but still unmistakably there. "My love would say the same thing. She's always been the clever one between the two of us."

Idunn smiled. "Clearly. You came all this way for immortality, not for yourself but for someone else, a mortal as fickle as all the rest. What if you fall out of love with her? Won't you regret your foolishness?"

"Never." Her conviction was so forceful that Idunn raised her eyebrows.

Then, she smiled and opened the box, presenting Astrid with a golden apple entangled in vines. "Go ahead. Take it. But you must cut it free."

Astrid blinked. "As simple as that?"

"As simple as that." Idunn sighed. "I am so very old and tired. Let me to my rest."

Drawing her sward, Astrid slowly approached. Her instincts told her that something was amiss, that no one would simply give up the last of the immortal apples.

Be wary and do not trust your eyes. It is not as it seems. Her love's words echoed in her head.

She stopped short. If the bellowing and the earthquakes were an illusion, what else might be a trick? In their time talking, Idunn had never once moved from her seat by the fountain. In fact, she had barely moved at all.

The goddess tilted her head, regarding Astrid with impatience. "Well? What are you waiting for? Your prize is right here. Come and take it."

"Come to me," Astrid said, refusing to take another step.

Idunn's eyes flashed furiously. "You dare speak to the Aesir like this? I should smite you where you stand."

"Then do it," Astrid challenged. "Come to me and strike me down where I stand."

Idunn grimaced as though in pain and the earth shook beneath their feet. Memories of the stories Nessa would tell came bubbling to the surface of Astrid's mind. There was a god she knew, one that had been bound inside a mountain and tortured with the venom of a snake. One that made the ground shake with the agony of his writhing, a torture only ever abated by his wife holding a bowl to catch the poison.

Astrid adjusted the grip on her sword, steeling herself for a fight. "You're lying. Show me who you truly are."

Idunn's eyes widened in surprise for just a moment. But then she laughed. It was a low, cruel, bitter thing, like the taste of poison on Astrid's tongue. "You are far cleverer than you look. Which isn't saying much, I suppose, but still. Credit where it's due, mortal."

THE APPLE OF HER EYE

"Loki," Astrid said, "drop this illusion and tell me what's going on."

The trickster god glared and snapped his fingers. The illusion vanished, and in its place was a cave. A man laid bound to rocks by entrails. His ruby red hair was lank and filthy. The edge of his hairline looked as though it had been burned, and the marks stretched like rivers down the rest of his face. The corpse of a snake hung above him with its mouth open, fangs dripping venom into a bowl held aloft by the woman who sat beside him – Sigyn, if the stories were correct. This was Loki's punishment for killing a fellow god.

"The goddess in the garden was a much prettier sight, was it not?" he asked.

"In the same manner that cowbane is pretty," Astrid retorted. "That doesn't make it any less deadly. I prefer to see the truth of things."

He snorted, clearly amused. "Then why are you speaking to a trickster?"

"Because I was sent here by my love. She told me that I would find Idunn's apples and gift her with immortality." Astrid gnawed her lip thoughtfully. "But it wasn't her who summoned me here, was it?"

Loki arched an eyebrow. "Am I to answer that question?"

Astrid ignored him, feeling the pieces of the puzzle all slot into place. "Nessa is the granddaughter of a powerful völva and sensitive to the magics of the world. Though your powers have diminished, she must have been a simple target to curse. Then, it was a simple matter of sending her a vision of the apple and the cave. You were going to trick me with the apple so that I could cut you free, believing that I was saving her."

The woman holding the bowl chuckled. "It seems that you underestimated this one. She saw right through you, husband. Very clever for a mortal."

"Silence, Sigyn," Loki snapped.

The goddess obeyed and fell silent, though Astrid could see the ghost of a smile still on her lips.

"Now that you've been found out, it's time to release my Nessa," Astrid said. "Free her from your curse."

"No." The reply was so simple and so blunt that Astrid felt taken aback.

She gripped her sword hard enough for her hands to ache. Outrage burned through her like a wildfire. "What?"

"I said no. I still hold her as leverage, so unless you cut my bindings, I will break the curse, and let you leave this mountain alive." If she freed him, that would usher in Ragnarök, the end of the world, but if she didn't, her own world would end. She thought back carefully on what he said. Loki was known for his tricks and cleverness, but he was desperate for a reprieve from his punishment, and that made him more likely to agree without thinking through his own words.

"Cut your bindings?" Astrid repeated.

"Yes."

"Let her go and give me your oath that you will never curse her again and that you shall leave me alone. Then, I will cut your bindings."

THE APPLE OF HER EYE

"I solemnly swear on my honor as a god to leave you and Nessa be," he said.

She jerked her head up and down in a stiff nod. "Free her first."

Sighing, Loki snapped. A wave of power washed over her, and Astrid had to trust that he held up his end of the bargain. (Trust a trickster? The idea of it made her want to laugh.) "Your turn," he said.

Slowly, she approached and hefted her sword. Then, she ran it across the entrails binding him. Flesh split open, but only so far. She had been careful to apply the lightest touch possible for this.

Loki stared at the nicked bindings with a look of astonishment on his face. Then, it morphed into outrage. "You failed to fulfill your end of the bargain. The curse is back on."

"No, I did not," Astrid replied, unable to hide her smug smile. "You said to cut the bindings, so I cut them. You never specified that I would cut you free."

At that, Sigyn threw back her head and laughed while Loki shouted obscenities at her. Astrid gave them both an ironic bow and left the cave, ready to return to her love and put the whole sordid business behind her.

Captain of the Ship

Justin R. Hopper

The gaming board caught Hrym's eye the moment he entered the ale-house. It was edged in white gold that reflected the light of the nearby fire, on which logs and turf smouldered. He and his crew had come to Dublin for the slave market and now that they had sold all their goods – the men, women and children they had captured on their raids up and down the Scottish coast – there was time for drinking, feasting and fighting before they put back out to sea. Yet the moment Hrym saw the hnefatafl board he knew he would have to play.

Hrym Hammer-Fist was a huge man – strong of back and broad of shoulder. His crew liked to say that one of his forefathers must have bedded a giantess. Yet despite his size, Hrym was as quick in a fight as any man and his brain was as agile as his body. That was why he had survived for so long, at a time when so many other sea-wolves and outcast Viking captains had set up rival camps in the islands of the Hebrides, Orkneys and Shetlands. And for Hrym, the greatest expression of a man's speed of thought and cunning was the game of hnefatafl.

Hrym approached the gaming board and saw its owner clearly for the first time. He was a slim man with fair, shoulder-length hair and delicate, almost feminine features. In the firelight, his

CAPTAIN OF THE SHIP

eyes glittered with a hawk-like sharpness and Hrym knew he was not to be underestimated, despite the welcoming smile on his face.

"I would play hnefatafl with you, friend," said Hrym.

"Yes, and what would you play for?" the man replied.

Hrym held up a bag of recently acquired gold coins. He tossed it casually onto the table, where it landed with a clunk. "Will this be enough?" Hrym said.

"It will be a start," the owner of the board replied.

Before they began, Hrym and his opponent, who said his name was Loftur, agreed the rules of the game (for hnefatafl is a game with many variants). The board was laid out in a grid of squares and the King piece placed at the centre, surrounded by twelve defenders. Twenty-four attackers were then arranged in four formations on each side of the board. Their objective was to capture the King by hemming him in on all sides. The King won if, aided by his warriors, he could escape to a corner square. Any normal piece, apart from the King, was captured and removed from the board if caught between two of the other players' pieces.

All that remained was to decide who played King and who the attackers. Loftur gave Hrym the choice, and he opted for the latter, having always preferred to be hunter rather than prey. The game commenced and Hrym began to set up blockades, prepare ambushes and use his pieces to craftily herd the King towards them. He played confidently, having rarely been bested at hnefatafl, and some of his crew-mates drew near to watch: Thorfinn Half-Hand, his steersman; Asvald Bear-Claw, the berserker; Sigfast Long-Reach, the deadliest swordsman on his ship. All three expected Hrym to win. He had a reputation for coming out on top, which is why so many had thrown their lot in with him. Northmen. Danes. Even some renegade Saxons. They formed a mongrel crew that was feared like no other around the islands. The sight of their ship, the *Fire Drake*, meant slavery or death.

But as the game of hnefatafl progressed, it became clear that Loftur was no ordinary opponent. His King was wily, slipping and shuffling across the board, dancing through the gaps until he found the safety of the corner square.

Loftur grinned, and Hrym fought the urge to strike that handsome face – to drive his nose bone into his brain, the killing blow that had given Hrym Hammer-Fist his nickname. Instead, he reached to his belt where he found another bag of coins. He slapped it onto the table.

"Now we play again," Hrym growled.

"As you wish," replied Loftur, resetting the board.

The second game went differently. Instead of simply being content to avoid capture, Loftur played aggressively, decimating large swathes of the attacking forces while Hrym struggled to react. There were clever pincer moves and unexpected assassinations and all the time Loftur's King remained serenely on its throne until a corridor to safety opened up. Hrym felt like he'd been toyed with. Humiliated. He demanded a third game, and when that was lost too, a fourth. By this time, the ale-house had filled with Vikings from other camps, curious to see Hrym Hammer-Fist losing all his wealth to a stranger. He felt the thick press of their bodies crowding in around the table, heard their

CAPTAIN OF THE SHIP

whispers and stifled laughter. The smoke from the turf on the fire stung his eyes and he had a bitter taste in his mouth.

"Another game," he said.

"What will you stake?" said Loftur. "I have already taken all your coin."

This was true. Hrym had gambled away all the money he had made at the slave market, together with his favourite sword, Bloodgusher, its bejewelled scabbard and all.

"At my steading I have more treasures than you can imagine," Hrym said.

"They are no use to me. But I will play you one last game for something you do have here in Dublin. Your ship and crew. Lose and you must agree to undertake a quest for me. Win, and I will repay everything you have lost, thrice-over."

"What is this quest?"

"There is an island, far to the north on the Whale Road. On the island is a cave. And inside the cave is a great hoard of treasure guarded by a serpent. I wish you to take me to the island and kill the serpent. Then we will share the treasure."

Hrym stared hard at the other man. He spoke like a skald, though his voice sounded sincere.

"Who are you, Loftur of the gaming board?" he said.

"Only a merchant, who has been to many places and seen many things. Do you agree to my price Hrym Hammer-Fist?"

"You won't catch me going on any wild goose-chase," came a voice from the shadowy throng crowded around table. It belonged to Svein Smooth-Face, a recent addition to his crew. Hrym answered with his fist, driving it suddenly into Svein's guts.

The force of the blow lifted Svein off his feet. He collapsed to the floor, groaning.

"You are my wolves, and you will go where I say," bellowed Hrym.

He turned his attention back to Loftur.

"Let us play then, and if I lose, I will put my ship and crew at your service. But this time, the King may be captured by two."

He watched Loftur considering. A rule change that allowed the King to be captured by just two pieces rather than four was a major advantage for the attacking side. If Loftur agreed, Hrym felt certain he would win back his gold and more besides, before taking the man's head.

"I agree to your terms," said Loftur, nimbly arranging the pieces.

The game took place in near silence. All eyes were fixed on the board and the only sounds were the click of the pieces, the crackle of the fire and the gasps of the onlookers. The normal ale-house cacophony had been reduced to the hush of a god-house. Afterwards, the men who watched said it was the longest game of hnefatafl they had ever witnessed. This time Hrym sent more of his forces behind enemy lines, picking off the defenders to increase his numerical advantage, while always preventing the King from finding an avenue of escape. Gradually his pieces formed an unbreakable ring, that drew ever-closer towards the throne. Whenever Loftur's King attempted to move or break out, Hrym countered, denying the defenders breathing space or options. The game narrowed and Hrym's grip on it tightened. Loftur was forced to move his pieces into a defensive shell around the King. But Hrym had broken many a shield-wall, however strong. He harried and pressed. He compelled it to stagger around the board like a drunk, until the King and his remaining bodyguards were pinned against one edge. Escape seemed impossible, until...

Out of nowhere a fly began to whine in Hrym's ear. Some gnat or midge that buzzed about his face. He tried to swot it away, but his hand only found air, and the insect danced around him, ever more annoying. He made an effort to ignore it, to focus on the game and regain his concentration. He moved a piece.

Almost immediately he knew he'd made a mistake. A gap had opened up. The King dodged towards it. Hrym tried to block. The last defenders sacrificed themselves to keep the passage open. And now the King was away, fleeing through swathes of empty squares, reaching the safety of the corner square before Hrym's troops could catch him.

The giant Viking rose abruptly, like a great bear rearing up to its full height. Around him, men instinctively backed away, unwilling to be caught by the force of his fury. Hrym looked down at Loftur and saw the smaller man smile up at him, calm and unflinching. He shook his grizzled head.

"Let us hope we find something at the end of this treasure-hunt of yours," he said.

* * *

The following morning the *Fire Drake* slipped out of Dublin harbour and began charting a course for northern waters. The sea was rough, and Hrym hoped that the slender man who now travelled with them would quickly lose the contents of his stomach. But Loftur seemed unaffected by the swell and spent his time aboard amusing Hrym's crew with stories, songs and ribald jokes. He seemed oblivious to the fact that the moment this voyage was over, Hrym would leave his body for the crabs and fishes. Pride demanded it, if nothing else.

They passed the Hebrides with the weather worsening by the hour. Loftur stood below the dragon-beak prow, watching storm clouds gather in the distance. Hrym approached him from behind, resisting the urge to shove him overboard.

"Worried about the storm, friend Loftur?" Hrym said.

"The storm we will survive. You should worry more about the three dragonships in our wake."

"What?" Hrym swung about but could see no sign of another ship astern.

"That is a dangerous jest to play, Loftur."

"No jest. They have been on your trail ever since you left Dublin. I have a way of knowing such things."

It took another half a day for their pursuers to show themselves. In that time Hrym had come to think of them as phantoms, shadow-ships that haunted the mind rather than the northern seas.

Then, as they surged towards a darkening sky, with lightning flaring on the horizon, the first sail was glimpsed. It was red and soon it was joined by two more like it.

"The *Red Wolf*," said Thorfinn to his captain.

"Aye, and the *Sea Stallion* and the *Salt Bear* besides," Hrym replied.

CAPTAIN OF THE SHIP

"Who do they sail under?" asked Loftur.

"Garald Redbeard. He fancies himself the sea-king of these parts, but Hrym kneels to no man. Long has he sought out my camp in the Orkneys. Last summer we caught his brother Tostig, and put him to the blood-eagle. He has sworn to give me the same death."

Hrym knew that Garald's ships must have picked up their trail as they sailed north from Dublin, just as Loftur suggested. Perhaps he had spent too long in that ale-house playing hnefatafl, allowing word to reach the Redbeard. All his choices were now unenviable ones. Garald's longboats were as fast as his own, and if he tried to outrun them, they would be hanging on his stern all the way to his Orkney camp. Nor could he turn and fight at odds of three to one. Hrym knew his only choice was to forge onwards, into the storm, and hope that the weather gods would shift the odds in his favour.

* * *

The squall hit them like the breath of a frost giant. The sail was down now and all the men save for Hrym, Loftur and Torfinn manned the oars. The *Fire Drake* rose and fell with the sea swell and each time a burst of lightning illuminated the bruise-coloured sky, Hrym caught a glimpse of the longships off the port bow, doggedly maintaining their pursuit like a wolf pack on the scent of a stricken elk. They were gaining all the time, and by the time they were through the storm he was certain Garald Redbeard's fleet would be on him.

"Thor help us!" said Thorfinn, clutching the tiny hammer that hung around his neck, symbol of his namesake god.

"You're doomed if you think the Thunderer will aid you. He's too busy swilling mead to hear the prayers of a half-handed steersman," said Loftur. Lashed by the wind and rain, his face seemed to shine in the storm light.

"Then what would you have us do?" snapped Hrym.

"You must go through the fjord of Pictland, and head for the Swelkie if you wish to escape."

"Madness. We will be sunk for certain," bellowed Thorfinn.

To Hrym's ears, Loftur's plan sounded a wild gamble. The strait between Caithness and the Orkneys was the most dangerous passage a ship could take, and the Swelkie was the whirlpool off the northernmost point of Stroma, a maelstrom from which no boat could escape. Yet, had not the little man managed to extricate his King piece, when Hrym's own forces seemed certain to overwhelm it?

"Do as he says! Toward the Swelkie. We shall see how hungry the swallower is today," Hrym roared.

* * *

By the time they reached the Swelkie, the worst of the storm was behind them. Garald Redbeard's dragonships, however, were now no more than an arrowshot away, the steady pounding of their rowing-beat sounding over the waves.

Before them, the Swelkie churned with a fury few of them had ever witnessed.

"We cannot pass through that," said Hrym.

"We can if old Fenja allows it," Loftur replied.

He opened a cloth bag and drew out its contents. Hrym glimpsed a golden hair comb, silver thimble and necklace made from beads of amber.

"What are those?" he asked.

"Gifts for Fenja, the sea witch down below. The one who grinds the salt for the sea."

Leaning from the prow, Loftur hurled his gifts far out into the swirling foam. Almost from the moment they hit the salt spray, the broiling, heaving, wheel of water began to stop its violent gyration. The churn slowed then halted, the maelstrom becoming more like a millpond.

"See, Fenja is pleased, she stops turning her grindstone. Now go through swiftly," said Loftur.

"Lift her! Lift her! cried Hrym to his rowers. They struck hard on their oars as the *Fire Drake* shot across the Swelkie and emerged safely on the other side.

Behind them, the pursuers increased the speed of their own strokes to keep pace. The *Sea Stallion* and the *Salt Bear* were half way across the Swelkie when the whirlpool began to spin anew. It was as though a giant had suddenly begun to stir a cooking pot. Caught in the vortex, the two longships spun helplessly until they collided and smashed apart. The tearing of timber was soon replaced by the cries of terrified men as they were sucked beneath the surface of the raging whirlpool.

The *Red Wolf* quickly reversed direction, its rowers striking hard to avoid the same fate as the crew of the *Sea Stallion* and the *Salt Bear*. Hrym's men stood and jeered as it retreated further from lip of the maelstrom.

"Run, Redbeard. Run and leave these seas to their true master!" Hrym shouted across the steaming cauldron.

* * *

That night they feasted in Hrym's skáli and toasted the destruction of Garald's ships. Hrym's steading was on Eiday, the isthmus island, where they had stopped to take on the provisions for the voyage north. Inside his skáli, under the smoke-blackened rafters, Hrym showed Loftur the spoils of his raiding. There were golden crosses and reliquary boxes stolen from Christian churches; brocades and bales of rare silk snatched from merchant ships; drinking horns and arm rings plundered from his Viking enemies.

"These are fine, but nothing compared to the treasures I can lead you to," said Loftur, as he toyed with a filigree brooch.

"You are bold, Loftur. Asvald here thinks I should have already killed you and taken back my coin." As he spoke, Hrym glanced at the bear-skinned berserker who formed part of his bodyguard.

"You would never have survived the Swelkie if you had. Besides, you need me to find the cave of treasures."

"Do I? What is to stop me torturing the route out of you?"

The idea had occurred to Hrym. It would not have been the first time he'd employed torture in this hall. He had taken men's ears, eyes and noses. On one occasion he had peeled off a man's entire skin. He still had it somewhere, drying in a chest.

"It is not something that can be told or set down. Or a place you can find with a sun-shadow board. You will need my living eyes to see the movement of the waves and colour of the sea. My nose to smell the breeze and two ears to hear the sea-birds' cries. These are the things that will guide us there."

"Then that is just was well for you," said Hrym.

In truth, he had already decided to keep Loftur alive until they had reached the island and found the treasure. The passage through the Swelkie had shown Hrym that Loftur was a man with useful skills and knowledge. Only when this treasure (if it existed) was properly in his hands would Hrym give this man the death he so richly deserved.

* * *

It took them three days' sailing to reach the island with the cave of treasures. On the final day, a dense fog descended which mantled the sun and blocked out the stars at night. It was thicker than anything they had ever encountered and some of the men were afraid they might have strayed into Niflheim, the place of freezing mists. But Loftur reassured them they were still in Midgard, and guided Thorfinn Half-Hand on a course that eventually brought them to land.

They came ashore at a lonely place, where sheer cliffs rose from soot-black sand. The land was desolate, with no trees or signs of green. At Loftur's insistence they brought torches from the ship, and he led Hrym and his men to a narrow cleft in a huge black rock. They lit their torches, and followed Loftur through the cleft into a stony passageway, its walls thick with slime, that spiralled down until it opened out into a vast underground cavern. At its centre were three sharp slabs of stone that stood upright, each of them with a hole through its middle. Above the stone hung massive stalactites, cold and dripping.

Yet it was the objects heaped around the stones that drew the attention of Hrym and the others. Glittering in the gloom was a hoard beyond imagining. There were mounds of gold and silver, ornate weapons and finely wrought armour, jewelled cups and engraved serving plates. It was everything that Loftur had said it would be. Eyes widening with delight, Hrym was all for striding across the cavern when Loftur stayed him with a hand on the shoulder.

"Wait. You forget about the treasure's guardian," he said, lifting his torch to better illuminate the central stalactite that hung directly above the three upright stones.

At first, Hrym had simply taken it for a particularly bulbous cave formation. But looking harder, he saw that the knots that bulged around the main column were no mineral. They slowly shifted, and he saw they were in fact the coils of a serpent, a great worm that curled around the pillar and was now aware of their presence.

A soft slithering sounded, as it began to unwind itself and glide in their direction. Its head lifted up, large as a mule. Its eyes were golden and the fangs that sat in its gaping jaws were as long as daggers and dripping with poison.

"To take the riches, you must first kill the worm," said Loftur, with a smile.

CAPTAIN OF THE SHIP

* * *

Forty warriors had sailed with Hrym that day, and not one of them hung back when they saw the treasure that was to be gained by the death of the worm. Only Loftur remained in the entrance to the cavern, to watch Hrym and his men do battle with the scaly horror. They shot arrows into its curling neck. They thrust spears into its thick coils. They hacked and slashed with swords and battle-axes at its twisting body, which was as long as their own dragonship.

For its part, the worm fought with a serpentine speed and cunning. It rolled and lashed and battered. It crushed men or sent them flying with a flick of its gigantic tail. Some were lifted up in its jaws, where they hung, kicking and screaming, before disappearing down the monster's glistening gullet. Others perished as the black venom that dripped from its fangs fell on them, causing an agonising death.

Thorfinn Half-Hand was slain, still using his good hand to stab at the great worm's golden eyes, as its cruel mouth plucked him up and tore him in two. Sigfast Long-Reach skewered it over and over with his biting sword, until he was lifted up and smashed against the roof of the cavern. But it was Asvald Bear-Claw who did the most damage to the beast. Taking a long spear, he thrust it through the worm's neck so that its jaws were pinioned together. The stricken creature lashed wildly, mashing Asvald under a writhing coil, killing all in its frenzy until the only two living men left were Hrym and Loftur.

At last, the Viking chief saw his opportunity. As the worm swayed, bloodied and weakened, Hrym swung his battle-axe in a wide arc. Putting all of his strength into the blow, he sent the blade deep, slicing through scale and flesh, almost severing the worm's head from its neck. It toppled sideways, and as its lifeless body hit the ground, its jaws juddered open and released a slew of black venom that spattered over Hrym.

He sunk to his knees, knowing that he was dying.

The world swayed, and as it did, he saw that the coins and treasures that had been heaped around the three upright stones were no longer there. All that remained were heaps of pebbles, and three long strips of iron, torn asunder.

And in that moment Hrym knew who Loftur really was.

"You are Loki," he gasped.

"Yes," said Loki, who now seemed much bigger and brighter than before. "As you see, it is hard to kill a serpent without it killing you. This, the thunder god will one day discover."

"But…why?" said Hrym, his voice now weakened to a croak.

"Because I am finally free of my bonds. This serpent I despised, for it delighted in torturing me with its venom. An enchantment meant I couldn't kill it, that it might only be slain by the hands of men. Now you have wrought my vengeance and bound yourself to my service."

"Service?" murmured Hrym, the light going out of his eyes.

"A ship is being built for me in Hel. A mighty ship called *Naglfar,* made from the fingernails of the dead. It will need a captain, the very worst of men, and I have chosen you, Hrym. You shall be my captain. Go now, to Corpse Strand, where the

Naglfar is waiting. Your crew will join you there. On the day of the Ragnarok, we will loosen her moorings and sail together to Asgard to destroy the Gods.

These were the last words Hrym would ever hear. He fell sideways and as his body crumpled to the cavern floor, his soul fled out of it and went straight down to Hel, where even now it is waiting on the deck of the *Naglfar*, captain of the ship that will bring Loki to the final battle.

Degrees of Truth

Michelle Kaseler

The wind kicked up fast food wrappers as Emily walked past a broken window.

"Eyes on the prize," she muttered and picked up her pace.

There was only one reason to visit this section of town: designer knockoffs. Right now, that was all she could afford.

Trash cans overflowing with garbage baked in the afternoon sun, smelling just like the park where she'd played as a kid. Emily froze in the middle of the sidewalk, no longer a twenty-six-year-old with a law degree, but a tear-stained first grader.

Emily Smellily. Trailer trash.

But that girl had nowhere else to go. Grown-up Emily did.

It had been hard, leaving her mom, but going to school out of state had been the right choice – she'd gotten a glimpse of a better life.

Now it was time to repay her loans. She needed a job, a good one, and she was going to get it.

Emily continued down the street.

At the dead end, a man leaned against a vintage black Thunderbird. The license plate, framed by two metallic snakes, simply read 'LO'. Lowrider? With his greased ponytail and leather

DEGREES OF TRUTH

jacket, he looked like a bad boy from another era. He slid his sunglasses down his nose. His emerald stare could pin a moth to a wall.

"Mr. Key?" Emily asked. No one knew his real name, but he had a reputation for being the key to getting anything you wanted. "I hear you have Clouture bags."

He responded with a knock to the trunk. It popped open with a waft of leather, revealing rows of perfectly stitched purses. "Even better than the real thing. They have features you won't find in the originals."

"I just need something that looks authentic and doesn't cost five grand."

"See for yourself."

So many gorgeous colors – robin's egg blue, sea-foam green, electric flamingo – but Emily selected the practical black. It was perfect: luxurious and supple with the trademark Clouture angled bottom seams and red satin lining. She pictured herself breezing into the office, head high. "I'll take it."

"Three hundred," he said.

She sighed. "I don't have that much right now, but I have a job interview tomorrow. I need the bag to look the part."

Emily had graduated magna cum laude, but top firms hadn't been impressed by her degree from U Went Where? This next interview would be different. Several Emily Smiths had graduated the same year – including one from Yale.

"Lucky for you, I offer a financing plan." His teeth, while perfectly white and even, somehow reminded her of tombstones. "One hundred now, five at the end of the month."

❈ 237 ❈

Emily frowned. Six hundred was more than she'd planned to spend on a fake.

"Try it on for size before you decide," Mr. Key said.

She slid her arm through the straps. It melded to her side like it was made for her.

"Black is an excellent choice," he said. "Very professional."

The top grain leather was sheer heaven. Dessert for her fingertips. "Would you take fifty down?"

"Deal. But if you don't pay, we renegotiate."

"There won't be a problem." Emily handed him the cash. Her whole body felt buoyant. She would get the job, pay him back, and never step foot in this part of town again.

"Enjoy your purchase." That smile again. "It's going to change your life."

* * *

Back at her apartment, Emily put her mom on speaker while she transferred everything from her worn purse to the new bag.

"The firm sounds amazing," Emily's mom said. "I've been telling the bingo gals you'll be working with celebrities. Are you nervous about the big interview?"

"Just a little," Emily fibbed.

She wanted the job for her mom as much as herself.

When she was a kid, they'd lie outside on a blanket and gaze at the night sky.

"Always remember," her mom would say, "we see the same stars as the rich folks across town, so don't be afraid to reach for them."

DEGREES OF TRUTH

When Emily had struggled with algebra, her mom picked up extra shifts to pay for a tutor, and no matter how exhausted she was, she was never too tired to proofread Emily's papers.

"I wish I could give you more, sweetheart, but one day, you'll get it for yourself."

Emily was the first person in her family to earn a degree, much less go to law school, but so far, the only thing it had gotten her was a mountain of debt.

She reached for some Pepto.

"You're going to do great," her mom said. "And ring me the second you meet Brad Pitt."

"You'd be my first call, but I don't think they represent anyone *that* famous. Would you settle for one of the guys from Game of Thrones?"

"Only if it's one of the cute ones."

"Sorry, Mom." Emily laughed. "Besides, I don't have the job yet."

"Well, I hope Caden takes you out for a nice dinner either way."

While Emily missed living close to her mom, at least the distance made it easy to fake a boyfriend. Her mother meant well, but years of dateless nights followed by pep talks (You're a knockout! Any man would be lucky to have you!) made her feel pathetic. Telling the worst kid on the team they're amazing starts to ring hollow if they keep striking out.

"He already sent me flowers and made reservations at a new sushi place."

"You've got a keeper, hon," Mom said. "When do I get to meet him? I'd love to have you for Christmas."

"I'll see what he has planned."

After they said goodbye, Emily opened her calendar app and scheduled a break-up with "Caden" one month from today. She could say they disagreed about having kids.

Emily sank into the couch and pulled the rainbow afghan to her chin. While all of her furniture was Ikea or second-hand, it still had a modern aesthetic. The crocheted blanket didn't go at all, but her mother had made it, and it was one of the few things from her childhood that brought her comfort.

Ding-dong.

Emily frowned as she walked to the door. She wasn't expecting anyone.

On the other side was a bouquet so large she couldn't see who was holding the vase. It had all of her favorites, from purple dahlias and forget-me-nots to white and lavender roses.

Arrangements like that weren't cheap. Who could have sent it?

"Emily Smith?" The delivery man peeked around the lush blossoms.

"That's me."

She took them inside and opened the card.

Best of luck tomorrow.

Love, Caden.

* * *

Between interview nerves and the mysterious flowers, Emily barely slept. Thank goodness for Visine, concealer, and espresso

DEGREES OF TRUTH

– although the latter only amplified her jitters. The elevator rose, but her stomach remained on the ground floor.

Ping. Emily was greeted by the aroma of premium coffee and essential oils. The view from the floor-to-ceiling windows stretched for miles. She was in the heart of downtown. On top of the world.

Panic ballooned in her chest, pushed against her ribs. She wore mass-market shoes. Her designer blouse came from a thrift store.

Emily clutched her new bag like a security blanket and took a deep breath. She hadn't come this far to quit.

Emily approached the receptionist. "I have an interview with Alicia Summers."

"I'll let her know you're here."

Moments later, a thirty-something woman in a Diane von Furstenberg dress entered the lobby and said, "Emily Smith?"

Emily rose. "Alicia?"

"I'm her assistant."

Did she just roll her eyes? Emily's face grew hot. This interview was off to a fine start. "Sorry. I saw her picture on the website and you…"

"She says I look like the daughter she was too busy to have." The assistant smiled. "She really needs to update that photo. It was taken when I was in middle school."

She led Emily to Alicia's office. "Your ten o'clock is here."

As Emily entered, Alicia, the firm's founder, looked up from her cherry wood desk.

"I was just reviewing your resume," Alicia said. "Very impressive."

"Thanks." Emily took a seat.

241

"One of the partners, Charles Clark, attended Yale at the same time you did. He's going to try to duck in. He didn't know you personally, but said he recognized the name."

"I wish I could say the same." Emily smiled while her stomach writhed. "I had my nose buried in a book most of the time, so I didn't make many friends."

"That's what he remembered. Quiet, academic type." Sunlight bounced off Alicia's salon-perfect highlights. "Office rapport is important. We're a tight-knit firm, like a second family. Of course, that's partly because we spend so much time working."

Emily's laughter sounded tinny and nervous to her ears.

"Love the bag, by the way," Alicia said. "I'm planning to pick one up after I win my next case."

"It was my graduation gift to myself." *Breathe*. She was fitting in just fine, and if this Charles person didn't recognize her, she'd say she'd changed a lot since she was an undergrad. If he really pushed, she would sheepishly say she'd had some work done. That should make anyone back off.

Should. Such a flimsy word.

A film of sweat coated Emily's palms.

"So, tell me why you chose to study law," Alicia asked.

"My mom is a lawyer and my role model. She works in Manhattan, and while some girls fantasized about prom dresses and wedding gowns, all I wanted was a closet full of power suits."

Alicia beamed. "I'm the daughter of a successful career woman myself."

Emily smiled back. She had researched Alicia before the interview and carefully crafted that answer.

"The downside of growing up with a brilliant mother was I couldn't get away with anything."

Alicia laughed. "I feel that."

"Eventually, even New York became a little small for the two of us, so here I am."

A man peeked into the room. His face was nondescript, a map without landmarks. "Hey, am I interrupting anything?"

"No, Charles," Alicia said. "Come on in."

Emily swallowed hard. Moment of truth. Time slowed as he approached like a manatee in Hugo Boss.

Charles extended his hand. "I'd recognize you anywhere, Emily."

The crinkles around his eyes told her his smile was sincere.

"I'm sorry. I don't quite remember you." She wiped her palm on her skirt before shaking his hand.

"People say I have a forgettable face, but I don't mind." He grinned. "It helps them underestimate me in the courtroom."

"I'll be sure not to make that mistake." Her smile was also genuine. She was in the clear.

The rest of the interview went very well. Alicia closed by saying she had one more applicant to talk to, but she had a great feeling about her.

* * *

The smell of "Caden's" bouquet wafted down the hall of Emily's apartment complex. It must have come from Amber. She knew about Emily's fake boyfriend, and she loved a good gag. Emily would thank her friend after she talked to her mom.

Emily went inside, grabbed a sparkling water, and collapsed on the sofa.

Mom's number wasn't showing up in her contacts, but Emily knew it by heart and dialed it manually.

"Hello?" A strange-sounding man answered the phone.

"Uh, hi," Emily said. "I'm looking for Ann Smith."

"Sorry, wrong number."

Emily double-checked the call log. Yep, it was right down to the last digit. Her outdated phone must be glitching.

Buzz. A text from Caden.

How was the interview? Can't wait to see you tonight!

A chill ran down her spine. Texting from a fake number crossed the line from funny and sweet to creepy and weird. Not Amber's style.

Who is this? She wrote back.

In the mood for role play? I like it.

"I don't need this right now." Emily's voice rose.

She texted Amber directly. *Clever joke, and I love the flowers, but stop already.*

Flowers??? Amber replied.

What was going on? Amber wouldn't lie. If anything, she'd want credit for the idea. Emily reached for her afghan, but it wasn't there. It wasn't in her bedroom either.

I'm losing it. I need Mom. I'll message her.

But she couldn't find her mother in Messenger, either.

Emily opened her laptop to check Facebook, but the profile didn't exist. What the hell was going on?

She scoured the website of her hometown paper for news of an accident or fire or an alien invasion, but couldn't find a damn thing.

If only she had the number of one of the bingo ladies.

Hands shaking, she switched to Google and typed Ann Smith.

Dozens of results, but nothing about her mom. That wasn't surprising, though – she wasn't exactly a headline-maker. Emily kept scrolling because she didn't know what else to do.

Ann Smith knows LA real estate

Ann Smith, MD. Internal Medicine

She stopped mid-scroll.

Lawyer Ann Smith perishes in World Trade Center attack, leaving daughter Emily behind.

It had to be a coincidence, but something compelled her to click.

A photo of her mother stared back at her from the computer screen.

No. It couldn't be. Her mom was a cashier. She'd never been to New York. She was *alive*.

A bolt of pain split her down the middle. Emily cried out.

Across the room, light winked off the metal accents on the fake Clouture bag.

* * *

Mr. Key, dressed in a royal blue tracksuit, waited next to his Thunderbird. His hair flowed wild and loose. Had it always been red?

"I'm returning this." Emily held up the bag. "You can keep the fifty bucks as a rental fee, but get it far away from me."

"Oh, child, child," he said, his voice both soothing and sinister. "That's not how it works."

"Then how does it work? I want my life back."

"But you weren't happy with your life. I changed that, and now you complain to me?" He lifted his hand like a traffic cop. "Even so, I stake my reputation on exemplary customer service. Five thousand dollars by the end of the month, and everything goes back."

"That's ridiculous!"

"Call it a restocking fee." He shrugged. "You should be able to swing it with your fifteen-K signing bonus."

Emily gulped. How did he know that number? "But I haven't been offered—"

Emily's phone vibrated. An email from the firm.

Offer of employment from the office of Summers, Klein, and Bancroft.

Twenty-four hours ago, it would have made her day, her year, but she didn't feel a thing.

"You're welcome," Mr. Key said.

"You'll get your five thousand," Emily said through gritted teeth.

"Why the venom? There will be enough left to buy a real Clouture."

She wanted to pummel his smug face, rip through his chest and pull out his heart – if he had one – but that wouldn't bring her mom back. He had all the power. Her arms hung limp at her sides. "Was it all about the money?"

"It doesn't hurt." He held his diamond pinky ring up to the sun. "But mostly, I like to have fun, and people rarely disappoint."

"You call this *fun?*"

"Like watching rats in a maze."

"You're sick. Sick, sick, sick."

"Low key, sick, maybe."

"There's nothing low key—"

LO.

Key.

"Loki," she whispered.

Loki Meets His Match

Mark Patrick Lynch

It happened that Loki, the Trickster God of the Aesir, woke in his rooms in the palace citadel of Odin the All-Seer, and was bored.

This was an unknown condition for him and a vexation. He looked at his hands, tracing the lines on his palms as if they might hold an explanation. But for all the study he put to the job, it didn't show him why he felt as he did. He sighed. The excitement with which he usually greeted the day was nowhere in evidence. His blood did not fizz, his eyes lacked fire, and his body refused to spring to life.

When he searched his feelings, thinking he had simply mislaid his brilliance and all he need do was retrieve it, he felt oddly glum. But for what reason? Had a prank gone wrong and left him with nothing to show for his lies and inventions? His memory was no use there. He couldn't think of any game he'd set in play that had collapsed in ruin; worse than that, he had the hollow notion that no one was newly annoyed with him today.

How strange.

And this new morn? What were his plans for wreaking havoc with it? He searched for a riddle or puzzle, a joke he'd put aside

LOKI MEETS HIS MATCH

to fish out and play on someone, and found himself lacking on all counts. His purse of wrongdoings was empty.

"By the All-Father himself," he muttered. "What is this that I should not be sparking with merriment, ready to dish out a jape or some foul trickery to bewilder the nine worlds?"

He put his hand to his chest, searching for the beat of his heart. It was the only proof he had that he was alive, given how dull and unappealing the rest of him appeared. Even his hair fell lank and greasy around his deceiver's face. There *were* thuds beneath his palm, though they were dry and weary. He was struck, then, as if with a malady. A sneeze, sudden and without warning, confirmed this.

"Woe be to this condition," Loki said, for he had never been brought low by a cold or some sniffle of the nose. The flu was as unknown to him as was contrition. He turned to whomever he had bamboozled into his bed for the night, thinking to tell her so as well. To his belief, a complaint shared was a burden relinquished. "You know, it really will not do," he told her.

And was answered by silence.

His eyes may well be lacking their usual fire, but they still had light enough in them to see. They told him something he didn't want to know.

He lay alone under the deerskin blanket.

The side of his bed, usually rich with a fuming partner threatening retribution (this would be after his trickery had led her to sharing her body with him), was bare.

"Now this I do not believe." He scratched the crown of his head in consternation, the skin itching and flaking. Perhaps he had misremembered, and his plaything had already fled his chambers. "She is gone, stormed out earlier," he reassured himself. "That is the explanation."

But when he put his palm to the empty space beside him, he found the bedding as cold as a lake in the land of the Frost Giants'. As if – and perish this thought for what it might mean to him – as if it had been unoccupied all night.

"That cannot be."

It was not just unheard of, it was anathema to his very being.

"Something," the half-God whispered, "is wrong."

* * *

Loki crawled out of his forlorn bed and dressed in a sludgy, sorrowful way, as if every bone in his body was made of lead and his arms and legs weighted with rocks. He did not know why. He was a muddy thing of a being, a star without brilliance, a God without tribute. How feeble he was, how he felt old and done with. He creaked as he moved, and his face, when he caught its reflection, was pitted with the sorrows of age. Ugh. By the All-Seer.

Why not remain in his pit until he felt better; that was a fair question, was it not?

"Because someone has done this to me," he answered himself. "This is no natural ailment."

The fire had burned away overnight, leaving ashes behind, with not a stray ember to kindle to life and warm him. He huddled before the empty grate, shivering and wondering at the wounds inflicted upon him and who might have downed him in such a way.

"It must be someone of wit and cunning," he reasoned. Which meant he could dismiss most of the Aesir. "So who is it?"

With his body dull, and a tattered mist greying his thinking, he would need help in finding the culprit. So he pulled on his thickest jerkin, the one with the fur lining and the ragged-stitches across its length, and stepped inside his deepest boots before throwing a hooded cloak across his shoulders. This done, and judging himself as ready for the worlds as he could be, he pulled back the twin doors in the archway to his room – this was an act that required far more of him than it usually did – and went in search of help.

* * *

The citadel of Odin the All-Seer is the largest and most impressive in all of Asgard. Within its walls there are castles and palaces and bathhouses and gardens, there are theatres and statuary, and courts upon which games of sport can be played. Trees grow hither and yon all about it, and they are the trees grown from the seeds of the life-tree Yggdrasil. Thus do they grow quickly and with more leaves than many a forest can claim. The resin from their trunks can be taken as a drink and gift those brave enough to sup of it dreams of eternity or nightmares of the underworld. In summer the trees are in full bloom and bring a heady fragrance to the citadel and green shade to soften the quick rays of the sun. But come the autumn, as it stands now, when their leaves burn russet and then shed, they show cruel skeletons to the world, are themselves undone and naked.

And it is a skeleton I feel like now, the glum God of Tricks thought as he huddled in his cloak and was troubled by every breeze and turn of the wind as if he were but a mortal Norseman and a hundred years old at that.

The flaking trees did nothing to improve his mood, nor distract him from a twinge of pain in his elbows and knees as he shuffled forth. This business of walking, of swinging his arms as he went, of simply *being* had never been so terrible. How he yearned for normalcy, when he could leap and bounce and dazzle upon the earth and laughter was as quick to him as breathing.

The effects of the trick being played upon him were worsening, and he came to his half-brother's hall a thing part-crooked and hunched. He tapped on the door with knuckles so bony and sharp they sliced his skin and bled.

"Thor," he said in a voice gone feeble at his lack of resources. "Open up, it is your brother, come to seek your favour."

From behind the grim doors, doors that were made of wood blasted to a charred solidity by lightning bolts, his brother answered him. His voice, always loud, carried easily through the thickness of the wood.

"You, Loki, come to me for help? You jest. You are not coming in."

Loki had to raise his own voice, painful as this act was, to be heard. "Not this day. There is no joking to me this hour, I promise you. Let me in."

252

LOKI MEETS HIS MATCH

"And why should I do that, when not four nights have passed since you shaved the beard from one half of my face while I slept, leaving me to wake in the morning and be laughed at and mocked by all because I didn't notice?"

"No injury was done to you, brother. And you brought much joy to the maid-servants who tended you."

Thor seemed to think on this. "I suppose I did. But it was no thanks to you."

"It was *all* thanks to me. Had the blade in my hand not done its work, you would not have thought to dress your beard in such a manner, and no one would have smiled, no one would have laughed."

Thor said, as if it had just struck him, "You sound tired, Loki."

"I am. And shouting to be heard through this door doesn't make things better."

"Mm. But to the matter of my beard…"

"Must we?"

"It is important."

Loki didn't think it was, not at all.

"Were the maids and servants not laughing at me?" Thor asked. "Were their eyes not filled with mirth, when looking upon a God of the Norse?"

"They were laughing *with* you, even if you are slow to see the jest and only now understand it."

Thor's silence suggested that he was pondering this. Some time passed, for Thor was not the sharpest of Gods, which was probably why his weapon of choice was big and dumb and blunt.

253

"Protector of Asgard," Loki said hoarsely. "Am I not one of the Aesir, albeit by upbringing rather than birth? Am I not worthy of your protection when a wrong has been done to me?"

"It's doubtful," said Thor.

"Not even now, when I am stricken and brought low by an assault?"

"You only say you are."

"Then open the gates, see what has become of your brother."

Another passage of silence, which Loki hadn't the strength to break. Thor did his thinking much as a boulder grows moss, and came to his conclusion.

"It's a trick, isn't it? You are in some disguise, pleading illness or a poisoning. And when I let you in you will leave behind a vessel that you have hexed me blind and dumb to, and it will stink of flatulence or some such and fill my halls with its stink, and all will come away from my rooms saying that I, Thor, Lord of Thunder, cannot contain the belches from my arse. This door remains closed, at least until my beard has grown back and people do not laugh at me. And to you, it remains bolted forever more. Or until I forgive you. Whichever comes first. Good day to you, and pleasant trickery elsewhere."

Loki hung his head, defeated by his own reputation.

* * *

He tried Freyja next. Freyja whose beauty was beyond question and known throughout the worlds. It was as hungered after in Alfheim where the elves of light live as it was in Midgard where the men and women of the Norse live. And it was hungered after by the lovelorn, the romantics, and the dreamers. Many a heart was said to have shattered for contemplation of Freyja's fine looks and many were the lovers that had been spoiled at a glance of her.

But Loki was a God, and a Trickster God at that, and thus immune to such weaknesses. He would not flatter her heart by swooning before her, or widen his pupils just to make memory of her profile.

He somehow combusted his frail, stick-like bones and parchment flesh from Thor's lodgings to Freyja's own, threatening to fall and come apart as he crossed once more the All-Father's great citadel. He fouled his mind when he thought about why he'd pulled on his stoutest boots (he'd done it to save himself from the cold) instead of his winged heels that morning. And so, because he could not fly, he was left with no choice but to shuffle and sway in an uncoordinated lurch. People skirted him, thinking him a curse or a pox made flesh, however cloaked and hooded and humbled he might be. Some made spirit signs at him, or spat an entreaty to the All-Father for protection. Loki must look like sin woven into flesh.

But somehow he survived the trip, slow of heart though he might be, with blood so sluggish his veins might be clogged with whale blubber. Breathing heavily and with a pronounced rasp, he arrived at the palace Odin had bequeathed to the fairest of all the Gods.

Freyja's gates were open, and the only trouble Loki had in gaining access to her was through his own infirmity. He stumbled midway up the flight of stairs to her rooms, which floated above the lower floors so that they were nearer the sky through which she had loved to fly in her cloak of wings...until of course he had spoiled that pleasure for her.

"Loki," she said, upon spying him there, a crawling thing slowly edging up her stairs like damp spoiling a wall. "I had been informed a plague was seeking me, and I see it is true."

The Trickster looked up, paining further his dry flaky eyes, and from her expression surmised he must look like a seal that had been eaten by a bear and shat out afterwards.

"Such a disgusting thing you are," she said.

"Freyja," Loki managed, for she might have greeted him in such a manner any day of the year. "I have come for your help."

"In climbing the stairs?" Freyja asked. She sounded as if he had tried to persuade her that a stick with a stone on the end was Mjollner, mighty hammer of Thor himself. (To be fair, he had once attempted this, and nearly succeeded in the act.) She said, haughtiness in her every word: "Do you really think me so feeble of mind that I don't know what you are doing?"

"Sister..."

"I am no sister of yours, half-thing."

"Let me at least plead my case."

"Stand up, if you mean to do so. But I tell you now, I would sooner drop off the edge of the world than fall for anything you say."

Loki wanted to weep. And not with tears of laughter. This was a new thing for him, to be overcome with sadness. Even as a child, when his Frost Giant father spurned him and abandoned him to be reared by Odin as both brother and son, he had not shed tears. Some of the more contemplative Aesir had opined that this might be the reason for his tricks and deceptions; Loki, they had come to think, needed chaos, so he'd never be caught in a moment of calm that demanded he look into himself and contemplate his life, for then he might see who he was and just why he was as he was. That would be too much for the orphan, they decided, and might break him beyond repair.

When the tears came his weeping was a shock, wracking the body that he had transformed into a thousand fake images over the years in his pursuit of merriment and trouble.

"Do not think," Freyja said, "that I am fooled by some dollops of ice you have pressed to your eyes to melt there and feign tears. How easy it is to see through your mummery."

Loki lifted a feeble hand, dismayed to learn that it was now as withered as a chicken's scaly claw.

"Freyja, I have been wronged, and wronged grievously, and I cannot fathom who did this to me."

"You? Wronged? Tricked, do you mean? And who would have the nerve to attempt such a thing? Who would find the wit to come up with some bedevilment that you had not already conjured and dropped on some unsuspecting soul? No, half-thing, I will not be fooled into believing this impossibility."

So saying, she turned to leave him, only to be stayed by a memory. She looked down on him again. "My cloak has yet to dry and the sky is still denied me. Be gone with you."

* * *

Loki crawled down stairs made slick with his tears. Were he his usual self and these the tears of someone upon whom he had flourished a trick, he would have been delighted and thought to ride them like the rapids on the wild river that coursed through the mists of Nifleheim. As it was, they were his tears, and there were so many of them he feared he might drown the whole of Asgard.

But somehow, for some reason – perhaps he had used all the water in his body (and those born even of only half of the Frost have so much water in them) – the tears came to their end. He fortified himself.

"I will not be defeated," he said. "I will triumph over whatever adversary has chosen to blight me."

Those were just words, however. They might hold conviction, but they could not bear him aloft. For that he needed the help of a wizened length of wood fallen from a nearby tree. Hobbling with the aid of the stick, he sought help elsewhere, passing the smithy, the stables, the kitchens and their aromatic airs, and dismissing all as places of refuge and aid.

He did not know where he was going, but when his feet could shuffle him along no more and he thought his strength gone, he looked up, seeing he had brought himself to the branch and leaf home of Ullr, the Hunter God and stepson of Thor, who lived wild in the citadel's forest garden.

"It has come to this," he told himself sadly, and wondered if he could be brought any lower.

Ullr pulled back the tattered cloth that hung at the entrance and greeted Loki with all the enthusiasm of someone finding mould on a slab of cheese.

"Oh, not today. Whatever it is you want."

"Brother, do not close your, uh, door. It is your good friend Loki standing before you."

The Hunter God put a finger to his chin, unconvinced. "It doesn't look like Loki to me. He can change his shape, call forth deceptions for the eyes. He can be a tree, a dog, a woman, a man with hair and a man without hair. Big noses, small noses, ears or no ears. He can do all of that. I'll grant you it's so. But even then, no, you don't look like him."

"This is…" Loki's patience, like the hair he usually wore so luxuriously long and thick, was thinning. "This is unbelievable."

"Aye, and so are most of Loki's tales. When you think back on them. But when he tells them to your face, no, they're all to be believed. Which is why I know you are not Loki. If he had come to trick me, I wouldn't know it. He's sly like that. You, though, you can't be him because I know you are lying and here to fool me."

"Can you not see that I am wearing Loki's best jerkin, his finest cloak?"

"Aye, and I am holding my bow, and if I were to nock an arrow to its string and pull it back and point it at you, you'd know not to steal from me. And here's some more advice. I'd make sure you give those clothes back to Loki. He won't like it that you've stolen them. I tell you, for all he's a pain, no one of sound mind would do such a thing for fear of what he'd visit upon them in return."

Loki's head, barely raised as it was, sagged further. "I am surrounded by fools," he said.

"Now that sounds like something he'd say. But even if you were him, I wouldn't help you. Whatever he'd have coming to him, he was due it. Take your poor trick elsewhere and show it to someone who'll believe it."

* * *

Angry at being turned away by Thor and Freyja and Thor's hayseed stepson, Loki fumbled through the forest garden and rested against the bare bones of a tree losing the last of its leaves. There in its web of shadows he put what little remained of his mind to his predicament.

The problem was this: If the only Gods who would help him were the ones upon whom he hadn't played a trick, he was in short measure of friends. In his time he had brought a plague of spiders to his brother Thor, had hidden Nanna's jewellery in the innards of her favourite wolf, and had stolen Freyja's flying cloak and left it hanging from a cloud out of reach (until it rained, and the cloak fell sodden to earth and was no good for the air and wouldn't be for a good many weeks still to pass). He had painted the mirrors in Baldur's home so that he thought there was only a black space where he stood, and tied a knot so thoroughly complicated in Sif's hair after he had stolen it that even the elves who laboured at making complex magics could not disentangle its ribbons. And it had been many years ago that he had lost the trust of the All-Father himself and had sworn to stay out of his way for fear of punishment.

"I am alone, weakened, and pitted against the finest trickster of them all," Loki told the fallen leaves around him. "To be brought so low is a humiliation and I shall not live it down if I cannot pry myself free of this one's game and best him in return. What say you, leaves – is there a riddle to all of this we can unpick, just you and I? Is there a way of returning the favour of a prank, and tenfold, so I'll not be challenged again?"

The leaves, as was their way, said nothing to him. Perhaps in the flush of summer they might have spoken, for in summer the trees whisper to one another and know many things, and the wise can hear wonder in their musings. But this was autumn, when all across the worlds things fell, including, it seemed, the Trickster God of the Aesir.

* * *

As the sun began to sink, and with it Loki's hope of releasing himself from the trick ensnaring him, he set his mind back on his day. He did it with the intent of cursing all who had turned him away, even if he could not bring some pestilence to their lives. Shy of mischief he may be, but he could wish it upon them.

"Thor," he said. "Biggest and strongest of the Gods, who believes I do nought but play tricks. Freyja, pretty of face but ugly of heart, who contends that no one would play a trick on me. Ullr, as dumb as his stepfather, who says he sees through my truthful body and calls it a lie. May the sky come down upon you all and…"

Here the thin rasp of his voice fell silent.

Here the Trickster God of the Aesir lifted his eyes to the heavens.

Here Loki, the Marvel of Mischief, began to laugh.

"Oh, you devil," he said through his laughter. "Oh you slyest of all sly things! Of course! Of course! My fool brothers and sister are right. They knew without knowing. And through them I have my answer. Who but a trickster could fool a trickster? And who but the best trickster the nine worlds have ever known could fool Loki, the Lord of All Tricks? I have done this to myself! Of course I have! Now, to be free of this trick…"

He stretched and shuffled, and in doing shucked off the failing, broken Loki, the hunched and aged thing of brittle autumn leaves and scabrous bark for skin. The new Loki wriggled free of his stricken twin and stood, transformed into his old brightly cunning and mischievous self.

"Devil, you are," he told himself approvingly. "Devil."

For he had tricked himself! Loki had drawn a veil of forgetfulness across his own face and fooled himself for a full day that he was glum and withering!

He leapt up and twisted around, seeing the discarded husk that had been the put-upon, dreadfully wronged and painfully tricked Loki. What an old man he had turned himself into. A wrinkled face, strands of once-thick hair, skin used up and spotted with age. Its body sat there, sagging and soiled and soon to flake to nothing, like the brittle leaves of the season.

"Oh, what a tale this is," Loki declared. "With the worlds so easy to trick, I wanted a bigger challenge. And who would be the hardest of all souls to flummox but myself? And yet I did it. My brilliance is shown in all its glory!"

He shouted this to the worlds, so that all might know it.

"Loki is back and ready to play!"

LOKI MEETS HIS MATCH

And when he was sure they had all of them heard, he fell quiet and his mind went to hatching plans and stringing together deviancies and drawing up articles of distrust.

"Now," he wondered, "just how do I get revenge upon myself for this trick that has been played upon me?"

He pondered this long and hard before coming to a satisfying answer.

But that is a matter for another day. There are many tales of Loki, the Trickster God of the Aesir, and this has been but one of them.

A Knot for the Hawk

Nico Martinez Nocito

"Beware, my friends – the trickster is awake again!"

I sat up, rubbing my head. A pounding headache had intruded upon my consciousness, an unfortunate byproduct of my capacious enjoyment of Odin's best wine, and so it took me a moment to sense the binding.

That moment was more than enough time for Sif's maniacal laughter to swell to a ferocious pitch.

"Little brother, I regret to inform you that your games must be – ah – abandoned, for the time being."

Little brother was what she always called me, though I was neither her junior nor her brother, nor even certain that a word of that persuasion could ever apply to me. Either way, that irritation was quickly replaced with an understanding of what she'd bound.

Most forms of binding might as well not even apply to gods. We are, after all, fixed in certain ways simply due to our nature. The greatest of these bindings is that we cannot change.

Oh, certainly, some of us can shift from form to form, but there is a world's difference between turning from a wolf into an eagle and learning kindness, or empathy, or honesty. We are set in our ways, gods. The only bindings that should bother us are the ones that hold us stationary, and those are mostly irksome because as you are held in stasis, you know that someone else, some enemy, holds more power than you do.

Accordingly, this binding should only be a minor irritation.

Such a laugh, such a lark. A party trick to irk wily, irreverent Loki, to irritate him the way he always irritated everyone else. Get him drunk and wait until he was sleeping and then bind him to his current form so that he couldn't keep spying as a hawk or a fly, couldn't play his usual tricks, couldn't, couldn't, *couldn't*.

The problem with godly jokes, the ironic reason that perhaps made me such a trickster to begin with, is that they are very difficult to undo.

And why, after all, did I even care so much to try? To try is to make it obvious that the prank accomplished its goal – to irk me. And I'd always preferred not to admit defeat.

After all, I knew full well that this was Sif's revenge. I had already replaced the lengthy, gorgeous locks I'd stolen from her with a golden headdress, and delivered my most polished disingenuous apology to her pouting face. I'd thought that, by accompanying my delivery with new weapons for Odin and Thor, I would have bought enough grudging appreciation that the other gods would outwit any revenge before she got too far.

Obviously, I'd miscalculated.

"Do you miss it yet, Loki?" She beamed down at me, offering a slender hand to help me to my feet, as if this entire situation wasn't her doing. "If I were you, I wouldn't stick around to see what I do next. But no – you can't just fly off anymore, can you? What a shame. Your wings have been…ah…*clipped*, it seems."

I rose, without Sif's help, and dusted off my clothes with what little disinterested charm I could muster. "What a genius, Sif. I expect you were jealous of my hair?"

Her face colored, and I enjoyed the twisted struggle in her face: attack me again, or preserve her rather cleaner reputation.

Disappointingly, she chose the latter.

"Don't worry, little brother, I have none of your ruthlessness." She patted me on the head. I swatted her hand away. "The binding will lift on the final day of Yule – a festive gift for you, Loki. In the meantime—" She turned to face the room at large, and I remembered, the headache worsening, that I'd had the good sense to get drunk at a gathering featuring half of Asgard. The approval in Odin's gaze smarted more than the heavy binding knot in my chest. "My friends, I welcome to you half a year where you will be able to enjoy all the beauty of Asgard free of the tricks and the unexpected!"

The cheer her words trigger was, frankly, offensive.

Then again, the gods only liked my trickery when they benefitted.

* * *

For a god, six months' wait is almost laughable, a period so brief that it spoke more to Sif's incompetence and inability to bind my shapeshifting for any longer than fully functional revenge. I left the hall with an easy, mocking swagger and finger combing my admittedly scraggly beard in my best impression of a human male, my mind already spinning with ways to get my revenge on Sif without needing to transform into anything.

I wasn't expecting the nightmares.

They arrived that night with a flamboyant entrance I might've applauded under different circumstances, theatrically surging into a pleasant nighttime recollection with a fierce energy that, in another life, I might've found commendable. I was chased, or in battle, or simply inconvenienced, a door that I wished to get through barricaded from the other side. Usually, I found these adventurous dreams delightful as I outwitted wily creatures and defeated my enemies; in my sleep, such escapades always went rather more smoothly than they did in reality.

But tonight?

Tonight, I was trapped.

No wings waited for me when I leapt off a balcony to make my escape, and no matter how hard I tried, I couldn't squeeze myself into fly-form to sneak beneath the heavy door. I found myself plummeting through empty air, drowning underneath the weight of the ocean, helpless, stuck stubbornly in a single form.

And yet among all those nightmares the worst moment of all was when I glanced into a mirror and saw that man's face staring back at me.

When I finally rose in the morning, my hands were clammy and my mind spun. I chalked my disorientation and poor sleep up to last night's inebriation. *Childish*, I told myself, and *ridiculous*, like self-deprecation would humiliate my discomfort into evaporating, but this peculiar irritation was nowhere near as easy to dispose of as Sif's golden hair.

* * *

Weeks dragged by. A month passed.

On some days, I woke with blithe content and my usual mind for mischief. To present an unbothered façade at my inability to shapeshift, if only to irk Sif, was an almost laughably easy choice to make. If I was to be stuck in one form until Yule, I reasoned on those mornings, at least I wasn't confined to the body of a flea. I made trouble. I tricked Sif into believing I'd stolen her hair again. I drove Odin to nearly throw me out of Asgard.

Other mornings, I awoke with my entire body feeling itchy. I glimpsed my face in a mirror and felt as though I'd been speared through by shock to find anything other than a woman's face staring back at me. I was used to shapeshifting in my sleep, to always waking up in a body that felt right to me on that particular day. I'd thought that variability was far more to entertain myself than out of a genuine need.

Perhaps, I considered, I would be far less irked if the form I'd been locked into was somewhat more desirable. Being perceived as a human male objectively did not have tremendous appeal. But then, I had always chosen this form with moderate frequency, if only because it made the other gods less confused than when I materialized with a willowy frame and long, golden hair that I favored twisting between my fingers.

How could it be that I could be so content with my body one day, and then wanted so desperately to have the appearance of a woman?

Surely, I decided, the root of my discomfort was that even simply shapeshifting made me feel different from the other gods, permanently fixed in their consistency. My character or desires were not truly variable; they couldn't be – I was a god. Surely, I was simply inventing my discomfort because I was used to shapeshifting so regularly.

Not even my best act, though, could hide how much I hated this particular binding from Sif.

Her laughing gaze skipped over my face at every possible opportunity, and she twisted her now-restored hair into careful knots every time I passed, a cheering reminder of the fact that she'd successfully engineered a binding over me. I forced myself to deliver stubbornly suave responses to her various jibes, because the only thing more humiliating than my current condition would be admitting it to the person responsible.

Unraveling the source of my discomfort, alas, would require facing a problem head-on, which was something I'd spent several thousand years perfecting the art of *not* doing.

So I set myself to resolving the problem while entirely avoiding its root cause: breaking the binding myself.

* * *

If the world was a rope, each of us was a knot along its expanse, two or three smaller threads tethered together to create the human, or the monster, or the god. Like any good knot, most of our places there were immovable, the individual threads properly secured to avoid the kind of sliding and chaos that made ships lose their sails, and treaties their promises.

And so naturally, to move outside of that stubborn predestination – or break a binding a jealous relative had placed upon you – one had to be a master with knots.

I twisted a thin strand of grass into a tight square knot and pulled it tight; the blade broke abruptly, leaving green stains across my fingers. Last night, fed up with the monotony and irritation, I'd spontaneously declared my intention to leave Asgard for a few months, something that usually would have terrified Odin, but that, thanks to the Aesir's firm belief that I was in no shape to cause significant mischief, he had granted without question. Even Sif had only delivered a patronizing pat to the head, clearly none the wiser that I was leaving specifically so she wouldn't notice when I started to fray the knot of the binding she'd created.

Being in the lowlands was torturous without the ability to shapeshift. I'd always liked this part of the world, where the cold ebbed if only a little, and the people still had its harshness in their bones, but I was used to traversing it on a hawk's wide, powerful wings. I felt like a fraud of a god walking the shepherd's paths on two tired feet.

Then again, I'd never tried to break a binding before, and if there was anyone who could teach me enough about knots to manage it, it was the fishermen of this coast. Perhaps, while I was at it, their constant ephemerality would also remind me just how consistent and godly I was.

They changed. I didn't. This was how the world worked.

The village was quiet when I arrived. The sun had only recently crested over the horizon, but the cluster of huts might as well be completely uninhabited, the only sound coming from them the thin hiss of smoke rising from multitiered chimneys. I entered, feeling extraordinarily conspicuous.

After all, even when appearing as a human, I was not in the business of making myself particularly ill-looking; typically when interacting with humans, I would take it upon myself to shapeshift into whatever form best suited my needs. The only aspect departing me from my typical appearance of Asgard, the one related in all the best myths and stories that include me as their protagonist, was the blonde hair I'd rather grown out since Sif's inopportune binding, a small concession to lessen the sting when I looked into the mirror on those odd days where I just wanted to shapeshift into a woman.

So when I knocked on one weather-worn door, I was fully prepared to be recognized, welcomed inside, and perhaps offered a restorative drink, a welcome properly befitting a god.

I was not expected to be greeted by a spear point.

I blinked and took half a step back, my eyes narrowing at this unexpected greeting. A boy stood in the doorway, leveling the heavy weapon directly at my chest, his gaze focused unequivocally on me.

"Who the hell are you?" he demanded.

My lips parted to tell the truth, but then I stopped myself. Today, knowing the words this boy would use for me when he learned I was Loki – words like *he* and him – just felt wrong.

So I said, enigmatically, "A traveler."

The boy's eyes surveyed me, and understanding entered them abruptly. I expected him to greet me by name, but instead, he lowered the spear and extended one hand, giving me a path to enter the hut.

"Come inside," he said.

The room was small but cozy. Furs and thick tapestries cushioned the walls.

It was only then, beneath the glow of the candlelight, that the boy was rather older than a child by human standards – thirty or forty, perhaps. The soft curves of his face had fooled me into approximating a far younger age.

"Wine?" he offered.

I winced, recalling the inebriation that had led to this unfortunate situation to begin with. "No thank you."

He shrugged and poured himself a cup, the stark wooden vessel reminding me painfully of home in Asgard. "Well, *traveler*," he said, placing almost humorous emphasis on the identifier I'd provided, "you aren't the first wanderer directed here looking for answers. The best I can give you is this: there is nothing whatsoever wrong with how you're feeling."

I frowned.

"Not everyone fits well into their body on the first attempt," he explained. "Some grow up with no inclination otherwise, but not all are so lucky or – perhaps, so cursed. It took me far longer to come to an understanding of myself. There are many ways to find yourself, some more straightforward than others. There is nothing wrong with you if you know that you're a woman, or neither that nor a man."

I snorted. "Perhaps for you there isn't."

In Asgard, you were who you were; the nature of all there had been firmly set since the beginning of time. For Odin to truly be a woman was as impossible as me being anything other than a trickster. Those truths were unequivocally fixed in the stars.

He blinked, and his mouth unexpectedly twisted into a smile.

"You're not some odd traveler," he said. "You're a god."

It was my turn to look surprised. "You didn't know?"

"Gods don't typically entertain notions of stringent self-examination."

"Then who did you possibly think I was, to welcome me in like this?"

He shrugged. "My birth, you could say, was a mistake – everyone around me supposed I was a woman, when that couldn't be further from the truth. My story spread, rather like one of the legends of you that I suppose have circulated about you throughout the country. People started coming to me for advice – others like us, born unakin to what others expected of them. I presumed that you were another like that. And was I wrong?"

I found myself shaking my head.

"No, I don't think you altogether are."

Gods were not supposed to feel commonality with humans, let alone when one was the sort of trickster god who most of their peers seemed to regard as having sympathy for absolutely no one. But why else, after all, would I feel such solace in shapeshifting between genders if one form fit me all the time? Certainly, that was not a normal feeling among the gods.

And yet, perhaps it didn't have to be so foreign.

"Do you know anyone whose sense of themselves…shifts?"
I asked. "Perhaps someone who feels like a man one day, and a
woman the next?"

"Certainly," said the man. "As well as those who feel like neither.
There is no strictness to this system, not like others might lead
you to believe. To understand yourself is to acknowledge that
there is no such thing as normalcy there."

I felt something shift within me as my sense of self settled
into this new mold. I didn't have to constantly stick myself in an
uncomfortable dichotomy, attempting to fit into the expectations
the other Asgardians had set. My nature, my character as a god,
didn't change – it just had an unexpectedly more expansive
quality than that of Thor or Odin. And why, really, should it even
surprise me that I, a trickster to my core, couldn't be condensed
and streamlined into a single thing?

I'd never been so stubbornly simplistic to accommodate that
kind of single-minded thinking.

I didn't have to choose. I didn't have to feel off-kilter at the
other gods' odd looks, because my being a man and a woman was
as natural as Sif's gold-spun hair. My trickery, my unpredictability,
extended even further down to my very fundamental nature. Even
I didn't know what gender I might wake up as on a given day.

And there was nothing wrong with that.

My shoulders settled, and unexpectedly, at last, I found the
binding knot.

I'd scanned every inch of myself – or so I'd thought – for the
tiny spell. But Sif had tucked it into a place no other god would
ever have thought to examine: self-reflection.

To tug apart the thin knot was the work of a moment. The consequence of it hit me with all the speed of a cliff face smashed into by an unassuming, hawk-formed god.

After half a year trapped in a single body, a thousand forms erupted out of me in a moment: I was a salmon, a gnat, a woman, and then a hawk, perched on the back of the chair that the man had offered me. I stretched out my long-absent feathers, my tired muscles reaccustoming themselves to this variety of movement.

I was free again, to be myself, whatever that meant today.

"Farewell, Loki," said the man, a smile blossoming across his features.

I raised one wing in goodbye, and then the hawk spiraled out across the sky.

Loki and Pickled Herring at World's End

Mark Oxbrow

I remember nine giants
born at the dawn of time, they nurtured me
I remember nine worlds, nine giant women,
and the World-Ash, Yggdrasil,
growing beneath the earth.
– From *Völuspá (Prophesy of the Seeress),* from the
Poetic Edda

Hekla Archaeological Institute, 73 miles east of Reykjavík, Iceland

"Have you met him?"

"What?" Harpa blinked.

Ingibjörg fidgeted with her lambswool skirt, "Have you ever met Professor Haelstrøm?"

"No." Harpa shook her head. "I heard he's a bit…"

"…a bit what?"

"A bit kooky." Harpa shrugged.

* * *

LOKI AND PICKLED HERRING AT WORLD'S END

Loki was quite fond of being Professor Haelstrøm.

Professor Adelin Haelstrøm was imaginary. The latest of a hundred guises that Loki had taken in the last thousand years. He'd lived as an Elizabethan spy, a Parisian ballerina, a Finnish sniper during World War II. Loki conjured identities out of thin air, shapeshifting bodies like he was changing his hat.

Loki whistled a medieval Icelandic rímur as he hopped out of the taxi. There, across the road, was the Heklustofnun, the Hekla Institute: an unassuming single storey building of glass and stone. It rose out of the earth like a breaching whale.

Being Professor Haelstrøm gave Loki prestige. He lectured internationally on Norse mythology, staying in fancy hotels, sleeping in one-thousand-thread-count cotton sheets, and visiting universities. Haelstrøm was widely regarded as a leading expert on runes, both the Elder and Younger Futhark. He'd gained a reputation as a troublemaker, an outspoken mischief-maker that revelled in humbling his fellow academics.

And bedding their partners.

"I saw him debate once at Oxford," Harpa said. "He took Professor Kensington down a peg or two."

"Woah," Ingibjörg grinned. "Wish I'd seen that. Kensington is a pig."

Glass doors glided open as Professor Haelstrøm strode into the lobby.

"There he is," Ingibjörg said. "Game face on."

Professor Haelstrøm loved tailormade shirts and Saville Row suits. He was wearing a vintage Vivienne Westwood coat, a tweed waistcoat dyed purple with heather, and tartan trousers. One rule Loki always lived by: wear the finest shoes you can afford – you'll spend half your life wandering about in them. His shoes were Italian leather, handmade in Florence.

His eyes were dark, skin pale, his hair silvering. There was a spring in his step and a crooked smile on his lips.

"Professor Haelstrøm!" Ingibjörg reached out and took his hand. "Welcome to Hekla."

Loki read her ID badge: Ingibjörg Björnsdóttir | Forstjóri Heklustofnunar | Director, Hekla Institute.

"Delighted," he smiled.

"This is my colleague, Dr. Guðmundsdóttir." Ingibjörg introduced Harpa.

Loki spotted Harpa's ID badge: Archaeologist Elisabet Harpa Guðmundsdóttir; two Kuromi stickers; a tiny rainbow; a picture of a donut.

"Doctor." He shook her hand.

"Please call me Harpa."

"Outstanding," Loki grinned.

"I got you something," Ingibjörg held up a Visitor Pass sticker. She peeled off the backing and stuck it on his lapel.

"Too kind."

"Can we get you a coffee? Water or something?"

"I'm good, thank you." Loki shook his head. "Keen to see the dig site."

Ingibjörg talked as they walked. "We uncovered the farmstead three years back. It was inhabited between the 700s and the early 12th century. We've found a farmhouse, a small private chapel and the graves. In Iceland we can often identify the builders of sites as they're named in the sagas. But there's nothing written about this place. It's keeping its secrets."

"Do you like mysteries, professor?" Harpa said.

Loki nodded, "Absolutely."

"You'll love this."

She pushed open the double doors to the dig site. It sheltered under a soaring glass dome.

"Welcome to the dig."

Loki took a breath. The earth was bare, the grass stripped back. He saw a dozen trenches and excavated burials. The foundations of stone buildings. Three archaeologists huddled around a finds table, processing and recording artefacts.

He looked out, through the glass. Saw tufts of wild grass, thrashed by the fierce spring winds, and there, looming above them, Hekla Volcano.

"The settlement was buried when Hekla erupted in 1104CE. Farms up to 70 kms away from the volcano were abandoned." Harpa led them across the dig site. "Everything was buried in lava and volcanic ash."

Ingibjörg carefully edged around a trench, "I like to think of this as Viking Pompeii."

"You've got to see this," Harpa stopped at a finds table. "We found it six weeks ago. In the ship grave."

She picked a tiny silver artefact up off the table and handed it to Loki.

He stared down, turning it over in his palm. Inches from his face.

His heart leapt. He was surprised how hard it hit him. He choked back tears, taking a ragged breath.

"She's small, but fierce," Loki whispered. "A Valkyrie."

He cradled the gilded silver Valkyrie in his hand, as if it was as fragile and delicate as a raven's egg. She was little more than an inch tall. She held a miniscule round shield with a circular boss, and a sword. Her hair was parted in the middle, long, plaited and tied back. She wore patterned skirts. But it was her huge eyes that stared up a Loki.

"She's similar to the Valkyrie at Hårby." Loki said softly, never taking his eyes from the figure.

Harpa nodded. "Ours is a little smaller. But they have a lot in common."

Loki paused, fighting back tears. "You said she was found in a ship burial?"

"Yes," Harpa said.

Harpa wondered if Professor Haelstrøm was always so emotional. She knew the feeling: standing knee deep in a trench, crying her eyes out after months of fruitless digging, holding a pottery shard in her muddy fingers. Peers used words like 'passionate' and 'mercurial,' but she suspected they meant 'overemotional.'

"Follow me," Harpa smiled.

Loki handed back the Valkyrie. She carefully placed it on the finds table.

"Harpa found the ship burial late last year." Ingibjörg said. "We've spent the last two months excavating. Uh…that's one of the reasons we invited you. We're seeking ongoing funding, and

LOKI AND PICKLED HERRING AT WORLD'S END

we were hoping you might endorse our proposal. Your name would definitely help to…"

"…Of course," Loki interrupted. "Whatever you need. And if you need more money, I want you to call me. I have plenty of dirt on the executives at the World Monuments Fund. And I know some philanthropists with deep pockets. Always happy to put a knife to their throats. In a manner of speaking."

"Uh…" Ingibjörg blinked.

She was wearing her lucky toe ring, and she'd beseeched every goddess she could think of for divine intervention. She'd expected to spend hours trying to persuade the professor to help. But there he was, endorsing their bid without a second thought.

"That's uh…" Ingibjörg struggled to compose herself. "That's incredible!"

"Think nothing of it." Loki smiled. "It's the least I can do. You are doing such fabulous work. You shouldn't have to waste your time scrabbling about for money. It's nonsense."

"I just, I…" Ingibjörg was looking for the right words, but she wasn't finding them anywhere.

"Thank you." Harpa grinned.

"Yes," Ingibjörg nodded. "Thank you."

Loki had stopped worrying about money after looting Constantinople with the Venetians.

"The ship burial?" he smiled.

"It's this way," Harpa led him across to the far side of the dig. "The stones surround the grave, in the shape of a Viking ship. They vanished under the lava almost a thousand years ago."

Loki stopped dead at the edge of the stone ship burial. Two boulders marked the prow and stern posts. Two dozen smaller stones traced out the curve of the hull. But Loki barely noticed the stone ship or the grave goods. He stared down at the skeleton and its broken skull.

"She was a woman," Harpa knelt, down in the grave. "We can tell by studying the os coxae. It's part of the pelvis. And she was buried with two oval bronze brooches, a cloak pin and the household keys. See?"

Harpa pointed out a clump of ancient keys, half excavated from the earth.

Loki hesitated, not daring to step across the boundary, into the grave. He saw the keys and remembered the sound they made. They sounded like bells as they jingled on her belt. He remembered her smile and the pink in her cheeks on winter nights. He had bought her the cloak pin at the midsummer market. Traded a dagger for it. He had made the inch-tall Valkyrie with his own hands.

It was a gift.

"You need to see this," Harpa said, leaning over the bones.

Loki made his foot move, treading lightly between the stones, into the grave. He watched his shoe touch the ground. Felt the damp earth under his feet. He walked the path from the world of the living to the realm of the dead.

"You see here?" Harpa held a pencil in her hand, waving it around like a wand.

Harpa twirled it between her fingers, pointing at the skull with its sharpened point.

"There, you can make out carvings in her teeth," Harpa said excitedly. "Those horizontal grooves and that crescent. They may have been dyed red, to intimidate enemies. But the thing is, this has never been found in female remains. Not ever. She's the only Viking woman in the world found with teeth carvings."

Loki smiled. His hands trembled as he knelt by the skeleton. She had filed her teeth because it was forbidden to her. Her father never did forgive her.

She seemed so small now. Her bones were fractured, cracked under the weight of lava and ash. Loki gazed deep into the empty eye sockets in her skull. There was nothing but dirt.

"Her eyes." Loki whispered. "They were blue."

Harpa leant closer, "What?"

"Her eyes. Sharp. Piercing." Loki said. "Blue like the winter sky."

Harpa blinked. *Kooky* she thought to herself.

She brushed away a little loose earth. "We found this three days ago."

There, resting on the dead woman's breastbone, was a necklace. Gold and gemstones. Intricate spirals and knotworks. Tiny dragons and interlaced serpents. And a swirling line of miniscule runes.

"The necklace," Harpa said. "I've never seen anything like it."

Loki nodded. "And you never will again."

"Can you read the runes?" Harpa asked. "I don't recognise them as Elder Futhark, but the burial has got to be 8th century. It doesn't make any sense."

"Do you remember how Óðinn learned of the runes?" Loki said.

"Yes, but…" Harpa stopped. "Odin sacrificed himself on the World Tree."

"Óðinn," Loki grinned, "hanging from the boughs of Yggdrasil for nine nights and nine days. Like a dead crow. And why? Because the All-Father envied the Norns. Because he yearned to see the future as they did."

Harpa listened close, bewitched.

"And in his delirium Óðinn saw the runes: where the branches of the ash tree met. He saw the tiniest of twigs split and touch. Saw sticks make the shapes of the runes."

Ingibjörg moved closer to hear as Loki lowered his voice to a whisper.

"But Óðinn would not share all that he saw. Fé and Úr he shared. Íss and Sól. But there were other runes…wyrd and odd runes that Óðinn kept secret."

Harpa frowned, "Are you telling me that these are Odin's secret runes?"

Loki grinned, "Yes."

"Can you read them?" Harpa said.

"Yes," Loki nodded.

He leant close to the necklace, pointing at a tiny rune, "You see there? That rune is Seiðr – magic. To see and shape the future."

"How?" Harpa said. "How do you know this, professor?"

Loki noticed something.

The sky was darkening. Storm clouds swirled around Hekla. They swarmed down from the volcano, blotting out the noonday sun. A shadow fell over the land as if a giant cloak was drawn across the sky.

LOKI AND PICKLED HERRING AT WORLD'S END

Loki sighed. Darkening skies were never a good thing.

"Professor Haelstrøm?" Ingibjörg stared out at the gathering storm.

The blizzard hit the glass dome, snow billowing.

"You'll want to be someplace else," Loki said.

Harpa blinked, "What?"

The three archaeologists edged towards the doors. Snow drifted up against the glass, three feet deep. Hulking shapes moved in the blizzard.

"Oh dear," Loki sighed.

A dozen polar bears smashed into the dome. Gigantic paws, round and furry and huge as dinner plates, battered on the glass. Black noses snuffled and wiped snot on the windows. Teeth gnawed and claws scratched.

"What the Hell?" Ingibjörg gasped.

Loki stood, wiping dirt from his clothes.

"I think you should probably be running," he said.

Polar bears cracked the glass.

"This is impossible," Harpa said. "There's no polar bears in Iceland!"

Loki gave her a crooked smile. "You should tell them."

The glass splintered. Icy winds and roaring snow crashed into the dig site. Polar bears shattered the windows, breaking the glass dome apart.

Three archaeologists ran, scattering papers behind them.

Ingibjörg eyed the door. She wanted to bolt for safety, too terrified to hide. But her feet had stopped listening to her brain as it screamed at her to run.

"Professor Haelstrøm," Ingibjörg mumbled. "Perhaps…uh, you'd like to see my office?"

Polar bears rampaged into the dig site. Claws digging through snow and tearing up the earth.

"My name isn't Professor Haelstrøm. My name is Loki."

Harpa blinked. It took her a moment to realise her mouth was hanging open.

"But…" she stammered.

Two gigantic things stomped out of the blizzard.

Loki recognised Vörnir. The colossal jötunn was hard to forget. He was an immense frost giant, cut from ice and snow. Fists like boulders and razor-sharp teeth like icicles.

The second jötunn was King Eldr, the fire giant. He had dug his way out of Hekla. His body was a monstrous mass of black volcanic rock. Molten lava seethed from cracks in his flesh. Eldr's mouth was a furnace.

"Hi." Loki waved at the giants.

"Loki?" Harpa squeaked.

"Yes," Loki grinned. "And these are jötunn. Giants. Hired thugs."

"Hired?" Harpa said. "Hired by who?"

The two jötunn towered over them, breathing frost and flame.

Loki spotted something raging out of the snow, "Hired by her."

The chariot sliced through the blizzard, cutting deep furrows in the snowdrifts. Two gigantic Norwegian forest cats buried their claws in the earth. They strained against their reins, dragging the chariot into the dome.

A shining goddess rode high in the chariot. She wore jewelled armour, twilled silks and cloth of gold. A falcon-feather cloak draped about her shoulders. Her skin was milk white, her hair like spun gold, plaited and woven with strands of silver.

"Hey Freyja." Loki sighed.

"Freyja?!" Harpa gasped. "What?"

Harpa's mind glowed, synapses sparking like lightning, as she fought to make sense of a hundred impossible things.

"Loki sly-god." Freyja's voice was like honey. "Hawk's child. Adversary. Slanderer and trickster. Cunning-wise Loki. Thief of goats. And of giants."

"Freyja," Loki bowed with a flourish, "Goddess of love and war, gold and sorcery. Valfreyja, lady of the slain."

Freyja hissed, "You have something that belongs to me."

"Do I?" Loki mocked surprise. "I don't think so."

"Where is Brísingamen?" Freyja snarled. "Loki, I want my necklace."

Harpa peeked down at the skeleton and the golden necklace.

"I haven't seen it." Loki lied.

Freyja's cats hissed and spat, claws like scythes tore up the dirt. Fangs dripped with drool.

"Loki, Deceiver. Thief of Iðunn's apples." Freyja's feather cloak billowed as she stepped down from the chariot. "Should I feed your friends to my cats? Will that loosen your tongue?"

"Loki," Harpa squeaked.

Harpa always liked cats, but she'd suddenly decided she was more of a dog person.

"I don't think so." Loki shook his head. "I quite like these two, and I have never been that fond of your mousers."

Freyja took a step closer. She spotted the glint of gold in the grave.

"Is that Brísingamen?" Freyja glowered. "Did you bury my necklace in a bone pit?"

Loki glanced down at the skeleton, "Maybe."

"Who is that?" Freyja growled. "Wearing my necklace?"

Her cats seethed, spitting, hackles raised.

Loki took a moment, breathing deep. "She was someone I loved."

Freyja stared, tilting her head, teeth gritted.

"Loki mischief-maker," Freyja raged. "Did you give my necklace to your dead witch?"

Harpa looked down at the skull, at the cloak pin and the remnants of textiles she wore, at the oval brooches and her carved teeth.

"Seeress." Loki said. "Prophetess. Sorceress. She divined fates and foretold the end of all things."

"What?" Freyja choked on the word.

"Yes," Loki smiled. "She saw nine giants and nine worlds, saw the seed that germinated and grew beneath the earth into Yggdrasil, World-Tree. Heiðr they named her, bright, and minds she spellbound. She spoke of J rmungandr – Midgard Serpent, and Fenrisúlfr that will devour the moon. Hel will rise with her army of the dead. And fair Ásgarðr will fall. And you, Freyja, will die."

"Ragnarök?" Harpa gasped. "You're talking about Ragnarök."

"World's end." Loki grinned.

Freyja waved a hand at her two gargantuan cats. They fell silent.

"Do you think I fear Ragnar k?" Freyja scowled. "Óðinn has waited a thousand years for you to begin the end of all. You, Loki, Mother of Monsters, you must take up a sprig of mistletoe so Höðr will slay Baldr."

"No," Loki said.

"What?" Freyja snapped. "It is written."

"I don't care." Loki shrugged.

"But…" Freyja said. "What of Ragnar k? A thousand years we wait. Óðinn grows feeble. His ravens are too frail to fly. Þórr does nothing but drink and boast while Mj llnir lies idle."

"Mjölnir?" Harpa whispered to Loki. "Did she just say Mjölnir? And Thor?"

Loki nodded, "Yes, she did."

King Eldr stood, the snow at his feet had melted into a muddy puddle. He smouldered. Steam hissed and rose from his lava.

"I demand you give me back my necklace and you end the world!" Freyja fumed.

"No." Loki shook his head. "No way."

Vörnir the jötunn could feel himself melting. He took half a step sideways, away from the fire giant. Meltwater dripped from his gigantic fingers.

"What do you mean, no?" Freyja raged. "You have to!"

"No," Loki said. "I really don't. You see, it's like this. I came to Iceland in ages past to lose myself. To knit my wrath and plot and lick my wounds, like a dog."

Freyja stared, saying nothing.

"I never meant to fall in love." Loki said. "Me? Loki? Laufey's son? Born of goddess and jötunn? Fall in love with a mortal? Heiðr, with her crooked smile, and her red-golden hair, and her broad hips and that laugh. Yes, I took your necklace, and I made a gift of it to her. I would have given her all the nine worlds if I could have."

Freyja's necklace sparkled on dead Heiðr's breastbone.

"And she loved this world so deeply. Loved each flower and blade of grass, the whales in the bay and the seals. The puffins and the snowy owl on the wing. Wagtails and warblers, reindeer, foxes. The hills and rivers, sunshine and snow." A tear rolled down Loki's cheek. "And she made me love this world and all the things in it. Midgard. A precious isle in a dark and dead ocean. And you want me to kill that?"

Freyja wanted to say something, but she couldn't find the words.

"You want me to end the world she loved so much?" Loki shook his head. "No. I will not do it. You may take the necklace if you want, but you can tell Óðinn and the gods that they can rot, forever. Loki is not their plaything."

Freyja watched the tears streak Loki's face.

Freyja, Goddess of Love.

Her words were soft, her voice cracking, "Be at peace, Loki. Heiðr's arm-burden. I sorrow for your loss. A thousand years is long to grieve a fallen love. I hope your heart will mend little one."

Loki wiped his face with the back of his hand. "Thank you."

Freyja nodded and turned on her heel, swirling her falcon-feather cloak, and they were gone.

Cats and polar bears, Vörnir and King Eldr, vanished, leaving nothing but snow and cinders. Freyja's necklace faded and disappeared.

"Ok." Harpa slumped. "It's ok. This is all ok."

"What?" Ingibjörg felt dizzy. "That was real, wasn't it?"

"Yes," Loki smiled.

"And you, you're not Professor Haelstrøm?" Ingibjörg said. "You are Loki?"

"Yes. I'm Loki."

"And that was Freyja?"

"In the flesh." Loki said.

"So," Harpa's brain tried to piece things together. "This is the grave of Hetha, the seeress from the *Völuspá*? The *Poetic Edda*?"

"Yes," Loki said softly. "This is the grave of Heiðr, beloved."

"And she foretold Ragnarök?" Harpa said. "The world's end?"

"Hmm," Loki gave her a crooked smile. "About that…"

"About Ragnarök?"

"Yes," Loki looked rather pleased with himself. "The gods are petty and foolish. Óðinn? He desired wisdom, the gift of prophesy. The old fool gave his eye to see the future. Traded it away like some bauble. Battle-hungry oath breakers. Do you have any idea how tricky it is to get the gods to shut up and leave you in peace?"

"Loki," Harpa's eyes widened. "What did you do?"

Loki shrugged, "I made up a story."

"A story?" Ingibjörg frowned.

"I was lying in bed one night, over there, in the farmhouse. There was a fire smouldering in the hearth, and I was warm in

Heiðr arms. And I had an idea. I had just become a grandfather you see, Fenrisúlfr had three wolf pups, big as ponies..."

"...Fenrir? The gigantic wolf that eats Odin?" Harpa blinked.

Loki nodded, "Yes, well, I made that bit up."

"What?" Harpa squeaked. "You made it up?!"

"We made it all up." Loki shrugged. "That night, we lay in bed, eating pickled herring and making up stories. And I thought about my children. About Hel and J rmungandr and Fenrisúlfr – did you know they wanted to chain him up, like he was some... monster. And I thought about the baby growing in Heiðr's belly, and I wanted this world to live forever. I wanted my children and my grandchildren to grow up safe."

Harpa stared down at Hetha's bones. Imagined her as a mother. Cradling their baby.

"So, we made up Ragnar k." Loki grinned.

"You did what?" Ingibjörg said.

"It was quite easy really." Loki recalled. "Óðinn was consumed, obsessed with prophesies. So, we put out word of this wondrous seeress: a rival to the three Norns. And he came running. He hung on every word she spoke. The Doom of the Gods. A Great Winter. Splitting shields. An age of axe and sword. Trees and mountains falling. Serpents dripping venom in my eyes. The ship *Naglfar*, made from the toenails and fingernails of the dead. Poison and horn blasts, ravenous wolves, raging fires, war and the splintering of the rainbow bridge. It was quite a good tale."

Harpa stared, her mouth hanging open.

"And Óðinn sat there and lapped it up, like a kitten lapping cream." Loki grinned, eyes twinkling. "And then the old fool knew fear. And in his fright, Óðinn hid behind the walls of Ásgarðr, and left my children in peace."

Harpa blinked, "Ragnarök...was a lie?"

"Yes," Loki bowed deep. "For am I not Loki, sly-god, cunning-wise? Maker of mischief and weaver of lies?"

"Oh my god." Harpa mumbled.

"You are most very welcome." Loki grinned. "Now, I wonder if you might have something to eat? I find that I am quite hungry."

"Uh...yes." Ingibjörg muttered. "I ordered a lunch. It's... uh...it'll be in the...um. There's smoked salmon. Skyr I think. Hangikjöt, that's smoked lamb. Rye bread and butter..."

"...any pickled herring?" Loki said.

"I'm quite fond of pickled herring."

Just Because

Diego Suárez

By Ymir's breath and tears, he was terrified. Him! Loki! God of Mischief! Why would he ever be scared of something as ridiculous as *therapy*? He didn't need it! He knew his faults, he knew his issues, and he would deal with them on his own terms. Alas, Angrboda had insisted, even threatened with leaving him unless he went and did this, so he agreed to give it a try. A singular, lone try. After all, how could a mortal presume to know more than a god? So, he made the stupid, ridiculous appointment, and went to get this farce over with.

It was the twenty-first century in the Gregorian Calendar. The first chaotic, cataclysmic twenty years of the century were done, and Loki Laufeyjarson lived in a city as cluttered as a heart attack. It was the new world, where the humans ruled, not the gods. Turned out, the little ones, fragile and mortal, were just like the Aesir, and the other gods: possessors of the unbearable conviction of being the most important species in all of the realms. The difference was that humanity had blown the gods themselves out of the water in sheer hubris.

But this wasn't about humanity. It never was, and it never will be. This was about Loki, who knocked on the door of the alleged therapist for the divine. How does one even get to be that professionally? Probably a fake degree from a subpar education. If he got annoyed by this "doctor", he'd simply make their life utterly miserable.

Loki stood before the entrance door, wearing an elegant, dark-green suit, his red fire hair combed backwards, with his ears nice and pointed, and his burning eyes brimming with disgust. The therapist's office was part of a large building in the middle of the sprawling city's southern sector. It was on the fourth floor, down the rightmost end of a hallway, and opposite to an entrepreneurial start-up. Against the wall, a long couch to sit and wait was firmly placed. There was a table with a lot of magazines about myths, and their stories, beside it; a particular one, and one Loki particularly liked, was named after a flaming tree. He then looked at the plaque on the door, next, above the central doorbell. It read: "Ash Caledonia M.D.".

With a lanky, boney finger, he pressed the square button of the doorbell. The mechanical ring echoed like a bell toll.

Steps were muffled before the doorknob was turned, and the door pulled open. Ash Caledonia was a short, stout man with some white on his hair, wrinkles around his eyes, and was wearing a cardigan.

"Ah, welcome, Mr. Loki. Please, come in, come in!"

The human stepped aside, and the trickster god crossed the threshold into a small hallway with a bookshelf full of tchotchkes, books, and the lingering, earthy smell of a library filling the enclosed space. Past the hallway, the therapy room itself awaited. Was that the name? A therapy room? That didn't sound right. He'd keep calling it an office, and be done with it.

Said office was comfortably spacious, a lot of open space illuminated by big, frosted windows. A lounging couch was on the left, and a crystal table was on the right, which had accoutrements on it like a starry crystal orb, and a small statue of a pair of posing hands. A comfortable sofa was beside that chair for the therapist. There was also a small gong, a computer, some paintings, a wall clock, and a lot of various books and vinyl records on the shelves around the whole room. Spacious, yet full, and an interesting, yet not unpleasant décor style. The smell of an old bookstore remained in the air, which was its most endearing quality. It wasn't a bad place. Cozy. Like back when Asgard was his home.

Ugh, bad memories.

Loki sat on the couch, facing the sofa where Dr. Ash sat after him.

The two remained quiet.

I will not break, mortal.

Loki observed the doctor.

You think you're so clever, waiting for me to slip up.

The doctor simply sat calm, and cool, unaffected.

I'm onto you!

The ticking of the clock began soft. But it grew, and grew, and grew with every tick, and every tock. That sound gnawed at him, like needles through his eardrums. He hated this, the silence, but wouldn't allow himself to show that weakness. So, he would pivot, and start the conversation, make the doctor know he was outclassed.

"I know what are you doing," stated Loki, crossing one leg over the other, steepling his fingers together against his chest.

JUST BECAUSE

He leaned back, a smug smile on his face. "And it won't work".

"What won't work?" asked Dr. Ash.

"You. Fishing for any weakness, trying to tell me something I already know". Loki remained seated in his triumphant position. "You don't know me. *I* know me. I rule me." He added a particular venom on each syllable so he would be crystal clear in his intent. "Not you, mortal! You will not tell me anything about who am I! You understa—?!"

Then, he realized he wasn't sitting anymore. He had stood up, using a finger to threaten this man. A man who kept composed despite that. How many gods had he given therapy to in order to remain so cool headed? Loki's eyes turned into that of a snake, and he squinted.

"You're good," said the god, sitting back down. "What will you get out of this?"

"Just helping you. After all, you were the one that chose to come here, no?"

Loki squirmed in his seat some. It felt like hot coals on his backside all of a sudden. "Just because it would make my wife realize I'm fine," he defended himself.

"Is that what you believe?"

Loki felt his insides coil upon themselves. His face got warmer; the tips of his ears felt searing hot. What he believed was that he didn't need this, that he could handle it alone. He wanted to lie, it came to him as easy as breathing, but he found himself being honest for a rare change. This therapy business would, at the very least, let him vent. After all, doctor-patient confidentiality was a thing, right? So, he took the bite.

"No."

The doctor nodded. He wasn't taking notes, and this felt more like a conversation, not what the trickster expected. He did feel compelled to proceed, and he was sure no magic was influencing his thoughts. No, this was Loki wanting to talk, to have someone that would just listen to him in confidentiality.

"I *suppose* I could be better. It's just all this anger, this irritation in me. Like ropes on fire running through my veins." Loki just kept talking, uninterrupted. "And I know *why* they're there. Everyone thinks they know Loki. Everyone thinks, and swears, they know who Loki is! Well, they don't!" He felt a sting at the corner of his eyes, and his throat closing tight, forcing him to swallow. "I rule me. Me. I don't bow to anyone, nor to anyone's expectations."

Dr. Ash nodded. "We've established what you don't do, but what do you *do*?"

Loki found himself with no immediate retort. What did he do? He caused mischief, but what did that entail? All just to spite the blood brother that imprisoned his children, and the imbecilic, drunk thug with a mighty hammer?

"Chaos," he answered, frowning. The words that followed next surprised even Loki. "Pettiness. I'm like broken crystal, and I have nowhere to put all the shards."

"Could it be because of a betrayal? You reached out, trusted someone, and that person hurt you?"

"Maybe. I wasn't completely innocent, and I really came close to start Ragnarök."

"Can you tell me why you didn't, or haven't yet?"

That was the second time Loki found himself with no immediate answer. He wasn't a fan of such a feeling. Why hadn't he? Why hadn't he spelled the death of his treacherous blood brother, and his cohort of imbecilic bullies? Why hadn't he made the world end, and be reborn anew?

Because, at the end of the day, he couldn't bring himself to kill Baldur, and to doom his children to death. Because, at the end of the day, he loved his family more than he had come to hate Odin. Mischief or not, he was still a father.

Loki lowered his head, feeling a Jovian weight on his shoulders, and his back. He leaned forward, his hands held together, tight, trembling, and his arms resting on his thighs. His chest felt under a vise, a safe that was being crushed slowly. He felt the numbness on his fingertips spreading through his muscles. He felt vulnerable, open, and that scared him.

"I don't want to end the world," he admitted his voice barely above a whisper.

"What do you want, then?"

This human was good, really good! And even if it pained him to admit it, he needed this. He would never say this out loud, but he could at least stop lying to himself.

Loki found himself drawing a smile. It wasn't a clever one, nor a mischievous one. It was one born out of hope, and anxiety alike. "I want to keep coming here".

Dr. Ash nodded. "We'll set the schedule, and discuss payment options at the end of the session. For now, what do you expect out of your therapy process?"

Loki took a deep breath, and exhaled through his nose extremely slowly. To be fixed? No, he wasn't broken, he just needed someone he could let it all out.

"I guess we'll find out, doc. But, maybe, find a way to move forward."

He hoped so. He really did.

* * *

Six Months Later

Loki was at Dr. Ash's office for their weekly meeting. She was rocking a woman's shape now. Why? She hadn't been one since the Sleipnir Incident, right? So, the correct question would be: why not? Different species, different gender, a wonderful spectrum to explore. What happened with that giant's horse was in the past, it couldn't hurt her anymore, and she wanted to reclaim her femininity. So, she was a woman for the time being. She had a hoodie, red, some running shoes, and baggy pants. She had her red hair in a lazy ponytail.

"That's the thing," she said, elbows on her legs, leaning forwards, "I was betrayed first, so I would betray back. They wanted me to be a monster, so I embraced that, and became their worst nightmare. Who cares if they kicked me out of Asgard? They can go eat shit for all I care!"

"Would you say that if it didn't hurt you so much?"

She didn't have an answer for that, and the question briefly floored her. In truth, she cared, a lot. She cared that she had been kicked out by her blood brother, that she had to play the role of villain due to a stupid prophecy, and lost almost everything because of that. She cared about Odin's betrayal, and about her children being caged in places, and realms beyond her, and Angrboda. She cared a lot, so she didn't say a thing, and nodded as her answer.

She still didn't like the silence, it felt judging, and accusatory. But she didn't fill the space with noise anymore, and knew this was for her to stay with what she said, with what his question stirred inside her. So, Loki took this time to compose herself, to feel herself in that space. She knew this was an exercise in presence, in allowing herself to simply be, to let the anger wash over her without destroying her, and find a more measured, controlled answer. Wrath born from pain would never be truly gone, but she didn't want to be defined by it anymore. She was working to manage it better.

"I have another question that goes hand-in-hand with this one," added Ash. "Why is it that you insist on talking about the negative aspects in your life? Do you want to be defined by those moments only?"

"That's—" she began, but Loki quickly found out she didn't have an honest answer to retort to that. It was a common occurrence for her during therapy, she had noticed, and Ash was particularly good at leaving her speechless. However, she felt compelled to start talking about positive things.

"I'm happy with my Angrboda". It came out soft, shy, bereft of Loki's cocksureness. However, she was smiling an honest smile, and it made her seem at peace. "I especially love how patient she has been with me. I don't deserve her, doc."

"I don't like the word 'deserve'. Do you want her? Love her? Is your wife important to you?"

"Of course," she said, offended at the mere suggestion! However, she saw what he meant. *Always about the negative, right?*

"It's okay, Loki, to be part of things just because they matter to you. Not everything has to have any other motive beyond making you smile, being happy. If something is not to your liking, if it hurts you, you *can* remove it, be rid of it, and get something better. You can change yourself, and your world to be happy. You're not a prisoner to anything but your own expectations, and assumptions."

The clock kept ticking away after such a statement. Loki wanted to feel offended, to rebuke! To say she was prisoner to *no one*! She couldn't, though. She really couldn't. He had touched one of her biggest nerves, and they both knew it. She was an amazing liar, probably the best, but she couldn't deceive herself, and whoever truly knew her.

"I hate you," she lied after a resigned chuckle. What else was there to do, but accept it, and keep moving? That stout man, she could see why his clients were the divine.

Dr. Ash simply gave her a courteous, ambiguous smile in response. Always professional, that man. Loki would find out how to get a rise out of him before her therapy process was over. She promised herself, and the runes that made her name.

JUST BECAUSE

"So!" she exclaimed a bit, changing the uncomfortable topic. "I'm changing the topic because I want to. Why do you have a gong in your office?"

Ash looked at her pointedly, but silently acquiesced. He looked at the gong, then at her, and gave Loki a shit-eating grin that made her feel proud of this stout human.

"Just because," he replied.

Loki laughed out loud, her voice making the lights in the room turn on brighter for a second. Even her hair turned into tongues of flames and embers that burned nothing in their joy. She clapped loudly, and even stomped her foot on the ground.

"Good one! I really like that answer." Maybe it was a lie, but who cared? The answer had been so good, she took it at face value. "Just because, huh?"

He gave a nod, and a cheeky smile. "Correct." She respected that man. He knew what he was doing. He was wise, and with a firm hand to help her look at what needed to be done.

Loki had come to terms with the fact that she, indeed, needed this more than she had cared to admit beforehand. After all, the proof was in the pudding, and in only six months, she was slowly realizing the reasoning under her actions, of her anger.

Why were some mortals against this? It was so helpful!

That session, though, ended when the alarm beeped at the hour. She stood up, and shook her doctor's hand. "See you next week, doc."

"Of course. I will send you the name of a book I think you'd like, and that will help you with the anger."

303

She whistled at this. "Another one? You're either spoiling me, or dropping hints of a future institutionalization."

It was Ash's turn to laugh. It was a hearty, almost bellowing sound. "Guess you'll learn when you read it." He walked her to the door, opened the door for her, and let her walk off. "Goodbye, Loki."

"Bye, doc!"

She left, and walked down the hallway towards the elevator. With a wiggle of her fingers, she caused some problems in the start-up's office. Nothing major, just printers suddenly out of ink, and internet disconnecting. Why? Just because.

* * *

One Year Later

Loki had decided to ignore gender binary norms completely for the foreseeable future. They were a deity, a giant, and could change their shape, form, and even species! Why limit themselves to such a constricting zero-one system? That, and they wanted to. That reason held more water.

That day, they wore what was tantamount of sleeping clothing: baggy pants, fuzzy socks, and a baggy, warm shirt. They had their hair shaved on the sides, with the rest combed over the left side, with their pointed ears far more visible, too. They wore their *jötunn* skin with pride!

They were laying on the long couch, rolling the table's crystal ball between their hands. They now went to therapy once every other month, mostly for check-ups, and because they liked the conversations with Dr. Ash.

They were in deep thought, silence, their mind nowhere in particular beyond the moment. They had grown comfortable with quietude now. Silence was a pause, not a full stop. They still didn't like it, probably never would, but they could navigate it now fearlessly.

"You know what is funny, doc?" they asked, rolling the crystal ball between their hands constantly. Dr. Ash looked at them, encouraging them to continue with a small sound.

Loki stared at a point in the cream-white ceiling. "I should've left Asgard way before they kicked me out, shouldn't I? Life would've been so much simpler. Alas, what's done is done, right?"

Dr. Ash nodded. "Correct, there's no point in wondering about 'what ifs'. What else have you realized?"

That answer came easy, without any need for introspection. "That I'm incredibly lucky," Loki stated, lifting the orb with their right hand, looking how it broke the light filtering through the windows inside it. It was a rainbow, like the Bifröst. "Us gods don't need prayers to live, that's a misconception. We like being worshipped; it strokes our egos. I'm lucky because, right now, I'm loved by mortals. Sure, it has to do with that bizarre adaptation that made me Thor's stepbrother, but a win is a win. Not every god gets that luxury anymore. Hah! Look at me focusing on the positives. Slow, and steady, but got there."

"You're remarkably consistent in your conflicts, I'll give you that," said Dr. Ash. He didn't lavish them with praise. That was what they needed for this therapy to work. Angrboda loved them too much to be the kind of blunt he had needed back when they went by he/him. Yet it was their wife's love that ended up setting them in the right path. Imagine, being loved by someone so much that they sent you to get the help you needed. They were lucky indeed.

"I do have a firm Archetype attached to me, don't I?" agreed Loki with a mischievous smile. They were slow to change, like any deity, but once they gave that step? It was an absolute change. The irony of that slowness wasn't lost on them.

"Speaking of positives!" they exclaimed, lifting a slender finger from his free hand. "Me and Angrboda are going on a new date next week! Not just dinner, not going out for the theatre. Something big. It's been a while, and I wanted to do this with her. She's very excited."

"That's good!" agreed Dr. Ash. "Congratulations, Loki."

Loki then sat up, placed the orb on its little pedestal at the table, and stretched. "Thank you, doc! I do hate cutting this short," just fifteen minutes earlier, "but I have to confirm the reservation, and everything."

Dr. Ash Caledonia stood up, shook hands with the god, and said, "Understandable. Good bye, Loki. Enjoy yourself. You deserve it."

"That's definitely the plan!"

With that, they left the office with a pep in their step.

* * *

JUST BECAUSE

Once outside, and down the hallway, Loki waited for the elevator. Standing still, they felt a smile growing on their face. Oh, how had the doctor helped them in more ways than one. They would be forever thankful to that stout man that held no punches back.

Behind them, the start-up was having a lucky break, getting calls after calls, and deals after deals. They were on the rise, and weren't the only ones in that building.

They placed a hand on their face, covering just how much bigger their grin was getting, how many fangs were visible, and how much their lips stretched outwards, and upwards. They chuckled, softly, and while the light around them turned cold, their hair became licks of flame. They were excited, happy, and elated for what was to come.

"Hold on tight, my sweets," he muttered, "daddy and mommy are coming to set you free".

When the elevator opened, and the next patient of Dr. Ash's walked past him, Loki let her walk out first, and then stepped into the elevator. They were back to their human shape, sporting a polite and charming smile on their face. Once inside the elevator, they touched the button for the ground floor, and watched the doors close with pneumatic ease.

The Shape of Mischief
Jeffery Allen Tobin

The night stretched itself thin and frayed around the edges, a swath of deep gray running across the Nine Worlds. Loki sat at the edge of Asgard, perched on a crumbling outcrop that overlooked the realms below, a raven's form thinly cloaking his restless spirit. His feathers glimmered like soot licked with embers, and he eyed the flickering lights of Midgard below with the curiosity of one who knew every secret, every game, every pattern written into the weave of things. Yet tonight, even for Loki, the familiar glow of distant fires looked cold.

He flexed his claws, testing them against the stone, feeling the scrape and grit beneath his talons. For all the power coursing through his veins, Loki felt, in that brief moment, not like a god but like something far more fragile. He considered taking the shape of a serpent, the comfort of scales to remind him of the fluidity in which he usually thrived. But tonight, he clung to feathers – dark, brittle, a creature of air and fleeting moments, here one second and gone the next.

Below, he sensed the weight of Asgard, a fortress of stone and stars, where his presence was both integral and despised, as necessary as it was reviled. The other gods rested within, their dreams tangled with ambition and suspicion. None more so than

Odin, the All-Father, who bore the weight of secrets no mortal could withstand. Odin trusted no one. And Loki, least of all, had earned the cold gleam of Odin's one-eyed regard.

A low wind shuddered against the cliffside, stirring the raven's feathers. Loki closed his eyes, letting the wind wash over him, half a prayer caught in his breath – a promise of movement, of change, for that was all he truly understood. Beneath the shape-shifting, beneath the glittering guile, he was no more rooted than the air itself. The world wanted him to be one thing, but he was not made for such simplicity. To the others, he was treacherous, self-serving, fickle; to himself, he was merely free.

In his mind, the memory of an old oath surfaced, faint as smoke. He remembered the feel of it on his tongue – a promise he'd given with the same half-commitment that had colored most of his allegiances. But in that moment, sitting across from Odin in Valhalla, sharing mead and secrets, the words had felt heavier. An oath spoken to the All-Father carried a different weight, and Loki had felt that, somewhere beneath his playful mockery and glancing wit.

He had told Odin, once, that he would protect Asgard, though he did not believe the words himself. An irony, perhaps. Loki was bound not by honor or loyalty but by some tenuous thread of intrigue, a fascination with the worlds they governed and the games they played within them. Yet, as he perched now, watching the faint shimmer of Asgard's walls in the dark, he wondered if perhaps that old promise had sunk deeper than he knew.

He rose on black wings, scattering bits of stone from his perch as he swooped down into the night, his silhouette blending into shadow. With each beat of his wings, he felt the weight of the coming storm – felt the strain of those invisible threads binding him to fate, to Asgard, and to the gods who looked upon him with wariness and disdain.

The gods' worlds felt colder now, less familiar, and his own heart seemed caught between flight and fire. He realized, with a flash of insight as sharp as a blade, that his solitude was not mere distance from the Aesir but a creeping sense of misplacement, a rootlessness he could no longer ignore.

And as the raven's cry tore through the air, ringing harsh against the silence, Loki knew he would soon have to choose. For even the most unbound heart must, at some point, reckon with the price of its freedom.

This solitude, this edge of Asgard, was only the beginning. Loki sensed that his path led toward deeper entanglements, and perhaps, to that promise whispered in a shadowed hall of Valhalla, to be tested in ways that even he, the trickster, could not yet foresee.

* * *

Valhalla thrummed with the low, steady hum of voices, the heat of torches pressing close against the thick walls. Gods and heroes, alike in their bravado and thirst, leaned into the comforts of mead and laughter, a rare reprieve from the eternal vigilance required of Asgard. Loki found himself alone at the far end of a long table, absently turning his cup in his hand, his gaze distant, like a hawk sizing up prey across a valley.

Odin slid into the seat across from him, his single eye gleaming with the cool, calculating light that Loki both

THE SHAPE OF MISCHIEF

loathed and admired. The All-Father held his mead without drinking, letting the thick gold liquid slosh against the rim. For a moment, neither spoke, and the silence between them seemed to twist, an unspoken tension thrumming like the string of a drawn bow.

Finally, Odin leaned forward, his voice barely more than a murmur.

"You know, Loki, it's the same trick, every time. You slink into the shadows, hide behind a laugh and a jest, but I see you."

He narrowed his eye, and there was a dangerous warmth there, something bordering on kinship, though Loki knew better than to trust it.

Loki's lips quirked in a smile.

"Then perhaps I'll have to work on my craft. I'd hate for the magic to get stale."

A flicker of a smile crossed Odin's face, gone almost before it began.

"Stale or not, I have need of it."

"Ah, a need," Loki replied, his voice lilting with mock curiosity. "And what does the great All-Father need that his army of warriors cannot provide?"

Odin took a slow sip of his mead, letting the silence hang. When he spoke, his voice was softer, heavier, as if what he asked carried the weight of many lifetimes.

"There is a storm coming. Bigger than anything you've ever seen. The Jotnar are restless, and they've begun speaking of war. They're stirring in ways that even I cannot fully see."

Loki shrugged, swirling the mead in his own cup.

"And you think I should feel...concerned? Father, my loyalty is as changeable as my form. You know this."

Odin's eye held steady, unwavering.

"But you owe me."

The words landed hard, like a slap. Loki's smile faltered for a second, his fingers pausing on the rim of his cup. His mind flashed back to a dozen debts, a hundred ways he'd slipped past obligations like a snake shedding skin. He owed Odin for secrets kept, for slights forgiven, for the times Odin had shielded him, if only to use him again later.

But Odin pressed, leaning closer, his voice a low rumble.

"There will come a time, trickster, when all the masks fall away. A time when it will be impossible to stand apart and pretend to be neutral." He watched Loki's face carefully, his expression impenetrable. "For all your mischief, all your... flexibility, you are woven into the fate of Asgard. Just as we all are."

Loki scoffed, his laughter soft and sharp as a knife drawn from its sheath.

"Fate, Odin? I'm the one who unravels fate. I have no strings, no ties."

Odin's eye gleamed, a dangerous spark.

"Then humor me, Loki. See that storm in your mind – see the Jotnar marching, the end of Asgard clawing at the edges of all you know. Do you think even you can laugh as the worlds crumble beneath your feet?"

Loki felt a chill creep into his bones, despite the warmth of Valhalla, a flicker of something far more unsettling than fear. He met Odin's gaze, the silence between them a taut line strung between two opposites.

"Why should I care for this fate of yours? What has Asgard given me, except for curses and condemnation?"

Odin smiled, a grim twist of his lips.

"It's given you purpose. And you know it."

Loki looked away, feeling the weight of Odin's words sinking in. Purpose. For all his trickery, his endless transformations, there was a strange gravity that pulled him back to Asgard, to this hall and these gods, despite the scorn they heaped on him, despite the mistrust simmering behind every glance. There was something there, deep and silent, that bound him more securely than he would ever admit.

A spark of something darker flickered in Loki's gaze as he raised his cup, his smile as sharp as broken glass.

"Fine, old man. I'll give you your promise. I'll lend you my chaos, my cleverness. But don't be surprised if the price is steep."

Odin's gaze softened, almost imperceptibly, as he raised his own cup.

"I've never expected you to be anything other than what you are."

They clinked cups, and Loki felt a strange weight settle over him, something he could not shake. The promise hung in the air, sealed not with trust or respect, but with a dangerous understanding, one bound by unspoken terms. He could already see the first threads of the storm on the horizon, could almost taste the bitter tang of betrayal that lurked at the edges of this oath. And yet, he knew he would be there, at the center of it, both creator and destroyer, ally and enemy, for that was his nature.

As they drank, Loki allowed himself a final jest, his voice low and edged with irony.

"Be careful, Odin. You might find the trickster's help isn't exactly what you'd bargained for."

Odin smiled again, that dangerous gleam in his eye.

"I would expect nothing less, Loki."

And so, the promise was made – bound not by honor or trust, but by something far more dangerous: an understanding between two beings who knew the weight of their power, and the price it demanded.

* * *

The echoes of his pledge to Odin hung in Loki's mind like cobwebs, catching on every thought he spun in the days that followed. He took to wandering, slipping between forms – wolf, hawk, fox – letting the thrill of transformation blur the edges of his mind. But even as he moved, that promise stayed, like a stone dropped into a still pool, sending ripples through everything he touched.

It wasn't long before Odin summoned him. Loki arrived at the appointed place – an outcropping on the cliffs overlooking Jotunheim – draped in the likeness of a gray hawk, feathers fluffed against the bitter cold. The distant mountains loomed dark and forbidding, their peaks biting into the storm-thickened sky. Below, the shadowed lands of the giants stretched

THE SHAPE OF MISCHIEF

endlessly, a vast, broken wilderness that seemed as wild as Loki's own heart.

Odin, cloaked in a deep black robe, stood at the cliff's edge, his lone eye fixed on the horizon. As Loki shifted back into his own form, he felt the weight of that gaze settle on him, a cold, calculating look that spoke of centuries of watching, waiting, weighing.

Without turning, Odin said, "They're gathering. The giants sense weakness."

Loki let out a soft chuckle, his breath misting in the frigid air. "Weakness? I thought the great All-Father held all things in balance. Or is it that balance doesn't hold as firm as you'd like to think?"

Odin turned, his eye flashing with a dangerous glint. "Even balance has its limits, Loki. That's why I summoned you. I need you to cross the lines that we cannot. I need you to be…persuasive."

"Persuasive?" Loki smirked, folding his arms. "And by that, you mean I should stir the giants into discord? Play the serpent in their midst?"

A ghost of a smile flickered across Odin's face, a hint of the cunning that both gods shared, though Odin would never admit it. "Precisely. Get close to them, as only you can. And if you find the right ears, let them hear whispers. Let them doubt each other. Keep them fractured and feuding, and Jotunheim will remain no threat."

Loki feigned a look of shock, placing a hand over his chest. "You mean to say, the All-Father would ask his loyal trickster to deceive and beguile? I'm flattered, truly."

Odin's expression hardened, any trace of humor vanishing.

"Do not mistake this for sport, Loki. If you fail to do this well, it is not only Asgard that will burn. Even your precious Midgard will feel the giants' wrath. They would sweep the Nine Worlds clean if given the chance."

Loki's eyes narrowed, the cold light in them sharpening.

"And what of my reward, All-Father? I know well enough that you ask for more than my loyalty, and you offer nothing lightly."

Odin's eye met his, unblinking.

"Succeed, and I will give you that which you most desire: freedom from judgment. No more constraints, no more mistrust. You will walk freely in Asgard, untethered by the doubts of others. Fail, and you will be cast out, the door of Valhalla barred to you forever."

Loki's smile faded, and for once, his gaze grew serious. He studied Odin's face, the hard lines and the endless weariness etched into the god's skin. This was no jest. Odin's offer was real, and it bore the weight of an ancient promise – a rare currency indeed.

"Very well," Loki replied, his voice a low murmur. "Consider it done."

Without another word, he turned and leaped from the cliff, his form blurring, wings sprouting from his back as he dove into the wind, vanishing like smoke in the air.

The giants gathered in a dim hall carved from stone and ice, the walls flickering with torchlight that did little to stave off the chill. Loki slithered among them unseen, his form that of a small serpent with scales as dark as night, gliding through the shadows until he reached the ear of the giant-king.

The king of the giants was a towering creature with eyes like chips of glacier, cold and sharp, his massive hand curled around a horn of ale. Loki coiled himself near the giant's ear, his voice a sibilant whisper.

"Great King," he hissed, "have you heard the tales they tell of your strength? They say it is you who should rule the realms, that Asgard itself trembles at your power."

The giant-king's eyes narrowed, his brows knitting as he listened. Loki's words snaked their way into his thoughts, weaving themselves like a web.

"But tell me," Loki continued, his voice a purr, "why do your people murmur that another challenges you? That another is braver, stronger, hungrier for conquest?"

The giant-king's grip tightened on his ale horn, his knuckles pale and strained. "Who speaks of such things?" he growled, his voice a rumble that echoed through the hall.

Loki's smile twisted in the shadows, unseen. "Who indeed? These whispers travel like the wind, nameless and shifting. But I see you, mighty king. I see your strength, your rightful fury. Do not let such rumors fester in silence."

The king sat back, brooding, and Loki slithered away, his work done for the moment. He moved like a shadow, whispering doubts into ears, planting seeds of suspicion in those who had once stood united. He relished the thrill of manipulation, of watching the giants turn on each other with glances sharp as knives, their unity fracturing like ice beneath a sudden weight.

Yet as he moved, weaving his trickery, a strange feeling gnawed at him. He knew the role he played, the purpose he served in this grand design, but the thrill of it felt hollow, like biting into an apple that had gone dry in the core. For every seed of discord he planted, he felt the barbs of his own isolation, the knowledge that he was, as always, the outsider.

When he returned to the cliffs above Jotunheim, his work complete, he felt the weight of that promise to Odin settle over him. It was done – he had sown chaos, secured Asgard's safety, and upheld his part of the bargain.

But as he stood there, staring down into the dark valleys below, he felt no triumph. The lines he'd crossed – the deceit, the treachery – they were second nature to him. And yet, for the first time, he wondered if he'd lost something of himself in the act. Not freedom, not loyalty, but something deeper, something he couldn't yet name.

The wind shifted, carrying with it the faint murmur of distant voices, the sound of giants arguing, the tension he had spun beginning to tighten and snap. Loki closed his eyes, letting the wind wash over him, feeling the pull of that promise, the unyielding tether that bound him back to Asgard, to Odin, to the fate he'd tried so hard to outrun.

As he opened his eyes, he felt a strange certainty settle over him. He had done what was asked, but the debt had not been erased. For a trickster, a shapeshifter, the greatest chains were the ones he could not see, and they weighed heavier than he had ever imagined.

With a bitter smile, he turned back toward Asgard, knowing the next encounter with Odin would come with yet another price.

THE SHAPE OF MISCHIEF

This time, as he flew back to Asgard, his wings beat against the night with a heaviness he could not shake, and he wondered if perhaps, even he could not escape the cost of playing both sides.

* * *

The hall of Asgard gleamed with a harsh light, torches blazing along the walls as the Aesir gathered for a rare feast. Odin presided over the revelry, scanning the crowded hall with an air of imperious detachment. The gods sat in clusters, laughter and talk rolling through the air, a brittle gaiety that seemed to cling to the walls.

Loki entered quietly, his steps light, almost unnoticed, until he reached the heart of the gathering. His presence rippled through the crowd, muting the laughter as gods and warriors turned to look upon him with a mixture of wariness and intrigue. He knew how they saw him – a dangerous ally, a creature who bent truth like light through a prism. Tonight, though, he wore no smile, no mocking glint in his eye. Tonight, he felt the promise he had made, not just to Odin but to his children, who lingered in his mind like silent witnesses.

Odin watched him approach, his gaze as inscrutable as ever, though Loki sensed the sharpness behind it, a readiness like a blade waiting to be drawn. Loki stopped before the high table, bowing with exaggerated elegance, his voice smooth and edged with something dangerous.

"All-Father," he said, letting his words carry across the hall. "I bring you news from Jotunheim. The giants are restless, but they remain divided. They bicker among themselves, feuding over petty slights and old grudges. I have…persuaded them to keep their swords turned inward for now."

Odin inclined his head, a hint of a smile flickering at the corners of his mouth. "You have done well, Loki. You've secured Asgard's peace – at least, for the time being."

Loki straightened, his gaze steady, his own smile thin. "A curious word, peace. It has a way of shifting, slipping through fingers the moment one reaches for it. But I suppose we each have our way of keeping it close."

The hall fell silent, the other gods watching the exchange with a mixture of amusement and tension. Odin's smile faded, his expression sharpening into something colder. "Speak plainly, Loki. If you have more to say, say it."

Loki let the silence stretch, his gaze moving from Odin to the other gods seated around him. "Very well," he said softly, his voice carrying the burden of withheld truths, secrets that had smoldered in his heart for too long. "Perhaps it's time we consider what this peace is built upon. Perhaps it's time we speak of secrets held in shadow, even here in the shining heart of Asgard."

Odin's eye narrowed, but he said nothing, allowing Loki to continue. Loki's voice grew sharper, each word a dagger.

"You all trust Odin, of course. Why wouldn't you? The great All-Father, who holds our fates in his hand, who spins the threads of our destinies with such careful precision." He paused, letting his words settle into the room. "And yet, what do we know of the secrets he keeps? What do we know of the bargains he's struck, the promises he has made and broken in silence?"

The tension thickened, the gods glancing at one another, uncertainty flickering in their eyes. Odin's gaze remained steady, but there was a dangerous edge in his voice as he replied, "You tread carefully, Loki. Remember that even you are bound by oaths, bound by the threads that keep this realm whole."

Loki laughed, a cold, mirthless sound. "Oaths? And what of the oaths you have broken, Odin? What of the price others pay for the power you wield? We all bear the burden of your choices, your sacrifices made without consent, without even a hint of warning."

Thor's voice rumbled from across the table, his tone thick with contempt. "Enough of your games, trickster. You sow nothing but discord, as you always have."

Loki turned to Thor, his eyes gleaming with a dangerous light. "Discord, Thor? Perhaps it is not discord to tell the truth, to unmask the illusion you all cling to so tightly. And if discord lies in that truth, perhaps the fault is not mine but in the shadows you refuse to see."

Odin's voice cut through the hall, cold and final. "Speak your accusations plainly, Loki, or be silent."

Loki met his gaze, a strange mixture of defiance and sadness in his eyes. "Very well. I will speak plainly." He took a step closer, lowering his voice, yet letting it resonate in the great room. "You hoard a relic, a weapon of unspeakable power, one that could turn even the strongest of us to dust. You keep it hidden, even from those closest to you, for fear of losing control."

A ripple of shock swept through the hall, the gods shifting uneasily, murmurs rising like the hiss of a snake. Loki could see the spark of doubt in their eyes, the small fissures of trust beginning to crack. He had planted the seed, and now he let it grow.

Odin's face remained impassive, but his eye held a cold fury. "You are a fool, Loki. This power, this relic – it is not something to be wielded lightly. Its very existence threatens the balance we have fought to preserve."

Loki's gaze held steady, his voice soft but fierce. "And yet, you keep it hidden, as if it were a mere trinket. You hold it close, unshared, unchallenged. And for what? To preserve a peace that is built on secrets and fear?"

Odin rose slowly, his presence filling the hall, his voice a low, terrible rumble. "Enough of this," he said, his tone like the first crack of thunder before a storm. "You think yourself clever, Loki, but there are forces at work that even you cannot understand. You meddle in matters beyond your reckoning."

Loki stepped back, his face a mask of defiance and resignation. "Perhaps. But I will not stand by and pretend that this is peace. I will not be silent while you hold our fates in your grasp, hidden in shadows you control."

Odin's gaze hardened, a finality in his eye. "Then you leave me no choice, Loki. By your own hand, you have broken the bond that held you in Asgard's favor. From this day forward, you are cast out. You will no longer find welcome in these halls, nor refuge in this realm."

The hall fell silent, the gods staring at Loki, some with pity, others with satisfaction, as Odin's words settled like stones. Loki looked around, feeling the vast emptiness of his exile even before it had fully taken shape. But there was no regret in his eyes, no hint of submission.

THE SHAPE OF MISCHIEF

Instead, he laughed – a soft, cold laugh, filled with irony. "So, this is how it ends, then. The trickster cast out, the truth silenced to preserve a lie. But remember this, Odin." His voice grew sharper, carrying a warning that lingered like a shadow. "Even in exile, even in darkness, I will not be silenced. I am a part of this realm, woven into its fate, whether you like it or not. And when the storm comes, as it always does, you will remember my words."

With that, he turned, striding out of the hall, the eyes of the gods following him with a mixture of awe and fear. He could feel the weight of his banishment, the cold emptiness that lay ahead, but he walked forward with a fierce, unyielding pride. He would no longer be bound by the rules of Asgard, no longer held by the silent bonds of oaths he had never fully believed in.

As he stepped beyond the gates, the night stretched out before him, vast and unyielding, a wilderness waiting to be claimed. Loki breathed in the cold air, feeling it settle into his bones, filling him with a strange, liberating calm.

He was alone, yes, cast out and unwanted, but he was also free – a trickster unbound, his fate now his own to shape, as wild and changeable as the wind. And in that freedom, he felt the first flicker of something he had not known in centuries: purpose, sharpened by the very exile that had once seemed his greatest fear.

He would carve his own path, one step at a time, with no allegiance but to himself and the truth he bore. And as he vanished into the darkness, he knew that Asgard would not soon forget him – for even in his absence, his presence would linger, like a shadow that refused to fade.

323

MYTHS, GODS & IMMORTALS: LOKI

And so, with a final, defiant laugh, Loki disappeared into the night, the storm of his own making gathering quietly at his heels.

* * *

Loki wandered beyond Asgard, the weight of exile pressing down on him like a cold wind. Yet, despite the sharp pang of rejection that lingered in his chest, a peculiar sense of lightness accompanied his steps. Asgard's constraints, those unspoken boundaries and silent rules, no longer held him. He could feel his own nature, raw and unfettered, humming in his veins.

Days passed in silence. Loki moved through Midgard and beyond, his form shifting like a dream – sometimes a raven soaring against gray clouds, sometimes a silver fox darting through woods dark with pine. He felt the world shifting around him, the Nine Realms vibrating in their eternal dance of light and shadow. But within him was a growing realization, a quiet question gnawing at his thoughts like water eroding stone.

What was he, without Asgard's watchful eyes and his place within its schemes? For so long, he had defined himself by what he opposed, by his role as a foil to the Aesir. But here, alone in the silence, the familiar patterns began to unravel. There was no throne to challenge, no eye upon him, no bonds to strain against.

And then, on a cold night beneath a canopy of stars, he found himself once more at the edge of the Nine Worlds, staring into the endless void that stretched beyond. He looked out, a solitary figure standing on the cusp of existence itself, and his laughter echoed into the emptiness, bright and wild.

THE SHAPE OF MISCHIEF

It was here, at the edge of all things, that he heard a voice.

"You laugh, even now?" It was a voice soft yet potent, familiar and strange at once. Loki turned, seeing a figure emerge from the shadows – a tall, robed woman with a face as unyielding as the cold night itself. The Norn Skuld, keeper of the future, stared at him with eyes that seemed to pierce through his many shapes and guises.

"Ah, Skuld," Loki replied, his smile wry. "I wasn't aware my laughter required approval."

The Norn's expression remained impassive. "You stand on the precipice of realms, unbound and unshackled, yet you linger here, as though awaiting something."

Loki shrugged, feigning indifference. "I am merely enjoying the view. Some of us aren't as bound to our threads as you Norns might think."

Skuld stepped closer, her eyes narrowing as she studied him. "Do not lie to me, Loki. You search for purpose, even now, though you would rather laugh than admit it."

Loki's gaze drifted away, a hint of the smile fading.

"Purpose," he repeated, the word a faint whisper in the vastness around them. "Strange thing to seek, don't you think? It's a cage, as binding as any oath."

"And yet," Skuld said, her voice sharp, "you have been running toward it your entire life. You, who would play the trickster, the outcast, the instigator. All this time, you have sought something more than freedom – something to make that freedom bearable."

Loki felt the truth of her words settle over him like frost, chilling yet clarifying. He looked back at her, his expression devoid of the usual slyness, stripped down to something raw and unguarded.

"Tell me, then, wise Norn," he murmured. "What lies ahead for one such as me? What thread could possibly hold one who slips through every net?"

Skuld's gaze softened, and for the first time, her voice carried something close to compassion.

"Fate is not merely a thread, Loki. It is not fixed in the way you imagine. Each choice you make, each act of defiance, weaves new paths. Even now, in exile, you shape the destiny of Asgard, of Midgard – of all realms. It is in your nature."

Loki laughed again, though this time the sound was quieter, almost rueful.

"You speak as if I have a choice. As if I could choose to be anything other than the trickster."

Skuld stepped even closer, her gaze meeting his with fierce intensity.

"It is not the role that defines you, Loki, but what you make of it. The storm you bring is not a curse, nor a blessing. It is simply the truth of who you are – a force, a shifting, an unmasking. And in that, there is freedom."

Loki considered her words, allowing them to sink into him.

A force, a shifting.

He had always thought of himself as trapped by fate, bound to play the trickster's part, but here, at the edge of all things, he felt something strange – a glimmer of purpose not tied to deception or opposition, but to transformation itself. His laughter was not a rejection, but an invitation to see deeper, to unmask and reveal the hidden.

THE SHAPE OF MISCHIEF

He looked out once more over the dark, endless void, a feeling rising in him that was neither joy nor sorrow, but something vast and resonant, a sense of belonging not to any one realm, but to all realms. In his exile, he had discovered the truest shape of his freedom – not as an escape, but as a calling to shape and reshape, to bring light and shadow into sharper relief.

Finally, he turned to Skuld, his gaze calm and certain.

"Thank you," he said, his voice soft. "For reminding me of who I am."

Skuld inclined her head, her gaze gentle.

"Then go, Loki. Go, and bring your truth to the realms. Shape them, unmask them. This is your purpose, if you would claim it."

Loki smiled, a deep, genuine smile that felt as natural as breath. And with a final nod to Skuld, he turned and stepped forward into the unknown, his form shifting into a raven, his wings spreading wide against the star-strewn sky. He flew across the expanse, a solitary figure moving through the endless tapestry of the Nine Worlds, a trickster no longer bound by the roles others had cast for him.

Now, he was a creator of his own making, a force that would not merely challenge but reveal, his purpose as vast and changing as the cosmos itself.

And in that boundless freedom, Loki knew he would never be alone, for his path was the very edge between shadow and light, chaos and order, a constant reminder to all who would see: there was truth even in trickery, meaning even in mischief, and in the laughter of the unbound heart, a song that would echo through all things.

Laufey's Son

C. Adam Volle

One blow, that was all it took – one blow upon his raised shield, and the thin, red-headed boy fell to the grass with a grunt.

"This," his brother Helblindi pronounced, lowering his club, "is hopeless."

Outside the fighting circle, their father Fárbauti frowned, but he noticeably did not disagree. Beside him, their older brother Býleistr smirked.

"I think that's enough for the day," Fárbauti said after a moment, rising from his crouch. "Býleistr, Helblindi, why don't you go in? We'll be along."

The two older boys turned and made for the nearby hill, mumbling to each other once they were close enough to not be overheard – though there was hardly any question as to what they were saying. Their sibling watched them go with a dark expression.

Then the shadow of his father fell upon him and said, "Get up, Loki."

Loki did as he was asked, though he could not help groaning in the process. The past few hours of practiced combat had left him shaky-limbed and covered in bruises.

"You know what I'm going to say," said his father.

Loki said it aloud anyway. "I can't come with you."

"Not this year."

"It's a dishonor."

"You have more growing to do."

This was a kind twisting of the truth. In recent years Loki had grown as tall as his brothers, but his torso and limbs had stubbornly refused to thicken. The boy clearly took after his mother, whom his father had always affectionately called "Needle." So yes, there was more growing to do, certainly, if Loki were ever to join the men of his family in their forays abroad. But it was unlikely there was more growing to be done.

Fárbauti picked up Loki's club and handed it to the boy, then started for the hill himself. Loki hurried to fall in beside him while slinging his shield across his back.

"But it's good that there will be a man of the hall here," said Fárbauti as they walked. He gestured at the fields to their right and left with an arc of his hand, where figures could be seen at work. "It keeps the thralls in line."

Loki rather doubted that the slaves would obey him at all, were they not magically bound to do so, but he held his tongue. His father was still trying to make him feel better. The least Loki could do in gratitude was not argue with him.

"As for tonight, tell one of your stories," Fárbauti was saying, "and nobody shall be able to hold the slightest ill will against you. What's that one about the jötunn who recognized Odin…?"

This question, of course, resulted in Loki having to retell the tale, which took up the rest of the time that the pair spent walking up the slope, just as it was meant to do. By the time that Loki had finished, they had reached the summit, and the small village atop it had shimmered into view. The invisibility of the feasting hall and its surrounding houses was one of several illusions that had been recently cast in preparation for the absence of their defenders. The grass beneath their feet turned to well-worn paths leading toward each home, but Fárbauti did not step onto the one for theirs. Instead he continued the ascent toward the mead hall that capped their village's hill like a great helm. He gave a wave and said, "I'll prepare for the feast later. I'm going to speak to your uncle."

Loki suspected otherwise, but he said nothing.

Inside the one-room longhouse that Loki's family occupied, the boy found himself alone; married with children, his brothers had stepped out from under Fárbauti's roof years ago. The thralls had readied a basin full of water for him and he washed himself with it, then put on what he considered to be his finest tunic, trousers, and robe. He felt as he did as though he were indeed girding himself for war, for he knew that he would be either ignored by the other young men that evening, who would talk excitedly of the glory they would soon be winning on the battlefield, or be the easy target of their dull wit, roundly mocked for remaining with the women.

It was as Loki added a necklace of glass beads to his attire that the door opened and his mother Laufey entered the house. Her appearance confirmed Loki's suspicion that his father had returned to the hall in order to report Loki's failure to his wife, not to confer with his brother. Naturally, she had now hied to Loki's side to comfort him – aggravation of the injury, though she knew it not. He picked up one of the arm bands he had set out to wear.

"Loki," she said.

"Mother."

"I heard from your father. I am sorry."

"Are you?" he asked, clasping the arm band.

"It is true that no mother finds pleasure in sending her sons to war, but yes. For your sake I am sorry."

"Mm. Well, thank you."

"Next summer," she began.

He sighed.

"Next summer, he will have you," she insisted.

"And if he does not?" Loki asked. "Then what place is there for me here? Right now I have my seat at table because I am Loki Fárbautason. But I will soon be mocked if that is the only reason, and eventually, I will be hated. Men will refuse my friendship, women my love. Mother – I would rather be dead."

"Show the bravery now that you would if you were on the battlefield, my son. Do not cower before your future any more than you would the warriors of the Aesir. Instead, plan to defeat it."

"And how might I do that?"

The air in the room changed. He had frustrated her.

"That is your own challenge," he heard her say, her voice retreating toward the door.

He thought the conversation over, but then heard his mother say, "Loki Fárbautason."

The boy stifled another sigh as he turned. "Yes, Mother."

"We are named the jötnar," the woman began.

"Kin of Ymir's blood," Loki continued instinctively.

"Feared by men and gods."

"Mighty and wise."

Rather than proceed to the poem's next line, Laufey repeated, "Mighty…and wise."

Then added: "I know many warriors who could be called the former, Loki, but few the latter. Yet I see that potential in you. While your father and your brothers are gone once more to uselessly break their bodies against the shields of the Aesir, consider how you might fulfill it."

And without waiting for her son's response, she left.

* * *

The farewell feast would play out in much the way Loki expected. Later he would retain dim memories of responding to his peers' jests with barbs of his own, ones that he knew even as he drunkenly spewed them would result in his receiving a beating, and not just a beating but the kind of thrashing that he might have normally avoided, due to his older brothers' protection – only, his brothers were themselves the targets of his insults, for they had recalled with much mirth how, as a child, Loki had sometimes transformed into a girl, so that he could join the daughters of the village in their discussions and games. Loki's memories of the toasts, on the other hand, would be clear: how all of the men at the table who were going into battle had toasted each of their number in turn ("Fárbauti Flosason!" "Býleistr

Fárbautason!" "Helblindi Fárbautason!"), one after the other, and how they had passed over him.

The next day, Fárbauti led Loki's brothers and the other warriors of the village down the hill, through the fields, and into the forest, on the other side of which they would unite with other jötnar on the road to war. The women, children, and thralls all watched their departure, waiting until the last of the men had disappeared into the trees before setting about their duties for the day. Loki remained a little longer yet, as though one of the men might soon reappear and motion for him to come. When he finally did break away, he returned to his house, and he did not emerge until night-meal.

* * *

Death came to Fárbauti's hall three nights later.

It found Loki absent. The previous evening, Loki's mother had finally spat at him that if he were going to spend all day sulking indoors instead of working, he could feed himself. Loki responded by not showing up for the following meals. A battle of wills had thus begun, which was the happy gossip of the table that night, before all talk dwindled and finally ceased at the creaking of a slowly opening door.

The face of a troll filled the building's entrance; its bloodstained smile extended from post to post as it said, "Health and happiness, Dear Jötnar." Then its claws and those of its fellows pierced the hall's ceiling, and there arose many screams.

When Loki cracked open his own door, he saw that the roof of the hall had been split apart, and that three trolls loomed over the torn-open structure, peering into its interior as if into an opened chest. To his horror, one troll already held a corpse within one black-nailed hand. The body lacked a head. This troll – the one who had first given greeting, though Loki did not know it – now grinned down at the women and children inside the hall.

"One of your thralls tried to escape," it said. "When we found him, he attempted to purchase our favor by telling us your whereabouts."

"But we have our honor," the monster added, raising the headless corpse higher now for their inspection. "Never would we reward such rank treachery. Here is your unfaithful servant, Jötnar, justice done."

The troll dropped the body into the hall. Loki heard its weight crash onto a table.

"Now, who is in charge here?" asked the beast.

A moment passed before a voice called up from within the hall, "I am!"

Loki recognized it as his mother's.

"The lady of the hall, I presume," said the troll.

"I am," said Loki's mother, and: "My name is Laufey Ljótrdóttir."

"Well met, Jötunn. I am Róg. My comrades are Drepa and Glymja. We bid you well."

"Well met," said the troll to Róg's left – whether Drepa or Glymja, Loki was unsure.

"Well met," said the troll to the right.

"Not so well as to spare our roof, I see," said Laufey, putting into her voice as much defiance as she could muster – or perhaps that she felt she could dare.

334

"But perhaps well enough to spare your lives, Lady Laufey, if you will hear us out."

"I am listening, Róg Roof-Wrecker."

The troll chuckled.

Then it said, "We are both children of Ymir, Lady; we are both risi. As the Fates would have it, however, we are but brutes, while you possess talent for all manner of arts. We have come to ask that you put these gifts to our service."

"And in what way might jötnar serve trolls?"

"By settling a debate," said Róg. "You see, Drepa and Glymja have only eaten the raw meat of animals, humans, and yes, jötnar such as yourselves. They do not believe me when I tell them that the finest taste in the world is to be found in the jötunn's kitchen."

"You want us to cook for you," said Laufey, dumbstruck.

"Yes. A stew. You call it skause. Once I laid waste to a hall of your kin and found a full pot of it boiling over a fire. Never before had I experienced such a taste. I would do so again, and share the delight of it with my brethren."

"And if we make you what you wish?"

"Satisfy our appetites," said the troll, "and what need is there to feed upon you? We will leave you in peace."

"Then we agree to your request. But it will take time to make enough for all three of you."

"Time we have; the sun has only just set. But do not tarry, my lady, and do not seek to escape. You and your fellows may do as you please in order to make your preparations, but we will keep the children here before us – and we will not depart from this place with empty bellies."

The night grew relatively quiet, then, as Laufey ceased to shout at the trolls and instead began talking to her peers. Quietly, Loki closed the door to his house again. He went to the back wall of his home and took down the shield hanging there, which he pulled over his arm, then the sword hanging above it. He unsheathed the sword and set the scabbard to the side. He gave the weapon a single, experimental swing. It felt as awkward in his hand as it had the last time he'd practiced with it. Turning, he crossed back to the door, whereupon it opened.

His mother entered the house, terror written across her face – and then suddenly fury, as her eyes took in the sight of him.

"What are you doing?" she hissed, slamming the door closed behind her.

Loki raised himself to his full height, but whatever manly resolve he hoped to project was undercut when he stuttered, "I— I have to—"

She slapped him across the face.

"You stupid boy," she said. "They would make a snack of you while they wait."

It took Loki a moment to answer, for to his horror his eyes were welling up, and he realized his voice was in danger of breaking.

"And after you feed them, they will make you their dessert," he finally said with a sniff.

She locked eyes with him. "Not if they are dead."

Loki hesitated.

"You have a plan," he murmured.

"I do. Put down your sword and shield, Loki," she said. "You know that in your father's house is one of this family's greatest possessions – a flask of eitr. A single drop will kill even one of those trolls. We need only poison the skause with it. Go and retrieve it while I go to the pits."

Loki frowned, doubtful. "How am I to bring it to you?"

"What?"

"For the moment, they are willing to let women and children live. They are not likely to afford the same grace to a man."

"Then do not come as a man," Laufey said, just before she reopened the door.

Loki watched her step back out into the night.

* * *

Loki understood her meaning. Still, some moments passed before Loki did as he was bid, setting down his sword and shield, then walked to the little library of scrolls in their home to find the necessary runes. He had not spoken the magic words in years – not since his father had sat him down one day, called his use of them "perverted," and forbidden him from ever using them again. The scroll was where he had left it.

He unrolled the parchment, cleared his throat, and began reading the figures aloud. As he did, his red hair lengthened, growing from his neck down to the small of his back. The mass along his throat shrank. His chest grew, softened and rounded; his hips widened.

By the time he had finished pronouncing all the symbols on the scroll, the transformation was complete: He was a young girl. The immediate feeling was two-fold: a familiar comfort that he had dared not explain to his father when the old man had confronted him, alongside a terror at that first feeling and what it might suggest.

But there was no time to meditate on either emotion. Putting aside the scroll, Loki crossed to the chest in the house that contained his father's personal effects. Rummaging within it, he eventually found the small flask of eitr, that primordial poison out of which life itself first formed. He wondered where his father had obtained such a treasure. Perhaps if he survived to see the man again, he would ask. He placed the flask in a small bag and departed the house.

Outside, the night was abuzz with activity. As the trolls watched, all the inhabitants of the village – first the women, children, and thralls of the hall, but soon everyone who had not departed with Fárbauti – were swarming the outdoor cooking pits. These had last been used for the men's farewell feast, three nights beforehand, and so they were no longer ready for use; firewood had to be procured, then the fires set and stoked, and afterward the largest pots placed upon them, which needed to be filled with water. Meanwhile the ingredients required preparation: the carrots, the turnips, the cabbage, and the leeks – and of course the meat, which meant slaughtering one of the cows. It would indeed take some time to make the trolls their meal.

Loki's mother was taking part in this process when he found her, dropping an armful of small logs into the pit for arranging by Angrboda.

"Ljúfa," Loki's mother said before he could utter a word. "Did you bring the seasoning?"

Angrboda looked up at Loki, her face clearly questioning the sudden appearance of this girl she had never before seen. Loki did his best to ignore her by fully facing his mother, whom he presented with the flask.

"I have," he said.

"Good. Keep it," she said, "and you can add it when the time is right. For now, help us with the fire."

Loki nodded and placed the little flask back in his bag. To avoid any questions from Angrboda, he assigned himself to the woodpile.

The work took hours. Loki's limbs eventually grew tired, as he imagined the others' did – particularly the younger boys and girls, none of whom the adults dared to dismiss. But though the work may have slowed, it never stopped; it could not stop.

Finally, the meat and vegetables were boiled in the mead, the herbs applied. All of the individually cooked pots were carefully drained by the weary women into one big cauldron, the largest in the village. Beside this cauldron were placed three great water jugs emptied of their contents, which the women hoped would serve for the trolls' dishes, since no bowl or plate in the village was of a sufficient size. When these jugs were lined up beside the bubbling vat, Loki's mother nodded to him, and then she returned to the mead hall. Loki took the flask out of his bag again as his mother climbed onto the table.

"Róg. Drepa. Glymja," she yelled.

As the trolls turned their attention to his mother, Loki poured the eitr.

"Your night-meal is ready," he heard her say.

The trolls made noises of hunger as they looked down at her, then over at the cauldron and jars. One troll – Drepa or Glymja, Loki did not remember – said, "It certainly smells good."

"But we will see how it tastes," said the other, approaching the vat.

"One moment," said Róg.

The troll's fellows frowned. Clearly, the wait had drained them of patience.

"We do not doubt your hospitality, Lady," said Róg. "Nevertheless, we would have you take the first taste. Just to ensure the skause has been correctly prepared, you understand."

Loki's mother nodded, hopped down from the table, and returned to the cauldron. She gestured at Loki, who produced a wooden spoon for her. She dipped the spoon into the skause and retrieved with it a dollop of the brown stew, which she blew to cool. Then she ate.

After waiting a moment, as though to allow her stomach enough time to thoroughly appraise what it had been given, she looked up at the trolls and nodded. Róg clapped and rubbed his hairy hands together.

"Wonderful," it said, and reached down to take the cauldron in his massive hand.

One would have thought the great pot would have burned the troll's palm, but Róg seemed untroubled by the iron's heat. With care, the troll picked up the cauldron and evenly divided its contents into the three jugs while the other trolls watched. Once the cauldron was completely empty, he set it down again and took up one of the jugs. The other trolls did likewise.

With a toothy grin, Róg raised his jar into the air.

"Skål," said Róg.

"Skål," the other two trolls repeated.

And they drank.

Even the largest jugs in the village's possession were but cups to the trolls, so each one downed its portion in one pull. Róg lowered his jug first, a smile spreading across its face. He looked at his fellows, searching their countenances for confirmation that the skause was all that he had described to them. He received it: Both trolls emitted groans of pleasure as they finished their portions. They lowered the jugs licking their lips.

"Delicious," said one troll – Drepa or Glymja, Loki could not say.

"Incredible," said the other.

The three trolls briefly stood in silence, clearly savoring the taste in their mouths.

"But it does not satisfy," added the first troll.

"No, it does not satisfy," agreed the second.

"It is a morsel rather than a meal," Róg admitted. "If we wish to fill our bellies tonight, we will have to do so on more standard fare."

And the three trolls looked back down at the women and children in the hall.

"You said that if we prepared your skause, you would leave us in peace," said Loki's mother.

"I said that if you satisfied our appetites, there would be no need to feed on you," Róg corrected her. "Alas, we find ourselves unfilled. But I acknowledge you are deserving of consideration, Dear Lady, and so I will make you one more promise..."

The troll extended one of his hairy arms down into the hall. The screams began again.

"We will save you for last," he said as his claws closed around Loki, "and if we are full by the time it is your turn, we will leave you be."

Róg lifted Loki into the air.

"But I confess that is unlikely," the troll added.

He opened his mouth.

"No!" Laufey cried.

The troll closed his mouth.

The beast's change in course occurred not due to the anguished cry of Loki's mother, but a curiosity – a wet sensation on his cheek. The troll raised a finger to his eye and withdrew from it a tear – dark red, iron-smelling.

"No," Róg muttered, then looked at his fellows. The two other trolls looked back at him, each of their faces already crimson-streaked.

"Poisoned," whispered Róg. And: "How?"

"The jugs, of course," said Laufey.

Róg sighed. "Of course."

He dropped Loki, who landed in the grass below.

One by one, the three trolls sank to the earth, the blood pouring more freely now not only from their eyes but their noses and mouths. One by one, their breathing slowed.

"A costly meal," gasped one troll – Drepa or Glymja, Loki would never know.

"Hardly worth it," opined the other.

"My friends, I apologize," Róg coughed.

And they died.

Only after the three gargantuan bodies had failed to stir for some time did the occupants of the hall emerge from what remained of the building and cautiously approach. Loki's mother led them, the quicker to reach her son, who was already sitting up in the grass.

"Mother," he said when she stood over him.

She looked down at him. "Loki. Now, I think, it is time for you to get your sword."

He blinked. "Now? To what end?"

She smiled. "To claim their heads. You can present them to your father when he returns. Here, let me help you up."

"He will know I did not slay them," Loki said as he accepted her hand.

"He will know you did not kill them with a sword," she answered. "He will not know that the plan to use the eitr was not yours, when we say it was. And he will celebrate your wit."

Loki's face slackened as he realized the truth. "That is why you had me bring the eitr. You wished to make me the hero."

She leaned against him, smiling now.

"Loki Fárbautason," she said, as though speaking a name warriors cheered in their halls.

"I think," replied Loki after a moment, "I would prefer to be 'Loki Laufeyson.'"

The God of Lead and Blood
M.M. Williams

He didn't know how many years he'd been chained to this tree.

Iron bands bit into his wrists, his neck, his forehead. Flaxen thread kept his mouth sewn tightly shut. Drip, drip, drip. Burning, searing, excruciating. How long had she been gone? A minute? A century?

So monotonous was it that he instantly recognized the moment when, far outside these depths of Miðgarðr, far below the searing fire in his blood, he sensed chaos unlike any he'd ever known. Even from here, he could feel the screams.

Ragnarok.

Frantic footsteps echoed through the cavern, and the sound of a swinging sword. His serpentine torturer's head fell against his shoulder and tumbled to the ground. The ties in his mouth were also cut, allowing him to suck in a frigid gasp.

The haze of venom continued to cloud his eyes, but he saw her moving amidst the fog. Rosy cheeks worthy of poems and hair of fairest gold, just like all her brothers. She raised her sword above him and swung the blade down against his bonds around his arms. Again and again she brought it down, crying out in exertion. Upon the tenth hit, the iron encircling him cracked and fell, and Loki fell with it.

THE GOD OF LEAD AND BLOOD

"My…love," he rasped through a broken throat and an ossified tongue. Were it possible, he would reach for her, but fatigue weighed down his limbs, and his usual strength was not returning as it should have.

Sigyn wrapped him in his old cloak, the first warmth he'd felt since his imprisonment. "Even Fenrir and Jrmungandr could not defeat them. The stags have prevailed and chewed through the last branches of the world tree. Vili and Ve have fallen, as has Tyr. Ásgarðr is crumbling. There are no eyes fixed upon us now."

Loki's lungs grew tight. "…Hel?"

She paused in sympathy. "I don't know of any who fled Niflheim in time."

He'd known this time would come, yet that knowledge didn't make the arrival less bitter. His three most impressive creations. Gone.

"…the…children?" he asked.

"Safe. Ready to run."

That allowed his breath to relax somewhat. Heavy eyelids slowly wiped away the haze to behold her clearly. "Run where?"

"To the edge of this world," she whispered. "To a new land where wolves and snakes and horses run free. I swore to you that we would one day be free. Today, I keep that promise."

Loyal, honey-hearted Sigyn, who had always seen in him the good that no other could, had protected him when no other would.

Before anything else, Loki kissed his wife.

And they ran.

***

The barkeep had barely finished wiping up the spilled beer from the counter when the first stranger entered, brawny and bearded, with a patch over his eye. A long black feather stuck out of his hat, and a rifle was slung across his back.

After him came a woman in blue dress, with greying hair twisted into a crown of braids. The barkeep put his elbows on the bar, watching them warily as they strode inside, heads swiveling left and right, searching. Age hadn't been terribly kind to the pair, forming deep grooves across their skin, pulling their cheeks down into jowls.

The barkeep adjusted his glasses. "Just the two of you? Could've sworn I heard another horse riding alongside you."

"Ears are easily deceived," said the old man, voice bouncing with a heavy northern accent that caught the attention of everyone nearby.

"So," asked the barkeep, "you gonna buy a drink or just take up space?"

"Do you know a settlement called Holt?"

He'd known that question was coming – why else would these two be wandering through the San Bernardino mountains?

"Little town just north of here," he answered. "Keep to themselves mostly. Every now and again, one pops down here."

"What do you know of the man who leads them?"

The barkeep looked the old man in his one blue eye. "Lonnie's got lead in his blood."

THE GOD OF LEAD AND BLOOD

The old man sighed for a long time, and then reached for his wife, pulling her to the side – though not far enough for their conversation to become secret. "You should stay here," he told her gruffly. "Rest, my heart."

"We've traveled all this way," the woman said. "I shouldn't like to cower away from the battle now."

"We don't know that this is going to turn to bloodshed."

"When the both of you are involved, has anything ever not?"

As they spoke, the barkeep looked at the stock of the man's rifle, the grain of the wood ever so familiar. The corded muscle of Yggdrasil.

It wasn't a surprise to see Gungnir in this form. The sword and the spear had been outshone by far more destructive instruments, and in this wild land, there was no other option than to upgrade. Such was the way of things, that something greater would usurp what came before.

As the couple continued to mutter to each other, the barkeep backed into the shadows, into the storeroom of the saloon where the true owner of the establishment still slumbered. Once outside in the hot morning sun, he tossed away his glasses, knelt, and allowed his bones to stretch and break.

A few moments later, in the form of a brown appaloosa horse, Loki bolted for the mountains, tearing up dirt with each crash of his hooves against the ground.

How old those two were now. Not that it was particularly surprising. A god was nothing without devotion, without offerings given by mortal souls.

Thus, the great conversions to new faith had brought their end, slowly draining the hidden realms of their power as belief began to wane. Time had left them starved, surviving on the remnant scraps of hidden loyalty and passing curiosity. Worship had, for the most part, been forgotten. But the stories had lingered, and thus, the old gods had lingered too.

And these old gods dared to come here after what they'd done.

He didn't slow his breakneck pace as he came into Holt. Every eye in town watched as he tore through the street to get to his home.

When it came into view, he forced himself to stop and reared back into his truest form, tall and thin and beastly. Mousy brown hair fell in spikes over his forehead, sodden after his furious run. Every huff that left his mouth carried hot anger.

Not far away, on the porch of, was the beauty of the pair. Sigyn sat in the sun, golden hair loose and long, partway through weaving a yard of cotton fabric.

When she noticed his arrival, she sat up, wiping the sweat from a brow furrowed in concern. "You're early."

"Ring the bell, get the boys in from the field," Loki said as he leapt onto the porch. "Tell 'em to get their guns. And tell everyone else to get inside."

"What on earth for?" she asked in alarm.

He paused in the doorway, gritting his teeth hard enough to hurt. "Your father is coming."

* * *

When they arrived, he was already outside, dressed in his work clothes. He didn't feel like cleaning blood out of his good suit today.

Odin dismounted from Sleipnir, and Frigg from Glaðr. Only the wind spoke as all appraised each other for the first time in a hundred years or more. Two ravens flew overheard, their shadows slithering over the grassy ground.

"Wondered when we'd hear from you," Loki said simply, resting his hand on his Colt.

Sigyn came out of the house, dressed in her finest, and Frigg's chin wobbled at the sight of her daughter.

Sigyn gestured to the door. "Come in for some lemonade, Mother. The boys can fight outside."

She gave Loki a knowing look which carried a fair hint of warning, and he sighed.

"Follow me," he ordered Odin, pointing to the vast garden that stretched behind the house. "Don't touch her carnations, or she'll tan your hide."

As he walked forward, Odin surveyed the buildings and their residents, only a few of whom were jötunn, troll, elf, or dwarf. "I did not think there would be mortals here."

"Well, you clearly didn't know that Holt is home to the best doctor in the west," Loki answered, "and a man that not even the most ruthless gangs dare cross."

He and Sigyn had worked their tails off to build their reputations in the county – to find mortals who relied on them enough to act as devotees and give them back a fraction of the godly strength they'd once possessed. He robbed the corrupt rich. She healed the poor. Both of them kept the town in line. Together, they'd earned respect and power once again.

He walked with Odin to the end of Sigyn's garden, off into the hills, until they were surrounded by grass and brush. They stopped to look at the morning sky and the birds in it.

"What are you doing here?" Odin asked eventually.

"You expected me to sit and drink venom for all eternity?" Loki asked right back.

"Surely, you know you tread on land which is not yours. This is a forsaken place, bathed in sword-sweat."

"You can choose to rot next to your wooden crosses back in the frozen north," Loki said tightly, "but you don't get to choose for me. This is our home, and we're not leaving."

Odin's brow furrowed in frustration. "You cannot stay here. The war has gone too far."

"That's what brought you here?" Loki hissed, whipping toward him. "You hunted me down because you think *I* started the Great Rebellion, you floppy prick? The settlers here were spilling blood and worshipping gold long before I ever arrived in the New World, and they'll do it long after I leave."

"So, you expect me to believe you are living out your days as a simple farmer? That you do not draw any power from this chaos?"

Loki barked out a harsh laugh. "Is it truly so hard to believe that I don't spend my life manipulating every soul who skitters past me? Is it so terrible that me and my kin might enjoy some freedom from judgment here in our own damn town? Did you miss pointing a finger at me so much that you traveled around the world just to do it again?"

THE GOD OF LEAD AND BLOOD

Odin's jaw worked in discomfort. "I did not start the rumors about you, nor did I write the stories."

"You sure didn't stop them, either."

"You cannot say that they are all false."

"A blind goat could tell you I'm not a good man. Hell, I'll tell you myself. I've insulted all of you. I've played tricks, lied, stole. I've killed in cold blood. So have all of you. So did you, once." He paused to curl his lip. "You made me as I am, and you've punished me for it every day since."

A carefully chosen word. Loki had not been born, but made. An unwelcome consequence of the moment when Odin had, in pursuit of wisdom and glory, struck a bargain with a seeress. He'd wished to rid himself of all imperfection, leaving only wisdom and valor.

The völva had said that such a feat would require the loss of something he cherished, and on her orders, he had raised his knife and carved out his own eye. Anything to be rid of weakness.

Anything to be perfect.

The seeress had reached into his heart, and into his fallen eye, she'd poured his pride, his fear, his dishonesty, his excess of lust. For one heartbeat, Odin had gloried in his success. Truly, he was meant to be chief among the gods, for he had done what no other being could, and achieved perfection.

Until the eye had begun to grow into a body. Into a child, plain of face and unremarkable in build, with prominent ribs and scarred skin.

Loki had awoken and asked, "*Who am I?*"

"A jötunn's son, abandoned," Odin had said, the lie falling easily from his tongue.

But the völva had secretly given her memory of Odin's deed to Loki, and he knew Odin's statement for the falsehood it was. Both had realized then that the seeress had played a trick. All flaws still existed within Odin, and as punishment for his hubris, all his imperfections would haunt him in physical form.

Loki pulled a jackknife from his pocket, slicing across his palm to let black blood fall to the ground, every drop inhaled greedily by the arid soil. "Kill me, then. Spill my vein-tar all over this 'forsaken place.'"

"Son—"

"Don't!" he snarled.

That stupid title had plagued him for a thousand years. Were they father and son? Brothers of a sort? Was Loki naught but a shadowy reflection that had stepped out of a looking glass? For a thousand years, he'd questioned it, and for a thousand years, he'd arrived at the same conclusion.

Creator and monster, they were.

Not, of course, that the former of those titles was deserved by its bearer. With creation came responsibility to teach, to love, to guide – duties Odin had never taken upon his shoulders.

Odin could scarcely *look* at Loki without succumbing to regret.

"Kill me," Loki said again, "and finally rid the world of the parts of you that you hate so very much."

"We came to ask you and Sigyn to return home. I never wanted to kill you."

THE GOD OF LEAD AND BLOOD

"You never wanted me alive, either. As long as I breathe, I remind you that the darkness never left you. To you, I'm nothing but proof of a failed sacrifice. Of your bloated pride."

The taunting didn't work. Odin's expression was not fiery, but droopy, weighed down by sadness.

Finally, Loki's control snapped and he pulled his Colt from its holster, directing it right at Odin's remaining eye. "How dare you tell us to come home, when you watched in silence as they murdered your grandson?"

Gravel crunched nearby. With his free hand, Loki pulled his second pistol from its holster, raised it, cocked it. He didn't need to look to know who was coming.

Several pairs of feet were moving. A heavy stomping gait that could only belong to Thor, and the sure, steady steps of Hermóðr and Höðr, and the proud, pompous swagger of the one Loki loathed more than any other. He adjusted his aim to point right at the sound of clinking jewelry.

Loki laughed bitterly. "I should've known you'd bring them."

He turned to see Njörðr stepping forward from the sagebrush, his chest draped in heavy necklaces of woven gold. His suit and waistcoat were made of fine silk, his boots shiny and unmarred. Asgard lay in ruins, but heaven forbid that the king of the seas ever be seen without his riches.

Loki placed his finger on the trigger. "Take another step and taste lead, piss-drinker."

A thunderous growl rumbled inside Njörðr's chest.

353

"Oh." Loki allowed himself one moment of a wicked grin. "Still a tender subject, I see. Perhaps you wouldn't be wound up so tightly if your wife had ever knocked boots with you."

Thor stepped between them, burly arms spread wide, hairy belly poking from the bottom of his shirt. "For so long, we've bickered like children at the berry bush, all wanting the biggest fruit. After all we've lost, can we not have peace?"

"This is not bickering," Loki hissed, heart burning at the memory of Nari's belly pierced and emptied in front of him. "He killed my boy."

Njörðr lunged forward, fists tight, jewelry jangling. "You killed Baldr."

A gunshot shook the air. Like a flash of lightning, all the visitors drew their weapons. Odin pulled Gungnir off his back. Thor held up a shotgun.

But no one collapsed, and no other shots were taken. Salt-heavy blood streamed in a crimson sheet from a long cut on Njörðr's pale cheek.

"You try my patience, lord of earth-blood," Loki said with a wry smile. "Unlike all you oh-so-noble souls, I hold grudges. As do my kin."

With a flick of his eyes, he directed their attention to the nearest ridge. Two shadowed silhouettes stood at the top of the hill. Both Vali and Narfi had rifles against their shoulders, but Loki knew who had given the warning. The former had always been the better shot, because he'd always had the most to prove after the birth of Vali Odinsson – a boy of nobler birth and greater destiny, whose name was given specifically to cast Loki's own legacy in shadow.

THE GOD OF LEAD AND BLOOD

"Your grudge is of your own making," declared Njörðr. "I only took payment for your crime. A firstborn for a firstborn."

Loki took two dangerous steps toward him, gravel crunching underfoot, and pressed the barrel against Njörðr's hairless chest. "Your perfect little nephew condemned his own sister to eternity in a locked room for no other crime than loving me. I told him he'd die for it, and he did." He leaned in closer, dropping his voice to a whisper. "And I'd do it again."

"Don't say another word about my brother!" Höðr snarled, lifting a pistol of his own.

Blond waves of hair fell over a bandana tied around his eyes – or what had once been his eyes. Cloth had lived there since the day of his birth, when Odin had been so consumed by regret that he'd cried out for Huginn and Muninn to peck the babe's eyes, so that little Höðr could never be manipulated by the völva as his father had been.

Loki had discovered that day that he was more than weakness and imperfection, and that he was capable of goodness, because he had learned that his heart possessed mercy. Many secrets had spilled from his lips, but never this one.

He could not condemn Odin for loving his son.

"Back away, Höðr," he said, not moving the gun from Njörðr's chest. "My quarrel was never with you."

As always, Thor continued to shove himself where he wasn't wanted. He pushed Loki's gun downward. "If there cannot be peace, then let us settle the debt with blood, and move forward. There are other battles to fight."

"Let's settle it," Njörðr echoed smugly.

❈ 355 ❈

"Then come to town," Loki said, accepting the challenge, "and bring a gun."

* * *

He finished loading the revolver and left his workshop. Sol had nearly reached her apex.

It was time.

Summer heat beat down upon the town. On one side of the street was every ancient being who'd crossed the sea to find sanctuary here, as well as Loki's mortal devotees, all of them oblivious to the true nature of their neighbors and the significance of this duel.

On the other side stood the whole daggum parade of gods who hadn't perished in the fall of Yggdrasil. He hadn't spoken with the family in the last hundred years, and several faces from the old days were gone now. He wondered how many had died in the event itself, and how many had simply been forgotten by time.

His Vali and the other Vali were already sizing each other up for the potential battle to come. Sigyn, as always, had laid out a table with a spread of roasted meat, herbed bread, beans, corn chowder, beer and wine. He slid an arm around her back, brushing scarred lips over her neck.

"Refreshments and everything," he muttered. "Is this a duel or a debutante ball?"

"You know I never miss an opportunity to throw a party." She turned within his embrace and placed a hand upon his scruffy cheek. "You also know that things have changed since Ragnarok. We are, all of us, not the same as we once were."

He knew she didn't regret running away. He also knew she missed some of them terribly. What happened in the next few minutes would either close the rift or widen it permanently.

"Nari was your son, too," he reminded her.

"We knew this day would come," she said quietly. "Do what we talked about."

He pulled her tight against him and kissed her deeply, slowly, reveling in the fact that all who had opposed their marriage were now watching. "We'll see."

Njörðr already stood in the empty road, spinning a borrowed pistol around his fingers. They took their places, twenty paces apart. Loki nonchalantly adjusted his hat to block the burning sunlight.

Odin spoke with a booming voice as he counted down. "Three."

There are dark drops within my blood, völva.

"Two."

Take them from me, and leave only wisdom.

"One."

Take them from me, and I shall be perfect.

"Draw!"

The snooty little sea man never stood a chance. Loki yanked his Colt out fast, pulling the hammer as he did, and fired just before Njörðr. A new hole appeared right on his opponent's thigh, opening the crucial blood ways there. A few gasps rang out.

Njörðr fell to his knees, clutching at the wound, and Loki stalked toward him. Half the hands in the crowd drifted toward guns, bayonets, bowie knives.

He had every right to put a hole between Njörðr's eyes. To turn and put another one between Odin's. Maybe throw in a shot at Thor just for a laugh.

He, the god who wasn't born. He, a being grown from cruelty and rigid pride and unchecked primal appetites, had been made for this purpose, after all. The siren call of this Wild West hummed in his blood, begging for a storm of gunpowder and lead.

Loki raised his gun, pulled the hammer. Watched as his opponent shut his eyes in preparation for the execution. Smiled.

And he fired into the air, toward the nearest cliff face. Every tongue was silent as a small plume of dust burst from the rock.

He gave a quick wink to his wife. "Never was able to defy you," he said softly.

Grateful tears welled in her eyes as she stroked the wedding band upon her finger.

"The rest of you can stay as long as you want," he announced as he holstered his gun. "Maybe if you pull the spears out of your behinds, you'll find the New World as charming as I do. Build your own damn houses, though. I'm not doing it for you."

"You were always a coward in battle," Njörðr grunted from the ground, clutching at the bubbling wound. "Stop talking and be done with it."

"Nah," Loki grunted. He crouched, elbows upon his knees. "It's just nice to see you bleed."

Njörðr would heal, but the thirst for vengeance was satisfied. As it had always done, his lifeblood turned to saltwater, carving out a clear pond in the middle of the town. Tomorrow, Loki would craft a fountain to hold it and keep it flowing. A memorial to the son who no longer was.

"This world was never yours," Loki said, low and venomous, "and someday, when they speak your name for the last time, you'll crumble with it."

"And you think you won't?" Odin asked from the crowd.

In his heart, Loki knew that other devotees still lingered in hidden pockets of the world, praising him and others. It was all that had kept breath in their lungs. Still, he craved more, and he would have it.

He was far more than darkened blood and shadow. If they would not worship him as a god, he would continue to take their loyalty and respect in the form of a man, and he and his kin would not only survive, but *live* here in this land where wolves and snakes and horses ran free.

"No," he vowed, looking his creator in the eye as he walked to take his wife's hand. "I am the god of blood and lead. And I'm going to be remembered."

Biographies

Prof. Tom Birkett
Foreword

Tom Birkett is Professor of Old English and Old Norse at University College Cork, Ireland and an expert on Norse mythology and its modern reception. His publications include the book *Reading the Runes in Old English and Old Norse Poetry* (2017) and the edited collections of essays *Translating Early Medieval Poetry* (2017) and *The Vikings Reimagined* (2020). His popular retelling of the *Norse Myths* for adults was published in 2018 and translated into several languages, and his illustrated children's book *Legends of Norse Mythology* was published in 2023.

Chris A. Bolton
Loki: The Movie
(First Publication)

Chris A. Bolton lives in a house inside a cemetery in Portland, Oregon. His short film *Evil F—ing Clowns* won Exceptional Horror Comedy at the 2023 Portland Horror Film Festival. He wrote the all-ages graphic novels *Smash: Trial by Fire* and *Smash: Fearless* from Candlewick Press. His short stories have featured in *Portland Noir*, *ParABNormal Magazine*, and the *Odin* and *Morgana le Fay* anthologies from Flame Tree. Haunt him online at chrisabolton.com.

Drew Conners
Loki's Confrontations
(First Publication)

Drew Conners is a born and raised Kansas City native. As a kid, Drew always drifted into the world of storytelling, whether it be through the latest Percy Jackson book or adventure movie, leading to a lifelong love of story crafting. As an adult, Drew can be found researching mythologies of all kinds and chipping away at his latest project. This is his first publication. If you wish to see more, he is active on Instagram (@drewrcon) and Facebook.

BIOGRAPHIES

S. Cameron David
The Norn's Offer
(First Publication)
A self-described dreamer, S. Cameron David has had an interest in science fiction, mythology and all things fantasy for as long as he can remember. You can often find him watching the animals ambling about outside or seeking out hidden paths into Faerie.

Stephanie Ellis
Means to an End
(First Publication)
Stephanie Ellis writes dark speculative prose and poetry. Her novels include *The Five Turns of the Wheel, Reborn, The Woodcutter*, and *The Barricade*, as well as the novellas, *Bottled and Paused*. Her short stories appear in the collections *The Reckoning* and *Devil Kin*. She has a strong interest in, and passion for, folklore and myths and legends – and Norse mythology in particular.

Corey D. Evans
Eitrdropar
(First Publication)
Corey D. Evans is a groundskeeper living in the United States, but writing is one of his passions. He has edited theological works for Dispensational Publishing House and Trust House Publishers, and contributed short fiction to anthologies by Flame Tree Publishing. More of Corey's work can also be found at his Substack: Corey's Story Stack. When not working or writing, Corey enjoys adventures with his wife and six children.

Ariana Ferrante
The Ties that Bind
(First Publication)
Ariana Ferrante is an #actuallyautistic speculative fiction author, screenwriter, and playwright. Her main interests include reading and writing fantasy and horror of all kinds, featuring unconventional protagonists getting into all sorts of trouble. She has been published by Eerie River Publishing and Brigid's Gate Press, among others. On the playwriting side, her works have been featured in the Kennedy Center American College

Theater Festival, and nominated for national awards. She currently lives in Florida, but travels often, usually to ride roller coasters. You may find her on Twitter at @ariana_ferrante, and on Instagram at @arianaferrantebooks.

Cara Giles
Parent-Aesir Conference
(First Publication)
Cara Giles is a fantasy writer from southern Utah, where she lives with her husband and two daughters. Her writing has appeared in *Sun Rising Short Stories* and *Enchanted Living Magazine*. As a child, Cara was fascinated by a photo of the Snaptun Stone that featured Loki carved with his mouth sewn shut. It was a delight to cut the threads and let him speak in this volume.

Matt Ralphs
Ancient & Modern: Introducing Loki
Matt Ralphs has worked in publishing as an editor and writer for many years. He's helped create graphic novels, novels, short story compilations and coffee table art books. His writing credits include adult and children's fiction and non-fiction – including a lavishly illustrated book of *Norse Myth*s – and he has published works with Nosy Crow, Phaidon, Macmillan, DK, Big Picture Press, Anderson Press and OUP. He lives in England on a boat called *Nostromo*.

Sara Gonzalez-Rothi
Fraternized
(First Publication)
Sara Gonzalez-Rothi has served in the White House, the United States Senate, and an environmental non-profit organization by day. She is a late-night creative by impulse, with publications in *Boudin* and *NUNUM*, with forthcoming pieces in *Literary Mama and Creation Magazine*. Cuban-Norwegian-American, neurodiverse, and in all the universe, her favorite title is mom.

Kay Hanifen
The Apple of Her Eye
(First Publication)
Kay Hanifen was born on a Friday the 13th and once lived for three months in a haunted castle. So, obviously, she had to become a horror writer. Her work has appeared in over one hundred anthologies and magazines. Her

BIOGRAPHIES

first anthology as an editor, *Till the Yule Log Burns Out*, was published in 2024. When she's not consuming pop culture with the voraciousness of a vampire at a 24-hour blood bank, you can usually find her with her black cats or at kayhanifenauthor.wordpress.com.

Justin R. Hopper
Captain of the Ship
(First Publication)
Justin R. Hopper grew up in the Worcestershire countryside and has a longstanding interest in folklore, myth and the fantastical. He has written for film, TV and radio, and his BBC TV adaptation of the M.R. James ghost story *Number 13* was described in the *Guardian* as 'a dark piece of deliciousness'. His story 'The Raven and the Key' is included in Flame Tree's *Odin* collection. His Offie-nominated play *Bedbug* premiered in London 2024.

Michelle Kaseler
Degrees of Truth
(First Publication)
Michelle Kaseler is a software engineer from Tucson, Arizona whose love of the written word allows her to live several lives more interesting than her own. When she's hanging out in the real world, she enjoys funky shoes, hot sauces, and long runs. Her previous publication credits include Flame Tree's *Dystopia Utopia* anthology, *Daily Science Fiction*, and NewMyths. com. 'Degrees of Truth' was inspired by a Writer's Games event with the prompt 'Fatal Flaw'.

Mark Patrick Lynch
Loki Meets His Match
(First Publication)
Mark Patrick Lynch was born and raised in West Yorkshire, England. His short stories, mainstream and genre, have appeared in various publications across the world, from *Alfred Hitchcock's Mystery Magazine* to *Zahir*. His latest novel is *Walking Horatio* and his latest collection is *Cardinal Points*. His short story 'When Sleeping Wolves Lie' can be found in the Flame Tree anthology *Were Wolf*. Feel free to say hi to him on Bluesky if you like: @ markpatricklynch.bsky.social.

Nico Martinez Nocito
A Knot for the Hawk
(First Publication)
Nico Martinez Nocito (they/them) is a queer, trans writer of fiction and poetry, often with a speculative bent. Their work can be found in *Strange Horizons* and Flame Tree Press's *Morgana Le Fay,* as well as numerous other anthologies. They spend their free time running, blogging about books they love, and acting in local theater productions. Learn more about Nico and their writing on Bluesky and Instagram @ nicowritesbooks.

Mark Oxbrow
Loki and Pickled Herring at World's End
(First Publication)
Mark is a storyteller, author and ghostwriter. His books and stories feature Norse gods, vampires, ghosts, witch goddesses, Arthurian legends, poison gardens, folk horror, medieval monsters and secret treasures. Two of Mark's stories have been recommended by legendary editor Ellen Datlow as among the best horror short stories of the year. Mark was born and raised in Edinburgh, the world's most haunted city. Over twenty-five years ago, he founded Scotland's largest Halloween festival.

Diego Suárez
Just Because
(First Publication)
Diego Suárez is a Mexican lover of mythology, fantasy, science fiction, and a forever Game Master with over eight years of tabletop goblin-wrangling/ rearing experience. A fan of Ursula K. Le Guin, V.E. Schwab, Naomi Novik, and Terry Pratchett, he writes because storytelling is what makes us human; he writes because our stories are the one indelible, indefatigable thing we can point at, and say: "this is us. Forever."

Jeffery Allen Tobin
The Shape of Mischief
(First Publication)
Jeffery Allen Tobin is a political scientist and researcher based in South Florida. He has been writing for more than 30 years. His latest poetry

BIOGRAPHIES

collection, *Scars & Fresh Paint*, was published in 2024 with Kelsay Books, and his poetry, prose, and essays have been featured in many journals, magazines, and websites.

C. Adam Volle
Laufey's Son
(First Publication)
C. Adam Volle is a professional writer and editor from Rockmart, Georgia, in the United States. Typing up history books, magazine articles, and encyclopedia entries during the day and stories of fantasy, science fiction, and crime at night, he often describes himself as a writer of nonfiction for a living and of fiction to live. Visit his personal website at AdamVolle.net.

M.M. Williams
The God of Lead and Blood
(First Publication)
M.M. Williams is an author of Norse-inspired Fantasy novels and speculative short fiction. A native of the Pacific Northwest, she currently lives in Northern Utah with her spouse, toddler, and tyrannical tortoiseshell cat. She began writing fiction in 2018 while at university studying International Relations and Scandinavian Studies – and, to her keyboard's dismay, she hasn't been able to stop. When not writing or parenting, she can be found studying folklore and history, experimenting in the kitchen, or translating old handwritten documents.

Authors and Core Sources on Loki: Snorri Sturluson

Snorri Sturluson (1179–1241) is the name you will keep reading when learning about the core texts of Norse mythology. This Icelandic scholar, politician, historian and poet is commonly considered the compiler of all or most of the *Prose Edda*, to which we refer in this book, along with being the author of *Egil's Saga* and *Heimskringla*, an Old Norse king's saga. Sturluson had the good fortune of being raised by Jón Loftsson, chieftain of Oddi in Iceland and a relative of the Norwegian royal family, and thus benefited from a good education and connections. A favourable marriage bestowed chieftainships upon him, increasing his standing and wealth. He became known as a poet while working as a 'lawspeaker' in the Icelandic parliament, and was also cultivated by the Norwegian royalty, becoming an agent in support of union with Norway. As political events marched on, this relationship turned sour and Sturluson was assassinated by the very nation he had supported – not before penning the enduring chronicles of their kings.

Myths, Gods & Immortals

Discover the mythology of humankind through its heroes, characters, gods and immortal figures. **Myths, Gods and Immortals** brings together the new and the ancient, familiar stories with a fresh and imaginative twist. Each book brings back to life a legendary, mythological or folkloric figure, with completely new stories alongside the original tales and a comprehensive introduction which emphasizes ancient and modern connections, tracing history and stories across continents, cultures and peoples.

Flame Tree Fiction

A wide range of new and classic fiction, from myth to modern stories, with tales from the distant past to the far future, including short story anthologies, **Beyond & Within**, **Collector's Editions**, **Collectable Classics**, **Gothic Fantasy collections** and **Epic Tales** of mythology and folklore.

Available at all good bookstores, and online at flametreepublishing.com